Why Stay We Here?
(Odyssey of a Canadian Infantry Officer in France in World War I)

by

George Godwin

Author of *The Eternal Forest; Cain;* and *Columbia: the Future of Canada*
First published in 1930 by Philip Allan & Co. Ltd., London

"The Grecian soldiers, tired with ten years' war,
Began to cry: 'Let us unto our ships;
Troy is invincible; why stay we here?'"
Christopher Marlowe, *Dido.*

GODWIN BOOKS
Victoria, B.C., Canada
www.godwinbooks.com

Includes bibliographical references.
ISBN 0-9696774-6-4

I. Title.
PR6013.024W49 2002   823'.912   C2002-911250-8

autobiography, Canadian history, World War I.

NOTE TO LIBRARIES:
THIS BOOK MUST BE ORDERED DIRECT FROM THE PUBLISHER.
SEND E-MAIL FOR DETAILS:
rthomson@islandnet.com

Copyright: #1003636
ISBN: 0-9696774-6-4
Godwin, George Stanley (1889-1974)

Includes:
Preface by Prof. Reg Roy
Introduction by Robert Stuart Thomson (Godwin Books)
Footnotes
Illustrations

*"Who knows but life be that which men call death,
And death what men call life?"*

Euripides: *Phrixus.*

What readers have said about *Why Stay We Here?*

When the book first appeared in 1930:

"At the present time it is difficult to read another war book without impatience, without feeling already satiated; yet although all the facts which Mr. Godwin relates in this, his second novel, are known, the angle from which he approaches them is so quiet, so dignified, stressing continually the acts of man when part of a crowd and his difference as an individual, that this book should certainly be recommended to all young men and women who only know the war through the aspects of *All Quiet on the Western Front* and *Journey's End.*" (*The New Statesman*, Feb. 22, 1930).

At the time of republication, 2002:

"What tends to make Godwin's book different from the other war books of the time is his philosophical approach; he discusses the army as a relentless machine (especially for the soldiers in it), man as a herd animal, the eternal evil within man himself. On the positive side is Craig/Godwin's wife and children in England, his hope of finding a kind of Tolstoian love, and, above all, the healing qualities of nature" (Prof. Tim Travers, U. of Calgary, 2002).

"Precisely what it means to be 'so Canadian' comes out clearly in George Godwin's novel, *Why Stay We Here?* Stephen Craig (. . .) is posted to Kent and marvels at the contrast between the British soldiers and the men of his unit: 'No anaemic men, these, drawn from office stools or shop counters. No. But men whose clear eyes have that look in them that comes only in the eyes of those whose horizons have been wide. Men of the prairie, of the mountains, of the timberlands. Canadians.' Such figures are more than just individuals. They are distillations of the essence of Canada. Compelling and larger than life, they reveal the degree to which the myth had made the soldier and Canada virtually interchangeable. Innately peaceful yet willing to fight for a principle, the soldier possessed the same youthful vigour and vitality that marked his homeland out for greatness. He was the heir to the traditions that extended back three centuries. In his person he embodied the strength and soul of the nation. He was the complete Canadian" (Prof. Jonathan Vance, *Death so Noble: Memory, Meaning and the First World War*, p. 162).

"Godwin's words are the perfectly controlled, powerful expressions of a sensibility which has grandeur and intensity. Godwin is an excellent narrator and a sensitive observer. His obscurity is undeserved and should be reversed" (Dr. 'Toby' Jackman, Victoria, 2002).

"What is most remarkable about this book is the modernity of the writer's approach; Godwin could well be writing from a 2002 perspective" (John Cherrington, author of *History of the Fraser Valley*, Fort Langley, 2002).

"This is a particularly fascinating piece of fiction. The author does not miss much: the atmosphere at Ferguson's Landing at the outbreak of the War, the shift of position by potential pacifists, the isolation of the lone German in the community – all described in first-rate detail" (Dr. Charles Humphries, Vancouver, 2002).

Preface

by Dr. Reginald H. Roy, C.D., F.R.H.S.
(Professor Emeritus of Military and Strategic Studies,
University of Victoria)

THE eminent military historian C.P. Stacey wrote that the Great War of 1914 - 18 had a greater impact on Canadian history than any other event before or since. He was probably right. We entered that war as an agricultural country; the life-and-death demands of that war threw us headlong into industrialization. The War had a tremendous impact on the nation at large, but its impact was even greater on the individuals who served in the armed forces, particularly those who served on the Western Front. *Why Stay We Here?* is the story of one who fought in the trenches during 1916 - 17.

It is not your usual war story; rather, it is a story of war and its dehumanizing impact on an individual, his fellow soldiers, his family and the many people he comes into contact with. This is an aspect of the War which has tended to be neglected.

The author, George Godwin, appears in this book as Stephen Craig. Godwin was born in England (1889) and, like tens of thousands of British immigrants, came to Canada before the War. When the conflict broke out Godwin was trying, unsuccessfully, to make a living by fruit-farming in the Fraser Valley. A bad recession had appeared in 1913, and he could not make a decent living. Although he hated the idea of war (and had lived in Dresden during his adolescence), a Canadian officer's relatively generous pay would solve his economic problem.

Initially unable to join a local battalion owing to poor eyesight, he took his wife and two children back to England with the intention of signing up. In London Godwin barges into an elegant hotel, insists on speaking to Canada's Minister of Militia, Sam Hughes, and wangles a commission for himself in the Canadian Expeditionary Force. By October 1916 he was in the front line. Apart from a short Officers' Training Corps course, he was completely unprepared for the trials which he was to undergo.

Fortunately for us Godwin was a highly observant officer with a natural gift for writing. His descriptions of life in the trenches are as good as one will find anywhere: snipers, anti-aircraft guns firing at German planes, a (for Godwin, absurd) church parade in the fields behind the line, clandestine boxing matches, prisoners of war observed up close. Analyzing his fellow-officers (one of the many original aspects of *Why Stay We Here?*) he notes that their motives run a wide gamut: duty, adventure, boredom, herd-instinct; one lieutenant (from Victoria, B.C.) is even there to escape a bullying wife half his size. Godwin describes the fear and monotony, the mud, smells, lack of sleep, constant danger of sudden death, and the joy of relief when another battalion arrives to take over from his own unit. Underlying all of this, and a constant worry, is Godwin's concern for his wife and children in England.

Why Stay We Here? is no 'drum and bugle' narrative. At heart Godwin is a pacifist and a philosopher. (He decries the destruction not only of men but of the French countryside, as fields, orchards and villages are pounded by shellfire. Godwin questions everything and concludes that the generals are "criminal fools and (. . .) idiots." He exposes those French, Belgian (and English) civilians behind the lines who exploit Canadian soldiers by over-charging them. He wonders why men, including himself, enlisted, and concludes that they were stampeded into it and followed a kind of herd instinct. For Godwin there is a blackness in men's hearts which made them willing to enlist to kill. His own experience causes him to see things in an unusual way: in his teens he had gone to school in Germany; he knows German and the Germans and refuses to accept the attempts by propaganda (some of which, e.g., the articles in *Land and Water,* is quite subtle) to stir up hatred against them. Nevertheless, in warfare it is kill or be killed.

Why Stay We Here? gives a valuable account of war at the front as witnessed by a man who was unusually sensitive to the world around him. Godwin finds much kindness and generosity in his fellow soldiers and he sees some impressive bravery; he also discovers in those freezing trenches (1916 - 17 was the worst winter in many years) a comradeship stronger than anything he had ever encountered. This creates the kind of morale which can with-stand every test, every danger.

However, Godwin sees no glory in war. If we see glory Godwin suggests that we have been conditioned to do this from childhood, and in fact he traces this development in detail, starting with how he used to play with toy soldiers in the nursery. Godwin decries the losses which battle brings with it. There are few first-hand accounts by Canadian authors of life in the trenches. *Why Stay We Here?* deserves to be republished for its stark realism, its philo-sophical probing, and as a work of literature.

Introduction

George Godwin, *The Eternal Forest* and *Why Stay We Here?*

by Robert Stuart Thomson
Owner and Editor, Godwin Books
www.godwinbooks.com

THE STORY of George Godwin and his two autobiographical novels is a complex one and needs some explanation. His first novel, *The Eternal Forest,* was first published in 1929 and soon went out of print. Who knows why? The fact remains: until my reprint (1994) this book was confined to rare books rooms in a few universities.

Neither did there seem to be any mention of it – or of Godwin – in anthologies of British Columbian or Canadian literature. When I first read *The Eternal Forest* in 1993 I was astounded at how good it was. How strange, I thought, that both Godwin and *The Eternal Forest* had become unknowns! I knew that it deserved to be recognized so I published it myself in 1994. This was a big leap into the unknown.

Since *The Eternal Forest* re-appeared in 1994, its reception has confirmed my impression that many others felt as I did about Godwin: 2,500 copies have sold and there has been significant favorable critical reaction (George Woodcock's Preface, articles in *B.C. Studies* and *National History*). Before long (1999) I located and read the sequel to *The Eternal Forest: Why Stay We Here?* If anything, I found it better than *The Eternal Forest* so I knew I had to republish it too.

George Godwin (1889-1974) wrote 20 books between 1928 and 1957. They have unusual range and depth because Godwin had an expert's knowledge of a vast array of fields: literature, history, economics, sociology, political science, psychology, law, criminology, education, even books on mysticism, faith-healing and agriculture (see Appendix: 'Other Works by George Godwin').

The Eternal Forest tells of Godwin's experiences as a homesteader in British Columbia from 1910 to 1914; it is also a holistic analysis of British Columbia in what Godwin calls "its adolescent stage."

Why Stay We Here? (1930) continues Godwin's story as he hears the declaration of war (1914) and returns to England (1916) where he joins a Canadian Infantry Unit as an officer. Such is the overview. The details are below: Godwin's life, his two Canadian novels and how the three are connected.

I. George Godwin's Life

At first sight Godwin's life might seem ordinarily upper-middle class English; closer scrutiny reveals an unusual destiny. Born in England in 1889; steeped in music and literature through his mother's influence; bereaved at age five of his father; educated at boarding schools (Glenrock in Sussex; St. Lawrence College in Kent). Top of his class in English, history and biblical studies; bottom of the class in everything else; considered richly deserving of regular Friday canings on the grounds of "mental ineptitude."

At 15 Godwin quits school (he probably was expelled) and, following a decision of his 'family council,' is sent off to complete his schooling in Dresden (in-tow to his elder sister, Maude, who is going there to study voice).

Dresden witnesses a radical change in George. He applies himself to learning German and falls under life-long spells, notably Wagner, Schumann and Goethe. He makes close friends at the Realschule (Junior high school, approx.) How different the system is from England! Long walks with close friends. Serious discussions of music, literature, boxing. He finds in Germany no stigma against playing the violin or reading Goethe for pleasure. There is no pressure to participate in team sports; there is no cruel 'ragging' in the dorm at night. Godwin's experience in Germany will mark him for the rest of his life; it will certainly account for the many warm allusions to Germany in *Why Stay We Here?* Here is protagonist Stephen Craig's description of a young lieutenant whom he had tutored in English while in Dresden.

Would the Herr Lieutenant now be a full Colonel, boozing, shooting and raping in Belgium? Not easy to believe, that. Nor of his men, those spectacled boys of the old Realschule, now men and soldiers. Take Zeidlitz as a specimen. His greatest ambition had been to learn *Das englische Boxen.* That wide smile, those friendly blue eyes. Or Stolze, grave and preoccupied, anxious always for the examination [the *Einjahrige.* If you failed you had to serve three years – as opposed to one year – as a private soldier. – Editor] but absorbed in his hobbies, inviting you to share his pleasures, inviting you to accept his friendship, in the classroom, in his home, in his little sanctum.

"Here I paint." He pulls out the canvas, holds it up proudly. There he is, the Erl King upon his steed, riding through night and storm, clasping his child. But that is not all. *Ach, nein.*

"You like music, *nicht wahr?*" The fiddle is tucked under the chin from which yellow hair sprouts amid the pimples. "You like Schubert. Ach, he is the best." He plays *Ich Grolle Nicht, Du Bist die Ruh.*

And the words: *"Heine, ja."* And he is rummaging again, the fiddle forgotten. Here are poems neatly transcribed in slanting Gothic characters.

Romance, the fabled Rhine, troubadours, chivalry, gnomes and heroes, magic gold (*Why Stay We Here?*, p. 31).

About 1907 George returns to London and finds work in a bank. He also starts to study law, part time, at the Middle Temple (he will write a history of it in 1954). In 1911 (?) Godwin leaves for British Columbia; sends for his fiancée; marries; buys property and builds a house in Whonnock (pseudonymically called "Ferguson's Landing" in *The Eternal Forest*). This is a small community of farmers – mostly rather eccentric – eking out a living on the north bank of the Fraser River. All around is a great rain forest; to the south one can see, like some Bali Hai, the majestic cone of Mt. Baker.

The magic of the place will remain close to Godwin's heart all his life (it is the core of his Romanticism) and the recollection of it will calm his spirit in troubled times. Here the Godwins spend five or six years.

Their 500 pounds sterling is soon spent and they (like almost everyone in the community) find that it is hard, even impossible, to make a living. Using several characters (Dunn, the Newcomer, and Bob England) as spokesmen, Godwin analyses the reasons for this sad state of affairs in *The Eternal Forest* (as he had in *Columbia, or The Future of Canada* in 1928), laying much of the blame at the feet of government and big business, guilty in his eyes of mismanagement, greed and corruption.

By 1916 events and personal considerations (a bad recession in 1913, Godwin's poor opinion of the kind of education British Columbia could offer his children, the outbreak of World War One in 1914) conspire to lure him back to England. The decision to return to England was wrenching because it seemed an admission of failure; besides, the Godwins had come to love the beauty of the forest and valley and the sort of people they had lived with – neighbourly people, refreshingly without social pretense. As Newcomer (Godwin) says to his wife:

> "We have always bothered too much about manners and too little about morals. In the Old Country the polished cad can pass, at least for a time. But it is fatal to be plebeian common.
> What mucky thinking has gone before that standard!
> Look at Johansson – he belches across the table, picks his teeth, spits and blows his nose through thumb and finger.
> But consider the man himself! Good God! He is heroic! (. . .) He works like a horse. You never see him idle, doing nothing. Yet he will always lend a hand to a neighbour. It's Johansson who starts the [work] bees (*The Eternal Forest*, p. 210).

The Godwins return to England in the summer of 1916. Once there, George is helped by Dick, an older brother, to muster up enough courage to 'beard' Sam Hughes himself (Minister of Militia) and flatter him into giving George a commission. Soon George is off to France, where he is assigned to 'Tobin's Tigers,' the 29th Battalion from Vancouver, B.C. I will let not spoil your suspense but will let *Why Stay We Here?* tell you the rest of the story.

By the early 1920s the Godwins are back in London. George completes his training for a career in law and continues to write, prolifically, as one can see from the list of books in the Appendix.

Five children are born to the Godwins. Three of them go to St. Paul's famous school (perhaps as charity students – not that it matters) and forge fine careers (one in medicine, two in law). Educationally, the decision to return to England from Canada must have seem vindicated. George dies at the ripe age of 85 in 1974. His remains lie at Leatherhead (just outside south-west Greater London).

II. *Why Stay We Here?*

That *Why Stay We Here?* ended up on the slag-heap of dead and forgotten books is not entirely a mystery when one probes the historical facts. First, its timing (1930) could not have been worse: a huge, rich harvest of World War One books suddenly appeared about 1929. *Memoirs of a Fox-Hunting Man* (1928), *All Quiet on the Western Front; Death of a Hero; Good-bye to All That; Journey's End; Generals Die in Bed;* and Feilding's relatively unknown but brilliant *Letters to a Wife.* These were tough acts to follow. Another problem appears to have been satiety: the general public seems to have had its fill of World War One accounts and reminiscences. I think it is fair to infer this, if one can judge from the reaction of some very influential reviewers. They were thoroughly sick of the genre:

> "If this book *(Why Stay We Here?)* had appeared a year or so ago it might have made some stir: for it is well enough written in a jerky, impressionistic style. We have, however, had so many War novels of late dealing with infantry on the Western Front, all more or less similar in tone, that one finds it hard to raise much enthusiasm over another rendering" – *The Times Literary Supplement,* London, May 15, 1930.

Unfortunate timing for Godwin the novelist! 1930 meant unfortunate timing in a few other ways as well. The Great Depression wreaked havoc in most trades, including books. Also, it did not help that *Why Stay We Here?* was published in New York (Appleton) and in London (P. Allan) but never in Canada. There was little support for Canadian books in Canada at that time. Nevertheless, at least one important voice praised the book. Thus the editor of *The New Statesman* (Feb. 22, 1930):

"At the present time it is difficult to read another war book without impatience, without feeling already satiated; yet although all the facts which Mr. Godwin relates in this, his second novel, are known, the angle from which he approaches them is so quiet, so dignified, stressing continually the acts of man when part of a crowd and his difference as an individual, that this book should certainly be recommended to all young men and women who only know the war through the aspects of *All Quiet on the Western Front* and *Journey's End.*"

For 72 years (1930 to 2002) *Why Stay We Here?* has remained almost completely unknown. As I mentioned earlier, when I first read it (1999) I was riveted; it was as good as *The Eternal Forest.* Both books sprung from a need to search for meaning in life; in both the author seemed determined to see beneath the surface of things; in both he enveloped his fellow humans with the same broad empathy. Both books were the product of an unusually powerful poetic imagination. I knew that I had to re-publish *Why Stay We Here?*

Allies for this enterprise had to be ferreted out once they were inveigled or simply badgered into reading it (why is it so few people seem to take time to read challenging books these days?).

My most important ally proved to be Prof. Jonathan Vance. I just happened to read a glowing review of Vance's *Death so Noble* (1996), a subtle and illuminating study of Canada during World War One. Vance describes how Canadian public opinion (civilian and military) was encouraged to take an unquestioning pro-war stance through propaganda, censorship and the creation of a whole set of 'myths.'

Vance had high praise for *Why Stay We Here?*, calling Godwin one of the few authors (along with, for example, Peregrine Acland and his *All Else is Folly*) who had dared to speak out boldly against the prevailing mythology and at the same time suggest many new and insightful ways in which to assess the war; e.g. the following quotation from Vance's book shows how much Godwin had absorbed of Carl Jung:

"In 1930, Godwin published *Why Stay We Here?*, a bitter and powerful tale of Stephen Craig, a British Columbia fruit grower, and his wartime odyssey. The novel is full of protest against the use of religion in war. In one exchange, Craig and his (. . .) friend Piers ponder the existence of God; Piers concludes that 'if He exists at all, then He must be an impersonal God who doesn't care a hoot about mankind.' Nonetheless, Godwin concludes his novel by admitting that the soldiers were universal victims like Jesus; in the final chapter, he leaves us with a powerful image: 'what were these marching men as, if not as Christ, Archetype of all suffering, sacrifice? . . . A battalion of Christs bearing the sins of the world along a northern road of France.' Godwin had clearly agonized over the relationship between Christianity and war and had concluded that there was no place for organized religion in the carnage at the front. There was, however, a place for Jesus. He, like the soldiers, had been condemned to suffer for the sins of others. Christ, then, was the quintessential symbol of the man at the front" (*Death so Noble*, p. 43).

Vance's recognition confirmed my impression that *Why Stay We Here?* was indeed a powerful and original statement about the War (especially as it affected Canadians). Soon I was in touch with Vance and sent him a copy of *The Eternal Forest*. It caught the attention of one of his graduate students, Claire Campbell, who saw Godwin (who becomes many things to many people) as a prescient proponent of forest ecology decades before it became a widespread concern; she wrote about this aspect of *The Eternal Forest* in the (alas!) now defunct *National History* (summer, 2000). Her article is on my site: www.godwinbooks.com

In due course I contacted a number of other academics about *Why Stay We Here?* Most helpful of all was Tim Travers in Calgary who clarified many issues and arcane footnotes. Military historians Desmond Morton and Reg Roy made some excellent suggestions. Several well-read, discerning people read the manuscript and confirmed my impression that this was a book that deserved to be in print as part of Canada's heritage: Mr. Allen Specht, Mr. Ted Staunton, Dr. Shawn Cafferky, Dr. 'Toby' Jackman, Dr. Charles Humphries, Ms. Anne Yandle, Mr. Fred Braches, Dr. Jean Barman, Dr. Patricia Roy.

In short, I was starting to build a bridgehead through my guerrilla marketing. A convincing commonplace holds that there is no such thing as negative publicity; this is true (to a point) so I was pleased to read that Pierre Berton was at least aware of the existence of *Why Stay We Here?*, although he had a negative view of it, flippantly dismissing (in his 2002 *Marching as to War*) Godwin's book with one damning word: "bitter." Very strange, I thought, to dismiss such a complex book, a book so rich in empathy for the terrible suffering, both military and civil, with one lousy word, but then I recalled that Berton had pompously dismissed Louis Riel as "a traitor" on a David Ingram television interview, so no serious umbrage was to be taken.

It occurred to me that Berton (like Mr. William New, who in *Canadian Literature* had dismissed my editorial innovations in the 1994 *Eternal Forest* as a mere 'apparatus') needed to actually read the book. It is too bad that both Berton and New, giants on the Canadian literary-historical scene, are not above taking cheap pot-shots without doing their homework. Our national culture is a precious thing; it is continually growing and forgotten books are potentially an important part of this growth.

Presumably the reader has read the quotations on *Why Stay We Here?* which precede this essay. I would like to add a few points of my own concerning Godwin as a writer.

In my view the most striking thing about Godwin is a combination of acute observation and original analysis. Godwin questions just about everything. He accepts nothing at face value: neither God, nor Christianity, nor patriotism, nor education (such as he experienced it), nor the Military, nor the people he encounters (including himself). He has a driving need to understand things as they really are.

The following passage is typical: it starts with a casual observation, but this observation leads to questioning several issues on a broad, connected front: cowardice, bravery, nerves, the effects of surgical reamputations, the unfathomable limits of mind and body.

At the front Stephen notices the Colonel's batman flinging the contents of the Colonel's bedpan over the parapet and is tempted to conclude that the Colonel is a coward:

> "Stephen had encountered the Colonel's batman coming out of H.Q. dugout. He carried a German helmet upside down, and cast its contents over the parapet. So the Colonel, it seemed, did not leave his dugout, even to relieve himself.
>
> Was the Colonel, then, a coward?
>
> No, like his adjutant, who wore the ribands of the D.S.O. and the M.C., he was a brave man.
>
> It seemed, then, that a man had so much physical courage and no more. Nerves, like the stoutest ropes, wore through, became tattered, thin and unreliable. Piers had explained something of this, talking about those reamputations cases he had seen in hospital. The first time, doped with morphia, the patient went to the table cheerily enough. But the fourth time? The fifth time? Piers said that he had seen big fellows whimpering at the thought of it" (*Why Stay We Here?*, p. 115).

Stephen/Godwin is a perspicacious observer, but he does not allow himself to reach any conclusions until he has subjected his observation to calm reflection and logic. In the above quotation his conjecture (that the Colonel might be a coward) is merely tentative, and he will test it in the light of experience and superior knowledge (here his source is alter-ego Piers, who knows a great deal about the reality of this war, having fought through the bloody Somme campaigns of 1916 and having been promoted up through the ranks).

It is only after a careful cross-checking of evidence that Godwin allows himself to formulate conclusions. (In *The Eternal Forest* Newcomer analyzes the rough-edged Johansson in much the same way.) In short, behind Godwin the novelist there is a philosopher (and a barrister): seeking, sifting and testing for reality and meaning. Does our upbringing subtly condition us to like war? How? What are the Germans really like? What are the Allied 'brass' really like? Do they really think that this war can be won using their methods? Similarly, Stephen/ Godwin will probe the real reasons why his brother officers signed up to fight (there are some big surprises here); how the men under his command really think and feel; how civilians (English and French) really feel about Canadian soldiers. The questioning is thorough and it makes no room for propaganda or ready-made ideas.

Also striking is Godwin's lyricism, his poetic vein. In the quotation above he likens worn nerves to worn ropes. Such a comparison seems so natural as to go unnoticed *(ars celare artem),* but it is really unusual and appropriate: like rope, we all have breaking points, no matter how courageous our spirit.

One finds poems in Godwin's prose. Here is Stephen in his trench at the front; extremely ill and dead-tired, he soon falls asleep:

"Five hours for sleep. Stephen is in his bunk. He has loosened his belt The war has ceased for him. For a few hours. High upon the mottled alder is a green woodpecker. Tap, tap, tap. Hard bill on bark. Tap, tap, tap. After timber-haunting insects, there on the graceful alder, in the dappled forest. How beautiful both tree and bird. Tap, tap, tap. *Picus viridis.* Picus, why did you love Pomona so? Was it worth it, tapping bird? Tap, tap, tap. After insects. Such hammer blows with hammer bill.

Five hours? No, as many minutes. Stephen rolled over" (*Why Stay We Here?*, p. 99).

The reader is taken with Godwin back, briefly and poignantly, to the wilds of British Columbia. A serene day in the depths of the bush, and the sudden, mysterious tac-tac-tac of a woodpecker. For Stephen/Godwin the forest – eternal – represents serenity, peace, harmony, perhaps the closest thing man has in the way of a divinity, and it is in the forest that Godwin's spirit, at times deeply troubled and frightened (although he tries hard to hide it) takes refuge. In the passage cited, the short, staccato, jerky movements of the sentences conjure up the phenomenon described. Mimesis. There follows an obscure allusion to Pomona and the deities of rural, agricultural Rome. Not a word of explanation from Godwin. Again, it is typical. (In the text of *Why Stay We Here?* I enclosed a footnote on this allusion, and consulted a few professors of Classics. We all gave up on it; maybe some clever reader will enlighten us by e-mail (rthomson@islandnet.com).

Godwin does not explain his allusions; there is no condescension about him. The title is typical: *Why Stay We Here?* Godwin tells us that it is from Marlowe, but that is all; it is up to the reader to collaborate intellectually and make the necessary connections, reasoning perhaps in the following manner: "Here is Marlowe, an Elizabethan, writing about the Trojan War. The Greeks are trying to conquer Troy. An absurd war: a Trojan (Paris), abducts the wife (Helen) of a Greek King (Menelaus), and Menelaus has his brother invade Troy in order to get Helen back and exact revenge. But Troy is too well defended and cannot be conquered (the cunning Greeks have not thought up the idea of the 'Trojan horse' at this stage). So why bother staying? Better to return to Sparta. Then one makes the connection: Aha, the British, French, Canadians, etc. are in a similar position to the Ancient Greeks and Germany and its Allies are like the Ancient Trojans, unconquerable. The line cannot be 'rolled up.' This 'Great War' cannot be won this way. And so on.

It is a rich, clever allusion, and suggests that history, not always, but only too often, repeats itself; however, it is up to the reader to have enough general knowledge to make these connections. By the way, I hope the reader will pardon my intrusion in adding to Godwin's original title an alternative one: *Odyssey of a Canadian Infantry Officer in World War One* but Godwin's title seemed too obscure.

There would be much to say about the historical value of *Why Stay We Here?* In my opinion one of the book's chief historical merits is to invite the reader to reflect on certain victims of the War who are usually ignored: widows, orphans, parents and relatives.

Many hearts were broken. There is a particularly good passage about a French widow and her young daughter with whom Stephen billets when he is sent behind the line for respite:

> Stephen beckoned the little thing, and she came, shyly, and sat upon his knee. He kissed her, fondled her flaxen hair.
>
> Did he kiss her? Or, in her, did he kiss his absent little son?
>
> The child recognised in him the father-man and screwed his buttons round in little hands, flirting with her eyes innocently.
>
> A child. Innocence, trust, affection. Sweet things, indeed.
>
> A succession of men, remote and mysterious. Coming and goings. Some passed her by, big and creaking, with loud, alarming voices. But a few, like this thin man who came to her with his slow father smile, took stock of her. But none of them replaced the one who had gone without returning, the bearded man, with black strong hair, who slept beside her Maman. The man she had called Papa (*Why Stay We Here?*, p. 123).

There is also much in *Why Stay We Here?* on how World War One damaged individual soldiers, physically and emotionally; how it often made them authoritarian, prejudiced and full of anger; how it often led them into atheism, despair, and anomie. The important (and seldom-mentioned) point is that these effects are not just 'historical,' not just confined to the past; they have been passed from generation to generation and, although often disguised and almost imperceptible, continue to affect us. It is vital to understand them and Godwin helps us to do just that.

III. Connections between *The Eternal Forest* and *Why Stay We Here?*

It is not necessary to read *The Eternal Forest* (1929) first in order to appreciate *Why Stay We Here?* (1930) but some knowledge of *The Eternal Forest* will help to clarify certain aspects of *Why Stay We Here?* As stated earlier, *The Eternal Forest* is largely about a small community of homesteaders at "Ferguson's Landing" on the north bank of the Fraser River. Among other things, *Why Stay We Here?* is the story of the generally tragic effects of World War One on some of the people in this same community.

Several characters appear in both novels. There is the closest of links between George Godwin and the two protagonists: 'The Newcomer' in *The Eternal Forest* and Stephen Craig in *Why Stay We Here?* Similar backgrounds, intellects, interests, values, dispositions, and sensitivities. All three of them agnostics or at least skeptics; all admirers (and poets) of nature; all three critical of the established order of things, determined to expose its weaknesses and to explore how it could be improved.

Other characters appear in both books. Godwin's wife Dorothy, (resolute, loyal and practical, but inclined to be unimaginative, unromantic and distant) is, we suspect, the model for the wives of both the Newcomer and Stephen Craig.

Old Man Dunn is a pivotal character in *The Eternal Forest*. Widely-read, reflective, confrontational – Dunn becomes the Newcomer's chief intellectual-spiritual companion. The discussions of the two men reveal wide-sweeping interests: literature (Thomas Carlyle is Dunn's 'sage'; Francis Thompson and Charles Lamb are favourites of the Newcomer), history, current events, politics, economics and sociology; they draw on this knowledge as they analyze British Columbia and Canada from many angles. Their close relationship is, however, forever changed by events in *Why Stay We Here?*

Bob England is the local realtor who sells the Newcomer an over-priced forested lot on the steep slope above the Fraser River; Bob is also one of the Newcomer's main sources of information on the economics of Ferguson's Landing and British Columbia, especially the inexplicable boom and bust cycles (see Mr. Woodcock's preface to the 1994 *The Eternal Forest*). In the years of *The Eternal Forest* (1911 to August 1914) Bob is a great pal of the Austrian immigrant Stein (a model farmer and an asset to the community) but this relationship too is transformed by events in *Why Stay We Here?* Bob can't get into the War quick enough – "keen as mustard to get at Master Hun."

Writing to Craig first from Ferguson's Landing, then from England and France, it is Bob who keeps Craig posted on news about their neighbours from Ferguson's Landing.

A few minor characters figure in both novels: crafty Blanchard, who owns the general store (on pilings stretching out into the Fraser River) which is the chief meeting-house of the locals, the place where they buy goods, barter, and exchange ideas, news and gossip; feckless Heggerty – a hillbilly who lives with his huge family deep in the forest (he is the first of the locals to sell out to the Japanese).

A few final points: Godwin's pre-World War I personal journal (it was never meant by Godwin for publication but I included about a third of it in my 1994 *The Eternal Forest*) contains a number of entries which resurface, altered, in the text of the 1929 *The Eternal Forest.* This raises the likelihood that when Godwin wrote his two novels (presumably about the time they were first published, i.e. 1929 - 1930) he was well fortified with notes which he had made ten to twenty years earlier, i.e. 1910 - 1919. These two novels contain such a wealth of detail that it is hard to believe that Godwin culled such detail up from memory alone.

It is hard to know if Godwin planned, all along, to write two complementary novels. I think *Why Stay We Here?* was an afterthought.

Had both books been planned at the same time, would Godwin not have used one name – Stephen Craig – for the protagonists of both?

'The Newcomer' (which is Godwin's play on the Salish 'Chechako') is perhaps clever but rather vague. I suspect that Godwin was dissatisfied with it and changed it in *Why Stay We Here?* to something more specific and plausible. Some continuity is lost in the change from 'Newcomer' to Craig, but it is a small point and overall I think the two novels are well-integrated. The reader will judge.

Some readers will wonder at my use of photographs, footnotes, and other realia in a novel. The conventional (or traditional) view is that a novel should be able to conjure up its own world through the magic of words alone. So it should, but it seems to me that when a novel is clearly autobiographical and contains a great deal of historical fact (and some of these facts are not well known and for the sake of the historical record need to be made accessible), then it is justifiable to treat it as history and illuminate it with historical realia.

Another reason for editing this book as an historical document is that the author is now dead and almost unknown. Readers who like Godwin will want to know many things about him, things which never came to light because his books disappeared. Did Godwin have two brothers like the ones described in *Why Stay We Here?* Yes. Was his wife like Craig's? By all accounts (including my own impression, because I had supper with her and George once, in 1970), yes. Did George have a son named Eric, born in 1912? Yes. Is Piers a portrait of Ben Gray? Probably.

Many footnotes have been necessary; I hope the reader finds them useful. As I mentioned earlier, Godwin does not usually explain esoteric or time-specific things; military jargon, slang, the significance of *Land and Water,* the role of the Officer's Field Book, etc. Notes and pictures were needed in order to clarify many allusions which seem obscure from the vantage-point of 2002.

Robert Stuart Thomson, Victoria, B.C., October 2002

CHAPTER I

1

"HERE'S the mail!"

In the dimness of Blanchard's store there was a stir among the men who idled there in the close air that smelt of cheese and apples and decay.

Those who hearkened turned at the booming voice of Old Man Dunn and saw beyond the door the limping figure of the lank store-keeper. He struggled with the mail-sack which had just rolled to his feet, a missile fired from the hurtling through express. The sack was heavy, and the day was hot.

Yes, there was the mail.

Ferguson's Landing,[1] half hidden by the great trees of the forest, dreamed beside the Fraser river, now bright as a snake uncoiled upon the valley floor. Beyond the river, the door framed a green sea of timber that vanished over the southern horizon somewhere in Washington State.

Blanchard's store was the centre of the settlement. Did you need new boots, maybe, or a canvas shirt, or the stuff for a dress? A few sacks of wheat, harness or an axe? Then Blanchard, smiling enigmatically, served your needs, with mock servility.

Would you barter eggs or a butchered Berkshire pig, for flour or fence-wire or paint for the shack? Then Blanchard, brushing the flies aside, would cipher on his blood-stained counter, and make a reckoning.

Now, at the approach of the mail, the men of the settlement stirred. There would be letters for some of them, and, maybe, the odd cheque from a Sapperton[2] cannery. Or there might be a roll of reading matter, *The Farmers' Home Journal, The Poultry World, The Saturday Evening Post.*

Blanchard, the store-keeper, was now Blanchard, the postmaster. He tossed out his sack's contents upon the dirty floor and stooped among its booty.

"Letter for Mr. Dunn," he announced. "And one for Mr. Preedy."

A burly, bearded man, with shaking hands, was Old Man Dunn; he took his letter, greedily.

And so it went, each man taking his mail or demanding mail that was not there, making a grievance of it. Nothing much on this hot August afternoon, it seemed.

They drifted, gossiping, out into the sunlight, tanned men, in open shirts, and old breeches thrust into the tops of high laced boots. But a few there were who settled down again in the dim store to gossip a bit before taking the dusty trails that would lead them home. They exchanged the small talk of the settlement.

"Wid eggs at this price, how can a man buy chicken food?"

"Say, I reckon it's time the ole wharf gotta few new piles. It stands to reason, piles don't last for ever."

"Where's the pile driver?"

"At Carlyle.³ I guess there's some hokey-pokey a-going on. The Landing don't ever git its fair share. No, sir."

"Don't never feed hens mash first thing, that's wot I say. Why? Sure, they'll loaf all day and a loafin' hen don't lay. No, sir."

Little Heggerty, there, weakly truculent, began taunting Bob England, stolid, solid old Bob. O, yes, they did say it of him that he grafted, being the Party man in those parts. Could one help what they said?

Bob England sucked his cob-corn pipe. He did not care. He came to his newspaper and he opened it.

"Wot's the price o' eggs in Vancouver?" asked Heggerty, peering over Bob England's shoulder.

"Eighteen cents."

"Eighteen cents? Say, what kind of a swindle do they call that?"

A figure stood in the door, black against the blaze of the afternoon.

Blanchard put his dark face to the wire of his cage. Customers were of more importance than His Majesty's mails.

He said: "Good afternoon, Mr. Stein," and: "Yes, there're letters for you, Mr. Stein." And said it so respectfully, adding, examining the stamp: "One from Germany, I see."

Mr. Stein moved into the store with assurance and dignity. He owed Blanchard nothing, and he paid cash for what he bought. Under his wide-rimmed hat, his sallow face looked handsome, set off with a neat vandyke beard. He suggested other times and other places.

"So," he exclaimed, taking his letters and examining them with curiosity. "Did many people get letters today?" he asked. "Did Mr. Dunn?"

Blanchard smiled.

"Not much mail today, Mr. Stein," he replied. And his smile seemed to say: "You are altogether too curious, my friend; but Blanchard is up to you."

Bob England and the Schleswig-Holsteiner were old cronies with twenty years of tried friendship behind them. They talked together as old friends do, simply and without restraint.

"What d'you think England is going to do?" Stein asked. "*I* think she will declare her neutrality."

But Bob England now looked up and pointed with his pipe-stem at the open paper.

"Then you think wrong," he answered. "England has declared war." And his voice was changed.

And Heggerty heard it, too. He said: "Aw, what's that to me? What I'm worryin' about is the price of eggs."

Stein said nothing. He was thinking, and his sallow face darkened. And presently he ejaculated a prolonged "So!"

He looked around, and was suddenly aware that Bob England was no longer there; aware, too, that his friend had gone without a word, and that Blanchard too had disappeared.

He was alone.

He walked away, slowly. And now there was less assurance, less dignity about him.

2

Stephen Craig was first at the wharf. He wiped the sweat from his eyes and looked down into the flashing water below. After a hard day's work, a swim. He felt a queer excitement in his blood. It had been the same when he was a boy. Water; it increased the tempo of the heart just to look at it; this element, water, that seemed to have so close an affinity to blood that when it called the other answered like a friend.

Where were the other fellows to-day? Bob England? You could never tell, with him; he was so often late. And just when you gave him up, there he was with his slow smile and cob-corn pipe, sturdy, serene, imperturbable.

He would not wait . . .

How glorious to be alive, to be swimming!

He rose to the surface, snorting, a grampus head.[4] Sweat of the day's dust washed away, pores breathing, drinking, talking. Little open thirsty mouths. Flashing body, flashing blood.

After the heat of the day, after ten hours of toil!

He swam luxuriantly on his back, wet eyes half closed, the blinding sun a dancing iridescence seen between lashes.

Someone on the wharf, someone shouting.

The other fellows, late to-day. Ha, ha! he was in first. There was old Bob England, lazy beggar, always late for everything, up there on the wharf.

He waved, shouted and plunged down again, head over heels, wallowing.

Bob England's voice came over the water, and this time urgently. Stephen paddled swiftly to the bank.

Bob England, leaning over the towering wharf, was calling: "Craig, come here, come here." He watched impatiently the purposeful strokes that brought the swimmer to the wharf.

Bob had not come to swim. One did not need to be told that. Something was up. Even so, holding a pile, Stephen looked up to the face turned down to him:

"Coming in?" he asked. "It's marvellous."

Bob England ignored the invitation.

"England has declared war!" The words were shot out of him. "It's right enough. Tom Preedy got the news by wire from Vancouver." Bob England exulted.

Stephen paddled slowly to the bank. It must be true enough. But why be pleased about it?

Bob England had already disappeared when he clambered up to the wharf.

What news is like unto news of war, speeding across the world from the cities to the towns, from the towns to the villages and the sleeping hamlets; passing beneath the seven seas, piercing the mountains, echoing at last through far-distant valleys?

Stephen dressed slowly, thoughtfully. On the way home he would drop in at Old Man Dunn's. Old Dunn, full of Karl Marx, was all against Capitalism. And, surely, this war was a child of Capitalism!

MacDonald, the smith, twisted round as Stephen passed the forge, one steel arm about an upraised fetlock, his square face begrimed with the sweat that ran down into his eyes, over his cheeks. He, too, had heard.

"If they want to fight," he said, "let them get on with it. I'm not interested." And he turned to his job.

Stephen, troubled in his heart, said: "But you must stand somewhere, Mac."

The steel arm worked like a flail, the smith intent upon his task. The new-shod hoof came down, struck sparks from the smithy floor. And the smith straightened up his back. An immense man, hairy and black, with dangerous eyes.

"Stand?" he repeated. "Here I stand in my smithy. War? What's a row in Europe to me? Let 'em go to it." He thrust out an arm for the bellows, and the fire breathed fiery sighs.

3

Old Man Dunn often overlooked the milking of his cow Maria until she protested dolefully with oozing udders, pain in her mournful eyes. But he never forgot favourite passages from *Sartor Resartus, Beyond Good and Evil,* or *Sesame and Lilies;* even turgid periods of *Das Kapital* stuck like burrs in the fabric of his mind. His notorious absent-mindedness was really a very present-mindedness. He lived with ideas, did Old Man Dunn.

Burly, bearded and slow in his movements, with the broad accents of Yorkshire that not even forty odd years of exile could change by a single cadence, he was the rebel of Ferguson's Landing.

Stephen Craig had often sat in the hot little kitchen listening to him while little Mrs. Dunn darted about the hot wood stove. Like a little hen she was, darting here, darting there.

"All war," only a few weeks ago Old Man Dunn had said, "for whatever purpose, is wrong and wicked. In the old days there was at least an extenuating chivalry to regulate it. But that's gone. Modern wars are ferocious – and why are they fought at all?"

What is more easy than to find the answer to one's own question?

The old man said oracularly: "In the interest of the capitalist class, of course."

He quoted Tolstoi, pointed, with a hand long since palsied in the lead mines of Nebraska, to *War and Peace,* a battered tome upon a wooden shelf.

"Condemned by God and man," he boomed. "You can't decide a moral issue by force of arms. The mightier side wins. That proves its might, nothing else."

The old man was standing at the broken gate of his picket fence, against the background of his neglected orchard when Stephen, wondering at the vehemence of the smith, came along. Heggerty and Bob England were with him. The old fellow's voice was audible; it travelled through the still air down the dusty road.

So the arguments had started already? Sooner or later Old Man Dunn would find himself in trouble with his talk against war.

Then the words became clear and Stephen unconsciously slackened his pace.

"War," the voice of Old Man Dunn was booming, "is the only way. We must meet force with force. There's no other way with these German swine. Why, man, it's unthinkable that England could stand aside and watch the rape o' Belgium, little Belgium. It's a terrible business, but it's the only way."

4

When Stephen Craig had come to Ferguson's Landing with his wife, Old Man Dunn had set to work to make a convert of him. And he had succeeded. Other influences there had been. The reading of Tolstoi and the appeal of the forty days of bread labour for all who would break bread. Henry George and the single tax idea.[5] But most, the rough schooling of the bush – those years before the place was cleared or near its present promise of fruitfulness. Once Stephen had tried to sell out. But nobody would buy.

Now he was glad. The young orchard was now planted, graftings from the ancient Gravenstein in the old man's meadow. Yes, the younger man had been drawn to the older by the common bond of books, by kindred interests. Both liked talk, and new ideas.

So, after four years both saw eye to eye as socialists, agnostics.

Now, hearing these words from the old man, Stephen Craig stopped involuntarily. He turned upon his heel and walked quickly away. Well, after all, there were things one had to settle with oneself, with one's own conscience.

This was one of them.

Walking slowly, he took the rutted trail that led to his ranch. How beautiful the valley as one rose upon the northern side until it lay green beneath one, severed by the silver river.

After all, war was not an easy reality to grasp without experience of it. What exactly did the word 'war' evoke in his mind?

First, boxes of tin soldiers, red and blue, with pivoted arms. Toy forts of wood painted grey. Little leaden cannons that fired broken match sticks. That had been great fun on the nursery floor. Playing at killing. One row of red opposed to a turbaned row of heathen warriors. Arms got broken, and lead stands and rifles, but that could not be helped; war was like that, it was breaking things. That was its charm. War, then, was a game that one learned along with 'Ring-a-ring o' roses' and 'Here we go round the mulberry bush.' In childhood. In the nursery.

Then there was that picture in the first history book. A snow-storm, a blizzard in the Alps. Troops fighting their way against the storm up a precipitous path. And Napoleon, looking glum, riding upon a stout little cob. In the deep snow beside the struggling column lies a little drummer boy. He beats a tattoo upon his little drum as the troops struggle past.

Yes, one understood that. It taught courage, courage in the face of death. Those soldiers could not bother with the boy. He would have to stay there and die. And he knew it. But still, he drummed, and courageously accepted his fate.

But now one might consider the object lesson of the dauntless drummer boy from a different angle and give the picture a different interpretation, say: "Napoleon, unmoved, murders a drummer boy."

War, then, was as much a part of childhood as Gentle Jesus. The small head accepted the game of killing along with the God of Love without effort. That was why people grew up without feeling the incongruity of Christian armies, of war, of organized murder.

What else was there? Yes. That photograph.

He had been rummaging furtively among the intriguing oddments of an old box in his elder brother's[6] bedroom when he came upon the print. And there he had been found gazing at it, fascinated.

"You've no business . . ." There had been a queer look in his brother's eyes. "I took that."

And he had asked: "What are all those? Dead men?"

"That's the Boer garrison of a captured blockhouse," he had been told.

They lay, those Boers, in abandoned attitudes, like sleeping men who somehow lacked the peacefulness of sleep. Bearded and clad in homely clothes, with bandoliers slung about their shoulders, they lay sprawling beside their rifles, their dark faces turned to the sky.

"Why are their faces black?" he asked.

Stephen's brother took the print in his hand and looked at it with curiosity.

"Black?" he repeated, perplexed for a moment, then : "Oh, I see what you mean. No, they're flies."

Then Mafeking Night, a roar from the street below, a howling and a yelling that had excited strangely the small boy in the quivering dormitory of small boys.

What else did he know about war?

Collecting the fortnightly parts of the *Russo-Japanese War History*. But then those countries were so remote that there was no horror. Soldiers slaughtered at Port Arthur were no more real than soldiers fighting on the plains of Mars.

He had arrived at the end of Old Man Dunn's meadow that ran with the rutted road. He turned his eyes and looked upon the ancient Gravenstein. For four years, every day, Stephen passed the old tree. It stood, gnarled and twisted, in the roadside corner of the field, propped upon a wooden crutch. Each Spring the Gravenstein burnt, a pink flame, and in early September the fruit was red upon the dark green boughs.

For Stephen the Gravenstein was not just an apple tree: it was a friend, and today, more friend than ever, so trusty there, beside the road, greeting him. He stopped and looked at it. And the tree looked back at him, knowing him.

5

Maple Grove,[7] the municipal district of Ferguson's Landing, was to have its own infantry company, officered by its own men. Bob England, who stood in with the political people, had gone down to Sapperton on the local to fix things. He returned with everything arranged. Ferguson's Landing would guarantee one platoon and would be allowed to nominate one officer. Bob, the lazy, the lethargic, became energetic. From somewhere he unearthed a Manual of Arms. Drilling was started in Old Man Dunn's meadow. He would stand, leaning upon his broken fence, approving.

Nobody understood the directions, but each tried to direct the rest in turn. There was much laughing. But underneath there was great earnestness. Getting ready to be soldiers. They stood there in the meadow like ramrods, men in soiled and worked-soiled clothes, men tanned by the open air, men hard as nails.

But the simplest manoeuvre was too much for them. Directly the straight line obeyed the order, advanced, wheeled, changed direction right or left, all became confusion and a new start had to be made.

Whereas a few weeks ago a calving cow, a runaway sow, or a five-cent drop in the price of eggs would have provided ample talk for the gossips at Blanchard's store, such events passed unnoticed now.

There was but one topic: war . . .

It would be all over in six weeks.

No, it would last till Christmas.

Well, yes, perhaps it might take that long to fix the Kaiser and his horde of Huns.

But what about the Navy, the British Navy? Wait till that had a go at 'em.

What was the good of drilling when it would be all over before there was a chance of going overseas?

Ah, remember the Boer War. Two years and more.

Yes, but that was different. We had to chase those Boers all over South Africa. Besides, they knew the country inside out and we didn't.

Sending redcoats to be shot down. That was crazy.

But six months? Why, in that time modern artillery could wipe out millions. Yes, millions.

Capture the Kaiser, that would finish it.

So through the hot summer of 1914, while the green valley moved towards autumnal ripeness and the maples lit their torches and dripped blood, the simple settlers estimated the inestimable, pondered the imponderable, solved the insoluble. Mrs. Corley, the minister's wife, received a letter from the Vancouver Red Cross Society. It seemed that this far-off war could absorb all the bandages the women of Ferguson's Landing could make in their spare hours. The minister called a church meeting, and without more ado the women settled down to work.

6

Miserable days for Stephen Craig. Nobody saw much of him now. He stayed upon his own place, avoided, whenever possible, his neighbours. But Old Man Dunn sent word that there were Gravensteins for the picking. So he went, carrying an empty sack. What apple is so sweet as a Gravenstein, what apple has so fine a flavour, such firm flesh?

Yes, every day, for four years, Stephen had passed the Gravenstein and greeted it. It was not a tree as other trees were trees, not a mere growth from graft or skilful budding. No. It was a friend, and a familiar, sharing with him the life of the valley. He would greet the veteran as he passed, not with words, but in that communion that has no need of them. For in this old apple tree he saw a symbol, the symbol of the lusty fruitfulness of the valley, of the earth.

Many years ago, he considered, some man had planted there this apple tree; maybe old Ferguson himself when the settlement was but a chip out of the bush. And now that unknown was gone. But the Gravenstein remained as his monument and memorial, a witness to his worth and usefulness upon this earth.

An acre cleared, surrendered grudgingly by the bush, roots grubbed up by hand, ploughing done and red clover in. And there the little grafted trees, each with its binding where he had clayed the bleeding graft. In five years' time there would be an orchard, blossom and fruit, shrill greens and dappled patches on the clover there. The pride of it . . .

Dear Gravenstein, so weighted with the years, yet bearing in that neglected corner the same sweet luscious fruit! Could it be that men might pass this tree without a thought for it?

Nearing its end was the old Gravenstein, but its sap would survive, for already it ran in those new graftings. A new lease of life; another generation. The old tree had sired the young trees in the clearing, where Stephen had made a home.

He clambered over the old fence, landing in the lush grass of the neglected meadow. It might be possible to fill the sack unseen and go without a word: thanks could be sent by note. He didn't want to meet the old man. The war had come between them. He was finding out already that to be even an unavowed minority of one carried its penalty, throwing up barriers everywhere, hampering friendly intercourse with neighbours. But somehow the magic of the Gravenstein dispelled all gloomy thoughts. How friendly were these laden branches overhead, how comely the red hanging fruit.

But when the fruit was gathered, the old man came.

He held a newspaper under his arm. There had been fierce fighting on the Marne. The casualties were heavy, very heavy. But worse with the enemy.

"If only I was young," he boomed, looking up.

And Stephen, looking down on him from his ladder, his face framed in the dark green of the Gravenstein's foliage, said with bitterness: "If only I were old."

The old man turned away. War had destroyed their friendship, ended that pleasant intimacy.

7

Tales of atrocities filtered through to the Settlement. The invading German hordes had violated the laws of war, had shot down old men and mere boys, bayoneted babies, raped women and young girls, indulged in drunken orgies, ravaging the occupied country.

Old friends began to look askance at bearded Stein who, only yesterday, all had held to be a credit to the Settlement, so honourable, so industrious, so clever with his hands. And Stein now went furtively, with trouble in his eyes.

Yet Stephen remained unmoved by these tales. He weighed the probabilities in his mind as he worked about his place, there on the slope of the hill, on the edge of the forest. Somehow such foul deeds did not square with long memories of a romantic land, a kindly people . . .

Dresden[8] in the Spring, with its broad clean streets garlanded with blossoming trees, pink and white.

Bummels. Bummels through the Saxon Switzerland. To Königstein. Long days tramping, singing in the sun. Beer gardens and fat waiters, dark, cool drafts of lager. Postcards, always postcards, even though one would arrive home ahead of them. *Grüss aus Königstein.*[9] *Wass für ein grossartiger Tag.*[10] Bummels to the Weisser Hirsch, up the hill crowned with white of cherry blossom, and, amid the trees, the little tables, each with its family group, each with its long thick beersteins.

Every Saturday, every Sunday. Happy days.

And everywhere friendly faces, the broad, homely Saxon faces, of the people in the streets, of the boys in the *Realschule.*

They had no playing fields, these German schoolboys, knew nothing of cricket on warm summer afternoons, or football in the tang of autumn air. For them sedate walks, two by two, in the Grosser Garten. Haunted boys, pursued by the spectre of the cursed *Einjähriger* . . .

"You see, if one fails in the One Year Examination, then one must serve the full three years as private soldier. If one passes, then only one year and concessions."

Was it dreadful to serve the three years?

Nun,[11] look at the drafts as they march along the Pragerstrasse on their way to the barracks with their bundles to serve their term. Do they look pleased? Ach, nein! The army is not pleasant.

They told tales, unpleasant tales, these boys. Tales of brothers who had failed and who, as conscripts, had been spat upon, who had been clouted with a sheathed sword, had had toes stamped upon. A woman known as Red Rosa had written a book[12] exposing these things and had been cast into prison for it. It was dangerous to have this book in one's possession.

Hard to believe, harder still when one had spent long evenings in the Herr Lieutenant's barrack quarters in the Alt Stadt. Six foot seven he was, and straight as a ramrod, the tallest officer in the Saxon Army. Already before the exchange of conversation *Stunden*[13] he knew his English well. But he would perfect it, *nicht wahr?*[14]

A large, white-washed apartment, plainly furnished, camp-bed in the far corner. A bust of Napoleon, a portrait of the Kaiser. Books . . .

"Every soldier admires Napoleon. He is the soldier's ideal, *jawohl.* One studied him, his sayings, his campaigns. And Clausewitz, and many others."

A student soldier, efficient, alert, eager.

Would the Herr Lieutenant now be a full Colonel, boozing, shooting and raping in Belgium?

Not easy to believe, that. Nor of his men, those spectacled boys of the old *Realschule,* now men and soldiers.

Take Zeidlitz as a specimen. His greatest ambition had been to learn *das englische Boxen.* That wide smile, those friendly blue eyes. Or Stolze, grave and preoccupied, anxious always for the examination, but absorbed in his hobbies, inviting you to share his pleasures, inviting you to accept his friendship, in the classroom, in his home, in his little sanctum . . .

"Here I paint." He pulls out the canvas, holds it up proudly. There he is, the Erl King[15] upon his steed, riding through night and storm, clasping his child.

But that is not all. *Ach, nein.* "You like music, n*icht wahr?*" The fiddle is tucked under the chin from which yellow hair sprouts amid the pimples. "You like Schubert, *ach,* he is the best." He plays *Ich Grolle Nicht,*[16] *Du Bist die Ruh.*[17]

And the words: *"Heine, ja."* And he is rummaging again, the fiddle forgotten. Here are poems neatly transcribed in slanting Gothic characters. Romance, the fabled Rhine, troubadours, chivalry, gnomes and heroes, magic gold . . .

Well, was one lightly to believe these things? Could one be expected to become enthusiastic over fighting these old companions of boyhood's happiest days, days far happier than any spent in the English public school, where such activities were suppressed.[18]

Imagine it: sticking a bayonet into friendly grinning Zeidlitz; imagine bombing romantic Stolze!

Another memory flashed back. Lowestoft on a broiling summer day, a troupe of entertainers in a garden of wide lawn. Deckchairs in the shade. And a thin man with bottle shoulders singing a song. What were the words? No matter. We had a Navy, a British Navy, and we would in due course trounce Kaiser Bill.

And another. Oxford Street, and hanging across the road, a great banner: *Blut ist dicker als Wasser.*[19] Presently the Kaiser was to pass. *Dicker als Wasser.*

Then Christmas in that pleasant land. The gay lighted trees of every home with their red, white and blue sparkling balls and twinkling candles. *Heilige Nacht,*[20] the old hymns. And Frau Schmidt, stout kindly soul, insisting that he take the sofa, place of honour, since he was an *Auslander* and far from home. A foreigner! as if one could be anywhere more at home than in Germany, ever among kindlier, dearer friends.[21]

So old memories crowded in as Stephen worked in the shelter of his great wood-shed, the scent of dry alder rising from the busy buck-saw in his hand. And each brought with it heartache, heavy pain, a nostalgia for those happy far-off days . . .

The dim auditorium of the opera house rose before him, electric with expectation. The first night of the *Ring*[22] and everywhere the hum of voices. Then utter silence as the conductor raises his wand and the first sweet notes float up to the gallery, up to those rapt students, each one marking the music[23] from an open score.

Magic nights of intoxication, there in the great theatre beside the slow, wide Elbe; there by the royal palace where ancient princesses of the royal line passed in and out in prim sedans, ignoring the passage of the centuries, clinging stubbornly to the romantic past.

All this was Germany, and these were Germans. How could one square the war, and the accusation of the world against these people, with such memories of those?

Yet, of course, there were aspects, even then. He remembered them quite well. What was the cowardly instinct which had prompted him, only the day before, to recount to an appreciative audience in Blanchard's store those other memories. What miserable spinelessness had held his mouth when he should have been a witness to so many kindnesses, so many happy days?

A craven, beastly thing to do. But there, one had done it, standing there with all those faces round one, each one hearing just what he would gladly know, and hearing believe, and later retail, embroidering copiously.

A man who could pander to the mood of other men like that was a poor thing. Stephen worked on, disconsolate. If only he had not told so many stories of the swaggering officers of the Wilhelmstrasse, Wiesbaden, and how they pushed civilians aside, both men and girls, like so much dirt. And why had it been necessary to haul forth and refurbish the incident in the Dresden shop when the two American ladies had been arrested for commenting disrespectfully upon the portrait of the Kaiser?

Those things were true enough. But one knew very well in one's heart that in telling them as he had done, and by telling nothing more, one bore false witness.

Going with the crowd, how easy it was![24] How infernally hard to resist! It was only when one was alone that one seemed able to be honest. Perhaps each one of those fellows at the store, tramping home through the steady rain, would shed the fierce, false hate of an hour before and think again in human terms of brother men. If only it might be so.

8

One evening, when the war was six months old and the prophets of the Settlement were already less loquacious, Bob England came up the steep trail to Stephen's place.

The fellows of the Landing had talked it over, he explained.

"They want you to take the commission."

"A commission? No thanks."

Stephen moved his pipe from his mouth and gazed miserably into the great open fireplace where a resinous root-prong spurted rainbow-tinted flames. "I prefer the ranks, but thanks for the compliment, just the same."

But when, an hour later, Bob England put on his oilskins and went out into the rain-swept evening, it was agreed. Stephen was to officer the new-made soldiers of the Settlement.

Not for nothing was Bob England a clever and successful real estate agent; not for nothing was he the Party man in the valley. Talk, and enough of the right kind of it, and one got results. He had proved it many times before. There are people who will accept humbug addressed to the ears, when there, in front of them, is the evidence of their eyes to give it the lie. That being so, one could sell land fairly easily. And when you had acquired the art of talking a man into one thing, it was easy enough to talk him into another.

Left alone, Stephen turned to his wife, miserably.

"Now I'm drawn into it," he lamented.

She stood, looking down on him without speaking. Thinking of the two babies, perhaps. Thinking many thoughts, but saying nothing at all.

If one had had the courage one would have said: "No thanks. I'm against this war and I'm against all wars. I've been reading Tolstoi. It's merely murder. I'm a Pacifist, so put that in your pipe and smoke it. Besides, I like the Germans. So put that in your pipe as well and see how the mixture smokes."

But one didn't do anything of the sort. No, one retailed anything that was of bad report of these people and denied them their virtues with a cowardly silence. And even that did not get to the bottom of it. True enough, without dishonesty or self-deception, he was dead set against it. But did it not so happen that moral conviction coincided with desire?

Suppose he had liked the idea of the war, had hankered to get into khaki and plunge into this adventure? How long would he have hesitated because of Tolstoi or anybody else? Not a moment.

No, one had to get into it. There was no way out.

With a heavy heart he rose, stretched, and looked out at the gathering night.

Far below, through the clearing, he could see the lights of the Settlement and the shadowy curve of the river in the dusk. Peace and beauty everywhere, and the voice of the rain, a monotone, winter's anthem.

They went to bed in silence and lay long awake without words. Outside they could hear the rain upon the trees and a soft sighing as the forest drank. Presently she said:

"I suppose it means all our work will go for nothing?"

"Yes," he assented, "it means just that." He sought her hand. It was rough and calloused: its gentle pressure answered him.

9

The examining officer at Sapperton was nearly done.

"Sound as a bell," he declared. But a few moments later he shook his head. "Sorry," he sympathised, "but I simply can't pass you with that bum shooting eye. You go home and wait. This war has only just commenced; they'll be glad of you later on, bet your life on that. As for now, I've got to reject you. I'm bound by the regulations. Suppose you wouldn't like to consider the Army Service corps?"[25]

But, no, Stephen did not care to consider that, somehow.

10

Stephen tramped the streets of Vancouver seeking a loan. But the war had made money tight. Nobody seemed to care to lend money on land in the Fraser Valley. He tried at the office of Ferguson Real Estate and Loans, the self-same office where, a year before, he had encountered the grandson of the Settlement's founder, turned from pioneering ways to be a "white-collar guy."[26] In the end he was grateful to the extortionate private lender who advanced him a thousand dollars at twelve per cent. It appeared to Stephen at that moment almost as an act of kindliness.

A thousand dollars, two hundred pounds, a slender purse with which to face the journey home.

From the wide window of the transcontinental, Stephen, his elder boy upon his knee, watched the panorama of Ferguson's Landing slide past. His heart was heavy. The great trees of the bush, in massed battalions, marched past, a pink orchard whose fruit he knew, and there a home amid the green, rough slashings, pitted by tree stumps and, more swiftly, a meadow in lush grass, a cow, a lichened roof. Smoke. There was the sand-pit, rust-red against the green, where he had sweated in summer weather, and there an ancient trail that took you up the slope into the forest, flickered past.

He shifted the boy and watched with a strange tightening about the heart. Swiftly sailing past upon its sea of green flashed the ancient Gravenstein. It was in blossom.

11

O Valley, what lacked your loveliness that they turned from you?

In the morning of the world the seas went back and gave me to the sun. And I conceived: within my fecund belly the first man leapt. I am man's mother. I am man's lover.

Food and drink of my body I gave him; toil, and, after it, repose. In the day, sweat, but in the evening I fanned him with a breeze. And presently he looked up and found the stars and the moon. He learnt to sing, and I sang with him and there were echoes in the hills about me.

Everywhere loveliness, fulfilment, until in his dark soul he fashioned a god and in his name launched the first murder on the world.

O Valley, mother, lover, pity them. Not men and women, these, but chips upon a tide, leaves before the wind, twigs beneath a heel.

Notes to Chapter I

1. "Ferguson's Landing": a pseudonym, most likely Whonnock, a small settlement located approx. 30 miles east of Vancouver, on the north bank of the Fraser River. With Vancouver, Ferguson's Landing provides the setting for the greater part of *The Eternal Forest* (1929). Much like Thomas Hardy (whose works he admired) Godwin used pseudonyms for many places (and real people) in this novel. His purpose is not clear to this writer, but many of his human portraits have been recognized as real people by residents of that area. Mr. Fred Braches' *Whonnock Notes* (Spring 2000), deals with these issues. As stated earlier, *Why Stay We Here?* (1930) is the sequel to *The Eternal Forest*. Both can be considered autobiographical novels, i.e. Godwin is present in "The Newcomer" of *The Eternal Forest* and in Stephen Craig of *Why Stay We Here?*
2. Sapperton: the original site of New Westminster, but located on its eastern edge. Named for the Royal Engineers (a.k.a. "sappers").
3. Carlyle: pseudonym for today's Ruskin.
4. grampus head: "a blowing, spouting, blunt-headed dolphin-like creature" (Oxford Dict.).
5. Henry George and single tax idea. Henry George (1839 - 1897) contended that only lands and buildings should be taxed. Income tax he thought unnecessary.
6. "his elder brother": one of George's older brothers, Donald Godwin (1880 - 1922) had fought in the Boer war (see photo). He is the editor's mother's father.
7. Maple Grove: Godwin's pseudonym for today's Maple Ridge.
8. Dresden: Godwin's "family council" decided to send him to Dresden to attend a Realschule (approx. junior high school) there. Godwin stayed for about two years, learned the language and became familiar with the culture.
9. Grüss aus Königstein: A greeting from Königstein.
10. "Was für ein grossartiger Tag!": What a splendid day!
11. Nun: Well now.
12. Red Rosa's book: *Rosa Luxemburg Speaks.* Luxemburg (1871 - 1919), was the co-founder of the Spartacus party and the German communist party. Arrested and shot by soldiers while en route to prison (1919).
13. "Stunden": lessons.
14. "nicht wahr": wouldn't he?
15. the Erl King: the Elf-king. Poem by Goethe.
16. *Ich Grolle Nicht:* from Schumann's *Dichterliebe.*
17. Du bist die Ruh: lit. You are peacefulness/tranquillity; to paraphrase: In you I find total peace of mind.
18. ". . . such activities were repressed": for similar views see Godwin's *Journal,* which is found in the form of an appendage to my 1994 edition of *The Eternal Forest.* See also Godwin's *Queen Mary College* (1944).
19. "Blut is dicker als Wasser": Blood is thicker than water.
20. "Heilige Nacht": Holy Night.
21. ". . . kindlier, dearer friends." For similar pro-German sentiments see Godwin's *Journal* (p. 305) and his *Japan's New Empire* (1942), p. 1. *Japan's New Empire* is out of print but you can read passages from it on my site: www.godwinbooks.com
22. "the Ring": Wagner's. See *Journal,* p. 304.
23. "marking the music": i.e. following the score while listening to the music.
24. "Going with the crowd . . . it was." See *Journal,* p. 304.
25. Army Service Corps: handled supplies and equipment.
26. "He tried at the office . . . a 'white-collar guy.'" This event is described in detail in *The Eternal Forest.*

CHAPTER II

1

THE long train clanged through the valley, climbed into the mountains, dived through the heart of them, and presently slid down into the flowery prairie.

The over-heated tourist car, first a magic place of mysteries and delights to the small boy, became his stifling prison. All day the baby plagued his mother, never a moment still. And at night they tossed restlessly in the tiny cabin behind the swaying curtains.

Between whiles they talked of the future and how things could be arranged. There would be around eighty pounds when they stepped ashore at Liverpool.

"I'd better go home to mother with the children."

"Well, yes." That was inevitable, the only way. Just the same: other people's houses, even the old home. Not the same. The bread would taste less sweet. Taking second place, no longer mistress, placating others; keeping these two active children quiet . . .

Small shrill townships, lakes, long desolate stretches of wastelands, and then Toronto, like a handsome young man in clothes too new. And Buffalo, a blowsy, vulgar wench. And New York, the city of a dream, and that dream fantastic. They walked the roaring canyons of its ways with their children and were bewildered after those years in the silences of the valley. They were strangers passing by on their way to war. The great city knew them not; neither did they know it. These swarming millions who poured in human tides up and down these shadowed ways were not going to war. The war was an item in the news, a big item, but not so big after all beside the baseball World Series.

They were people apart, the man, the woman, the child, the babe. Folk sucked back into the vortex of that old whore, Europe. America, that was something to be thankful for.

And so they left the monstrous city in a haze and passed into the east, became a smudge upon the dim horizon. Vanished.

2

They parted at Liverpool, a Liverpool unaccountably changed, pressed down and flattened.

"Look at the Liver Building! What has happened to it?" What is it, after all? A pepper pot, no more.

She took the two children to await the Irish packet; Stephen took the London train. In a toy carriage, drawn by a nursery engine, he sped through tiny fields whose trees were no bigger than big bushes. England had shrunk, become an absurd little land, yet primly beautiful.

And the valley had vanished, and the quiet life of the valley. The timber house among the trees, the little half-done clearing, the young apple trees of the new-planned orchard, and silent watching bush were fragrant memories and no more. And now those three familiar faces gone too, moved with the shifting panorama, the finished life of yesterday.

So war began the stripping process, the uprooting, the work of destruction. The little ranch was empty now, a year would see it derelict, for the jealous bush that yielded it up so grudgingly would claim it back, hungrily. Rank weeds and bracken, forest vegetation and sturdy saplings would reconquer the taken ground. House and outbuildings, fences, all would now start the inevitable processes of decay.

The train slid into Paddington. Darkness enveloped the city. The great station was a cavern, a cavern of many echoes, of shadows that came and went in the gloom.

And in the Temple the old planes loomed dimly with each its warning whitewash band.[1] The ancient hall was a silhouette against a sky across which moved the skeleton fan of searchlights, ghostly fingers pointing an accusation. No familiar mellow lights in the high windows of the hall, no robed gossips in the lighted door, awaiting the call to dine.

Dear, dear familiar place: and yet how changed. It was as though he came upon an old and solid friend with a tale of penury and woe.

He climbed familiar stairs, wide and shallow. Yes, all was just the same, even the hard knots that generations of feet could not wear away: they stood out from the worn boards like little fortresses, defiant, invincible. The third flight, and that familiar oak, and there his own name in large black letters looking back at him. Stephen Craig. Nothing changed, nothing at all . . . The door stared back at him.

"So there you are at last, and a fine time you have been. Well? Did you expect to find some changes, then? You, there, with the twitching lips?"

Stephen knocked; the door opened.

3

A slow business, getting into this war. And little wonder, since it was conducted by lunatics. In Sapperton they had discovered a disqualifying right eye. Now there was nothing right at all.

Stephen had completed his training in the Officers' Training Corps. It had begun with a medical examination, and ended with one. In the three intervening months, so it seemed, the A.1 human machine had become derelict, below even the C.3 grade.[2]

"There are plenty of fellows who would give a lot for that little card," he was told. "It lets you out with a clear conscience."

He considered that. It was certainly a view. Three months had been long enough for the discouraging revelation that war enthusiasm a day from the guns burnt less fiercely than war enthusiasm five thousand miles from them. Ferguson's Landing was baying for the fight. England was like a nervous, apprehensive terrier.

The O.T.C. had been the school cadet corps all over again, glorified, redeemed here and there from boredom. As, for instance, by advanced ballistics expounded by a professor (with German *bas reliefs* to illustrate bow-and-stern air waves and the like) for those who were curious enough to probe the mysteries of flying death.

What an end to that exalted resolve taken there in cold blood in the shadow of the forest!

That must have been something strong to wrench a man out of the frame of his life, to carry him five thousand miles. Anti-climax. It ended with the very problem that had so often posed him in the valley: the problem of getting a living.

What was left? Sullen anger. Disgust. Money worry.

During the training period, so familiar were uniform, routine of drill and instruction in lecture hall, that it was as though one had slipped back into the familiar setting of the old school. In that matter-of-fact atmosphere (so little do sergeant-instructors vary) the Great Moral Issues which had loomed so large as one leant on an axe and meditated in the silences of the bush, dwindled and disappeared. Tolstoi and his teaching went clean out of mind.

Stephen, rejected, had taken a small room in a side street in Soho. He wore a borrowed suit of checks, having sold his clothes three months before. It was tight under the arms, too short in the legs. He looked like a scarecrow as he went about in it. Conscious of this, he interpreted the looks upon the faces of others, that now and then seemed vaguely hostile, to his absurd appearance.

The explanation came later. A girl with a bottle-shouldered youth in khaki. She threw it over her shoulder as she passed: "My boy's in khaki. Wot's your girl think of you?"

A pretty little thing, too, with fair hair and wide blue eyes. How happy she was, how proud of her pimply soldier boy!

Well, what did his girl think of him? She had never told him. He had often wondered himself. Perhaps it was best to judge by actions rather than words. Certainly this last letter from Ireland overlooked the question the fair girl asked. Perhaps that was because it had matters more important to communicate.

And the last of his money was gone. At Ferguson's Landing there had been times when the temptation to write home for financial help was overpowering. But they had never done it. Now it would be necessary to surrender. He would have to borrow. Stephen boarded a bus. Best get it over.

4

The bearded old gentleman stood up in his office, adjusting gold-rimmed glasses and thereafter inconsequentially looking over their rims.

A loan? But why? Stephen could pack his bag and come out to Putney. Hospitality, yes. A loan: it went against the grain.

How to explain the case clearly so that this old man would understand? No case could be clearer. One wanted money because one had none: one wanted it, not for oneself, but for one's wife. And one wanted it for her because this thing called the British Empire temporally required one's whole time, had for the time taken away freedom to work and earn. And this pink-faced old man was part and parcel of that monstrous entity. He might have stood as its symbol: solid, stolid, hard-headed, obtuse. If one got to France and fought, it was for him, for his wealth, so small a part of which one now desired to borrow.

A reasonable request, surely.

I, Steve, on the first part, forego my home which I have made with my two hands, leave wife and children, surrender liberty and forthwith smother personality, undertaking to obey my superior officers, and those set in authority over them in turn, in all things. And I undertake, further, to ignore all personal danger, to accept all bodily risk, and, if necessary, to die in the process or suffer mutilation.

Lastly, my wife, who makes her sacrifice without protest, and my children, who are too young to know anything about the matter at all, are also partners to this contract. Signed, sealed and delivered.

And on your part, dear uncle, since contracts are matters of give and take, you will eat less butter than you did and sell your saddle horse for army purposes.

But be of good cheer, you will make money. And this is one of the peculiar consequences of war against which your philosophy will arm you.

Even so, you, too, as patriot, have your duties. Your country, uncle, needs you. At least, it needs your money. But it is no more unreasonable with you than with me. Of me it asks youth, home, a warm place in bed beside my wife, the caresses of my children. Perhaps more. So you, good uncle that you are, will buy your War Loan. The interest is your due. Meanwhile, ten pounds is an urgent need.

Well?

Something wrong here, surely.

Uncle (grasping prospective borrower with avuncular heartiness), "A loan, my boy? Of course. Nobody appreciates more than I all that you have done, all that you are doing for your King and country." (Rummages in strong box). "Fifty to get on with and more when it's done. Not a word. Not another word. This is not a loan. Merely a partial liquidation of my indebtedness to you, to your generation."

Something wrong here, most certainly. Bearded age had missed its cue.

Stephen, his face scarlet, tears of mortification in his eyes, signed the I.O.U. placed before him, gulped his thanks and hurried away from that old man.

So this war left one nothing, nothing at all. Not even one's self-respect, one's pride, one's independence.

5

"Go right in to the old bird. But come into the hotel. God, what clothes!"

They passed into the tea lounge of the Hotel Cecil, where the war was not permitted and all went on as usual, the tall, lean man in khaki, sporting the thin gold badge of the wounded; the thin, tanned Stephen in his absurd checks.

A brother out of nowhere. But a brother at an opportune moment. They swiftly etched in the gap of years, eyeing each other as only the children of the same loins can, a half affectionate, half critical appraisement.

Stephen thought : How well he looks in his uniform! Three stars. A Captain. Wounded. A hero. Well, well. And that absurd moustache. It suits him.

And Ricky, the wanderer,[3] the man of many parts, took in this scarecrow. Poor old Steve, so quiet always, remote beggar. He *would* get left.

A waiter of obvious military age brought tea, set the table before them, and moved off, for the first time blessing the affliction of flat feet.

Ricky, for whom life was a matter of tightrope walking, who waited like the fox he loved to hunt for the long chance. Ricky, weak, lovable, roving Ricky. He launched upon his scheme.

"You want a commission? Right. I'll explain how you can get it. You've got to go straight to the Minister. Old Sammy is at the Savoy surrounded by chocolate majors.[4] Never mind them. Shove in. But wait a bit. Get an intro from – D'you know anyone useful? No? Ah, the Agent-General for British Columbia. That's him."

Useless to point out that both Canada and England had turned him down. Ricky brushed those obstacles aside.

"Look here, it's understanding human nature that gets you through. How the hell d'you suppose I bluffed a rubber company to bring me back from Kenya and pay me a thousand quid to survey a plantation in Peru? And, by the same token, how d'you suppose I wangled a passage to New York?"

He lit a cigarette and leaned back luxuriously. "Steve, you don't understand life, my lad. How did I travel to New York? On a millionaire Johnny's de luxe steam yacht."

He described a depreciatory gesture in the air. "Of course I've had my ups and downs. You bet. I got stuck in the Hudson's Bay country with a dog team sick on me. That's how I came to be with the Canadian outfit. I just knew something would turn up. And it did. A trapper blew in with news of war. Did I hump it? I did."

Dear old voluble, plausible Ricky. You had to listen. It was good as a tale. A tale of Stevenson. All action. *Treasure Island* walking about, come to life.

"At the back of everything you get to the human element, Steve," he continued. "That's what is going to fix you. The intro. is easy. Get it right away. Don't ask for an appointment with the Minister. Breeze right in. A particularly snotty chocolate major will push his silly face out of Sammy's door. Walk in.

"And now for the important part. You must bear in mind that old Sam is only a man under his Piccadilly chest. And quite a good old scout, too.

"Here is the line of country. He is vain. He is pledged to rise to the patriotic appeal. His reaction will be automatic. He is kind-hearted. But vain peacocks aren't in it.

"Now what you've to do is to appeal to him for a commission. 'Your wellknown good heart, sir, has brought me here. Everybody told me that I should get a square deal from you. We've all got to do our bit. I've come from B.C. to do mine. I want a commission with the C.E.F.'"

Sitting in the Cecil lounge, listening to Ricky, now dramatised into the part himself and working his way to his objective with the aggressiveness that had saved his bacon so often in the past and landed him right side up from many an awkward dilemma, it seemed easy enough.

And so it proved. Amazing Ricky! What a gift wasted! True, it took two weeks to get into the presence. True, too, that the chocolate major put up an unexpected resistance as guardian of the door. True, *sotto voce,* rude remarks were made upon the appearance of the persistent applicant for audience.

But the Minister rose to the bait, melted visibly before the flattery. Gave the word. Stephen was to have his commission.

Why did he jubilate? Because he was about to close with the hated Hun? No. No. Because he was about to receive the King's Commission? No. Because the objective that had brought him across half the world was about to be realised? No, again.

Stephen rejoiced because a subaltern in the C.E.F. received good pay and a generous allowance for wife and children. Stephen walked on air because once again, as so often in Ferguson's Landing when things seemed desperate, he had won a way to bread and butter, had solved the immemorial problem of making a living.

6

Fifty pounds would buy a splendid kit. But then, there was so much else to be done with it. This would have to be an elastic fifty pounds, the most elastic fifty pounds ever known. That sum was to perform miracles. It was to companion the lonely, to draw together beneath one roof, for some time at least, the members of a small divided family. It was to establish a temporary home of sorts and restart the idle wheels of the old domestic machine. And, incidentally, it was to fulfil its ostensible purpose – was to provide full service kit for yet another subaltern: uniform, boots, field glasses, compass and a weapon. Certainly a magic fifty pounds.

7

They are united again.

"How that boy has grown!"

He takes the child and holds him out. He is really heavy. Such a lump. But baby? Baby is puling. Tired after the long journey by boat and train. Teething, too, with a rash upon his body.

"How do I look in uniform?"

"Very nice. Turn round."

She takes the slack of khaki cloth that sags behind the shoulders where, in the great second-hand Jew dealers, he had not noticed the defect.

"But it doesn't look absolutely new."

"It isn't."

He displays a triangular piece of leather, liking to teach her these new secrets. "This is the monkey," he explains.

"The monkey? What a queer name."

"Well, I'm not quite sure about that. Anyway, it's named after some sort of creature."

"Isn't it called a frog?" she suggests.

"Of course. Frog."

They pass away into gales of laughter. Oh dear, what a man for getting things all mixed up. A monkey!

"Well, is it really any more funny than frog? But what it's for, God knows. I'll have to find out." He puts on the Sam Browne.

"A decent bit of leather," he observes, expertly.

Yes, that fifty pounds had stretched and stretched, but there are limits, even to the purchasing power of magic money. It was a skeleton kit he had acquired, so unlike those magnificent outfits with which proud parents and relatives were equipping their schoolboys for the war.

No tailored tunic or 'bespoke' breeches. No service revolver, no compass, no binoculars, and, naturally, no periscope or other gadget without which Eighteen Years in Khaki would seem improperly dressed. Puttees of the regulation pattern out of Ordnance Store. No beautiful long, soft leather field boots, but a pair of Tommies' black barges of boots, hard as iron, but later to become upon long marches kindly and sustaining as the companionship of old friends. No boot like an Army boot, once broken, for real service.

Weapon? Glasses? Compass? Later on. Enough for the moment that they were together again.

"What a tiny flat! What ghastly sticks. Bamboo. Anyway, we'll just remove these things from the mantelpiece and hide them. The old dame probably treasures them. They make me feel rather sick."

He surveys the little bedroom next.

"Where is baby to sleep? There's no bed or cot."

"Yes, there is." She pulls out the bottom drawer. It is now a cot.

"That's an idea." Stephen is all admiration for her ingenuity.

The war seems quite a long way off.

And now she is beside him. He puts out his arm and throws it round her, and so they lie, warm body to warm body. He can feel the steady beat of her heart beneath his sheltering hand.

The family unit. Primeval instincts satisfied. Harmony. Contentment.

Very, very faintly through the open windows comes the sound of the sea breaking on the shore. And another sound with it: a low, just audible rumble from across the grey waters of the Channel.

The guns.

8

A Kentish town of narrow streets, low houses. And everywhere soldiers. No anaemic men, these, drawn from office stools or shop counters. No. But men whose clear eyes have that look in them that comes only in the eyes of those whose horizons have been wide. Men of the prairie, of the mountains, of the timberlands.

Canadians.

Big men, husky men, simple men. Their voices echo in these narrow ways and there is a twang in them. Their friendliness is moving in its childlike assurance. They take their welcome for granted. And in the little shops, where they spend their plentiful dollars, they are greeted with smiles. Landladies with apartments to let refuse all save Canadians living out of camp.

"The soldiers must come first, nowadays," they explain.

And why not, when one can charge them double?

The war has awakened the little town from a slumber which fell upon it after the Napoleonic wars; it is thriving, growing rich, catering for these burly, bronzed men from Canada.

So there are smiles for the soldiers who swarm into the little, low-ceilinged shops, filling them with their loud voices, with their bulky bodies. But there are two prices, also: one for the inhabitants; another for these generous spenders.

But the little town does not care for them. It likes their money. But it will be glad when they have gone. That is, the last of them, finally. For as the drafts march away with blaring bands, others come to take their place. More and more . . .

"Where are you from?"

"Vancouver, Missie."

"Ah, I *thought* you were American."

"American? *Hell!* I'm a Canuck."

"But surely Vancouver's in America, isn't it?"

"Say, that's a good one, Sister, but quit yer kidding . . ."

Still, whatever he is, this big bronzed fellow who takes such liberties, he is a generous spender, no doubt about that at all. And he has a way of making love. Different it is from that of the local lads, bolder, just a trifle alarming, but very pleasant in the evenings, down by the canal that was to stop Napoleon, down there under the prim willows.

They fell into the way of it all. There was now no worry about money. They had very little, but it was enough. For they were now part of that great maintained population which, being consecrated to death, was absolved the natural function of productive toil upon the open market.

They were at once a sheltered family, and a family exposed: they had sure bread, but a bread-winner without secure tenure of life.

9

Long days up by Caesar's Camp. On the square, minus Sam Browne. In the lecture room. Cocktails in the canteen. Shovelling in trenches. Taking part in a mock raid on a dark night. Easy enough, pleasant enough in its way. But just a trifle boring.

And always the evenings to look forward to. Evenings at home, with Alice, with the children. No need to think about jobs now; no need to worry about next month's bread. It was assured. The pay came as promptly as the rations.

Orders for France came on an October day of wind and rain, with grey clouds a-scud over a dreary waste of Channel. Stephen was to report at once at Sandling Camp.

He said: "Well, this isn't really 'good-bye' at all. I'm only going to Sandling, a mere mile or two away. No need to worry yet."

"I know," she nodded. "Besides, you might be there for months and months."

"I might," he said. But he knew better. Officers, that is junior officers, were badly wanted.

And so he went off and reported himself to a colonel who, handling many draft officers, had neither time nor inclination to welcome them. A dreary mess, its nucleus a padre and M.O., both on the cadre, but for the rest composed of transitory members unknown to one another. Four dreary days of boredom that ended with final leave.

Stephen was out of the camp in a flash.

France at last. Well, it was what one had been preparing for. It was what one had come across Canada, across the Atlantic for. Still, to leave them now, to go, when it came to going . . . It wasn't pleasant.

The future loomed up darkly with a thousand possibilities, and none of them pleasant.

10

They dressed by gaslight.

There was so much to say, so short a time for the saying.

What are words at such a time?

There is sympathy, close and real, so that thoughts become words that need no speech, or there is no communion.

She stoops over the long drawer wherein the baby sleeps. What long thoughts are in her patient heart? Here, in the flesh, is the blood of the man who goes, and her blood, mystically made one. Yet not alone the woman or the man, nor the fusion of both, this sleeping babe. This softly pulsing heart beats out the music of ten thousand loves.

She rises and goes: "I must get breakfast. It is late."

It might be any day.

He is dressed now, a tall man, slight and sinewy. Creaking belt, creaking boots. He can hear her in the kitchen, moving about. Familiar sounds, china against china, steel on steel. And presently the smell of food.

He glances at the sleeping baby and passes quietly into the tiny room beyond. The last few minutes with his boy . . .

Remember them. Stamp them upon your mind and in your heart engrave them. Carry this memory with you when you go, and keep it with you. It may be the last long look. You may never see again this little head of yellow hair, this baby puckered face, this soft, sweet mouth. It is not yet four o'clock; quietly, then, lest he wakes. There can be no final smile, no kiss, no wide blue eyes. No close hug, heart of father to heart of son . . .

He kneels down beside the narrow bed and stares into the baby face. Very lightly he puts out a finger, touches him. So warm, so soft, this boy, his lovely one.

He buries his head in the bed-clothes.

Divine Intangible Mystery, keep him. Do not let me fall, so that I may return. Give me my life for him. Do not leave him fatherless. For who will care for him as I care? And who can shield him as I can shield him? Who can stand between him and the world?

He rises slowly.

"Breakfast is ready."

Her voice from the kitchen. He goes quietly out. His face has changed. He sits down at the table.

"Ricky is coming for me in the sidecar. Pass the bread, dear."

"I do hope he shows up. You never know with Ricky."

"He will come."

They eat in silence, but their thoughts are everywhere. There is no need of words.

And Ricky comes. He is sounding his horn, out there in the windy darkness, a grin on his face. There is his old machine, its headlight thrusting a yellow cone into the darkness.

She comes with him into the narrow passage. It is Good-bye. He holds her close.

The last embrace? Who knows? Then let it be long and ardent. But then go quickly, for there is a breaking point.

He waves to her from the pulsating machine; it starts. The last impression: a woman standing in a lighted doorway.

Notes

1. "And in the Temple . . . whitewash band." London lawyers' residences are located in the ancient inns of court (Lincoln's, Inner Temple, etc.) of which 'The Middle Temple' is one. According to Mr. William Godwin, one of George's sons, George took coaching in law for a few (pre-World War I years) while working in a bank. He finished these studies after World War I thanks to a dispensation granted to students who had served in the War. Godwin subtly evokes the Middle Temple with strange contrastive effect in the woods of *The Eternal Forest* and, as mentioned earlier, wrote a history of The Middle Temple. The 'Temples' take their name from the famous Knights Templar of the Crusades. The whitewashed bands served to make the trees visible at night (during the blackouts which were imposed because of air raids) so they would avoid collisions.
2. C.3 grade: unfit for active service overseas.
3. "And Ricky, the wanderer . . ." George's elder brother Dick (1885 - 1964), wounded in one of the Somme Battles. See photo. Dick is mentioned several times in Godwin's *Journal.* It was a complex relationship: as a teenager George had carefully planned to murder his brother but his plans failed. See *Journal* in *The Eternal Forest,* p. 302.
4. chocolate major: "They look splendid and taste good, but melt in the heat (. . .) The Canadian Expeditionary Force had created 258 battalions but needed only 48 [majors] for its four divisions. This left a lot of officers surplus but reluctant to return to Canada. They struggled to get staff jobs. Their plight was a little sad, but to CEF soldiers, they were despicable poseurs" (Prof. Desmond Morton).

CHAPTER III

1

THEY sat in the dim light of the Paymaster's office in the transport lines: Stephen, O'Reilly and Piers, three draft subalterns.[1] A whisky bottle stood on the bare table, and each man has his glass; the Paymaster, the guide, and the three draft officers, just in.

This was actually the front, Stephen told himself. In half an hour they would go up to their trenches. It seemed impossible.

"Aye, that was a game," the paymaster was saying, savouring again the joy of victory. "There was I . . ." He launched upon a postmortem of a great poker victory. They listened in silence. The poker game took precedence over this other business of war. They waited, as men wait who have all to learn and would feel their way. And just now it was poker that mattered, not war.

A pleasant man who took life comfortably, this Scot. Bland and smiling, with a little trick of sucking in after each observation. It was as though he tasted and savoured his words as he tasted and savoured his whisky.

Just what had one expected? That was not easily defined, but one had expected noise, terrific shattering noise. Tenseness. One had come up to the front line braced for it. And there was no noise, only astonishing inaction. Uncanny silence. And talk of a poker game . . .

But from behind this surface talk emerged gradually an old preoccupation. A sentence here, a sentence there. Whisky and poker, after all, were but devices of the waiting period. Presently there was to be a battle. The Ridge[2] was to be taken, that low hump that was lost by the sorely-tried troops under Sir Henry Wilson.[3] The impending battle lay like a cloud upon them.

2

During the preceding weeks, Stephen now realised, he had been school-ing himself for this ordeal; and no ordeal was here. Mud, yes, and a wintry sun, and the discomfort of the shrapnel helmet. Very little to suggest the most bloody war in all history. Why, this village of the transport lines seemed nearly normal, and that air of normality was enhanced by the matter-of-fact fosse that rose like a stunted pyramid on the left beside the skeleton superstructure of the coal mine.

The interminable talk of the Paymaster came to an end. The guide, a nonchalant lieutenant between whom and the new arrivals was fixed that great gulf that divides those who have been in the line and those about to go into it for the first time, rose. His tunic was soiled and shabby, and on his arms the battalion badges were an eloquent rain-washed blue.

They left the village behind and were walking in file along the communication trench, upon the duckboards, stooping now and again to dodge wire. Here was desolation. All sign of green was gone from the landscape. And soon there was only the uniformity of a shell-churned earth, an ochreous yellow, or deeper dun. Tree stumps, here and there, stood like witnesses to man's crimes against the earth and the life thereof, and the sweetness thereof, and the fullness thereof.

Conversation was spasmodic. Each thinking his own thoughts; or intent upon taking in these new surroundings.

Suddenly the guide stopped. He pointed skywards with his stick. "Look!" he exclaimed.

The little party halted there in the trench beside the Arras road, and gazed up into the watery blue sky.

Far overhead, high above a bleared sun, a tiny speck travelled across the sky; it moved with the precision of a heavenly body upon a fixed orbit, and there was majesty in its purposefulness.

"An enemy plane," laconically the guide, his stick pointing at the scudding machine. "A Red Devil. We've had a bit of trouble with those blighters lately."

Up there, in that tiny machine, in its cockpit, there was a Teutonic intelligence, keen, fearless, determined. Skilled hands were on the controls. What was there about this steadfast instrument of destruction? It was baleful, sinister, evil.

Suddenly, white balls of smoke appeared in the sky, and the snap of the anti-aircraft guns travelled over the barren earth. Presently the little machine was surrounded by smoke balls. No longer now upon its fixed orbit. It was a gadfly on a summer day, dancing, there, under the watery sun, following no course at all, dodging, with amazing skill, the guns of the Archie[4] teams below.

"Where the hell are our fellows?" growls the guide. And at that moment, as it seemed, there was another machine in the sky. Very faintly the roar of engines came to the little party in the trench. Crackle of machine gun fire. They are engaged.

How soon it is ended! Higher and higher rises the victorious machine, while below it, a fiery comet trailing dense black fumes, the vanquished plane spirals down and crashes a mile or more away.

"Another Red Devil done in," observed the guide with deep satisfaction. That is all. The little party proceeds upon its way.

After all, there was a war here. The silence had been broken.

3

Only a week had passed, but it seemed to Stephen years ago that he had sped through the darkness in Ricky's sidecar to the crowded station on that dark morning.

Southampton, and pink-faced lads in khaki, waiting in the cold gloom of great wharf Sheds; schoolboys dressed as men, as soldiers, officers, lads with schoolboy faces, graces, airs. Beautifully turned out, they were, with amazing varieties of luxury kit. They seemed to be festooned with leatherware. Beside them the Canadian officers looked like elder brothers.

"Christmas trees!" A patched and faded trench coat has spoken. He carries nothing, this fellow. Good God! After a year of it one learnt something. "They'll soon dump that junk." There is good-natured scorn in the voice.

On the boat, black and sinister, a lad with the badge of the Royal Fusiliers on his lapels came up to Stephen, stumbling over the feet of sleeping men in the darkness.

"Is this any good to you?" he asked, holding up a khaki article from which hung tapes. But Stephen decided against the patent bullet-proof waistcoat.

"Thanks," he said, "God knows I'm no hero, but I'd rather hate to be picked up with that thing on."

The youth nodded comprehensively: "I know, that's just what I feel myself. But you know what mothers are."

Stephen nodded: "Yes, and fathers, too."

"You're right, I'll have to chuck the bally thing overboard."

Havre. And now already those three ghastly days in the camp upon the hill seemed remote and unreal. Havre. The café at the corner of the big square. The American bar. Chevalier. Drinks. Too many drinks. Painted girls at little tables with callow English boys. Disappearing. Where?

"Don't you know?" Perched on his high stool at the bar, Experience explains. "Rooms provided upstairs for short times. Regular business here."

They disappeared in couples, the girls with a businesslike air; their khaki-clad companions, sheepishly, flushed with unfamiliar wine, full of curiosity, desire.

And then the train at last and O'Reilly and Piers. Both bound for the same battalion, brothers. O'Reilly taking nothing seriously, with always a droll story in that Canadian drawl that had about it a hint of Dublin.

And Piers, slow and whimsical, startling you when you least expected it with a bawdy story; then later, mood changing, talking books, poets. Something lovable about Piers, thin and gaunt and melancholy.

At Rouen there had been twelve hours of waiting. They loafed about the quays.

"Wasn't it along here that the Ball of Suet[5] travelled with her basket of edibles upon a memorable occasion?" asks Piers.

O'Reilly had spotted a large café. He indicated the door.

"What a commentary on human nature," remarked Stephen, thinking of the Ball of Suet who, of course, was a woman and a fellow creature while her shared provisions lasted, but only a woman of a certain kind when her body became the price of liberty.

They sat down by a wide window from which they had a full view of the ancient city's river front. All was grey – river, sky and city.

O'Reilly said: "Of course. I had forgotten that the Germans had been here."

"And the English, for that matter," added Piers.

Beyond the slow grey Seine, against the dun sky, the hill of Bon Secours was etched against the skyline.

"They love to show you the place where they burnt the Maid," remarked Piers. "And for a franc or two will tell you many lies. And if the Maid doesn't thrill you, they know something better than that. Have you noticed, French guides think an Englishman in France is only happy in a brothel? And if that one doesn't work, why then they produce their postcards."

Stephen said, "The Ball of Suet must have been a fairly prosperous lady. Perhaps that is why, when everybody fled, she was the only one with provisions?"

But O'Reilly had been thinking of the Maid, twiddling his glass.

"It was a dirty crime, the burning of Joan," he announced.

Piers shrugs his shoulders, languidly.

"It was. But like the crucifying of Christ, it was a long time ago. Tragedies are only tragedies when they are near enough to touch us personally."

O'Reilly disputed that and looked as though he were ready either to fight or weep over the Maid.

"She had a fair trial," argued Piers.

O'Reilly snorted. "That's what the Germans say in defence of the execution of Nurse Cavell,"[6] he retorted.

It was evening when they rose from the marble-topped table. They were the best of friends now, cronies already, philosophic. And just a little drunk.

4

'A' Company H.Q. dugout; a mouth in a sandbag face. The guide stooped and disappeared within. They followed in file. It was dark, and the uneven steps were steep and slippery. The dugout was thirty feet below trench level.

The guide pulled aside a rough curtain of sacking, and a tired, handsome face peered out at them. The Company Commander was sitting sideways at a rough bench upon which were papers, a holster, an empty tin mug and plate with fat-smeared knife and fork. A candle, thrust into a bottle-neck, lighted his work and filled the dugout with moving shadows.

The guide saluted. "The three draft officers, sir," he announced, and passed into the shadows beyond.

The Major greeted them with a slow smile of welcome. Not a man of words, this dignified veteran of the Somme, about whom there is an air of detachment, serenity, remoteness. He is in the war, this man past middle age, but scarcely of it. He indicated the bench, and Stephen slumped down beside him. He pointed an arm and O'Reilly and Piers lurched towards the wire bunks beyond.

Stephen was trying to remember. He had met this man before: but where?

"What part are you from, Craig?"

"Ferguson's Landing, sir, in the Fraser Valley."

The tired face lighted up.

"Well, well, you don't say? Then you'll likely know my brother?"

"Andy MacDonald, sir?"

"Why, yes."

For a moment the dugout faded to twilit unreality. The valley burned vividly in the heat of a summer's day. Cling, clang, and the harsh breath of forge bellows, glow of red roaring fire. There are the old gossips in the smithy and sweat-grimed Andy is entertaining them with his unending riddles and lewd stories.

The Major, head propped on arm, murmurs: "Well, well," as one who wakes from a dream. They look into each other's eyes and they share the valley of their vision. Hot and still it is in the summer sun, the river burnished, the green forest very still.

The candle burned steadily. Only the creaking of leather, where O'Reilly and Piers sit hunched upon the chicken-wire bunks, listening.

"Has the place changed much?"

Stephen opened his mouth to answer.

There is a shattering crash, an ear-splitting detonation. A blast of air gushes into the dugout: they are in total darkness. Somewhere debris is falling, and from the dugout walls earth cascades down in little avalanches. They can see nothing, only hear and smell. The stench of spent high-explosives is in their nostrils.

The Major's voice comes out of the darkness. It is level, tired, matter-of-fact.

"Anyone there?" he asks, turning towards the direction of the invisible sack-screened doorway.

"Yessir."

"Oh, you, Sergeant Glenny. Well?" A torchlight frames a dark and brooding face beneath a forward-tilted helmet. The sergeant is rubbing his elbow. He has been blown down the steep steps head first.

"Coal-box, sir,"[7] he explains laconically. "Jerry isn't playing fair this afternoon. It's only four o'clock."

The Major strikes a match, applies the dancing flame to a candle.

"No," he agrees laconically. "Not playing fair." For weeks the Saxons in their trenches, forty yards away, had been taking things easy. But every afternoon around five o'clock the battalion had come to look for the evening hate, a sporadic activity of machine guns, bombs and coal-boxes that lasted half an hour or so. But never before a sporting signal: a flippant tattoo of snapping machine-gun fire high overhead in warning.

"Go and have a look."

The Major is fastening his belt. He is going to have a look, too.

5

From the Kellett line, facing to the east, the conformation of the ground was visible, a reach of mud, pitted with craters and shell holes, littered with wire entanglements. A hump, like a monstrous slug, Vimy Ridge broke the arc of the eastern skyline. To the south the flanks of Notre Dame de Lorette rose steeply, scarred by abandoned trench works.[8]

Once cattle, driven from the village by aged men, had watered at the meandering Souchez, but its banks had been bombarded until the flow of the little stream filled shell holes, craters and the network of the trenches all about the low-lying ground. And, having watered there the beasts were wont to move up to Bois en Hache to shelter from the sun. That was the wood, over there, a few totem poles of charred and splintered wood. Trees, once upon a time.

Over this desolation, now lit by a watery sun, the tide of battle had washed backwards and forwards. And would wash again. The coming battle brooded over the trenches and the men in the trenches.

6

"In some places Jerry is only thirty yards away." The corporal, rifle slung, was piloting Stephen on his first duty round. "It's easy enough to walk into his lines in the dark, too. Even the old-timers lose their sense of direction now and again."

Thus one came late in the day to learn a job of one's subordinates.

Their progress was very slow because at this part of the trench the duckboards were sunk two feet in yellow mud. They wore thigh gum-boots and at every step pulled their legs up out of the sucking mud and let them sink back again.

They came up to a man, standing on fire-step, eyes glued to periscope. The corporal said: "If you look, sir, you'll see what I mean."

Stephen looked. In the periscope he could see a wide section of No Man's Land. There was something hanging there across the enemy's wire.

"You see what I mean, sir?" said the N.C.O. at his elbow. "He lost his way, though you'd think it was impossible. Been there three days. We can't get him in. Not that it matters much. He's dead. But still . . ."

Stephen nodded. But still . . . No need to say more.

They moved along. The trench took a right-angle turn, and rose in an easy gradient. Here the mud was even deeper, and each step meant exertion, drawing one leg up, sinking it again in this yellow mud.

The corporal went ahead.

He said: "Keep your head low here, sir, we're open to enfilade fire."[9]

Stephen turned. He saw that now they stood fully exposed to No Man's Land. Across the trench, every few yards, were piled sand-bags on beams from parapet[10] to parados.[11] Below curtains of sacking hung. Some protection. But not much.

Somewhere over there, among those tangled wires of the enemy's trenches, there was a watching eye. Stephen felt it on the back of his head. Now he was aiming, finger on trigger, eye close to telescopic sight. In a moment . . . But no. They reached the first curtain of sacking and passed beyond. A machine gun emplacement was revealed. The crew turned round, saluted.

"Anything to report?"

"Sniper's pretty busy, sir, but nothing else." They moved slowly on.

Every inch of this interminable way would have to be retraced, including this stretch within the German sniper's field of vision.

An hour later, the tour nearly done, Stephen, ploughing slowly through the mud, pulled aside the sacking. A report, sharp as a whip crack, snapped above his head, a wet stinging impact of bullet into sandbag. The corporal pulled him back. The curtain fell to.

"Nearly got you, sir," said the corporal. "The bastard!"

Stephen smiled crookedly.

What does one do? Officer and N.C.O. Of course this fellow knew infinitely more about the game than he, Stephen, did. But Stephen wore two stars upon his shoulder straps. They made all the difference, even if his was a Tommy's[12] tunic, just like the man's beside him.

Officers lead, other ranks did what they were told. Impossible to stand here all day. On the other hand, waiting, with his rifle lined on that sacking, was a watchful sniper. Nor could one ask the N.C.O. what should be done under the circumstances. Stephen felt anger rising, the anger of the impotent.

Now, if it had been a matter of taking a club and having a go at a visible enemy likewise armed with a similar club, then there would be something in it. One might almost enjoy that. Anyway, one would not funk it.[13] And Stephen was funking it now, funking it on a day when the line was quiet as a Sabbath afternoon. What would he be like when the rough stuff began?

"Well, we'll be getting along."

They moved slowly forward through the mud. The divided sacking revealed a desolation.

"Keep well down, sir," counselled the following corporal.

Stephen's heart throbbed with a sobbing beat against the wall of his chest.

Perhaps now? No. Well, then, he is taking extra special care to get him this time. But no. Two more steps, three, four, five. Stephen swallowed a lump in his throat. Of all abominations: to pitch head foremost and die in this polluting mud!

The first tour is done. Once more the dugout, now already wearing a homely, friendly air. Stephen shook a bulky form that lay on the lower bunk.

"Your tour, O'Reilly," he said. Then, turning to Major MacDonald, he added: "I suppose I might turn in for a bit myself, sir?"

But the Company Commander pointed out that first he must report. Report? Report what? Your round. How queer, such formality in a wet dugout in the front line!

O.C. 'A' Co.

Sir,
I beg to report as follows (8 a.m. - 11 a.m.)
1. *Everything quiet.*
2. *No. 3 M.G. crew report a sniper busy at a point roughly from their emplacement N. 20 or 30 rounds fired.*
3. *Another sniper is operating at a point so far as I can judge E by SE from M.G. No. 2.*
S. Craig.

The Major read the report. Then he handed it back.

"What about the wind?" he asked, eyebrows raised.

"The wind?" Stephen is uncomprehending.

"Have you never heard of gas?" And there is a tinge of contempt in the tone.

Stephen took the flimsy squared paper.[14] He was ashamed. And that gong above the dugout door to remind him, the Klaxon, and his own gas-mask.

He left the dugout chagrined, carrying the major's compass in his hand. He had been so pleased to know just how to write his report.

When he returned he wrote again.

4. Light wind. NNE.

He was learning his job.

In the afternoons, after days of inactivity, when it seemed as though the war had become a matter of alert watchfulness and nothing more, the enemy's evening hate would begin. But always first that friendly warning: the music-hall tattoo of the machine gun, facetious, grotesque in this place. It seemed to say: "Sorry, fellows, but our officers make us do this, so keep your heads down."

A humorist, but a man with a heart. Perhaps many men with hearts? Over there, behind the wire, behind that parapet.

Their machine guns traversed the trenches, scattering mud and sand, splintering woodwork, but beyond that, did little harm. For that a man well entrenched would scarcely stop from scratching.

But the sausages[15] were another affair. They came sizzling across No Man's Land in a drunken parabola, their sterns waggling. You could watch them as they came. Dodging sausages was a science more easily learned for having played Fives,[16] Stephen decided. They gave one time, a sense of direction, so that one could dash for the next traverse[17] and there shelter, crouching down. A little shaking, a ringing in the ears. But nothing worse.

But when they exploded, as they sometimes did, right in the trench, there was a hole big enough to house a transport wagon comfortably. Now and then, they caught a man unawares; and when that happened, there was little left of him.

7

Life shared in the dugout was a community life. There were no comforts. There was no privacy. All ate at the narrow bench which was also the Company Commander's office; slept in the two-tiered bunks. And as they ate food which had been hot when it left the battalion kitchen half an hour before, but was hot no longer, rats, scurrying insolently among the beams, scattered dirt upon the food. Sometimes the bread ration ran short.

"Hey! Is this bread meant for four?" It is O'Reilly, whose burly frame needs food, holding up a meagre piece of bread.

"Yessir."

"They're shelling the Arras Road," explains the tired, even voice of Major MacDonald; "you can hear it."

"What you need, my lad, to cheer you up is a nice hot cup o' tea," chirped

Stephen. "Here it is. Or shall I say, here it would be if that Primus could be made to function."

O'Reilly tilted the tin mug and put it down promptly. "I suppose one gets used to it in time, but that dope they put into everything we drink makes me feel sick."

"I'd like a word in the ear of the M.O. who doctored this lot," growled Piers. "He's too conscientious."

8

At the Canadian Military School the science of trench warfare had seemed plain enough. The blackboard made the theory clear, and in the practice trenches, that showed as white scars chalked against the green of the Sussex Downs, the application of that theory had been easy enough, for there the trenches were laid out symmetrically. One saw trench warfare as a game of chess, not easy, but played upon a prescribed board, and in accordance with known rules.

But what could one make of this actual trench map, this intricate white mesh across the blue-print? How could one apply those carefully assimilated theories to this tangle of defences?

Here, for instance, was Kellett Line straggling southward like a worm to meet Company Trench at right angles; and Company Trench, in turn, linking with the Arras Road at an obtuse angle, and that road, or what remained of it, stretching two thousand yards to the Colonel House where, by an eastward turn, you took Angres Alley and zig-zagged down to Cooker Alley, and so to Mustard Corner and the Kellett Line. Roughly, the four sides of a square, and that square veined with trenches and entanglements like the back of an ancient's hand.

9

It is dark. But the corporal had a reputation as guide. They climbed out of the trench and disappeared. The ground was slimy and now and again they stumbled over unseen obstacles, over potholes, shell-holes, filled with muddy water, cold and foul. Presently they should come out somewhere on Rotten Row.

The corporal led. "Wire there, sir," he cautioned, or, again: "Bad place, go easy there."

Presently he halted and moved his head about. His tin helmet, mud-smeared so that it will reflect no light if flares are fired, moved like a monstrous bloom in the gloom. His face showed phantom-like through the darkness.

"Sorry, sir, but I guess I've loss my bearings. If I'd been right we'd be up to Rotten Row by now. I must 'a gone wrong."

His voice was the voice of a man whose vanity is touched. To go wrong like this, and with a new officer!

Faintly came a muffled sound. Over there, in the direction to which they were heading, a German working party was labouring silently. At any moment this darkness might be broken, cleft by the arching stalk of a flowering star shell. At any moment the machine guns might open up.

"Let's go on." Stephen moved as he spoke.

The corporal slung his rifle. Now he followed. A chagrined man.

Well?

There it was again: officer and N.C.O. The N.C.O., at the end of his resources, merely had to say so. But the officer, why, he must find a way, take the initiative, the responsibility. Act. Yet this corporal was a noted guide, a seasoned soldier while he, Stephen, was the veriest amateur in war.

It was cold, and the night air was moisture-laden; mist floated in torn shreds about the trenches. The muffled sounds continued. They slid and scrambled, breathing heavily.

Men, working there unseen. Stopping now and then to listen, apprehensively. Men with fast-beating hearts, or men indifferent from usage that dulls the instinct of self-preservation, but dulls it last. Men with beating hearts, alert for that star shell that may cleave the night and give them to the hungry waiting guns, the merciless machine guns.

And men at those guns, too, peering through the gloom, watchful, waiting.

Stamping half-frozen feet on fire-steps. Waiting for the coming of the rum. Thinking of home, of warmth, and comfort. Of their families, their girls.

Wire, more wire, something hard that took skin from shins. Then the dim outline of a parapet. Their trenches. They scrambled over the parapet, breathing heavily.

"How did you make it, sir?"

"I worked by the Dipper – the Plough, we call it[18] – but it was mostly luck. The stars are useful. But it was luck, mostly."

The stars, the same stars. Beyond the great trees, as one looked up out of the silent, shadowy valley. Most beautiful. Over the ship, too, as she pulses on her eastward course, following. Following stars, watching stars. Old friends who had come with one across the world and would return again – alone? Other stars, maybe, other worlds, other wars. Soldiers on Mars, looking with longing at that steadfast star serene, that star, the Earth.

Through the darkness a phantom gleaming forest rises, and ghostly trees clothe the naked, violated earth in a kindly garb of green. Rain descends, beating a loud tattoo upon the forest's trees. The kindly rain.

The ghostly forest has vanished. Not rain at all. Lights are winking away there to the rear. The air is alive with sound. It is the guns.

And now the trench seemed a sweet and homely place, familiar, welcoming. As for the dugout, it too wore the friendly face of home.

10

Blue smoke filled the dugout. The Major slept, head on arms outstretched upon the littered bench – the bench he only left to prowl the line. O'Reilly and Piers squatting opposite one another on their bunks. Both chuckling.

"Hallo, Craig. Listen to this: 'There was a young man of Mysore' –"

"That is one of Piers' little efforts; he's quite a poet."

O'Reilly rose, his great bulk filling the narrow companion-way between the bunks, buckling his Sam Browne. A corporal, from nowhere, already awaited him, a nose and mouth beneath the curve of helmet, there in the doorway.

Stephen loosened belt and tunic and slumped on to his bunk. Those stars, confound them. He fumbled for Field Message book, humped himself and wrote. Piers smoked, lying upon his back, tall and thin, a bag o'bones of a man with a woman's hands. He quizzed silent Stephen.

"Letters?" he asked.

"No, only an idea," Stephen dissembled.

"Verse?"

"Sort of, I suppose."

"I say, that's interesting." Piers sat up and swung his legs down.

"D'you know, between ourselves, I write 'em, too."

This was a private affair, after all, something not too willingly shared.

"Do you?" said Stephen, in a colourless voice. But he was interested, and now regarded the wistful face of Piers with a new alertness and interest.

The Major stirred, sat up, listened. He turned, and they saw a haggard face. He jerked his wrist and frowned at the glowing dial of his watch. In sleep his ears have heard the guns and sent the message to his brain.

A detonation shook the dugout, scattering dirt.

"What's that?" He is only half awake now, his poor head muzzed by fading dreams.

A red face peers through the sacking of the doorway, answering him:

"Our guns, sir, firing short. They'll be right on top of us in a moment." Then, with reproach in the voice: "The second time this week. Dud gunners, they are."

The Major leapt. "As though I'd men to throw away," he snarled.

He is through to H.Q. The staccato voice of the buzzer fills the dugout with its urgency.

"Show me?" Piers extended a thin arm.

Stephen hesitated. "It was only an idea," he deprecated. And Piers, tilting the page to the light of the candle, read:

The Seven Stars that form the Plough
I marked five thousand miles away.
I watched them as the long train sped
Across the prairie, day by day.
They followed on, far out at sea,
The great ship as she eastward sped;
I saw them from the deck each night:
The Seven Stars which followèd.

And lo! there, high above this trench,
I see those stars, immobile now,
They know that though I take the sword
My heart is faithful to the Plough.

Piers scratched his stubbly cheek; nodded his head slowly, an understanding expression upon his sensitive face.

"That happen to-night?" he asked. His voice was surprisingly gentle.

Stephen grunted. Piers had poached upon his privacy. He felt resentful.

11

An infinity of Stephens: the Stephen of the trenches, conscientious, matter-of-fact; and Stephen, the husband and father, who broods apprehensively in secret for the final issue. The officer and the man.

And was that all? No, for the officer was but a pretence, while the man was real, real and many-faceted. There remained other Stephens. There was the objective observer of the other two, a Stephen standing back a little, a spectator with understanding heart. A philosopher who pondered the inverted moral values of a world at war. A rebel who protested impotently. A mystic who brooded apart, sensing vaguely behind this obscenity the veiled splendours of a world elusive and unseen, yet very real.

Who shall know this man, so various, so complex? No one.

Notes

1. Subaltern: lieutenant or second lieutenant.
2. The Ridge': Vimy Ridge (see map).
3. Sir Henry Wilson took command of the IV Corps December 22, 1915 and was thrown back by the Germans from his position just west of Vimy Ridge.

4. "Archie" (battery): anti-aircraft gun battery.
5. "Ball of Suet": Guy de Maupassant's novel, *Boule de Suif* (1880), about a buxom young woman of easy virtue.
6. Nurse Cavell: Edith Cavell (1865 - 1915), head nurse at the Berkendael Medical Institute in Brussels. Shot by the Germans for aiding Allied prisoners, etc.
7. "Coal-box": large calibre artillery shell.
8. See map of area.
9. Enfilade fire: bullets fired at you from the sides.
10. Parapet: a built-up bank extending along the front of a trench.
11. Parados: a built-up mound extending along the back of a trench.
12. "Tommy": British soldier.
13. "funk it": to shirk, avoid taking action.
14. "flimsy squared paper": a reference to the Field Message Book carried by officers. It was used to write requisitions (aka 'chits') for equipment, to grant permission to lower ranks, etc.
15. Sausages: heavy trench-mortar bombs.
16. Fives: a game played with a ball against a wall, resembling squash, but played with the hand ('a bunch of fives').
17. Traverse: a built-up bank at the side of a trench and extending forward towards the enemy lines; used to block bullets from the flank.
18. "the Plough": i.e. the Big Dipper or Ursa Major. It contains the North Star.

CHAPTER IV

1

THE tour is over and the battalion withdrawing to the support trenches. It winds along a labyrinth of duck-walked trenches, and those trenches deep in mire.[1] The men breathe heavily, talking but little. Tired they are, wet, cold and hungry. The harsh bark of coughing betrays their slow progress. Now and again a warning word travels from man to man along the file.

"Wire!" And every man stoops.

"Busted slats!" And every man steps warily.

There is little other talk. It has been an uneventful tour, with but one casualty: the boy from Sapperton, who thought it fun to draw the sniper's fire, and succeeded too well. A wasted life.

But the autumn had seen much hard fighting. And now winter, with cold and the misery of perpetual wetness that brought hacking coughs: fever. And spring so far away.

An hour's steady crawl to the jangle of equipment, clank of steel, creak of leather and then the hump of Notre Dame de Lorette, high against the dark night sky.

Shadows pour slowly from the end trench, a dark fluid from an aqueduct, and flow over the muddy ground. They are out of the line. They are in the support trenches.

2

In the front line dugouts a man might generally stand erect. True enough, there was often inches of water underfoot, but a little ingenuity, a few scrounged Mills bomb boxes and you could contrive a flooring of sorts. Besides, there were the bunks, high above the dirt where, by candle light, a man might smoke and read in peace.

But here the century was no more. These billets would have grieved a cave man.

Huddled like a pigmy village in the open, the sandbag hovels, roofed with corrugated iron, are really sties, igloos of mud, kennels no more than four feet high. The men go into them on all fours, like dogs, dragging their equipment with them. They spread their ground sheets, muttering, search for candles, matches.

"Christ!"

"Je-sus."

They do not like it, not at all. They looked for something better than this. Even these sandbag walls are bursting, spilling forth their slimy contents. How could a man sleep like this? How could a man clean up? It wasn't to be done. Suffering Christ, it wasn't.

3

Boots, gas masks, goggles, steel helmets, puttees, mess tin covers, holdalls, comforters, trench tool handles, webb equipment, caps, tunics, pants, coats . . .

How is No. 3 platoon for shortages? Well, where is No. 3 platoon?

On the parade ground of the military school a platoon was a platoon. There it was, standing in front of you. You could count the men, move them about, check their equipment. But in the line there were men here and men there, men on fire-steps, men in dugouts, men out at the advance post, runners, cook-house men. The rigid unit of the text books and parade ground had vanished, and in its place were men scattered anywhere at all.

Yet one must see to one's men, and care for them. Stephen slid and stumbled in the darkness. The rum ration could be issued right away. Magic rum that burnt like a hot flame in the blood; wonder-worker that wiped misery away.

Who carried the rum? This man? That man? Loud voices arguing, casting blame, the one from the other. The rum is mislaid. The rum *must* be found. An hour passes. Why isn't there a rum ration?

Angry voices.

The rum is found: two stone demijohns half buried in the ooze of a burst sandbag.

Rum! Wonder-worker, burning, aromatic; stinging the larynx, scalding a man's guts. But good rum. The best. Jamaica rum, dark, dark brown, pungent-smelling comforter. Drink it down. In one gulp, head back. Who cares about these kennels now? What is this misery, when the body sings like a bird, when the heart is uplifted?

4

Sergeant Glenny came along for a green envelope.

If the men were kennelled like dogs, the officers now fared a little better;

their semi-dugouts were built half into the slope of the hill and finished off with sandbag walls. They were fairly dry, had good bunks, a bench for table.

Sergeant Glenny, then, Stephen now realised, was his right-hand man. A good man too, as he had sensed in the line. But now to be a rod and staff, reservoir of vast stores of knowledge, humbly offered superior ignorance. For such is the Army.

"A green envelope?" Stephen does not even understand.

"Yes, sir. They issue a limited number for specially private letters. They're liable to be opened by the base censor, but aren't censored here."

Stephen understood. What a decent idea.

"You want one especially, sergeant?" he asked.

"Well, sir, yes, I do. You see, my wife is expecting."

Who should understand now better than Stephen?

"I'll get one from the Major," he promises.

But there are no green envelopes available. Still, there is a way out. It is quite simple. The sergeant returns; Stephen explains. The big fellow's face falls, his eyes look reproachful.

"No green envelopes?"

"Is the letter written?" Stephen asks.

The sergeant fumbles in his tunic: "Yes, sir."

How many tender things were in that letter? How many things meant for but one other human creature? To have those lines read by this man whom one would see day by day, one's immediate superior officer.

"Very well," announces Stephen, "I think we can get over this little difficulty. Seal the envelope."

The man licks the envelope thoughtfully. Stephen holds out his hand for it. He has written his signature upon the corner.

"That goes through like that, sergeant."

The sergeant's face breaks into a smile, his eyes speak gratitude. Stephen waves his thanks aside.

And regulations? Well, good things in their way, and necessary. Good things to break now and then. Certainly that letter contained no information of use to the enemy. And there the Army's interest in it ended . . .

Little women somewhere over there waiting for their babies. How damnable to keep their men from them at such a time. Well, consider all the armies, all the married men, all the leaves, and all the expectant mothers without their men. What vast reservoir of anxious love was there!

There must be a power of praying going on, Stephen conjectured. But to what purpose? The war went on. And men went down, went down and never saw those fragments of themselves that beat beneath their mothers' hearts, their unborn children. Certainly there would be less praying hereafter.

The support trenches have disclosed his platoon to Stephen. And now a batman materialises. Pilk, a little reed of a man sporting the two ribands of the Boer War. Sharp features, bottle shoulders, and false teeth that decline to stay in their place. An alert little man with the springy step characteristic of the weakling.

But Pilk is swift and efficient, quiet and orderly, good-humoured. He understands the boning of leather. He sets to work on the Sam Browne.

"Plenty of bones about here," he remarks, "but a bit green."

Stephen looks up. "What on earth are you using?" he asks in a horrified voice.

"Only a bone, sir," answers Pilk, soothingly.

"Yes, but d'you know what sort of bone, man?"

Pilk continues to strop the belt with the bone.

"Can't say that I do, sir. Human, likely as not."

"Yes, it is. That's a tibia."

Pilk looks mildly interested.

"Is it, sir?" he asks, with polite interest, continuing his work.

Not far to seek for bones in that Golgotha where sixty thousand Frenchmen fell. There is a tibia just outside the door where a little gutter drains down off the hill. And later a skull adorns the landscape. Some wag has mounted it on a stick and beneath it placed a pirate's cross-bones. When Death is a familiar, one jests with him. Why not? Presently another skull and cross-bones appear above the dugout door. Pilk has his own ideas of nattiness. Stephen says nothing.

5

The men went overland to Ablaine St. Nazaire[2] to clean up unwashed bodies, to draw from the Q.M. store grey shirts, clean and smelling of the bakehouse. To bath. There were lice upon these baked shirts, it is true, but they were dead lice and therefore of no account.

Ecstasy of hot water under the showers of the field baths.

The battalion headquarters were in the cellars of a demolished house, once the *mairie*.[3] Here the Colonel, short and sturdy, pink-cheeked and very spruce, sat before a littered table; on the opposite side of the road the shell of the old grey church raised two sides of a half-demolished tower, a battered tombstone for the dead chancel. Little of the village remained; the ebb and flow of battle had washed over it, and the guns of two armies had pounded it until there was not a single dwelling left unscarred, and the few standing walls that had withstood the fury bore the pock-marks of shattering steel.

The village was dead, but it was alive with men. Painted signs stuck out from every ruin. Y.M.C.A., Signals, Q.M.S. Stores, H.Q, Canteen, Latrines, Dressing Station. Khaki figures looked out from ruins, crawled out of cellars, scuttled about the ruined road.

The shattered village carried on. A shell burst on the pitted road, scattered debris, brought tumbling precarious walls. Well, one could not stop them getting the range. But curse those fellows who would walk in the open, for they told the enemy plainly that Ablaine St. Nazaire was still worth his shot.

Every day this road was shelled half-heartedly. But the prospect of delousing, of bathing, made the men out of the line indifferent to the hazard. They scarcely turned a head when a column of smoke and flying debris spurted from the scarred road as they moved towards the village from the toe of the hill of Notre Dame, but marched openly towards clean shirts and running water; towards coffee and chips, fags. What were mere pot shots from somewhere back of Lievin? Why, nothing to get excited about. To hell with it!

The bath house has canvas walls, duck-board flooring and rows of iron pipes overhead from which hot water, scalding water, falls. The place is full of steam and naked men, men with spotty bodies, little sores from scratching, lousy men soon to be cleansed, but soon to be verminous again.

The bath house shakes and the stoker pokes his head round the boiler.

"A near one that," he grins, as the noise of falling debris subsides.

What do they care? To hell with it!

"Got a bit of soap, Shorty?"

"This is the stuff."

Latherings, rubbings, snortings. Luxurious! Toes, pick at 'em.

"Ever see a bunion like that? A bitch on the march, I'll tell the world . . ."

Piers, O'Reilly and Stephen walked back to the village and bathed luxuriantly.

Yes, the baths were popular.

6

They are to be a week in the support trenches; beyond taking shortages, and the supply of working parties, there is not much to do.

Stephen got his orders from Major MacDonald when they returned from the bath. He was sitting before a little bench in the hill-side dugout from the open door of which were visible the desolation of the valley and the hump of grim Vimy Ridge beyond. Vimy the coveted. Vimy the impregnable, dark and brooding. Vimy the prize to be won by the price of battle.

"You're detailed to take charge of a working party," he explained; "the work is somewhere beyond Headquarters Trench. A sapper[4] will take charge when you get there."

That was a relief, anyway, that sapper.

There had been working parties on the green slopes of the Downs by Caesar's Camp.[5] But Stephen suspected that a working party in the line would be, like a platoon in the line, a very different thing from the working parties of the military school. The thought of the sapper was a comfort.

At five o'clock it was already dark; a fine soaking rain fell. The men fell in, and they were peeved men, hating working-parties above everything; clean men, spruced up after hours of patient toil, and now soon to be befouled with mud again, out there in the quagmires of No Man's Land. In five minutes those communication trenches alone would leave them slimy and wet from the knees down. A couple of hours would see them wet and muddied to the middle. The rain would soon complete their misery.

Stephen stumbled behind the guide. He was in charge, but if there was a man there who understood less about his job than he did, he would have liked to shake hands with him. An hour's heavy going brought them to Head-quarters Trench, where a sullen sapper awaited them beside a dump of shovels. The downpour had increased.

"Bloody awful night," he greeted Stephen.

Stephen nodded. "Where are the gumboots?" he asked.

"Gumboots? That's just it. There are none, and a fouler place I don't know."

A fed-up man, this sapper, a little man who in other days had watched a hydro-electric plant grow under his hand, marking the relentless harnessing of roaring cataracts, and who was now contemptuous of this niggling work, messing with wire and corkscrew stakes.

He took over the party as one who accepts a liability, and they straggled out into No Man's Land, each man with his shovel. The ground over which they slipped and slid was a quagmire pitted with watery shell-holes and craters. Soon every man was soaked to the thighs, lifting with every step a weight of clinging mud.

The work began. But it was only a pretence of work. The men moved about slowly, without apparent purpose. Stephen saw shapes dimly in the darkness; men – they were doing nothing in particular, scrimshanking,[6] making a pretence of digging, working slowly into the slime the corkscrew stakes, lifting, laggardly, drums of spiteful barbed wire.

Poor devils!

Well, it was up to the sapper to get whatever the job was, done. And Stephen had no notion of what it might be. If it was to get order out of this chaos, then certainly the men might as well be back there at Notre Dame de Lorette writing letters, playing poker, telling smutty stories.

The rain was coming down faster now, a drenching soft rain that soaked them furtively. Now and then the silence was broken by the sharp report of a sniper's rifle. Shots in the dark from that trench over there, from the rifle of a man who was seeing in every shadow the shape of an enemy. Nervous shooting.

Out of the blackness a yellow light wavered up. Somebody trying to light a pipe with cupped hands, stooping low.

"Put that light out! Put that light out!" Stephen and the sapper speaking with one voice, and that an angry one.

"The fool!"

"The criminal idiot!"

The darkness is split by a hissing, flaming rocket of light. It curves upwards across the desolation and shadows race before it; it descends in a curved and graceful arc, hisses a moment in the mud, expires. It has fallen in the centre of the group of figures that stood out for that brief moment in etched clearness against the blackness of the night.

And now the night is filled with soaring lights that taper upwards like phosphorescent plant stalks, crowned with flowering luminosity. The enemy has spotted them. He has opened up with his machine guns. Slap, slap of bullets in mud and the crescendo of traversing guns, now somewhere over there, now approaching, passing, returning. An unseen hose played up and down No Man's Land, a hose that squirted lead.

It was impossible that one could escape death for long. Stephen felt an impotent rage surge through him, a blind fury that nothing could be done by way of retaliation, that all one could do was to flop ignominiously and endure! Now, if one could only get up and come to grips . . . But no, that would not work either. He was unarmed. That elastic fifty pounds had worked wonders, true enough, but it had not run to a service revolver. On ceremonial parades Stephen had worried through apprehensively with an empty borrowed holster. And, anyway, if it came down to it, how could one level a revolver and empty it into another man? No thanks.

Stephen had crawled instinctively to a shell-hole, knowing that in this declivity no shot could get him. His two arms were under water and the wet had soaked through his clothing.

He became aware that another man was crawling to the same shelter; he could see the outline of the body as it came over the rim, a moving hump. And presently he detected the sound of suppressed sobbing.

"Come on down here, you fool!" he shouted. The figure slewed down.

"Oh, Jesus! Oh, Jesus! Oh, Jesus!" A young voice, a voice full of abject terror.

The guns continued to traverse up and down, the mud flew, the lights rose, stately and beautiful, and cast their blue radiance over the desolation. Stephen saw the young face darkly, under the rim of the tilted steel helmet. A boy, or little more. One of those fellows who had come up that very morning, a draft man. What was his name? Yes, Cullen, that was it.

What a jar for him! Fresh from the "Finest Battalion Ever Raised," and now that battalion broken up in England to feed the necessitous divisions already in the line. Rough luck, that! Chums separated, pride cast down; friendly, familiar officers scattered to strange line battalions.

And Stephen felt perfectly cool, self-possessed. The boy's fear was, after all, a blessing; it banished his own.

"You're all right, lad," he comforted. "But never stick your behind up like that when you are crawling on high ground under fire, or one day you'll get a packet where you sit down."

The lad was whimpering softly now, quite unashamed. Not the weeping of a child, nor the harsh tears that are sometimes wrung from a man, but a sound like the grief of an animal.

Stephen put his arm on the lad's shoulder, patted him. "Show a little guts, lad!" he shouted.

Had he suddenly gone stone deaf and blind?

No, the last flare had burnt itself out and, as suddenly as they had opened fire, the machine guns had become silent. He stood up and looked about him, seeing nothing in a darkness intensified after light. Had anyone been hit – killed? How could he find out?

The sapper stood beside him. "Call it a do," he said.

The word passed from mouth to mouth, and figures loomed out of the blackness, shambling with trailing shovels. And presently a group of bemudded spectres stood in the shelter of friendly Headquarters Trench. Were they all there? Or were some lying out there somewhere wounded, dead?

He called the roll. And each man answered. That was something. He breathed a sigh of relief. An hour later the outline of Notre Dame de Lorette loomed over them. They were back at the Spur, in the support trenches.

7

To the Adjutant –

Sir,

As officer in charge of working party detail from B and D Companies last night I have the honour to report that I took over at 5 p.m. at H. Q. and proceeded via Baffolle and Dugout Alley to H.Q. Trench.

Reported to Lt. Haig and obtained shovels. Proceeded to work under sappers draining old trenches on Kellett line.

The party was subjected to occasional sniping and at 11 p.m. the enemy put a flare into the party and opened up M.G. fire (approx. twenty minutes).

I would suggest that much discomfort to the men might be avoided if gumboots were supplied for this kind of work. The men were wet to the knees for five hours last night and this could have been avoided.

S. Craig, Lt.

8

Piers, O'Reilly and Stephen were sitting at ease in Stephen's dugout. O'Reilly suggested a party.

"We'll get the Major along and fill him with a little wholesome booze," he suggested. "I'll go along and invite him now; meanwhile you fellows pool the rum ration."

"I'll fix the drinks," Stephen volunteered. "Pass that mess tin, Piers. I've got a bright idea."

He poured the three rations into the flat tin, a dark and odorous liquid full of promise. "D'you think you could scrounge a few lemons from some-where?" he asked the hovering Pilk.

The batman scratched his head, raised himself twice on his toes rapidly, grinned his doubt. He prided himself on being the best scrounger in the brigade. But lemons!

"Well, I'll have a try, sir," he said.

He returned an hour later and produced three lemons.

"Great business," Stephen chirruped. "And now a bit of sugar and we're all set. As for you, Piers, you're a lazy hound, sitting there doing sweet Fanny Adams."[7]

Piers grinned, and turned a page of a small book from which he read, oblivious of the preparations, wreathed in blue smoke. Making his escape. Slamming a door upon the war, upon the present.

The primus, surprisingly, functioned. Soon the dugout was aromatic with the vapour of the hot punch. Rum, lemon, sugar. A King's drink, by heck! So it was. And plenty of it, *Gott sei dank.*[8]

O'Reilly returned, sniffed the atmosphere, exclaimed in his big, soft voice: "Oh, boy!" and slumped down heavily.

The Major came softly, pulling aside the sacking over the door. They stood up.

"Here you are, sir, just at the psychological moment. Fine."

They made him welcome, heartily.

"Craig is our new padre, sir," grinned O'Reilly.

The Major looked from face to face, anxious to enter into it all, yet preoccupied, feeling, as always in this war, just a little that he, the school inspector, was enduring an interminable nightmare.

Piers explained:

"Craig, sir, looks after the spirituous comfort," he drawled.

The Major smiled dutifully.

"A punk joke, isn't it, sir?" Stephen laughed, "but it's the best O'Reilly can manage. There's Irish blood in O'Reilly's veins. But not much, and what there is, is a bit sluggish."

9

The dugout became thick with tobacco smoke, heavy with the fumes of hot punch. The major took his tot since, all said and done, this was war and, somehow, the rules of life that prevailed in peace did not apply here or now. Everywhere it was the same. Men kicked aside the Ten Commandments. And they shrugged: "It's the war."

Somehow, it was the war; it was a complete defence. In one word: unanswerable.

As the fumes rose to his head they unloosed his tongue. Soon it was the Major who was doing the talking. All of it. He was re-living the days of the Somme, and his memory missed no detail of that stupendous battle.

An hour passed.

The three subalterns sipped their toddies and listened respectfully. Yawning beside the Major, Stephen saw that both O'Reilly and Piers were dozing. Presently he saw them lean towards each other. Their eyes closed. They slept, their mouths lolling open. And the even voice of the Major flowed steadily on.

And presently Stephen drowsed, heavy-eyed beside this silent man become garrulous, this man who now fought his battles not once but several times over again.

And then he, too, slept, leaning gradually more heavily upon the shoulder of the Major.

Suddenly aware that he was addressing himself to a sleeping audience, the Major stopped in mid-flight of reminiscence.

Three pairs of eyes opened. Three men spoke at once.

"By gad, sir, that's interesting."

"Well, we missed a whole lot of this war, but there seems to be plenty more of it left, sir."

And Stephen, sadly eyeing the mess tin: "I'm afraid the booze is all done, sir."

The Major rose. "It's been a great party," he declared, buckling his Sam Browne.

And they agreed heartily, stifling their yawns.

And as he went out they looked in wonder after him.

"Eat my hat if the Major isn't as near sozzled as may be," declared O'Reilly.

10

Malcolm MacDonald had been brought up in a Presbyterian home. His father had been a master carpenter, a first generation Canadian, with all the inherited traditions of a strait Scot. Ever since he was thirteen, he had had to think of life as a serious business. The eldest of seven, he had been for years his mother's mainstay. But somehow he had struggled through high school in the little Ontario town, had worked up for his school teacher's certificate and gone west.

Now he was the head of a home of his own. And that home was in the tradition of his Scottish Presbyterian forefathers. He had never tasted tobacco before coming overseas, and even now cigarettes had a way of becoming pulped in his mouth. He would never learn to smoke, and he knew it. He had never tasted alcohol before the war, had known but one woman in his life.

He felt, without being able to explain why, that dancing, theatres, and joy-riding were aspects of modern life to be deplored and discountenanced.

In the MacDonald home, in the half-made avenue out at Kitsalano, Vancouver, the Mission bookcases were locked. The sets of books that looked out of their imprisonment were leather bound: Scott (complete), Dickens (complete), Thackeray (complete), Foxe's *Book of Martyrs* (1811), and a *Popular Educator*, bought on the instalment plan. A narrow home, presided over by a thin little woman whose rimless glasses gave birdlike sharpness to the piercing eyes that looked out from behind them disapprovingly. An air of repression lay over the orderly little establishment. The children were seldom dirty, never rude; on the other hand, they did not laugh very often.

Life in the MacDonald household was real and decidedly earnest. It had manifold duties, but few pleasures. It imposed many obligations, but granted few concessions. And since it was part of the many duties imposed upon a man that he be prepared to fight for his country, from the early days MacDonald had been an earnest militiaman.

Who could have foreseen a war? Who could have imagined that war would be like this? Certainly not Malcolm MacDonald.

And now he talked about the Somme. His mind always came back to that battle. He talked about the war impersonally; but about the Somme he spoke in a proprietorial way. There was even affection in his voice. The battle, in memory, had become dear to him. He went over, again and again, every phase of it as he had lived and suffered it. It was the morbid affection of the leper for his sores, of the bereaved for the afflicting sorrow. The battle was his, and he would tell you of it because it was not yours, and you could share it only vicariously with him.

His life was broken in two parts. The Somme divided them. It had broken his life in two, so that it was like a bridge that was cleft at the crowning span. To get to the past it was necessary to think: before the Somme; after the Somme.

The battle became an orb, and the major revolved about it like a satellite. The battle, the battle that had got into his bones, into his flesh, into the whirling electrons of his brain's cells. He was dyed in the battle. Its living memory coloured his thoughts by day, his dreams by night.

He would sit at times, the papers of his routine work untouched before him, his calm sweet eyes looking out steadfastly, absorbed in the invisible. They looked out; yet they looked in. And he would stir suddenly and turn, like one continuing a talk in progress, continuing aloud his silent musings. And they would simulate interest, these subalterns, glance swiftly and furtively at one another. Humour him.

For the Somme belonged to the Major. It was his. He had a right to it. If he shared it with them freely, they were yet on sufferance and must remember it. What he gave of that experience they must accept, for he was privy to a mystery sealed to them.

And as suddenly as he broke into words, he would lapse back into abstracted silence, sitting still, his face clouded by memory, withdrawn from them.

Notes

1. "tour" refers to the time (about a week, usually) which soldiers had to spend in the front line trenches. The Canadian trenches were generally shallower and more vulnerable than the German trenches because the official Canadian Army mentality was "Don't get too comfortable because we will soon be attacking and leaving these trenches behind." Apart from their big attacks ("pushes"), the Germans tended to think defensively, with trenches often eight feet deep and connecting to tunnels and dugouts as much as forty feet below ground level.
2. "Ablaine St. Nazaire": see map at end of this book.
3. "mairie": town-hall.
4. "sapper": soldier expert in digging tunnels under enemy trenches, planting explosive charges in them; also used for building roads, fortifications, etc.
5. "Caesar's Camp": could be the escarpment looking out over Aldershot and Farnborough.
6. "scrimshanking": shirking duty.
7. "Fanny Adams": euphemism for "f--- all."
8. "Gott sei dank.": Thank God!

CHAPTER V

1

PIERS and Stephen climbed to the summit of Notre Dame de Lorette through a grey mist that enveloped the whole front, writhing sluggishly about the steep slopes of the scarred hill.

From this eminence, on a clear day, there was a clear view across the plains to ruined Arras. Vimy to the east, seemed to lie far below (though strangely, from Vimy, German eyes looked down upon this other hill). The ground between was hieroglyphed with trench works. Ablaine St. Nazaire was a mere pile of grey debris with one large dominating slab – the ruined church.

To the north, Liévin and Lens flourished untouched behind the German lines, two little oases of order in this desert of destruction and ruin. Too precious to the French, those twin mining towns, to be sacrificed to the guns. The Germans came and went in security. You could see them plainly through strong glasses, grey purposeful insects always on the move. Well, if the Allies were too tender to destroy these towns, let them push the line back and learn once more that thoroughness is the rule in war.

But on this chill morning the panorama was blotted out by the mist, grey-white and moist.

"What I particularly want to find," said Piers, "is the shrine they talk about, the one to Our Lady of Loretto. You know, this hill was a great place of pilgrimage. Every year thousands of devout and credulous souls came here to beg a boon of the flash plaster lady of the shrine. She was considered almost as great a wonder-worker as the Virgin at Lourdes."[1]

They reached the summit and found themselves amid a complete system of abandoned trenches, all fallen in and tufted here and there with coarse grass.

"A lot of our fellows come up here after souvenirs," Piers remarked. "'Frisking the stiffs,' they call it. It's pretty foul, isn't it? But I suppose when a man has been in the line a year or so he hasn't any sensibilities left. What he does to others to-day, somebody may do to him to-morrow."

Stephen was standing looking down into a collapsed trench from which sprouted tangled rusty wire and coarse grass tufts.

"If they want French equipment as souvenirs, they haven't far to look here," he remarked.

He stooped and picked up a rusted bayonet, and examined it. Then, idly, he kicked a boot that lay, sole upturned, in the mud. It rolled over and there in the gaping mouth was a skeleton foot. The snapped bone remained erect, a little stick, a little splintered tree, but one that would never come to leaf.

2

The boot lay there filled with the bony structure of the foot, and like a little mast, the shin bone thrust upwards from the sea of mud; yellow it was, like old ivory.

Mort pour la Patrie. Vive La France! Dulce et decorum est.

How would the Boot have been reported? As dead? Or among the missing? Probably among the missing, Stephen decided.

In little smudgy type, read through spectacles by a fat, dark woman with a black moustache . . .

Missing. Well, then, there was hope, *n'est ce pas?* Perhaps he is taken prisoner? Yes, that would be it. A prisoner. Hardship *avec les sales Boches,* but safe for the duration of the war.

Off to church.

Dimness; heavy, incensed air. And beyond that dimness: God. The good God who had arranged it thus. Candles before the tinsel shrine. The blessed saints protect him! Kneeling there, stout, short of breath, the Boot's mother. Praying, a little fat woman; perspiring, a drab little woman with a black moustache.

Praying for the Boot.

Waiting patiently for the Boot's return.

Scheming for the future of the Boot.

Marrying the Boot off.

Marie, yes. A nice girl, serious. And a *dot.*[2] How much the old man must have saved, such miserliness . . .

Well, as to that, was one not entitled to bargain a little for a gallant son like hers? She comes out into the great square of the little town. Little men with spotty faces, sallow faces, with stark yellow belts and leggings. *Les Portuguèses.* Allies.

And then – doubt. Doubt as she waddles through the *entresol.* Among the missing. Could that mean . . .?

Impossible! The good God would not allow it.

Aye, Boot, perhaps it is like that at home, eh? The good God has forgotten or has He taken you to that paradise of His?

Tears gathered in Stephen's eyes.

Well, Boot, can't you answer civilly? Poor Boot!

And poor mother woman. And sweetheart, perhaps. Yes, certainly a sweetheart, for the Boot is French.

Did he go with her on expeditions? Row her on a river. Kiss her in an orchard? Did he? Was she sweet? Did she yield?

And was Maman's choice, that Marie, a problem to be solved by common sense, a *dot, 'le business'?*

Ah, you are silent now, and all the ecstasies you knew have vanished in this misty air. A sorry fellow you are, lying there with your little garrison of bones, all that some shell has left of you.

Do you hope to rise some day and come together with all those missing bones, that vanished flesh? Do you wait patiently for the White Angel of the Lord to sound his trumpet call across this desolation?

And were you afraid at the last, were your toes in the right direction? And who did you call upon then, in that last agony of fear? Upon your good God, or little Angeline? Or upon the little Black Moustache?

Poor Boot, mouldering there, little coffin with its little skeleton. You did not want to come at all, did you? You loved life too much to wish to die. Even for *la Patrie.*

So different here, isn't it? No laughing girls, no booming bands to stir the quick blood. But only silence.

Ah, well, you travelled far. Many a weary mile you came. Did you start by proudly stamping up and down the parade ground? And then, less black, less shiny, along the weary roads of northern France? Then up this hill, and at the last, the journey's end? Here? In this caved-in trench? And here to remain?

But not for ever. Later on, they will reclaim you, bag of bones. And bury you with pomp and circumstance, and aged men will make orations. A little wooden cross will mark the spot and *immortelles* shall crown your chivalry,[3] and Black Moustache will come and she will weep.

That is how it will be. And with you all the other Boots and bones and bits and pieces.

You must not lie like this, you know. So untidily. That would not do at all. Did you not die for *la Patrie?* Of course!

No, it didn't do to think; it didn't do at all.

He turned away, suddenly chilled, but the debris of battle still lay scattered everywhere: rotted leather wear, pouches, belts, slings, rusted rifles, bayonets, haversacks, and shiny leather pouches cracked, but otherwise defying damp and time; yellow grenades and cracked and splintered grenade boxes, dull aluminium water-bottles, shaped like great lozenges. Wire, everywhere tangled, rusted wire.

They worked their way over the ground in silence. At length Piers remarked: "Imagine it. On this one small promontory sixty thousand Frenchmen have been killed. Then think of the whole front, from the Coast down to the

Argonne. Do a sum in multiplication, and then cast your mind to the boggy wastes around the eastern German front. Think of Tannenberg,[4] of the Italian front. And when you've done that, my dear Craig, take a long hop and consider Gallipoli.[5] Is the tale told then? It is not. There is still Palestine, the desert, East Africa. And even *then* there is still the sea. After all that it seems paltry to mention the few odd hundreds killed by the air raids at home."

They found the shrine, a virgin propped crookedly beside a trench whose sides had sloughed in. She held in her arms a Bambino, and both Mother and Child had chipped noses, revealing the plaster beneath the tawdry colours.

What devout soul had climbed the steep hill bearing this effigy? What sublime faith, what infatuated credulity, had set this Virgin here?

Piers said, "Queer, Craig, the hold religion has on men. Of all these dead fellows around us, I suppose each man called on God before he died."

"Some probably cursed Him," Stephen suggested. "That boot I kicked – did you see? That poor beggar must have been bowled right over, must have died with his head in the mud. D'you think he called on his God, Piers? I doubt it."

"Don't see how he could, if he wanted to," agreed Piers. He looked thoughtful for a moment, then he said: "I wonder how war eventually affects a man's faith. Take a man like the Major. Orthodox. Simple. Got his God complete with snugly furnished heaven from his parents. Hell and damnation, too. Everything cut and dried. Rewards and penalties. A heavenly book-keeper checking accounts. D'you suppose he feels the same after the Somme?"

Stephen nodded.

"Absolutely. I'm sure of it. He's got one of those watertight compartment minds. War is war. God is God and religion is religion. He has 'em all locked up in separate departments; he'd never let them out to mix and get all muddled up. That's why he's so calm. If he gets his packet[6] he'll go straight to his reward. And his God will look after his widow and children. No, it would never occur to MacDonald that God might say: 'Look here, my fine fellow, what were you up to, when you got killed? Killing your enemies? But don't you know that your enemies are My children? Haven't I told you to do no murder?'"

Piers grinned. "Lucky MacDonald," he said. "Well, personally, I've given up speculating about that sort of thing. I don't know, and I don't much care, whether there's a God or not. This place is enough evidence that He returns the compliment. If He exists at all, then He must be an impersonal God who doesn't care a hoot about mankind."

"Exactly what I feel lately," Stephen agreed. "Death in the ordinary course of things seems to fit in right enough with conventional faith. It's so darned well camouflaged that all it really means is the ache of missing for a while someone you liked or loved. But here mortality seems final, absolute. You can't hide from it here behind a parson's vestments and a nice mellow church, and 'The Dead March' in *Saul*,[7] and you can't become philosophic about it over the third glass of sherry."

"Yet I suppose if you brought the Major up here and put it to him, he'd insist that at the final trump this hill will become a swarming mass of resurrected *poilus.*"

"I suppose he would."

3

That evening Piers, who had been lying on his bunk with Field Message book and pencil, pushed a paper into Stephen's hand: "Horrible result of Socratic dialogue on the hill this morning," he grinned whimsically.

Stephen took the paper. It was covered with the minutest hand-writing and the little blocks of characters told him at once that Piers had been scribbling verse. He read:

Notre Dame de Lorette

Sixty thousand men lie still:
Bleaching bones upon this hill.

Some in groups and some alone,
Sitting upright, lying prone;

In the trenches, on the ground,
Yellow skulls and bones abound.

Bits of tunic, blue and grey,
Slowly, slowly rot away.

Water-bottles, haversacks,
Broken rifles, boots and packs.

Up from every disused trench
Comes that awful dead-man stench.

Aftermath of battle's tide:
Foul decay on every side.

But a shrine is tended still,
In a trench upon the hill.

In a little trench is set,
Our Blessed Lady of Lorette.

4

As men will, freed of the inhibitions that stifle normal life, Stephen, Piers and O'Reilly opened up and exchanged confidences such as they would have hesitated to extend to the bosom friends of normality. These gusts and bursts of frankness became more frequent as the days and weeks passed; these three men, strangers a month or more ago, were now more confidential than schoolboys.

O'Reilly unfolded his story, usually, released from reticence by his rum ration. Bit by bit, Stephen pieced his story together until he had it whole.

O'Reilly, it seemed, hated his wife, and that because, having once loved her, he could not forget that she had never returned his affection. He did not say so in so many words. It was the texture of his talk that coloured the pattern of the past.

Stephen had a clear picture of a thin woman, over there in Victoria, British Columbia. A woman with social aspirations whose concentrated resentments were against the husband who was so poor a go-getter as to stick in the managerial office of a local bank branch while other men climbed over his head to power and affluence.

O'Reilly good-humouredly admitted the truth: "Queered my pitch,"[7] he explained; "too easy with the overdrafts."[8]

Poor old O'Reilly: warm-hearted, affectionate, demonstrative, all bottled up those long years with that dried-up woman, bossed about by a wife half his size. And then suddenly this chance of escape. Freedom. Companionship, comradeship, change, excitement, and a chance to be his own unregenerate self. That was why O'Reilly was enjoying the war.

And Piers: one fitted together the facts of his life too, bit by bit, though Piers was reticent. But Stephen got the main outline. Scotch University, no money. The itch to write. Journalism. Restlessness. Travel. Three years in Spain. What doing? He shrugs. "Not much of anything. The Spanish tempo isn't fast. Poverty and sunshine don't make a bad mixture."

Then restlessness and off again. A job on a Glasgow newspaper. The sack.[9] Steerage to Canada. A job in a bank. Always scribbling verse. And then the war.

Stephen looked at the narrow face, the high austere nose, the sensitive mouth. Why had Piers done so little with life? And Piers supplied the answer to the question.

"No ambition. Never had. Like dreaming, and the sun. Sweat your guts out to do things and then spend the fag end of life chewing the cud of disillusionment. Whatever you do, you'll be disappointed. Hence the common sense of saving yourself the sweat of achievement. Do I regret wasted opportunities? Naturally. But then if I'd been Sam Smiles'[10] own little white-haired boy, would I be any happier? I would not. And think of all the drinks and women I should have missed."

And O'Reilly, sitting there so massive, would ponderously wag his head and come out with one of his favourite quotations:

"I warm'd both hands against the fire of life;
It sinks, and I am ready to depart."

"Like hell you are," from Stephen. "You know you're saving up for all the women you are going to have on your next leave."

"Which reminds me," put in Piers, "Grant is back from leave. Came up this afternoon."

Grant completed the 'A' Company complement of junior officers – an "Original," that is to say, one who had come overseas with the battalion. He had an M.C. to show for the Somme.

5

The battalion is going back into the line. The men are filing into the end communication trench, dim shadows in the protective darkness. Clank of accoutrements, muffled voices. An old French trench, this. No lumber supports, no chicken-wire to hold up bulging walls of soggy soil, but great bundles of twigs and thin branches gathered thriftily hereabout, likely enough, though now you might look in vain for a single living tree. Ancient women, thinking of their men and of their bellies, gathering sticks for these *fascines,* binding them with bark, with oakum.

Pilk, the ingenious, has fashioned a mighty stick from one of them. It hangs by a thong from Stephen's wrist. A stick for ratting.

How patient are these men who go into the line again! They are seeing this business through with a quiet resignation that has replaced the evanescent fever of the old enthusiasms. In Vancouver, in Victoria, in all the little places of the Fraser Valley, (yes, in Ferguson's Landing[11]), they are heroes: their home-town's own. But here they are only men: tired, rebellious in queer little bouts of childish anger, otherwise resigned.

The war has turned out so differently from the war of their imaginings; and they have either forgotten or forgiven those fierce patriots who first fired their ardour and enlisted their chivalry by pen or spoken word. They are so far away.

They will go back into the line and, maybe, the dugout they are quartered in will be sound and deep, or maybe it will stand derelict, comfortless and floored with yellow water. Maybe it will stink with the stink of some shallow, forgotten grave, there under the mud. If one could only find it and dig the offender up, dispose of him. A stinking stiff.

As they find it, so will they take it. A little cursing, but more joshing, good-humoured, facetious. After all, there is comradeship, the comradeship that makes all things endurable.

And hope, the invincible. Many have gone, but only to be replaced by others, fresh men drafted from all those "Best Battalions" that are coming across the Atlantic to feed the divisions in the line. And what is it that sustains each one, if not the secret conviction that for him the enemy looses death upon the air in vain?

6

There was Grant, jabbering now at Stephen's elbow. Not really here at all, but still in London, head drumming with the music of the *Maid of the Mountains,*[12] mind full of remembered nights: food, music, fizz and girls. In the flats around Shaftesbury Avenue, Piccadilly, astonishing adventures. And best of all the little amateur.

"Had 'em all beat a mile, that little kid. Her middle name was mustard.

"Before my leave was due I had a hunch I was going to get killed," he confided in the darkness of the trench. "I felt certain of it. And when I got my leave warrant I'd two days still to go. Was I scared stiff those two days? I'll tell the world I was! I played a sort of game at beating death to it. Fairly skunked about the line.

"Well, now I know those hunches are all bunk. I've got rid of that obsession. I feel I'm coming through. I'm not afraid in the slightest."

He stumbled forward in the blackness and vanished.

Rations might come short, but of food for thought there was plenty.

Intuition? What was there in it? Grant the reprieved, now cocksure of a charmed life. Didn't pause, apparently, to consider that this second hunch might be about as reliable as the first. A good job, perhaps.

The battalion took over the Calonne sector, but it might have been anywhere at all, so dark was the night. The guide led them. Not a sound from the German lines, but somewhere on the right the voice of the artillery, a throbbing, urgent and insistent, a beat upon the air, a fevered pulse, and there, against the skyline, a winking of lights: the guns.

Company headquarters were in Sunken Road. But it was no longer a sunken road, a cutting made through a fold in the ground to take the slow and heavy wheels of lumbering wagons. Grass and wild flowers were gone, birds and rabbits had withdrawn, and in their place the rats had come, monstrous rats that slid, fat and obscene, about well-beaten tracks.

The sunken road had become a trench, wide and deep, a little street of backward-tilted hovels, each with its low, dark entrance, holes that led into the banks or under them, sepulchres for the living. A street now crowded with moving shadows. But no, not a street at all, or a great trench: merely a sluggish rivulet of stagnant mud between malodorous banks of slime in which the shadowy forms of strange beasts floundered.

There are voices calling in the darkness; apparent confusion. But presently the figures melt into these sepulchres until only a few patrolling spectres move in the gloom. The battalion had made its disposition.[13]

Really quite simple, this job of taking over. The real work was done eight hours or more before they moved in file along the winding communication trenches from the spur of Notre Dame. Then two subalterns had met to check trench stores, had argued, amiably chaffered[14] over Mills bomb boxes that were revealed as empty ones; over shovels to be signed for that had mysteriously vanished; over those unending details with which the junior officer is never done.

Major MacDonald is sitting at the bench of H.Q. dugout. He is satisfied, content. A good dugout, this, made by German hands a year or more ago; bitten out of the solid bank and shored up with mighty timbers. And eight good bunks.

Here the *pickelhaubes*[15] sat, the square-heads, and *hoched,*[16] likely as not, and talked of Paris. Now they were over yonder, pushed back. They probably talked of something else. Between them and that so-near objective stood ten thousand guns, and how many men?

The Major looks up at Stephen, his face lit by the light of a single candle. Stephen being from home, from Ferguson's Landing, must make good. For junior officers, whisked on you from other units, you could not answer. But a man from the Valley, that was different.

"You got that job done quickly," he smiles.

Praise: laconic, matter of fact. Still, praise.

Stephen is pleased with himself. He produces his Field Message book.

"Here is the disposition, sir," he explains. And the Major, adjusting glasses and holding the paper at arm's length, says:

"Now that's fine, fine and dandy." He beams. Everything is plain.

Sunken Road was a good place after the Kellett line; a good place if the enemy opened up with his artillery; a good place to defend from an attack. A mighty parapet, that bank. It gave one a sense of security. You had to look right up to see the machine gun crews, the men upon the fire-steps.

But not all was beer and skittles.

There was the advanced post, out there in the open: the Souchez Post, to reach which you had to go overland, over the wrecked tramway that once linked Souchez with Lens, but now was only to be recognised as a trail of twisted steel.

"A sacrifice post," the Major explains. "Because if there was a surprise attack, it'd be wiped out. But it has to be manned."

Stephen studies the print.

"But how can one get across without drawing their fire? There is a clear field of vision."

And the Major smiles. How little this fellow knows after all!

"The reliefs are carried out before dawn and after dusk," he explains. "You will take over to-morrow. Two N.C.O's,[17] twenty men, two signallers and two stretcher bearers."

Notes

1. Godwin's *Great Mystics* (London: Watts, 1945) applies psychiatric and 'rationalistic' criteria to a number of 'mystics' (St. Paul, St. Augustine, St. Francis of Assisi, Luther, Boehme, George Fox, Swedenborg and William Blake).
2. "*dot*": French for dowry.
3. ". . . immortelles shall crown your chivalry." Not clear. Possibly suggests that great poets will enshrine "Boot's" memory. The feminine plural is puzzling.
4. Tannenberg: important Russian defeat, August 27 - 30, 1914. When the Russians attacked East Prussia a large part of their army was encircled and captured by the Germans. 90,000 prisoners were taken.
5. Gallipoli: (1915) abortive attempt of the Allies to seize control of the Dardanelles (Turkey), thereby securing a southern sea connection with their Russian allies.
6. "gets his packet": wounded (could be fatal, but not necessarily).
7. "Dead March" in *Saul* (1738), opera by Handel. This march was/is often played at funerals.
8. "Queered my pitch . . . overdrafts": i.e. I ruined my own chances for promotion by being too lenient with regard to customers' overdrafts.
9. "the sack": fired.
10. Sam Smiles: author of several books on the inspirational lives of "great men" (Wedgwood, Stephenson, etc.) Advocated hard work for success.
11. Ferguson's Landing: see note 1, to chapter 1.
12. "Maid of the Mountains": a musical comedy from 1916.
13. disposition: the stationing of troops for defensive or offensive purposes.
14. chaffered: bickered.
15. pickelhaubes: nickname for German soldiers, from the shallow-crowned helmet surmounted by a spike which they wore.
16. "hoched": "expressed loyal approval" (Oxf. Dict.).
17. N.C.O.'s: non-commissioned officers (corporals, sergeants, etc.).

CHAPTER VI

1

NIGHT paling perceptibly to the bleak neutral tints of dawn. Little puffs of wind now sending the wet mist swirling through Sunken Road. Rattle of equipment and the soft, sucking sound of boots in mud. Voices.

Twenty men and two N.C.O.'s making ready to go overland to relieve the advance post before dawn. And dawn at hand.

Hurry.

Sergeant Glenny falling them in, his clear voice rising above the murmur. Twenty-two steel helmets, discs wet in the mist, buoys on a lethargic sea.

Stephen standing by, hunched and cold, with sleep-laden eyes. Yawning. Waiting to take over from Glenny, waiting to lead with the guide, over the broken ground, towards the German lines, out to the advanced post.

Out of the harbour of the trench, into the sea of No Man's Land. The mist closes in behind them. Sergeant Glenny turns; his moustache is white.

"We cross the disused trench hereabouts," he explains.

Yes, here it is, festooned with wire, caved in and melancholy. They scramble over. It is a wave; twenty-two bobbing buoys ride over it. They drift forward, silent and preoccupied. Already mud, scraped off laboriously a few hours since, has risen knee-deep. A parapet shows through the mist. It is the outpost. The men are standing-to. The bulky form of O'Reilly blocks the trench. His eyes are swollen and he has a dilapidated air.

He says, "My God, Craig, but that deep dugout stinks!"

Day is now near at hand. But there is no need to hustle these gaunt men. In five minutes they are assembled in the trench; in six they have vanished in the mist.

The mouth of the deep dugout receives the relief. And presently, when daylight comes, there will be no sign of life upon this island in the sea of mud. They are hidden there; they will be hidden there all day. Putting in time, waiting. Waiting for nothing in particular. Yet for something very definite. A spearhead to take the first shock of possible attack; human signals to give the alarm and, having given it, to die and have done with it. A sacrifice post. In a war of millions, where a handful of men is of no account. Coming across the world for this.

The deep dugout is long and narrow, wet and malodorous.

This smell, what is it?

It is the smell of death and corruption, a stench that hangs heavy from the coast to the Argonne, where the battle front has cut a gash across the brow of France, a wound now gangrenous. A smell instantly recognised; not foetid mire, not excrement or a compound of these, but the unforgettable stench of men rotting in mud.

Somewhere near at hand, if one could locate it, was a shallow grave. Hicks sniffed, then spat.

"I reckon there's a stiff buried in this dugout," he asserts. "I'll get busy and see if I can locate him."

Hicks of the gipsy face works by the sense of smell. He plunges his hand into the mire, sniffs the sample, shakes a tousled head. "It's all sour hereabouts," he explains, "but where this stink is coming from, oh boy! There it will sure hum!"

He continues his self-appointed task.

The men have cast equipment on bunks and are settling down for the long day's inactivity. Already the signaller is seated, 'phones clamped to ears, a yellow novelette beside his buzzer. He reads by candlelight.

Somebody says : "Get the bogies[1] going, boys."

And yellow flames appear in the gloom. The smoke of pipes and cigarettes clouds the air. Somebody has got a primus going, six crouched figures are around it, a witches' circle. Presently comes the stench of melting tallow. They are holding an old cigarette tin over the flame. Salving tallow for bogies, for candles are none too plentiful.

There are to be twelve hours or so of this. Stephen decides that he will break them with a reconnaissance, very carefully carried out. He has only a nebulous idea of the lie of the land; of how he should meet a raid or unexpected attack (an improbability, but always a possibility). The men must stop below, coming up only to visit the latrine.

He blows up his air pillow. A small thing, that pillow, but what a difference it makes. He has come to love it, a treasure above price. He lies upon his back smoking. There is nothing else to do, but think.

He does that.

2

Now he must be a father in a wider sense, a father to these men of his platoon. He must be their mother too, and their nurse. He must see that they lack nothing of clothing or equipment; that they use the whale oil and keep their feet free of trench-foot.[2] And they are like children, after all, dodging the doing of things designed for their own good.

More. He must – so Stephen viewed his job – be even more than these things to them. There were those men who neglected their letters. They will be causing hours of anguish to women far away, to little old women, maybe, or to women young and unfulfilled; waiting women, girls.

"Hey, you, Robinson! Where's your letter home this mail? Nothing to say? Well, say that, and get a move on!"

And those, the youngsters, who have themselves still dramatised, who see themselves as those saw them who watched the troop train steam away. Heroes, off to do heroic deeds.

So these pathetic letters full of bombast, lies:

"Well, mum, I take up my pen to write hoping this finds you as it leaves me at present. Well, Ma, we are in the line and shells are bursting all around. Well, say, you just wouldn't believe what it's like. Fellows getting killed and wounded all along. But I'm fine and dandy, Ma, and say would you send a bit of that maple sirup and fags are always welcome . . ."

So it is.

And then: "You know I am obliged to read all letters? There's nothing here to censor for military reasons. But won't this scare your old mother, some?"

He shuffles. "Maybe," the writer grins sheepishly. He is caught out; he has never experienced a bombardment. He is new in the line.

Stephen understands. So much falsity about this war that this simple soul has not the courage to write the truth. It isn't what they expect, over there at home, this day-to-day monotony, waiting for some menace that never comes along. War meant bloodshed, fighting and gallant deeds. There were no gallant deeds to be done. Only routine, dirt, lousiness and, now and then, a bawling out for neglect of duty . . . a dirty rifle, a stubbly chin. Did a man come all this way to make a hobby of shaving out of a condensed milk tin, knee deep in mud?

"Now just you write a cheery little letter and say: 'Here a week and everything quiet just like it was in the barn way back home.'"

He nods, still sheepish, mollified. What'd they think at home? Why, just that there was nothing to this war, and that it was a pity that the boy went, what with so much work to be done about the place.

By the light of a flickering candle, heavy-eyed, tackling this pile of letters, in a bunk, in a hole, in No Man's Land.

Men to be comforted too, men with troubles at home. Poor Pilk, now, telling, with chattering false teeth, of that wife who neglects the two boys. Picture of boys from back of pay-book.

"Taken at Seattle, sir, where I was located a while back."

Pride. Love. Two nice little boys, with solemn faces, in sailor suits of velvet. The whole of Pilk's real life, there, the focus of all his thoughts, the subject of all his dreams, the spur of his ambitions. Pilk's ballast.

Yes, two nice little fellows. But a woman who drinks.

"Well, you know how it is when that's the trouble, sir." Poor Pilk shuffling there, getting it out with difficulty.

"Other men?" suggests Stephen.

Pilk nods. "Yes, sir. At home I could look after things myself. But here . . ."

Oh, it did not need a battle every day to make a tragedy of war. It needed no battles at all. These broken homes: were they not tragedy enough? And yet, after all, but a side issue; an aspect overlooked by those who weighed the cost of it all.

These letters of the married men. Here was that grizzly, silent fellow Martens writing to his wife. Hardly ever opened his mouth, except to bite from his chewing baccy. Taciturn, morose, stupid-looking, wooden-faced. And this his letter:

"DEAR WIFE,

"i take up my pen hoping this finds you as it leaves me at present the sox are dandy and i guess them new glasses come in handy that the peddler sold you for making of them but you mussent go adoing 2 much. has Girt carved yet you sed a carf was on the way if she went to old Moody's red bull it should be a good un and if heifer a fine milch cow later. keep her from the bracken thats where Mary Anne got the red water[3] sure as sure. tell Albert to lend a hand like i sed with the wood theres a bunch of alder ready felled and dry by now thatll keep the stove over winter and by spring i guses ill be on my way back. glad the hens is better of the croup well mother i must end, tell the children to be good and love to all friends."

Well, not difficult now to understand why Martens seems preoccupied.

Stephen looks at the weather-beaten face of this square-set man. He is over there, legs dangling from bunk, chewing solemnly. Admiration? Yes, but more than that: affection, tenderness.

All sorts of letters, and each revealing the writer. The family men, all anxious thought for those far-off little homes where their wives are making out as best they can. Victims of anxieties, these men, puzzling simple heads gazing out over No Man's Land by night from frozen fire-steps[4] and seeing little shacks in clearings, steamy kitchens, young orchards, or merely the silent bush, still and green, or a river, silver in the sun.

And thinking. Not of war, but of the problems of the old days that are still unsolved: that burning off that should have been done a year ago, that bit that ought to be in clover now. That pruning overdue. Corn on the cob for supper and flap-jacks. Hot tea that was tea and not a brown-tasting chemical filth – the tea of the trenches – doctored muck that made you retch, that turned a man's stomach.

But only from these letters did one know these men's secret lives, their inmost hearts. They did not share these things with each other. This new life they would share to the full, every one of them; but each kept to himself that other life, over there.

To share a short bread ration: that was one thing; to share a memory, something quite different.

3

Alice has moved from the seaside town to a Kentish village and tells him it is cheaper.

Lying there on his bunk in the deep dugout, he envisages her daily life, knowing her, for her letters are unadorned records of little events. They say nothing of the thoughts in her head. Well, he could understand that. She had not the trick of looking in at herself, so unlike those introspective ones who always were, and telling what they saw.

He reads the letter again. It is a bare outline, but upon it, lying there in his bunk in the dim light of the deep dugout at Souchez Post, he will build with his imagination a complete picture, detailed as a painted Dutch interior and as vivid, too.

"Eric," she tells him in that long, sloping foreign hand, "has made great friends with the smith. He is in and out of the forge all day, and generally as black as the pot. The smith says the child has no fear at all and will crawl between the horses' legs while he is shoeing them. He loves the bellows, too. He had two days in bed with a cold, but now his cheeks are rosy apples. My lodgings are nice and clean, the landlady is a decent woman."

Yes, that is how she writes. He can see her shopping in the village, peering with short-sighted eyes at the homely things she needs, fingering her purse, making calculations. He can see her begging the iron for an hour, for two hours, Such work these babies make! Then bed-time, dusk, and after, darkness, the little room yellow in the light of an oil lamp. Only the sounds that an old cottage makes, the rheumy sounds of age, for company.

Who will bother about this little woman with the two small children, a stranger drifted into the village? Who will look at her twice? Certainly not the squire, as surely not the vicar. She is a transient; she does not belong. She is a foreigner.

Would she make advances? No, for Alice made advances to no one. If you would know her you had to go more than half-way: you had to go all the way, and then you had to hammer on the door. Even then it was not always opened.

Hidden away in that Kentish village – shabby, poor, reserved and very proud; asking nothing, expecting nothing. Alice. And the children.

But the smith would like Alice. He would wipe the sweat out of his eyes, seeing her framed in the wide door.

"Come for the nipper?"

And his deep voice would be kindly.

Stephen, lying on his back on his bunk in the deep dugout. Dreaming. Twelve hours of forced inactivity, twelve hours forty feet underground, twelve hours with twenty men, twenty men passing away the time: cards, talk, argument and, here and there, a little smut. Twelve hours by candlelight, in an atmosphere that stank.

The telegraphist, in his corner, enters another world through the magic doorway of that yellow novel and Stephen has gone off to Kent. Both have escaped.

4

"Here you are, boys, here's the stiff!" It is Hicks' voice. He might have found gold, so delighted he seems.

Stephen swung down from his bunk.

The stench is found, there at the foot of the steps; a foot, no more, beneath the mud. Corruption. The spade is clotted with it.

It? This was a man a while ago. And now all there is to tell you so is that clot of scalp tufted with black hair.

"A Jerry. Pretty ripe. Phew! Smoke up, fellows!"

It is Hicks, the imperturbable.

But the deep dugout is more tolerable thereafter. The buzzer clicks. They climb back to their bunks. The turgid air is blue with smoke. The cause of the stench has been removed, but the stench remains. This is a stench more vile and stronger than all stinks put together.

For this stink is death. The distillation of corruption. Abominable. Never to be forgotten.

Haggard hours, but presently high noon. Mist gone. A steady drizzle now. Peering continually above the parapet, he can see beyond the German lines to the roofs of the houses of Lens and Lievin. Intact houses in intact towns, enjoying a charmed existence in this realm of destruction. A reproach too.

Then afternoon and the coming of darkness. A general stirring. Stand to.[5] And then, materialising out of the darkness, the guide of the relief, a figure muffled in a ground sheet.

5

Rats are everywhere. Not apprehensive marauders ready to run at a sound. No. It is man who is on sufferance here. The line is the metropolis of the rodents, their Canaan, their happy hunting ground. It is their kingdom, reaching from the Channel to the Argonne. There never were such times, never such endless feasting! Yes, life goes easily with the rats. They have built this unseen realm underground, a honeycomb of runs, and each one leading to a grave. You may see their beaten tracks, and sometimes at night watch them migrate, moving shadows. Battalions of rats, brigades, divisions, whole army corps of them: silent, stealthy, wise. They slide over the parapet and flash black against the earth into their holes. They sit, beady-eyed and insolent, returning stare for stare. Fat, oh monstrously fat, they are! Like cats, some of them. And others are diseased, with gaping ulcers on hairless flanks.

Sergeant Glenny grins.

"How goes the ratting, sir?"

"Good hunting this morning, sergeant."

He has learnt to use that big stick that hangs always ready from his wrist, the stick that Pilk fashioned for him, the stick that is his only weapon. His aim is improving every day. He has got tired of keeping count, so many rats beaten down into the slime, broken-backed, writhing.

6

The trench latrine is badly placed. The bucket sits crookedly in the mud in the recess that is too high. It is a humiliating ordeal, for it is necessary to crouch or take the risk of a sniper's bullet. An ordeal to be got through, somehow. Mud, chloride of lime, corruption.

Decay, what is it, but a moment of matter's eternal commutations?

Think of it like that. Be philosophic. In the open, in the privacy of the bush, the office of nature is without offence; an act of humility, an acknowledgment of the bond with Mother Earth. Soon decay will be cleansed, made sweet again. Manure. What fed the fruits of earth but corruption, after all?

And there a face, peering through the gap, beyond which the trench, regarding one's indignity stolidly, all unaware of it, seeing only a man in a latrine, and saying to him a necessary word.

"Keep your head down, sir; the snipers are busy this morning."

He is back in the trench. He retches as he adjusts his clothing.

7

Who was the warner? Hicks, by general consent, the dirtiest soldier in the battalion. He is whistling now as he drags a pump along the duckboards, a lock of black hair in his eyes.

"Hey, where's your tin hat?" Stephen calls.

"Aw, yer can't keep them things on when you're working. Can't be done."

He ignores the implied order and points with pride. "See that, sir? Pretty good job, I'll tell the world."

He has laboriously repaired the broken network that keeps up the sagging wall of the trench thereabouts. It is a neat, workmanlike job. And now he is going to pump a while at that dugout where there is a clear foot of stagnant water.

And when he has accomplished these tasks it will be time for him to take his stand on a fire-step, to keep a sharp outlook through the periscope, theoretically, but actually to keep bobbing up to take what he calls "a honest-to-God look-see."

The dirtiest soldier in the battalion, in the brigade, and, out of the line, a hard case. Stephen has heard stories of him. A roaring drunk. A hard hitter.

Hicks pauses, assumes a confidential air, says:

"I wonder if I might trouble you, sir?"

Well, they are all probably wrong about Hicks. Why accept the general estimate?

"Sure, you can. What is it, Hicks?"

"It's this gleet,[6] sir; it's pretty bad these days."

Stephen stares.

"Gleet? You mean you're V.D.?" he asks incredulously, shocked.

"Yep, and it needs treatment, too."

Stephen is indignant. A man carrying on without treatment in the line; probably ruining his chances of a cure!

"I'll certainly speak to the Major," he promises. And Hicks thanks him. But he seems now to have lost interest in the subject.

"This gol-darn pump jams," he complains inconsequentially, fumbling at the gear. His black head is still bare. An order, what are orders? His crime sheet is eloquent of his contempt for them.

But everyone knows all about Hicks, it seems. He is a tough guy, a hard case, a dirty-mouthed scallywag. As for his complaint, why, Stephen is just another victim of his joshing. Hicks and his malady are the battalion joke. His trouble is the legacy of youthful indiscretion; it will remain with him to a rheumy old age.

Notes

1. bogies: candles ("bougies" in French).
2. trench-foot: painful, swollen feet. Caused by having feet soaking for hours on end in flooded trenches.
3. red water: a malarial cattle disease of which the tell-tale symptom is red urine.
4. fire-steps: board or ledge in trench from which one fired.
5. Stand to: from just before dawn until daylight was the time when an enemy attack was most expected; during this time all armed personnel manned the parapet, ready for action (Fraser and Gibbons). Stand-to's could be ordered at any time.
6. gleet: gonorrhea.

CHAPTER VII

1

HOW could one grasp the design behind the apparent chaos of trench warfare? An expert wrote marvellously in *Land and Water*,[1] expounding the theory of war, explaining the strategy of the western front, masterly expositions that wrought design and significance out of seeming anarchy.

O'Reilly was enthusiastic. Stephen studied them earnestly, and presently he felt the beginning of understanding. War as a bird might see it, as those birds that still flew over the line saw it, those birds who, maybe, puzzled the riddle of their vanished woods. His reading lifted him out of this sector and displayed to his mind's eye the tortuous line that zig-zagged across northern France, and the lacework of feeding arteries, nerves, that converged, back there somewhere, in the central ganglion, G.H.Q. To think of this tremendous front as the General Staff must envisage it, as a whole . . . That hairpin bend now, down at Laon. How significant this writer made the turning movement there!

Yes, it was all so simple after all; scientific. Beautiful in their logic, they were, these weekly articles, carrying conviction to the mind. But this war somehow seemed unaware of the immutable laws of all war. It ignored them.

So Stephen ceased to read the strategist, for events proved the expert a poor prophet. After all, then, this war was not so simple an affair. *Land and Water* lay discarded, discredited. They ceased to bother with its oracle.

And the General Staff?

Those unseen masters of the army's destiny, somewhere there beyond the last battery and further still, in some secluded chateau where the routine of normal life was merely coloured by the war. Did they know much more about it all? It seemed doubtful.

And Stephen decided against it as improbable. The science of war, he concluded, was purely empirical. It consisted in winning. Who won knew this science; who lost lacked it. What was it then but the science of being powerful, which is, after all, no science at all?

He remembered, as a small boy, a reciprocal pinching contest with Ricky. Well, this war seemed about as scientific as that. It was childish. this exchange of shells.

Could those brass-hats think creatively? Had they original ideas outside the teaching of the military schools? Or were they dull schoolmen, following the old text-books slavishly, working by rule of thumb?

Might a man rise to supreme command of these vast armies without genius? Was it just possible that our leaders were merely old men decked out in uniforms, impotent old men, grappling desperately with a problem utterly beyond them? Old fools camouflaged in red tabs[2] and brass hats and buttressed up by the prestige of their military caste, high priests of mysteries and jealous of those mysteries, but comforted by the knowledge that the civilians at home knew even less than they. But old fools.

When the Major in his even voice talked of the Somme, it was not hard to find an answer to these questions. Our leaders were criminal fools and conscienceless idiots. Not that Major MacDonald criticised the conduct of that battle. He merely described it. It was enough.

But the Germans? The Germans had long made a serious study of war. Look at Tannenberg, for which the patient Hindenburg prepared for years. He got that down scientifically enough, so that when the hour struck the battle in those bleak marshes was already his. The defeat of the Russians had been a mathematical certainty.

That tall lieutenant in the great Dresden barracks. No polo. Always on his job. Thorough.

Well, and what more could the German General Staff do, for all that thoroughness?

Nothing!

So it came down to this: the text books were being used for a war whose problems no military mind had foreseen in the days of peaceful preparation. Yet why had they not foreseen? Under their eyes were all the factors that would go to the making of this conflict. Into this futile contest one had been sucked willy-nilly. Millions had been sucked into it.

What would Napoleon have made of it? A mess? Probably.

Stephen gave it up; it came down, so it seemed, to a matter of men and a matter of guns. Who had the most would stick it longest.

He paused in his cogitation. But would they? What of the human factor, that factor that no amount of material could cancel out? There was no answer to that. And he left the riddle unsolved, as wiser heads had left it, with the word *morale* forming itself in his tired mind.

2

Martens, beneath a stolid exterior, was considering the war from another angle. He was not exercised about the conduct of it; he had begun the painful process of trying to square it with his old idea of God. And he was experiencing some difficulty.

His thoughts took speculative flights, generally while he was on sentry. The immobility of a spell on the fire-step induced the necessary contemplative mood in him. Such moods he had in the old days of peace; they had come to him when he worked in the bush alone. Then it had always been easy enough to believe that God was love. The bush told him that and the affirmation brought great peace to his simple soul. To be the child of a heavenly father. It was something.

Here, especially at night, the mind of Martens took wing, while the voice of his protesting body, asserting its grievances, was muted.

The 'M. & V.'³ made Martens vomit. It made many men vomit. "It's the fat – my stomach heaves at it," he explained.

True, it is very cold, standing there with the smell of the damp earth in one's nostrils and a numbness of feet that no amount of whale oil will prevent. But thoughts come in at such times. And, strangely, an empty stomach seems to lure them.

It is on clear nights when the silent sky reveals its many splendours that Martens, numbed hand on rifle, looks up from the fire-step and contemplates the stars. And his simple soul is full of questionings. Things don't fit in; he has been deceived, has Martens. This war is not only wickedness; it is crass folly from which he would gladly escape, but cannot.

This land now, he considers, is fertile. One could get good wheat from soil like this. He guessed expertly that it had been in wheat before this evil had been done to it. In the villages behind the lines one saw pretty dud implements, but these Frenchies surely savvied farming.

Martens gazes fixedly at the indifferent stars, as though to read some secret hidden there. And then the shattering doubt: Was there really a God? A God like one was taught as a boy at home, and later by preacher? Easy to believe in God at home. He thought of the little woman with greying hair, his wife. She had no doubts at all. And she wasn't strong for war, wasn't Mother. How often she would come back to it, before he finally decided to enlist, saying:

"Look at them Mullers; they're Germans. Could you ask for nicer neighbours?"

And it was true. There was a bunch of German settlers back home. All friendly folk; honest too. Good workers. But now interned. Martens contemplated the dim outline of the German line, a white shadowy line beyond the black mystery of No Man's Land. Silent, lifeless. Fellows there like old Heinie Muller, watching on fire-step, same as him. Left alone, friends . . .

Yes, the thoughts came into Martens' head. And he would turn them over, examining them as a man might examine a potato, expertly, and with wisdom. And he would stamp, striving to bring the blood back to those lifeless feet of his; would stamp a while and then give it up.

It had been a folly to come. Mother had been right. Come to think of it, Mother generally was right. His real duty was right there at home.

Major MacDonald had no intellectual difficulties to wrestle with. One did not question the rightness or wrongness of war. One accepted it and got on with it. In life one did one's duty, and with Major MacDonald duty had always been associated with the unpleasant, so that it was by the degree of sacrifice demanded that one might gauge the imperative quality of that duty.

The God of his rigid Presbyterianism occupied another compartment of his mind and, happily, He stayed there. Major MacDonald, then, accepted the war without intellectual hesitancy. That the writ of righteousness did not run into the battle front was neither here nor there. After two years of heavy campaigning his critical faculties slept as soundly as they did in those far-off days when, an unblooded militiaman, he had pored over text books in the security of his home.

When subalterns and those of higher rank returned from leave with tales of the women they had enjoyed, Major MacDonald listened with a childish smile. He murmured: "Well, well," or "You don't say."

Presently, with any luck, they would go home and everything would be as before. This was war: one accepted it. Presently he would (with luck) open the door of this bewildering life and close it firmly behind him. He would enter the world of peace and normality. The Ten Commandments would once more become effective.

No, there were no intellectual problems for Major MacDonald, none at all.

As for O'Reilly, enjoying for the first time in his life a sense of release, warming to this new comradeship, he considered it, on the whole, quite a good war. O'Reilly was not a free man enslaved, but an enslaved man set free. Like a schoolboy out of school he was, his spirits rising triumphantly over danger and physical discomfort.

And Piers? Stephen often wondered how Piers felt about it all. He would say, often enough, that he had had enough of it before he got his commission. But beyond a confession of war-weariness, he said little.

3

The mail comes up. It has come up the Arras road under shell-fire; has been carried from battalion H.Q. in a shower of flying splinters. And the bringer of it, this strange muddied postman in khaki, with heaving chest, salutes and disappears. But not before he has wrought a miracle, there in the gloom of the dugout.

A pile of parcels lies on the dugout bench and, beside them, secured with string, the mail.

The mail comes first. All score. Rustle of paper, creak of bunks, little half-suppressed exclamations. Silence.

And now the dugout is thronged. Letters? Mere hieroglyphs? No. Living, breathing creatures. Dear absent faces look out from these pages, and scenes beloved rise magically from the written words. There is O'Reilly over there, with that girl of his, the one he clicked with in London in a casual mood and later found he really loved. The first woman who has given O'Reilly all that man can ask of woman: tenderness, loyalty, love.

And Piers there, listening to the Scots accent of his favourite sister, listening to her in the austere Edinburgh home he left so long ago, and visited a mere six months since. Six months only; is it possible?

And the Major with his wife, and hearing her calm, precise voice, her even tones, and standing all about him his children, neat and clean, a trifle subdued, perhaps, but smiling fondly.

Stephen is with Alice and his chicks, there on his bunk, Alice in the dugout, there beside him.

And now for the parcels. Awkward moment for Stephen, for he now knows what to expect. He lounges in his bunk, simulating interest in his single letter, re-reading it, absorbed. O'Reilly heaps his parcels on his bunk. Piers, too. The Major methodically unties the string of his. Presently he will roll it up very neatly and secrete it somewhere. For, after all, wherever we are, we take our characters along with us.

Oh, curse these parcels. What was one to do?

"Have a bit of maple sugar, Craig?" It is O'Reilly.

And Piers has shortbread, gay with lemon-peel thistle.

"No, but you must! Go on!" He holds it out, munching like an old goat.

And the Major: a regular shop! Chocolate, chewing gum, malted milk tablets, cigarettes, soap, all sorts of delightful things, and all so neatly parcelled up. He sets them out before him without haste. A methodical man. A deliberate man.

"Well, well," he says to himself. "Well, well." And that is all.

And Stephen? Well, there was only Alice to remember him. And Alice was too hard up to run to parcels. A job to make two ends meet with those two youngsters.

Astonishing how many friends these others have who remember them. O'Reilly says:

"They surely are wonderful women. Look at this." He holds up a pair of socks. "From our local women's war committee," he explains. "A parcel from them every mail. It's sure fine of them."

And Stephen? Well, yes, he has relatives and friends. But so long away, people forget. Or were of the kidney of that bearded old uncle . . . But no. This time there is a parcel for Stephen too. From Alice. He cuts the string and opens it. Oh, hell! She can't afford this sort of thing. There is a lump in Stephen's throat. The darling thing! But she shouldn't. So short of cash, hard up. Damn! She would be going without something she needed badly because of this extravagance. He screws the wrapping paper up and throws it down. He can do it now. At last.

"Hey, you, O'Reilly, try a bit of this. My Missis made it, and believe me, she is some little cook."

O'Reilly bites prodigiously. He says that it is good.

"Like Mother made, way back home," he grins, munching.

The maple sugar is sweeter now. Stephen's pride is restored. He is remembered too. His heart is full of tenderness.

4

They are so preoccupied that ominous sounds outside pass unnoticed. A voice is shouting:

"Stretcher bearer! Stretcher bearer!"

They abandon their feast and make for the doorway.

He is lying on his back, and except for the pallor of his drawn face there is nothing to show that he is hit.

Somebody says: "A Blighty[4] for you, Martens. Oh, boy! I'll say that's luck."

Suddenly from his blue lips Martens sends up a little urgent fountain of blood. He coughs and the fountain gushes. More than a Blighty for Martens.

Stephen says: "Don't lift him, fellows, slide him on flat. Careful!"

Martens's eyes are very hard to look into. What is it in their depths that hurts so? What there that wrings the heart? The reproach of a gentle animal struck down? Something very like that.

Do they not say: "Alas! I shall not see my ranch again; I shall not be with Mother in the Spring like I reckoned to be. How will she make out all alone?"

They lift him gently onto the stretcher. And now the Major comes hurrying. His jaws are working, his mouth is full of home-made cake.

"Steady now, lads," he says, "take him back carefully; they are shelling the Arras road."

They become surprisedly aware of this; the air is full of sound.

The Major says: "Martens, eh? A good soldier. A good soldier."

But so much of death has he seen, it means nothing to him now. And this is mercy. For in war the tender heart must be closed to overmuch compassion lest it break. So pity sleeps.

5

Stephen looked at the body and the sight of it made him bleed inside, made his soul bleed. He sought about in his mind, probing, seeking the enemy, hating him, raging against him, lusting to identify him that he might destroy him.

Who was this enemy about whom his mind was always occupied, seeking, searching, striving to understand. He sought the enemy: to know him, to identify and destroy. And over there, in the enemy lines, there were men seeking him too.

Where was this enemy?

Not here. Not over there. Nowhere in the battle zones at all. Where then? In Whitehall? In the Champs-Elysées? In the Wilhelmstrasse?[5]

In all those places. Yet in none of them.

The enemy was here. The enemy was the seeker, not the sought. The enemy was in the heart of man. There the evil seed had been thrust down in that darkness, fertile with the sperm of hate, of wickedness, watered with the waters of fear. And thrusting up out of that black evil soil, monstrous and terrible.

Yes, this was the enemy – not here nor there, but over all the world; they were the victims of themselves. Man was his own enemy, carrying that enemy under his breast, in his dark heart, like a snake, like a serpent. In this contracting heart, now filled with abhorrence of the thing begot of it. There was the enemy.

And that thing, death. Not death within the great law, after seeding, birth, growth and decay: the complete harmonious rhythm preordained. But death as an affront, stealing life yet unconsumed, consuming it. Martens, with full thirty years to run – the full course of life – dead. And the thing that had killed him, that had done this evil, there, within his own heart.

Man was the violator, the scourge, the curse of the world. In the abyss of his being, oh, yes, down there in the darkness a devouring beast, made more beastly by his power of thought, of invention. A beast enthroned over all other beasts, and the greatest of them.

War! What was it but the blackness of man's heart made manifest?

Thus Stephen grasped again what he had known before, in the valley, in the settlement, in the silence of the forest. Alone there, looking out over the wide horizon, looking in over the wide horizon: the wide horizon of the land, the infinite horizon of his heart. Then he had known, had understood. The law was Love. And Love was Beauty. And Truth. Tolstoi had taught him. And Christ. Only he had forgotten; had become unapprehending in his child's mind.

Christ and Tolstoi. All the great spirits of all the ages, unheard, unheeded. O the black heart of man, black heart seeded and spermed with hate; turning upon itself, self-consuming!

What was absolute? Nothing. All things were relative. There was no anchor anywhere, anywhere at all. The good of the race: that was to win this war. Yet it was the most evil thing of all for the members of the race, for the countless units of it. Of all the races. A contradiction, somewhere; and beyond understanding. No anchor anywhere; nothing to take hold upon.

Take Grant, now: Grant the hedonist. He had come into the war without a second thought. It was the mood of the moment, the thing to do; he did it. It was the fun, the excitement, the stimulation, the unusualness of it. It would be a junketing,[7] good sport. But it was not these things.

Grant was disappointed with the war, but was not disappointed overmuch. He was prepared to see it through, but he was unprepared to die. He wanted to escape, passionately. He wanted to escape in order to live. He had tasted many women, many girls. He hungered with his body to taste many more. He lived impatiently, for his leaves. He saved for them, for the women he would buy with the saved pay, for the champagne and the girls. And meanwhile he sustained himself by living again the past pleasures of dead leaves, contrasting the women he had slept with, comparing one with another, talking dirtily, but coming back always to the "little amateur," who "had the pro's beat a mile, yes, sir."

Grant, an animal, moving strongly with the herd. And underneath, Grant tasting liberty, fulfilment in the game of slaughter, responding to the urge of his black heart, to kill and destroy. But unconscious of that urge, all unaware of it.

Yes, surely, the enemy was not the sought, but the seeker. Men devoured themselves because they were divided.

6

The sector is no longer somnolent. The Saxons over there are becoming bellicose. Their evening hate no longer has that faint suggestion of apology; there is no prelude of warning fire high overhead, no facetious tattoo. Their machine guns open up viciously.

Their artillery too, sprays the Calonne sector, and the whine of shells is bitter on the air. Somewhere behind the little town of Lens their batteries are camouflaged against our aerial eyes. High overhead moves a plane like a black and buzzing midge, seeking them out; an eye, a travelling eye, up there. Photographing their back areas, flying low now, ignoring anti-aircraft batteries that spray the air all about with white balls of cotton wool. Swooping up now and returning, disappearing behind the line.

And soon our own artillery replies, whiplashes upon the air; a screaming: sinister and strangely exciting.

The infantry watch the exchange. They have a secret contempt for all gunners. Making work for them, the endless futile work of trench repairs. Leave the Boche alone, and he would soon get tired. Making work and causing casualties.

7

A 4.5 lands on no. 5 Machine Gun emplacement, and where a moment ago that little stronghold stood intact, with gun and crew, there is now a crater from which rises dense smoke and acrid, suffocating fumes of high explosive.

It is wiped out, is No. 5 M.G. Obliterated. And with it: how many men?

Stephen investigates, coughing as he stumbles in the miry wreckage. The fumes eddy, disclosing the contours of a crater. No gun, no crew.

Somebody says, "A direct hit." The voice is aggrieved, the face of the speaker dejected.

Yes, a direct hit. Another job of work.

Stephen considers with himself a little problem of trench engineering. They must rebuild, and at once.

The air is torn by the splitting scream of shells. The trench trembles. Head down, Stephen makes for the company H.Q. dugout.

O.C. 'A' Coy.

Sir,
I beg to report as follows (5 p.m. - 8 p.m.)
1. *No. 5 M.G. emplacement demolished. The gun is now withdrawn 25 ft. It has little protection.*
2. *Sergeant Glenny drew my attention to condition of trench at his post and asked for Primus and scoops.*
3. *Night very dark. Considerable artillery activity.*
4. *Suggest that No.5 M.G.E. might be rebuilt about 12 ft. in rear of demolished emplacement. There is now a natural parapet to start with.*
5. *Gleaned no information re Johnson and Holmes. Was a direct hit.*
6. *Atmosphere almost still.*

S. Craig

Five hours for sleep. Stephen is in his bunk. He has loosened his belt. The war has ceased for him. For a few hours.

High up on the mottled alder is a green woodpecker. Tap, tap, tap. Hard bill on bark. Tap, tap, tap. After timber-haunting insects, there on the graceful alder, in the dappled forest. How beautiful both tree and bird. Tap, tap, tap. *Picus viridis.* Picus, why did you love Pomona so?[8] Was it worth it, tapping bird? Tap, tap, tap. After insects. Such hammer-blows with hammer bill.

Five hours? No, as many minutes. Stephen rolled over.

"You, Piers?" he growls, blinking up into the dim face of Piers, that is shadowed by the rim of steel.

"Two o'clock already?"

Piers growls, "I thought you'd never wake. I've been tapping you for ages."

"Like a blessed – woodpecker," yawned Stephen, adjusting his gas mask.

8

Rumours are on the air; the strafe presages something. The long-expected attack on Vimy Ridge, perhaps, the shadowy battle that broods over the sector week after week. Month after month. Tunnelling companies have been at it a long time now, boring away beneath No Man's Land towards the flank of the scarred ridge.

Two o'clock and scarcely yet awake. Not very pleasant thoughts. And three hours of it to be got through.

And perhaps counter-tunnelling? Maybe thirty or forty feet beneath the Calonne Sector men are packing high explosives, piling them in that damp and earthy chamber; laying electric wires, mile-long fuses.

He jabs at a shadowy form upon the parapet.

"Missed him," snaps the following N.C.O.

Well, one would never know. It would be a swift business, a pressing of a button somewhere over there. Finish.

There is sporadic artillery fire. They ignore it. Two weary men, officer and N.C.O., making the rounds. Tired men. Dispirited, bored, and lousy.

The Major knows no more than his subalterns or if, maybe, he does, says nothing. He carries on as usual: phlegmatic, quiet, incurious. Dull.

Then you remember what he has been through. After that, any man's emotional wells might dry up, his reactions jam.

They are out of the trench now, for here the going is better and the chances of being hit not considerable. They stumble on in silence, thinking their own thoughts.

What makes it possible for this elderly man to carry on? Not animus against the enemy; he is indifferent to them. Desire for victory, the will to win? He no longer thinks of it; it is a mirage, vanished long ago. The war is everlasting. What then, if not that thing he calls sense of duty? And what is that, after all, but a fetish? How many fetish worshippers among these Christian armies? *How many fight because they cannot think?*

No philosopher ever wrote a treatise on the art of war; no soldier was ever a philosopher.

There is no moon, but the dark night sky is cloudless; where the dome rests upon the encircling horizon there is, here and there, an agitation of pulsing lights. The guns. But some distance off. The Calonne Sector has quieted down. It is long enough since the men were served their rum for them to be thinking of rum again. A new day, already; a light cold breeze blowing over from the north. Stephen halts in the trench to look at the luminous dial of his wrist watch. Five minutes to five.

A single candle burns on the dugout bench. The sound of snoring comes from the shadows where three men sleep. Propped against an upright, his legs along the bench, lolling to one side, the Major sprawls. Stephen stands a moment contemplating this figure of exhaustion. Poor Major. All in. What rings about his closed eyes! He suddenly realises that never before has he seen the Major sleep. And at that moment two steadfast eyes look into his. Not asleep, after all, or asleep like a watchdog, ears cocked. Stephen sits down, yawns, and pulling Field Message book[9] from pocket, writes:

O.C. 'A' Coy.

Sir,
I beg to report as follows. (2 a.m. – 5 a.m.)
1. No.5 M.G.E. fixed up, but still requiring more protection.
2. Shortage of bombs and S.A.A.[10] reported by Sergts. Grey and Campbell.
3. Several men seemed inclined to think our artillery was firing short.
4. Weather perfect; wind light, N.
S. Craig

9

Stephen is worrying his head. He does not grasp what is expected of him as a platoon commander if there should be an attack. Not enough to resist. Orders would have to be given, a plan of action seen clearly through confusion, co-operation with one's flanks maintained.

How could one impose one's will in confusion and turmoil?

He asks the Major endless questions and listens with a troubled frown to the patient answers. Trying to learn his job, but finding it none too easy. It seems a little clearer now, but he is still dubious, just a little fogged. Will he be able to handle the situation when it arises? How will he make out when the great attack on Vimy comes? He decides to make a note, and does so, in pencil, at the end of his Platoon Rollbook.

If enemy attack penetrates front line at any point, P.O.s on R & L of break fall back and endeavour to connect up behind and organize flank attack . . .[11]

Sitting here, quietly, this seems as easy as war seen from the bench of a classroom in the Military School.

He continues writing:

Division expects offensive.
Front line to be held at all costs.
Raids may be expected.
Gas attacks may be ditto.
Mines ditto ditto.

10

A general stirring in the dugout: eight o'clock, and the rations up. Bacon, bread, tea. The vileness of it!

They stir. Piers sits hunched on his bunk, and presently he's puffing contemplatively at a cigarette. Next he has a paroxysm of coughing that shakes his thin body. He will have such fits as this all day, but all day too he will light one cigarette from the butt of the last. Chain smoking: fifty, sixty, seventy a day. Woodbines. Not from little packets, but from tins of fifty. As good as Players.

O'Reilly shakes himself like a big dog. He wants a tin of water for shaving. He wants water to brush his teeth. He has got a brown taste in his mouth. Three days without a rear.[12] A No. 9 indicated.[13]

Upon Stephen sits a great weariness, lassitude of body, dejection of mind. If you could only sleep it out for once. Eight hours. Ten hours. Twenty-four hours. But you cannot. Sleep is rationed.

Another day. He contemplates the shrivelled rashers, held fast to the tin plate by congealed fat; he sniffs at the tea and the smell of chloride of lime offends his nose. Nauseating.

The Major has been writing, writing as he might write at his desk in his office in the great high school. He looks up now, and he smiles a slow, sweet smile, picking up knife and fork as he looks at Stephen's melancholy face. He indicates the food with his fork. Stephen shakes his head.

"Couldn't touch it, sir," he protests, "it makes me heave to look at it."

The Major smiles as one might smile at a dainty child.

"Now if you had your choice, what would you choose?" he asks, cocking his head playfully.

Queer little flutter of the Major's disciplined fancy. Playing at 'What Would You Like.' But Stephen knew at once what he would like. He said:

"First, sir, I'd like a long drink of cold water." He paused. The Major nodded, craning his neck towards the offence of the tea can.

"Then," Stephen continued, with rising enthusiasm as the images of delight coloured his mind, "I'd like a great big red apple, full of juice. And last, sir, I'd like a rose to smell, if there are such things as roses still."

Major MacDonald nodded. Then, raising his voice, he called his servant by name. The man came, standing in the doorway, blocking it.

"Go down to Aix Noulette," the Major ordered, digging into his pocket as he spoke, "and see if you can get a bottle of mineral water. And buy any fruit you can scrounge. Don't come back without something."

The quest is successful, for two hours later the man returns. He puts his booty on the bench: a bottle of Perrier water, four apples, six bananas.

There is the shining fruit in the dugout, on the bench, its beauty there beside the litter of the foul meal. And presently the fruit has disappeared. All save a single apple. This they ignore. It lies there blood-red and desirable. The odd apple.

Stephen is glum. That delicious water, that luscious fruit, has only made his melancholy more profound. Ripe fruit evokes so many memories. But most, memory of an ancient apple tree that stands in the corner of a meadow, like an old man by a cottage door. The Gravenstein.

"What are you thinking about, Craig?" asks the Major.

Stephen does not answer at once. But a smile is slowly wiping away the melancholy of his face. Then he grins, and it is a boyish grin.

"Well, sir, the truth is, I guess we all want that apple. What about dividing it?"

The Major does the dividing. Very deliberately he wipes the bacon fat from his knife.

He holds the apple and with meticulous care makes the division. They munch the final segments in silence.

O'Reilly says, "You didn't get your rose, Craig. It's an unjust world."

Notes

1. *"Land and Water"*: weekly newspaper specializing in the War. Printed in London from January 1917 to March 1919. Editor-in-chief: Hilaire Belloc. See photo of title page and extracts. Contact person for info.: Liliane.Lafleur@warmuseum.ca
2. "red-tabs": staff officers.
3. M. & V.: a stew with a high percentage of fat.
4. Blighty: usually a wound which is bad enough to get you removed to England and out of the fighting. From the Hindi word "belati."
5. Whitehall, Champs-Elysees, Wilhelmstrasse: centres from which government policy emanated.
6. junketing: travelling about in an adventuresome way.
7. Picus and Pomona: In ancient Rome Picus was held to be the god of agriculture; his name, Picus, means "woodpecker" in Latin. Pomona was the goddess of fruit and was married to Vertumnus, god of orchards and fruit.
8. Field Message Book: small book carried by officers. Used to take notes, make requisitions for supplies, etc. See photo of samples from Godwin's own Field Message Book.
9. S.A.A.: small arms ammunition.
10. P.O.'s on R. and L: Platoon officers on the right and left of the break (Prof. Tim Travers).
11. a "rear": bowel movement.
12. "a No. 9": laxative.

CHAPTER VIII

1

BOUVIGNY WOOD.

A camp on high ground among trees, such trees as have escaped the axe and an ignoble end down there in the trenches. Long wooden huts with little windows, bleak habitations, drab in their tar dressing; but for all that, most magnificent of dwellings. Magnificent after the trenches. Dry duck-walks to come and go upon, and with each free stride that queer half-articulated sense of release. Release from ever-present danger; release from the abhorred mud of the trenches that made each step a physical ordeal. Walking upright, openly, and without a care, as a fox might feel when the hunt is over or hounds are off the scent: time to squat awhile and lick oneself; time to breathe more freely.

A change, too, to clean oneself up, to delouse. Above all, release from those graves of trenches, those open graves that smelt of death. Joy of the sweet earth and beauty of dear, patient, waiting trees. Freedom of body and, with it, freedom of mind. So might a cripple feel miraculously made whole. Such freedom of movement, such sense of physical freedom!

The battalion had come out of the line on a night of utter darkness in the forlorn hours. Shadows moving in the murk.

Slowly, to the chink and rattle of equipment, 'A' Company drags wearily along the pock-marked road. They have stumbled along the endless communication trenches, a worm of moving men, and already they are half asleep upon their feet. At Ablaine, O'Reilly says:

"Better fall 'em out a bit here, Craig."

The column halts, breaks ranks.

"No lying in the road," Stephen bawls.

But the men lie in the road already, in the mud, and indifferent to it. What is mud to them whose lives are now lived in mud?

The sounds of coughing come from the ground, harsh and rasping. Stephen listens to these sounds and his heart goes out to the men.

"It's like a consumptive ward," says O'Reilly. "Tough on them."

"Makes you feel a bit disgusted with the M.O.'s,[1] doesn't it?" Stephen suggests. "The only thing that happens when you send a man out of the line is for him to turn up again with a No. 9 inside him. A purge is the cure for everything, apparently.

"The other day," he continued, masking a match for his cigarette, "I sent young Fellowes out to report sick. I noticed three or four gobs of blood in the trench beside his fire-step. Told me he had been spitting blood for days. But he came back."

O'Reilly said: "There was a general order, you know, which explains that. No men to be allowed out of the line unless their temperatures go over a hundred and three. A hundred and three! One used to go off the deep end for a temperature like that before the war."

Yes, it was a pretty tough war that garrisoned the front line with invalids . .
.

The worst part of the route lay ahead up steeply rising ground, a black wall against the dark night sky. It had been folly to allow this fall-out; the men would be stiffening up now, feeling it worse than if one had driven them on.

"Fall in," they bawl in unison.

Among the recumbent forms, the N.C.O.s move alertly. And they too are tired. But, as with the subalterns, they must not remind themselves of it. There is work to be done, the work of making men just as tired do just a little more.

The shadows move. Grunts and oaths, good-natured jests. Clank of equipment, as shoulders shrug the harness into position. Some sort of a ragged fall-in. They shuffle off at the word of command. Going out of the line: a pleasant thought, but they are too weary to savour the promise of it, its full sweetness.

And when they reach Bouvigny Wood, there are O'Reilly and Stephen, spent too, but both packing three weaker brothers' rifles: an extra forty-two pounds to hump, up the slippery hill, over the uneven ground.

O'Reilly and Stephen enter a long dark hut flanked with the familiar wired bunks; the floor is muddy here and there, but the duck-boards offer dry footing. The place is spacious, the only smell about it being the sourness of unclean human bodies.

The sound of a singing voice comes to them and O'Reilly halts by the door.

"Listen to that!" he exclaims. "Just listen to that!"

From a mousy little man, squatting cross-legged, and working feverishly with cloth and Blanco on his Webb equipment, comes the song in a weak tenor voice. He is throwing his soul into it, letting himself go. There is yearning in the voice, and a melancholy. That popular ditty, that sentimental ballad sung in a hundred canteens by as many lady amateurs amusing the troops.

"D'you hear the words, Craig?" asks O'Reilly.

Yes, Stephen can hear them now. A grin spreads over his face.

"Give me the right,
To sleep with you all night."

They stand a moment listening, watching the unconscious singer, and they shake with suppressed laughter. The sickly sentimentality of the ballad's melody; the frank realism of the words as revised by the troops.

But wasn't it this fellow's rifle Stephen had packed up the steep hillside a few hours before? Wasn't he the man who lay down and declared he couldn't go another step?

Only a night's sleep between them and that great weariness, but a full night, in shirt and pants, bootless, not a fragment of a night, doled out in rationed hours, and short rations at that.

A full night's sleep; a square meal of oblivion. Out of the line, cleaning up, in the open with the sane, sweet hinterland to nourish mud-weary eyes, eyes starved by months of desolation.

"Give me the right,
To sleep with you all night . . ."

Strange, resilient human nature. Forlorn and pitiable yesterday, and today absorbed by thoughts of amorous delight. A new grip on life, so differently the world looks in the huts, beneath the trees of Bouvigny Wood.

2

A week at rest is a week of work. In no more than two days this blessing, life above ground, with no danger beyond the chance of a stray shell, is accepted with no second thought, no gratitude. For what had every man yearned, there in the line, but for this respite? Yearning of body, yearning of heart. And the boon granted, they give no second thought to it.

There is grousing everywhere, such grousing as is never heard in the line, where a philosophy of resignation mutes such plaints as these.

They are grousing at the grub from the field kitchens that stand with their smoking chimney pots between the long huts. The cook is patient. There is no real grievance. But certainly the 'M. & V.' is no less fat. Can he help that? Does he make money tinning the bloody stuff? He does not.

They are grousing about the parades in the field behind the trees. They ask what the hell is the idea of them. Even the band of pipers does not cheer them. These sturdy makers of barbaric music are sons of bitches, never in the line. Whereas in the line a foot of water in a dugout will be the source of endless wit, a puddle in a hut is a scandal to be protested against.

Stephen remembered hearing a man say after a bad half hour of shelling that had left them all a little shaken up:

"If I ever come through this war nothing will ever look like real trouble to me again."

And he had recognised his own thought in those words, a thought that became, after a while, a sort of bribe to fate, a supplication and a prayer. It was the punished child of the nursery, promising to be good.

But now, with a sheer week of certain life, what was it worth? Not much, certainly, since there were so many petty grievances, so many grouses. The hardships of the trenches were gone; and now, like petulant children, they sought and found new grievances where they should have seen only the blessing of a week's respite.

And when the war was over – if one came through – would one live for ever after with the ever-present thought: No matter what my lot, I am alive, and it is enough? Over and over again, Stephen had made oath with himself that should he come through, the balance of his days would be spent in thankfulness for life. He wondered now whether this was but a mere self-deception to be cured by six months of the security of peace. The graph of gratitude, he decided, would show a steady downward curve. They would all be the same hereafter, those of them who came through, men who girded against the hard conditions of their lives, forgetting their blessings.

3

Pilk is now much about, in and out of the hut he comes and goes, and his face is always ready to break into a smile. Stephen is realising that in France a batman is a batman still. A born servant he is, this little man and, like all good servants, without subservience, possessing a dignity that survives even that long and narrow face, those loose false teeth. He now reveals a pride in his job he could not demonstrate in the line. Stephen's Sam Browne is resplendent.

"It's the bone that does the trick, sir," he explains. And there is pride in his voice as he holds the straps at arm's length, as a connoisseur might show a masterpiece.

But Pilk, how is he fixed?

"Turn round . . . Ah, puttees[2] on the blink and – trousers frayed."

Well, yes, it is true enough, the best of serge won't last forever.

To the Quarter-Master.
Sir,
Please issue Pte. Pilk, No. 187640, 1 pair trousers and 1 pair puttees. Those

he is turning in have been in use fifteen months and are worn out.
*   S. Craig, Lt., 'A' Coy.*

Pilk rises on his toes, smiles broadly.

"Thank you, sir," he says, and his teeth slip down and are smartly restored by a practised tongue.

Stephen is writing again. So many *details* to this job, no end to them.

Sergt. Glenny.
Gas Helmets. – Glasses not to be used on small Box Respirator as it scratches
*   the eye pieces.*
Salutes. – Orders are that the name of any man not saluting is to be taken. I
*   don't want any No. 1 Platoon men pegged for this. It does NOT apply to the*
*   front line.*
Smartness. – Men expected to be clean and shaved daily.
Gumboots. – It is now an offence to wear these anywhere but in the front line.
Defence Scheme. – Every man should have broad idea of this, and also with
*   regard to new drafts be told names of officers.*
Shortages. – Please report to me right away any shortages.
Gas Helmets to be worn at all times.
*   S. Craig.*

Detail, detail and more detail. A subaltern's job, a nurse's job.

4

Bouvigny Wood: how pleasant it is.

There, to the rear, open fields rolling opulently down to the folds where villages lie, still standing, undestroyed. People going about their business; looking to the nearing spring, making ready to sow the yellow seed, to cast it upon the earth. The round of man's most ancient occupation:[3] winning sustenance from the soil. But mostly old men and women who have no man at all.

And over there, a canker on the land, the battle front, like the edge of a leprous sore eating at the wholesome rim of the fat land.

And there are birds about. A ginger cat stretches his hindquarters luxuriously with head uplifted to the odours of the cooking stew, stalking the smoking kitchens with appraising eye, tail erect.

And what more natural than birds, than a ginger cat? Than blue-bloused men about the land? And ancient women over kitchen fires?

5

The Major talks about the Somme. For him the battle is, as ever, near, a vividly-remembered yesterday. It will be as yesterday with him ten years hence when he will be looking back across the flat days of peace as a traveller across a plain turns to behold the mountain that seems to follow him. The Major's life is divided into two parts, and they are cleft by the Somme.

Before the Somme, after the Somme: that is how he thinks of the past, and that is how he talks of it. Yes, that is how it is. He will not let you forget it. And if he comes through and lives to be an ancient man, it will be the same with him.

Will he be jostled then by younger men with new and bloodier wars to occupy them? An old fossil, babbling about that little show they had those years ago? Beside that experience all the events of life have been dwarfed to insignificance. Later, maybe, he will say: Before the War, or After the War. But it will be the Somme he will be thinking of.

When Stephen tries to draw Piers about his life in the ranks, a mask falls upon that lean face. He shrinks into himself like a mollusc before a probe. Piers was at Festubert, and on the Somme as well; in many raids, in many dirty places. He may – who knows? – be in many more. Why not talk of something else? A bellyful is what Piers has had. He says so bitterly.

So, when the Major, chin cupped on hand and elbow among his papers, there under the trees of Bouvigny Wood, starts once more upon this theme that seems to be for ever in his head, Piers retires into a restless silence. The Major is like Napoleon at St. Helena.[4] He must fight his battle over again and live again its terrors.

Stephen tries to visualise this battle. But it is not possible. Even those who were in it cannot do that, for they saw only a small part of it; registered only a tithe of its full horror. Multiply one of those hearty evening strafes a thousand times? But that did not get it. You couldn't do it. It was like sitting down to visualise the distance of Aldebaran;[5] you left the task reeling mentally.

But from the Major's eyes you sensed something of the battle, those eyes so much more eloquent than his terse, laconic phrases.

Yes, however wide the battle front, for each individual the horror of the whole would be localised and only dimly guessed at. It would be unendurable shelling, shattering tumult, death and mutilation, heart-rending cries, choking stenches. Utter anguish. Not for a brief spell upon a single day, but for day after day.

Stephen looked from Piers' melancholy face to the set, expressionless face of the Major. Admiration, affection, pity, and with them, a sense of humility.

Outside, O'Reilly, who has been silent, says to Stephen: "Shouldn't talk too much about Piers' time in the ranks and as an N.C.O. You see, he told me once that he never knew an N.C.O. who came back from England with his commission who did not get done in. He believes he will get done in. Oh, he doesn't say anything. But I know. Look at his face when the Major talks. That's enough."

Later, when the orderly had cleared the simple meal from the table, the Major said: "That show[6] is coming off to-night."

He had been over at the dilapidated house which served for battalion H.Q.

It is the show there has been so much talk about for weeks. Not the battle for the Ridge itself. No, not that.

Piers straightens up.

"Then we are not for it, sir?" he asks harshly.

The Major shakes his head. And Stephen is glad of it. No excuse for feeling like that about it, with no Festubert, no Somme, behind one. But yet there it was: a sort of reprieve, and one to be thankful for. Why not admit it to oneself? After all, one was a civilian and no professional soldier.

"They are going to attack on the right," the Major explains. "They want to straighten the line out and push it a bit nearer up to the Ridge. They are going to blow a mine."

He turned to Stephen and O'Reilly. "You two had better hump along with me and watch from the hill. It will teach you something. Zero hour is nine."

6

It is very dark on the hill so that the ground below them is a black pool. But the hump of Vimy Ridge stands out against the night sky like a sleeping animal. There is scarcely a sign of life, and the enemy trenches are silent except for the occasional bark of a Mauser,[7] or the harsh staccato stutter of machine guns.

What does that mean, if not that he has wind of something in the air? He can know nothing of these secret preparations, yet his nerves are jumpy. Why?

It is as mysterious as the sixth sense of a dog.

"Two minutes more." The Major, holding his wrist-watch before him, is self-contained.

"One minute. Half a minute. Keep your eyes over there . . . There she goes!"

There is no sound, no sound at all, but down there in the valley a thousand yards or more away the earth has opened and belched forth red fire. Flames swirl in bloody eddies and slowly die down. Then, travelling like a projectile across this uncanny moment of silence, comes the report – a deep, reverberating boom.

A black canopy rises majestically straight up into the air and drifts slowly across the sky. Compact and ominous, it drifts along the still air. Pandemonium breaks loose and the night, a moment ago serene, beautiful, is tortured with ten thousand lacerating sounds.

Five seconds, perhaps, from the sending of that unseen electric impulse, and the batteries come into action. A battery of eighteen-pounders lies snugly camouflaged under brush in the shelter of the hill. It opens up. The scream of shells passes overhead, a lashing like carters' whips, cruel and purposeful.

And with this high note now comes the deeper note of the 9.5's. Where is that battery? A well-kept secret. They could not say.

Lights rise and fall, red lights on pallid stalks, blossoming into crimson flowers. They proclaim in colour the enemy's distress. Flares waver up, pallid and wan against the bright lights of the many-coloured signals. The chatter of machine guns and the lower note of trench mortars, and, now and then, minor conflagrations as ammunition dumps are exploded by direct hits of the invisible gunners.

Have our men made their objective down there in that cauldron of death? Can any life survive that reeking chaos? Have they occupied the new crater? Are they clearing it even now of its reeking poison fumes?

A column of fire leaps skywards, shaking the ground with its sleeping dead and little group of silent spectators. A terrific detonation. A direct hit on an ammunition dump. Shells, S.A.A. and hand grenades detonate in one great roar. Ours or theirs? Difficult to say, for it is dark and the line thereabouts is tortuous.

An hour later all is quiet. The anguished red signals have ceased to waver in the air, the batteries are silent, and now only the lesser fry (machine guns and trench mortars, rifles), fire sporadically. Fired by men with lacerated nerves, fast-beating hearts.

They make their way back. They have seen a little show. What have they learned from it? Some conception of what a big show is like. Perhaps that, if nothing else.

Three hours later they are in their huts, the air blue with smoke. The Major comes with word.

"The crater has been occupied and consolidation goes forward," he says. And he says it as he might say: "A shortage parade to-morrow."

A crater has been occupied. Good God! Is that all that has come out of that cataclysm? How many men have died to secure those few odd yards of ground to gain that crater, that stinking hole in the ground? How many men? How many widows? How many orphans?

7

The week of rest is over and the battalion moves back once more into the line. Clean and spruce it is, but there is no hilarity. It would be strange if there were. First shattered Ablaine, then Souchez's razed walls. Desolate and drab it is, yet now it has a homely look that belongs to familiar things. And last, the first narrow entrance to the tortuous communication trenches. A signpost points the way. They need no signpost. The weary, worm-like crawl over the broken duck-boards, dodging the overhead wire. And soon the battalion is as muddy as before.

How many are thinking of Bouvigny Wood now?

The attack upon the right has started things. Now there is little rest. Our artillery is never quiet, and the men curse it heartily. They have no ill-will towards those unseen men in the trenches opposite; they are, like themselves, victims of the guns. The gunners are a common enemy. Their hatred is intense, concentrated on those unseen gunners. Cheerfully they would murder them.

Busybodies they are, raising those wasp nests, those hidden batteries that bark from behind the twin towns, Liévin and Lens.

Whose shells are those bursting bang against the parapet? Behind the front line trench? Just clearing it, and spraying debris and foul gas from No Man's Land?

They are our own.

Every man's voice is raised against these gunners who, so it seems, deal death to friend and enemy with supreme indifference. They are sons of bitches. They are bastards.

Yet these gunners have their troubles too. High overhead are 'planes searching out these secret batteries, and returning, directing their own artillery on them. The air throbs, a pulsation that ends at last upon the beating brain, a hated, abhorred sound.

The guns.

And at night there are the flashing lights upon the rim of the horizon. The bombardment continues.

Notes

1. M.O.: medical officer.
2: puttees: strips of wool cloth which were wrapped around the legs, starting at the top of the boot and winding upwards to just below the knees.
3. "man's most ancient occupation": farming, according to Godwin. This is a favorite theme of his, mentioned in *The Eternal Forest* and then developed in great detail in *The Land Our Larder* (published in 1939 but now out of print). *The Land Our Larder* is a blueprint to show the British how to organize farm production in order to survive the war with Germany and its allies.
4. Napoleon at St. Helena. Probably poisoned (slowly) by one of his own men, the Comte de Montholon, according the findings of Swedish dentist Dr. Sten Forshufvud.
5. Aldebaran: star in the constellation of Taurus.
6. "show": a battle, attack, raid, etc. Stoical euphemism.
7. Mauser: a German pistol.

CHAPTER IX

1

FEAR: there are so many shades of it. The shadowy forebodings of calamity that creep like fog about the shrinking heart; that terror which topples and overthrows the citadel of the human soul. And between these two conditions all those anguishes whose discipline is the triumph of the soldier's soul and the measure of his quality.

The man of imagination suffers most because he conjures up in his mind a thousand horrors that exist nowhere else, a thousand possibilities of evil. To him death comes not once, but many times.

The stolid man meets danger when it comes with courage or without it. For him death calls but once. And each man has his own especial fear.

For Stephen, shell fire, an ordeal, was endurable: it did not penetrate to that last defence where, like a flame burning in still air, the soul abides apart. It left him master of his own essential self. But when the machine guns opened up the flame wavered, and fear blew icily through the chamber of his soul. Shells were impersonal; machine gun fire searched for his entrails, making them turn in his belly while his blood curdled. Under such fire he was no longer Stephen, but one vast genital.

Those machine gunners fired with a single objective, their spluttering guns traversed hungrily seeking out Stephen's genitals. And they would find them. Horror! To be hit there. Become a eunuch, unmanned. Worse than death. No, not worse than death. Nothing could be worse than death.

And in the trenches, under fire, he would think: Why steel helmets for the head and no protection lower down? It was lower down that you needed it so badly. He wondered how many men there were in the hospitals who had suffered this outrage upon their manhood.

O'Reilly was pursued by the obsession of facial disfigurement; he was tortured by the fear of having his jaw smashed or blown away.

"Anything but that," he would say. "Anything but disfigurement; I'd rather lose a leg."

Piers said: "When I was in hospital there was a chap who had lost both arms from the shoulder. He was quite young and handsome, too. D'you suppose, O'Reilly, that he would trade his good looks for both arms, or even one of them? That's the very worst that could happen to a man, to lose both arms."

O'Reilly did not agree. He said: "What about your eyes?"

But Piers had seen more of war than the other two. He had, moreover, had long hours of observant inactivity in a hospital ward. He knew.

"If you lose both arms," he explained, "you are utterly helpless. You can't get out of bed alone, can't dress, can't feed yourself. Can't drink. Can't scratch your nose if it itches, can't put a smoke in your mouth. Can't write a letter or open a door, or read a book. Can't even perform the meanest act without somebody's help."

And as he spoke he was seeing that boy in his wheelchair in the ward, the handsome face with eyes that hurt you. He saw the nurse raising the cup to the boy's lips, saw her manipulate for him a cigarette. Such utter helplessness, such utter dependence upon another.

Yet this was not Piers' preoccupation. The cases were few; the odds against losing both arms were long, much longer than against losing one's life, or one's sight. And Piers, who thought in coloured images, who feasted on the beauty of the world, who loved its many-coloured splendours, was afraid of being blinded.

"Just a graze across the bridge of the nose can do it," he explained. "I've seen it happen on the Somme. Hardly a mark to show, but – blind. Optic nerve done in . . ."

Sergeant Glenny became one vast belly under fire. He had seen a man ripped open. "The blood just pumped out of him," he explained, "as if there was a great pump working in his guts. And you could see his guts, too, coils and coils of them."

He added darkly: "Abdominals hurt worse than anything. Hellish pain."

It made his entrails shrink to think of it. And as he talked he thought of the morphia secreted in his first-aid kit. He knew what he would do.

2

What did the Major fear?

Nothing, it seemed. Perhaps he was one of those men who held the secret conviction that they would come through unharmed. Perhaps that was how it was with him. Certainly he gave no outward sign of fear, even seemed at times oblivious of obvious danger, ignoring precautions that any man might take, stalking along the parapet like a lunatic.

What did the Colonel fear?

Everything, it seemed. Stephen had seen him only once for more than a moment. At Ablaine St. Nazaire, in a cellar, sitting on a bench before a table littered with forms and trench blue-prints. A little man with a ruddy complexion, wearing the ribands of the D.S.O.[1] and Legion of Honour. In the late fifties, Stephen supposed, but marvellously preserved. His actions were vigorous, his speech clipped and incisive. He had sent for O'Reilly, Piers and Stephen soon after they joined the battalion.[2] He had seen them singly. Stephen supposed that it was to size them up. He had asked a number of questions and, having considered the answers, summed up tersely with:

"I expect you to carry on as well as the officers you're replacing."

It might have been a challenge, an appeal for the maintenance of the Battalion's magnificent record. It might have warmed the heart, that phrase, but did not. It sounded like a threat and left only a feeling of resentment, because it seemed an unmerited warning, uttered obliquely. It seemed to imply that the Colonel did not really expect anything of the sort, was a hard-used man to have to put up with these three new subalterns, but was, nevertheless, determined to put the fear of God into them.

The Colonel had tried to frighten them into not being afraid. The Colonel, who lived in his headquarters, so that one rarely saw him in the front line, and then only as a hurrying figure followed by an orderly.

Once, coming back to headquarters along the communication trench under desultory shell fire, Stephen had encountered the Colonel's batman coming out of H.Q. dugout. He carried a German helmet upside down, and cast its contents over the parapet. So the Colonel, it seemed, did not leave his dugout, even to relieve himself.

Was the Colonel, then, a coward?

No. Like his adjutant, who wore the ribands of the D.S.O. and M.C.,[3] he was a brave man.

It seemed, then, that a man had so much physical courage and no more. Nerves, like the stoutest ropes, wore through, became tattered, thin and unreliable.

Piers had explained something of this, talking about those re-amputations cases he had seen in hospital The first time, doped with morphia, the patient went to the table cheerily enough. But the fourth time? The fifth time? Piers said he had seen big fellows whimpering at the thought of it.

Colonel and adjutant avoided the front line. But both Colonel and adjutant could, for the asking, go back to the security of the base, or retire to shine in a reserve battalion in southern England. Their courage consisted, then, in their contempt for that way out. They could escape, but would not.

3

Thinking thus, Stephen felt humbled. They were, both of them, better men than he. He would take the first chance to get out of the line that presented itself, but he would do nothing to bring about that release.

The Colonel had every right to put into that admonition the hint of threat. Stephen was being admitted to a company of men. He had to prove himself. There should be no resentment. Rather humility.

Stephen finally decided that what he was really most afraid of was of being afraid. You couldn't tell, couldn't guarantee yourself. Suppose, for example, he was reduced to the condition in which he had come upon Galway? True, he was little more than a boy and should have been at home; but there it was. He had been paralysed. And only a few minenwerfer[4] had reduced him to that pitiable condition.

Stephen had come up from a dugout to find a little group of men in a traverse jeering at the youth, whose face had turned grey-green. He stood there gibbering, unmanned, frank and unashamed in his terror. Oh! most pitiable.

Stephen had snapped at those laughing men, and turning to the frightened lad, had barked at him:

"Come on, now, show a little guts. This is nothing."

Why so rough a tone, why such impatience – which thrust aside the pity one felt, oh, in the heart, in the bowels, if one did not hate, in the person of this youth, the very thing one knew crawled somewhere deep down in one's own craven heart?

To whom was one making the appeal, if not to oneself?

4

What supported men in the line?

Many things.

The Major was a tired little boy dragging himself out to the wood-pile at the close of a long day to chop the needed kindling and stove wood for a weary widow woman. Only the little boy was now a grown man, and his mother had become his country. In a word, duty. Duty and love; piety.[5] Love of mother projected into love of country. Yes, that was quite easily understood.

What other mainspring of action thrust down so far into a man? And those roots in the emotions and not of the mind. One did not analyse love of mother; later, one did not analyse love of land. Yet either might be evil, surely. One might love mother at expense of wife. There were such men, walking through the world, yet ever in the nursery, mother-bound. And country, love of it, so it seemed, made its conditions, demanded, jealously, hatred of other peoples, other lands. Other mothers.

The Major, then, was in the war because he had so dearly loved his widowed mother, so faithfully laboured to alleviate her lot? And that, surely, was absurd.

He would have looked at you . . .

Many of the men were actors in a play. They played their parts before an invisible audience for whom they were heroes. The heroes of the popular songs.

We don't want to lose you,
But we think you ought to go . . .

Keep the home fires burning,
Though our hearts be yearning . . .

Oh! Oh! Oh! it's a lovely war.

When they took a chance, this unseen audience gasped. When they escaped, its cheering came to them, a mighty heartening roar.

War had to be squared. Somehow. This reality, grim, horrible, was not remotely like the drama that audience watched from afar; nor were there really such actors therein as that audience saw it. The war as it looked from England, from the prairie, from the bush: a thrilling affair, studded with great moments. What was it?

Only a drudging in mud, waiting for the inevitable packet. Dirt and vermin, heartache, ache of body, wet, sickness, a weary waiting – and then, the terror of gunfire.

Yet, with some, fancy triumphed in a way over reality, was masked by fantasy. Couldn't see how, exactly, but this was heroism. This was being a hero. For King and Country. Being plugged at,[6] sitting tight. Living underground or in an open grave. Suffering wet, cold, and – as when the enemy found the transport lines and opened up[7] – hunger.

Presently they would go over the top again and even that would be different. No matter, nothing could destroy those illusions of the home-folk which they carried with them, grafted into them.

They had left home for a war, and when they got home they would tell tales about that war. But about this business, well, about that they would keep silent. Presently it would fade from memory; perhaps. The reality they knew would become confused in their minds with the war the civilians sung about, would be wiped away by it.

Only, now and then, in dreams, it would return.

How could one explain to those womenfolk how one felt the first onset of nervous disturbance? What would they think if one sat back, there, in the old Mission rocker, and said, as one man had to Stephen:

"I was walking one day down a narrow road in a village behind the line. There was a shallow ditch on one side and a stone wall upon the other. In a field, nearby, an anti-aircraft battery was popping at an enemy 'plane and getting, per usual, nowhere near it. But that didn't interest me at all. You see,

I knew that in a moment the enemy would drop a shell into this road. Not an ordinary shell, mind you, but a shell that would just fit the road, like a bayonet fits its scabbard. The question was: Could I get cover in that ditch – was it big enough to allow me to squeeze in? I sweated over it."

No, they wouldn't understand; not with pictures in their minds of big men with neatly bandaged heads (a little blood, but not too much) holding up whole platoons of a craven enemy at the point of the bayonet.

For such exploits men got the V.C.[8] In that imaginary war. Stephen had heard a V.C. tell the story of how he earned that coveted honour. It was a strange tale.

And for the rest? There was the support and comfort of comradeship, the relief of humour. And hope. Beyond these, there was the knowledge that there was no escape. They became resigned. And there were those in whom suffering engendered bitterness. And hate. But not of the enemy.

5

The battalion was out of the line. It had come out mud-coated and bedraggled, marching at first over the hill raggedly and then into the open country beyond. Burdened men with aching shoulders, burning feet.

Slag fosses[9] stood forlorn upon the face of the grey land. Blue-bloused men in fields glanced up at the khaki column that moved like a worm across the flat country, and stooped again to their work without sign or greeting. Mining machinery sprawled, spider-like, beneath the pointing fingers of giant chimneys. An unlovely land.

They passed through villages, long and narrow, roughly paved and garbage-strewn, flanked by mean hovels from whose doorways shapeless women watched their passing with indifferent eyes. In time one gets used to anything. British troops from the trenches, what did they signify? The British, what were they after all? Bully-beef, biscuits, billets, coffee-chips, beer, wine. Yes, champagne, and much of it. Water to sell and, whenever chance presented itself, a claim against them for damage done to wattle cow-sheds wherein, side by side, upon their straw, they slept the sleep of utter weariness. And, perchance, kicked a little.

So it was: *"Malheur! Malheur!"*[10]

But just the same, there was profit in it. Especially was there profit in it when badges took the form of maple leaves in brass.

"Bon garçons. Plenty money."

"Malheur! Malheur!"

Apathy and ugliness. Women in vast crape dresses.

Old men, with faces like mahogany. Estaminets.[11] *Dubonnet. Caporal. Oporto Sandeman.*

Then open country once again, and the stink of dung-hills. Pounding lorries that squirted mud, thundering along the roads. Not that this mattered much, a little mud, more or less. But stolid faces of men squatting on tailboards, riding comfortably. Army Service Corps. Sons of bitches. Riding, clean and fresh, while they, the P.B.I.,[12] foot-slogged it from the line.

Later, there would be lorry-hops to such towns as Barlin and Bethune. Shops brightly lit and all the amazing life of a living habitation. Shops with bright windows, selling Burberrys, Dunhill pipes. Cake shops. Girls with smiling faces, flashing eyes, maddening breasts, so round, so soft. That one in the square opposite the tower with its demolished cupola. Everyone after her. A lovely creature. But chaste? Perhaps, or perhaps not. Probably a lover, but a Frenchman. Nothing doing with these *Anglais,* except just enough to keep them coming like bees to a honey jar. Spending their money. But no honey.

And little boys with pipe-shank legs and loose blue blouses, little following boys with impish faces: "My sister, ver' nise."

Signalling with dirty fingers dirty signals, pointing, making signs.

"Jig-a-jig, mistaire, jig-a-jig. My sister, ver' nise, ver' nise, my sister."

6

There is no band. Why is there no band? It was promised. They are too tired to sing, even to sing that lewd little ditty about the grasshoppers. Only murmur of flat voices above the rhythmic tramp of tired feet. Left, right. Left, right.

Nothing here to show for those many months of parade ground training. But isn't there? What keeps them going, if not that?

Word passes, magically, from nowhere, as all army rumours run, mysteriously: a band. A band to meet them and to play them into billets.

The last five kilometres, and the worst.

A wind rises and blows across the flat face of the land. Along the western horizon, against the grey of sky, another column marches, at attention. Wooden soldiers, trees. The band comes; and now it is playing, leading the battalion, the tired and foot-sore battalion.

Ah, music, and what a difference it makes! Putting heart into men, easing tired feet, softening the hardest road. And the wind blows in squally gusts, bringing fine, soaking rain, blows from the rear, catches up the music of the band, sends it down the road, sweeps it up and on ahead. After all, three companies hear no music, no cheering brass, no stimulating boom, boom of drums. Left, right. Left, right.

The wind has robbed them of the music of the band.

7

"March to attention!"

Down the column, voices in the wind:

"March to attention!"

And answering murmurs, growls.

The great car, flag fluttering from long bonnet, speeds past the column, spraying mud insolently. "Eyes right!" The Corps Commander. Fleeting glimpse: red faces beneath brass-peaked caps, flash of red tabs, flash of ribands. A driver smarter than their own commanding officer.

"That's him, the old son-of-a-gun. At the back."

The car is gone.

Left, right. Left, right.

A voice out of the column, blown by the wind:

"Poor bloody infantry!"

It is a bitter voice.

Notes

1. D.S.O.: Distinguished Service Order. After the Victoria Cross, the highest decoration in the British military.
2. battalion: on average, a unit of about 900 soldiers. One battalion was usually divided into four companies; one company was divided into four platoons; one platoon was divided into about four sections. Godwin/Craig commanded a platoon. See diagram of Godwin's unit; also the photo of an actual battalion.
3. M.C.: Military Cross. Like the D.S.O., it was awarded to officers only.
4. Minenwerfer: also known as "moaning Minnies." Approx. 80 kilos of high explosive shell. Short range, high arc. The concussion alone caused by them could be deadly.
5. piety: filial respect, dutifulness.
6. "plugged at": shot at.
7. opened up: started firing.
8. VC: Victoria Cross, the highest British medal for bravery.
9. "slag fosses": a raised pathway built of mine tailings taken from slag-heaps; this was a coal-mining area.
10. malheur (French): disaster, great misfortune.
11. estaminet: part informal restaurant, part 'drinking hole,' a favorite gathering place of the soldiers in France. Benches, wooden tables, are *de rigueur* to deserve the name.
12. P.B.I.: "poor bloody infantry."

CHAPTER X

1

MOTHER and father, too.

So one must see to the men's billets. There are ways and ways: turn the job over to Sergeant Glenny and go off to seek one's own, after a word with the billeting officer. Leave them to scrounge for themselves. One way or the other way.

To see every man fixed up, go over them all, and a word and a smile for each. Examine these damp wattle barns and consider the best arrangement of them, so that each man shall have the best accommodation possible and a chance of air. Seek out the source of each barn's water supply, walking the edge of the farmhouse dung-pile, considering seepage, filth. So many farmhouses, so many rectangular yards, so many dung-piles, walled round by wattle barns.

Look at that foot one heard so much about on the march; clean and dress that smelly member, making so intimate a service seem in order by matter-of-fact observations on the dangers of blood poisoning.

In short, to think and act for tired men, letting one's own exhaustion wait. Mother and father, too.

They have shed their equipment on the straw-covered earth which is half the dung of cattle; they are settling down, easing themselves, scratching chafed behinds, picking at toes, unwinding puttees; asking where the cook-house is; whether there will be a field cashier around later because they will be wanting something better than rations: coffee, chipped potatoes, fried eggs, beer, fags.

And here is Pilk at hand, faithful Pilk, dependable Pilk. He leads the way.

"Seventeen Rue St. Petersburgh," he says. "Yes, the wagons came up all right and I've got the sleeping bag and other gear. A good billet, sir. Magnificent. Bit of luck I call it."

Stephen's knees surrender, and every movement is an ache. He puts forth a final effort. A row of miners' tenements, looking bleakly towards a stark railway embankment spiked with signals: Rue St. Petersburgh. Pilk leads into the living room with all the pride of an explorer. A shapeless woman in shabby black greets them, standing there in the dark and airless room, a little girl peeping from the folds of her skirt.

She leads the way up the steep and narrow stairs. Here is the room. Yes, Pilk was not exaggerating: it is magnificent. A bed, puffed up like a balloon, with sheets, too, and a pillow. The woman turns it back and shows it them with pride; she stirs its loveliness with a red hand, and the crackle of straw answers her with promises.

The boards upon the floor are scrubbed; there is a mat beside the bed. Jug and basin, table, too. Magnificent. Voluptuous, intoxicating.

And suddenly the virtue[1] goes out of Stephen. A fit of coughing shakes him; he becomes red in the face, gasps for breath, subsides upon the bed. He is exhausted.

Pilk stands by, solicitous. "Better lie down a bit," he counsels, making signs to the watching woman. She nods in a kindly way, raises two expressive hands and murmurs: *"Malheur, malheur."*

Pilk bustles about the room, arranging things, keeping an eye upon the man upon the bed. The coughing has ceased: Stephen is now grey, his eyes closed.

"What sort of place have you got, Pilk?" He speaks without opening his eyes, wearily.

"Fine," Pilk tells him. "Mr. Piers has got the other room. He's had to go down to headquarters. I'm sharing with his batman, down below."

"What sort of place is it, Pilk?"

"Quite jake,[2] sir," disarmingly.

"Dry?" – suspiciously.

"Not a drop of water on the floor" – as one who asserts a thing hard to believe.

"Got a window?"

Stephen's eyes have opened. He watches the solicitous Pilk as he moves about, notes his hesitation.

"Well, no, not a window exactly," Pilk admits.

Stephen swings his legs off the bed and sits there a crumpled, collapsed figure of exhaustion, tunic loose, hair rumpled.

"Where in hell have they put you, Pilk? Show me . . ."

From the ground floor a dark flight of brick steps ended abruptly in a cellar. No light penetrated it; the smell of coal dust filled the stale and damp air of it.

Pilk lit a candle; Stephen looked about in silence. Brick walls oozed water and on the floor fine coal dust glistened feebly in the light of the wavering candle. In a corner stood Pilk's gear. Stephen pointed at it.

"Take that up to my room," he said. "You'll not sleep in this bloody hole. Fix my flea-bag up. I've got a bed. You can use my air-pillow, too."

2

They were now some miles behind the front line. The rim of the ochreous tide of battle that eddies across the face of the land is a bitter memory, and no more. But the sound of the guns flows along its aery avenues and breaks in little tremulous waves upon the ears. Now and again the windows oscillate and small objects become alive, with fast-beating hearts. A homely sound at other times, but now, the recitative of death; maker of humble hearts; remembrancer of mortality.

The guns.

Pilk explained the matter: he would draw rations for four and Madame would cook for them. And Madame would buy such extras as were needed, in short, do all the bartering, cooking, serving. And render an account weekly.

Pilk had succeeded in arranging everything with much language of the hands, the eyes and the toothy, friendly smile; but with no word of French . . . And Madame smiled her understanding and agreement. She soon set before Piers and Stephen such a meal as they had not tasted for many months.

"Marvellous cooks, these Frenchwomen," declaimed Piers, lean and gaunt, and now sniffing at the savoury dish. "And to think she's made this out of bully beef. Wonderful!"

The coffee, in a great pot, was fragrant. They drank copiously, savouring the good taste of it. Madame, meanwhile, had vanished to her own domain, a mysterious region barred by an immense cabinet. But the child remained, finger in mouth, wide-eyed and full of childish curiosity for strange men speaking words beyond her understanding.

Stephen beckoned the little thing, and she came, shyly, and sat upon his knee. He kissed her, fondled her flaxen hair.

Did he kiss her? Or, in her, did he kiss his absent little son?

The child recognised in him the father-man and screwed his buttons round in little hands, flirting with her eyes innocently.

A child. Innocence, trust, affection. Sweet things, indeed.

A succession of men, remote and mysterious. Comings and goings. Some passed her by, big and creaking, with loud, alarming voices. But a few, like this thin man who came to her with his slow father smile, took stock of her. But none of them replaced the one who had gone without returning, the bearded man, with black strong hair, who slept beside her Maman. The man she had called Papa. No, these foreign officers, they could not take her father's place; not even the gendarme who came evening after evening to sit abstractedly while her Maman bustled about her work, following her black figure with his protruding eyes, sitting there smoking his long, thin cigar, with his big drooping moustache and nose that drooped in sympathy. He never seemed to notice her.

And sometimes he would be there in the mornings, his indifferent face there on the pillow, beside her mother. But not her father. Her Papa had played with her, and she had played with him. He came pink and clean from the mines, pink and clean from the foot-baths where he laved his coal-grimed body. He would let her pull his beard and made to bite her finger. But he had disappeared. And one day her Maman had wept and, soon after, both she and her mother had become black creatures, heavy with crape.[3] Widow and orphan.

And now her Maman wept no longer. And the absent bearded face was fading from memory. And sometimes her mother laughed aloud.

The meal was finished; the debris of it lay before them. Stephen asked himself: is it possible that I once took such boons as these for granted, never giving them a second thought? Chairs and a hard dry floor; a table laid, and a woman near at hand to serve food? Warmth and security, ease, and, above everything, this coffee?

Had one ever drunk one's coffee absent-mindedly, thinking of other things? Of course one had. And so one had never known until this moment what coffee was. After all, it was necessary to eat with the mind as well as with the body; with the imagination and with the critical faculties. As one had done just now.

He took from Piers a cigarette and drew the smoke luxuriantly into his mouth, expelled it through his nostrils. And this, too. Tobacco: marvellous stuff.

They leaned back in their chairs, tunics agape, aching legs eased in soft comfort of slacks. The luxury of it! And more, lots more, to come. The evening, no less, and soon that waiting bed. Sleep.

The warm, dim room with its human smell increased their lassitude. Stephen felt the slow throb of his weary heart upon the wall of his chest, a muffled pounding, like a spent machine. Sleep coming, and not a few meagre hours hunched, fully-dressed, on chicken-wire bunk, with a stale awakening after a few fretful hours. No. But a long night's oblivion, naked between cool sheets.

He considered it, sitting back collapsed, with the yellow light of the lamp upon his drawn face. For months now one had been living with nerves at full cock. Now one had slipped them back to safety catch. That tenseness, that watchfulness, often subconscious, but always there; a taut wire, and that wire now swinging loose. Here, away behind the line, there was no question of surprise, of sudden shock, of waiting death. One's lease of life, reckoned by the day, there in the line, had been extended. Indefinitely.

Though, of course, even this village had been shelled, in a desultory way, by gas shells. Mostly the women and children must have suffered. Pretty foul, that. Little kiddies caught on the road, playing hop-scotch on the way to school. Then – zippp!

"Only one thing we need now," yawned Piers, "and that's a damned long drink of Scotch. Must see about that tomorrow."

Scotch? Stephen hadn't tasted alcohol since that day at Lorette Spur when they made the Major just the least bit drunk. There were, he now considered, a good many drinks coming to him. Well, he would have them. All of them . . .

Stephen undressed with all the delicious sensations of one experiencing a physical thrill, exploring a new physical rapture, for the first time. It was like the first kiss in which youth fuses ardent body and ardent soul. It was like the taste of bread to one long hungry. It was a rapture sweet as first love.

He stretched himself, there in the yellow candle light, white and naked, passing thin hands over the soft skin of his body, caressing it as he yawned. How beautiful, after so long, to make friends once more with it, this body, white and still uncorrupted.

Utter contentment. He slid down between the sheets, and the straw within the mattress rustled a welcome.

He was asleep.

And presently came Pilk, holding a candle, walking like a cat, eyeing the flea-bag, contemplating its promise with the eyes of a greedy child. And he, too, stripped thoughtfully, scratching his hide. A sleeping bag and an air pillow. What ho!

He wormed his way into the canvas bag. A sleeping bag and an air pillow and, nearby, an open window framing the night sky and the stars.

And Pilk slept too.

And out of the night came the voice of the guns, a tremolo vibrating upon the air, a throbbing, purposeful, cruel, evil.

The guns.

3

A brass hat[4] was coming to take church parade. The first day out, too, with the men all anyhow and needing rest. That meant lick and spit. And who had any cleaning gear, anyway?

Church parade! They cursed it thoroughly, and with it, the high officer who had no more sense or consideration than this.

They marched to a gently-sloping green and waited, standing easy, the coming of the mighty one. The Colonel fussed, like a hen he seemed, so anxious that his battalion should make a good impression. And who cared a damn what impression they made upon this unknown?

And so the tired battalion waited.

A car swung down the narrow lane and stopped. The black and red flag of Army fluttered from its radiator. A general officer in the Army car; that meant no less a bug than the Army Commander himself. And here he was, tall and handsome, dignified; an elderly man with expressionless face, a picture for the frame of a club bay window; remote, impersonal, having nothing in common with them, inhabiting a world remote from their world. And behind him younger men: brass hats, red tabs. Staff wallahs.[5]

And the weary battalion looked upon the great ones with eyes that were hostile or merely indifferent. Brass hats, what had the P.B.I.[6] to do with them? They belonged to another and an unknown world, these resplendent ones.

Stephen thought: the idiocy of having church parades, religious ceremonies, on active service. The absurdity of it! The damnable, hollow sham of it! And the Germans, they would have them, too, Lutheran and Roman Catholic. God was in all the camps. Well, perhaps they would sing a bit more heartily than the battalion was singing now.

The general held a little black book before him. How severe he looked, how handsome, how assured. He had no doubts, anyway. God would stand to attention along with the battalion, waiting orders, orders from the army commander. What a pain it did give you in the fundamental! Was God going to take sides in this filthy business? It was rank blasphemy; that was bad enough. But it was exhausting, standing still with swollen feet, and that was worse.

The general adjusted his glasses and began to read in an even voice:

"And the children of Israel did evil in the sight of the Lord: and the Lord delivered them into the hand of Midian seven years. And the hand of Midian prevailed against Israel: and because of the Midianites the children of Israel made them the dens which are in the mountains, and caves and strongholds . . ."[6]

Tactful and cheering, that, Stephen fumed. Dens, caves, strongholds – as if one hadn't had enough of dens, caves, strongholds.

And yet he probably meant well. Read the lessons in some village church at home, likely enough. Ramrod daughters, in the front pew. He would have bony daughters, and no son. Another watertight compartment mind. Like the Major's.

And presently he would take the salute and stalk off to his car, and a good dinner in some sheltered chateau. And later in the afternoon he would manoeuvre dividers over a map and, having plotted his move, deliver a few more troops to Midian.

Well, in a war like this, could you have generals prancing about the line? You could not. This old johnny was doing his best, no doubt of that. It was his job: a professional soldier. This war was the biggest thing in his life. His biggest chance. The longed-for opportunity. At the worst he would be sent home, lose his command, like the commander who had lost Vimy Ridge and left them the job of putting right his blunders with their blood. At the best, be made a peer, given a State money grant.

Best and worst for the P.B.I. were something very different. The Major said, "He is a gunner. He was on the Somme. He took Fricourt . . ."

The Major and his Somme! . . .

"He invented the creeping barrage,"[7] he added respectfully.

And Piers interjected:

"And sometimes it crept a bit too slow for my liking."

4

Back to billets.

Left, right. Left, right, left, left, *left!*

Overhead, a watery blue sky, and somehow, a smell of spring in the air, a promise faint as distant echoes. Stephen raised his head and sniffed. Yes, his blood told him so. Spring was drawing near. Your blood always knew.

Three blimps bobbing and nodding, black blobs against the blue, swaying and tugging at their cables, aerial buoys, those blimps; misshapen, vulnerable eyes, up there overhead, spying into the enemy's country, sending down messages to the blind batteries. Better than O.P.'s,[8] the blimps. Not so far behind the line, after all . . .

Beside the road, in a field, an Archie battery is making ready, the gun crew moving at the double. The swinging battalion becomes topped with pale discs. The men are looking for the target of the hurrying gunners, searching the sky with upturned faces.

There she is!

A tiny black speck high in the sky; and beneath her the bobbing blimp straining nervously at its cable as though striving to escape this buzzing menace, so high above it. The battery opens up: a short, sharp bark, smoke, and the clink of cartridge case on cartridge case.

Powder balls overhead, one, two, three. Those fellows in the blimp, sick as dogs at anchor there in the sky. Other things to think about now, though. Giving their parachutes the once over. A single hit and away she goes, a flying bonfire. Incendiary bullets. Ha, Midian would have rubbed his hands at that!

A murmur passes over the battalion as the machine dives in a long, slow, lovely swoop and flattens out then, like a leaf in the wind, tosses up and flutters away. The sharp staccato of her machine gun travels down the wind. She has missed. She is away. The blimp bobs like an old lady. A rather drunk old lady. The consequential Archie pops away. But in vain.

Left, left, left, right, *left.*

Untidy marching, this. But tired men, footsore men, men thinking of the cookhouse, wanting a feed, a smoke, an hour or two of ease. Not so far behind the line, after all – looking that way. But looking this: miles and miles.

An old man in a cabbage patch, hoeing along slowly in loose blue blouse. An old man with a bullet head and a face of bronze. Gnarled and bent, he moves very slowly, working his hoe. Doing the work, maybe, of three men nowadays. Deaf, probably, since he has not so much as raised his head at the uproar. Deaf or indifferent, or, maybe, both. It is true the battle lies beyond the ridge. But life goes on, and Spring returns, as in all former years. One must hoe a little, grow a little. For one must eat. And one must live.

But these fellows there behind the wire. They have been watching. Gave them moral support, maybe, to see one of their own machines behind our lines. A doleful-looking crew, these prisoners; their bodies seem too big for their heads in those little pill-box caps; and the grey field uniforms look too big for their bodies; their boots too big for anything at all.

Men in a wire enclosure. Prisoners. Moving about and looking out like animals in a zoo; looking out at the battalion as it swings raggedly down towards the village street. Not very dreadful-looking foes, these square-heads. Mostly decent-looking lads, with simple, honest faces. Staring out through the wire, watching them pass. 'Jerries,' 'Heinies,' 'Boches,' and by those names, good-natured or contemptuous, one thought of them; a breed of men first encountered in this war and with no existence apart from it. It is permissible to think of them as beasts about the earth; to think of them otherwise is very difficult, indeed. So many terrible things have been charged against them.

And yet, what were they but Germans? Saxons at that. You might go up to that wire and call to them:

"*Du – du mit dem Schnurrbart, kennst du vielleicht Dresden?*"[9]

"*Ja? Ich ging dort auf die Schule, weisst du?*"[10]

And it would be nice to hear about Dresden again. Zeidlitz might be there among them in that cage. Would he remember that time when the Herr Director boxed his ears for mimicking the class master with his: "*Schafskopf! Dummer Esel, Du!*"[11] and that dignitary, there in the doorway, an unseen spectator of the outrage upon his dignity.

Or Stolze? Did he dream of his *Gedichter*[12] still; yearn for his fiddle, and paint in dreams his Erlking, riding through the night?

What rot! These were Jerries, Heinies, Boches. Those others – Germans. Yet, mystery of mystery, one and the same.

The battalion halted, dismissed, and fell out.

Notes

1. virtue: strength and courage (same sense as the Latin 'virtu').
2. "jake": in good order, ship-shape, okay.
3. crape (sic): black cloth, symbolizes mourning.
4: brass hat: general or staff officer.
5: Wallah: used ironically in the sense of "big shot." Originally a civil servant in India.

6.   "And the children of Israel . . . caves and strongholds . . ." From the Bible, Judges 6:1 - 2. Although Godwin described himself as an agnostic, he was near the top of his class in English, History and Scripture, i.e. the Bible (see *Journal*, p. 304 of the 1994 *The Eternal Forest*). Godwin's mother's brother was Rev. Richard Free, an Anglican priest who wrote at least two books: *Seven Years Hard* (autobiographical account of his mission work with impoverished Cockneys on the Isle of Dogs in the Thames (near Deptford), published in 1905, and *A Cry from the Darkness*. According to Godwin family lore, Rev. Free once told Godwin (who professed Agnosticism) that he, Godwin, was one of the most spiritual men that he had ever met. Godwin's distaff side, the Frees, were originally Huguenots who settled in Norfolk. "Godwin and Free" would make an interesting Ph.D. thesis.

7.   creeping barrage: as the infantry attacked the enemy lines and advanced, their own artillery fired shells over their heads at the enemy, trying to make sure that the shells penetrated deeper and deeper into enemy territory without hitting their own troops.

8.   O.P.'s: observation posts.

9.   "Du – Du mit dem Schnurrbart, kennst du vielleicht Dresden?" "You, you with the moustache, do you know Dresden, by any chance?"

10.   "Ja? Ich ging dort auf die Schule, weisst du?" "You do? I went to school there, you know."

11.   "Schafskopf! Dummer Esel, du!" "Sheep-head! You stupid jackass!"

12.   Gedichter: Godwin probably means 'Dichter,' i.e. poet.

CHAPTER XI

1

A LETTER from Bob England, addressed from a reserve battalion at Seaford.[1] He wrote:

"Dear Craig,

"Here we are, the finest battalion that ever left Canada to fight the Hun. I am a full-blown buck private. You ought to see our outfit, there's nothing like it in the C.E.F.[2] As you may imagine, being fifty, I had a job to wangle overseas, but I dyed my moustache and passed for forty-one.

"There is talk of breaking up our battalion to supply drafts[3] for the divisions in the line. If they do this, there will be a riot, believe me. How are things in France? We hear that this summer there is to be a big push that will finish the business. I shall curse properly if it's all over before I arrive. I want my own particular slap at the gentle Hun.

"Have you had news of Ferguson's Landing? Here is some. Old Dunn and his wife pulled out for England. At last! As you know they had been talking of it for donkeys' years. They sold out to Japs[4] who have started in to clean up the old orchard.

"By the way, all the boys have joined up, at least, nearly all. Andy MacDonald hasn't. He says: 'If they want me they can come and fetch me.'

"Old Stein is believed to be a spy! They say he has been hand-in-glove with a German secret service agent in Vancouver, and that he was to have had a big job when the Kaiser took over. He always was a bit of a snooper, you remember. I hear they are talking of interning him.

"Well, we are all itching to be in France doing our bit, all as keen as mustard to get at Master Hun.

"So, until we meet in the line,
"Yours as ever,
"Bob England."[5]

Stephen, the letter in his hand, lay on his bed in the rue St. Petersburgh, with Pilk's voice coming up from the yard, talking to Madame in his international language of signs, signals, mouthings and pidgin French.

"Vous cherchez boogies pour moir, Madame, savvie boogie? Nong? *Comme ça*. Boogie. Like this. Oh, hell! Candles, you know: boogies. Don't you understand your own language?"

But Stephen was far away, in the valley, in the settlement, along the dusty road, by the old man's ranch, seeing what those cursed Japs are up to.

No, impossible, that they would chop the old orchard down. 'Cleaning up': that would mean sawing away the old wood, scything the grass, digging round, manuring. Things like that. Not chopping down, burning.

He held the letter idly in his hand, thinking. So over there in England they still talked that sort of stuff about the Hun, hating him?

What had come over Bob England, whose ranch had once been saved from a mortgagee's foreclosure by a timely loan from old Stein, that he could write of his old neighbour and crony thus? Old Stein, prim as a mittened old maid, innocent as a babe, hounded as a spy, threatened with the ignominy of a prison camp as an enemy alien! And Bob England telling of it with a hint of satisfaction!

That was what the war spirit did, then. It made a man go back on old friends, and accounted it a virtue in him. It demanded, as the price of this monstrous racial loyalty, the lovely loyalty of man to man, the loyalty of friends. It seduced a man from cherished standards of conduct; made him dishonour them, accounting that dishonour virtue.

Yes, it stole a man's judgment away, and, along with it, reason and heart. Loyal Bob, the soldier, was Iscariot[6] to Stein in his heart. Was Judas, because he withheld all sympathy, shut fast the door of his heart upon an old and trusty friend . . . Underneath, had he always hated Stein? Perhaps, for Stein was his benefactor.

And what had the war done for Stephen?

It had made an automaton of him, a cog in a vast soulless machine, a drop of water flowing in the irresistible flood-tide of war.

Piers had once asserted: "Only a saint or a sage could escape the mass emotions of a nation at war."

That was true. The race, unmoral, untouched by the shallow appeal of religion, tearing up the covenants of humanity; sweeping the members of it along, ferocious, without scruples, honesty, honour. The mass. The race, with its roots down there in the primeval slime: a brute fighting to survive, to survive at all costs, and in its frenzy casting away all pretence, all hypocrisy. Being itself: monstrous. Horrible.

Yes, that was what had happened. All unawares. He had ceased to think, to care. He had become a drifter. That agony of indecision in the solitude of the bush, in the silence of the forest, when it had seemed the most vitally important thing in life to decide aright upon this issue, now appeared inconceivably remote and of little consequence, like something once read in a book, seen in a play. Only the ghost of a remembered spiritual conflict now, yet then a burning reality.

With one's own soul, out there in the silence, in the sweetness and the innocence, how remote it now seemed. Yet it had been a spell alone with one's own soul.

Bob England's letter had revealed to Stephen his own ignominy. Why hold it against Bob England that, never having doubted, he was without doubts still? Bob had not ratted from any ideal. He had stayed by his ideal, which was: England, right or wrong. He, Stephen, could not say as much.

Why was it so easy to think of Germans as 'Huns,' as the outcasts of an outraged civilisation? Yet so it was: one side of one did that automatically, echoing the spoken and written word heard and seen everywhere. The thought and feeling of the war mood, tainted and tainting.

Was there a deeper self, dwelling apart, sane and sweet and whole, incorrupted? Yes, there was, only one had stifled it, let it go. Bob England's letter had done this, then: it had made the forest live again; it had restored reason, judgment. Tolstoi was real again. And Stephen was in the war, but not of it. He must not let go again. In it, but not of it . . .

Piers, cigarette in loose lips, lumbered in.

"Reading letters?" he asked. "Sorry."

Stephen held the letter up.

"From a full buck private in the best battalion that ever came overseas full of the fine fighting spirit of our magnificent troops," he declaimed.

Piers slumped onto the bed beside him.

"Poor fool," he said feelingly. "Poor bloody fool," commiserating.

From the yard below floated up the voice of Pilk. He had abandoned his attempts to communicate with the widow. He was addressing himself in pidgin French to the small child.

2

A field cashier was in town. Stephen, Field Message book on knees, wrote:

To the Paymaster.
Sir,
Kindly cash enclosed cheque and hand money to bearer, Pte. Pilk.
100 francs.

S. Craig.

He tore the serrated leaf out, Pilk standing there, waiting orders. Then he wrote:

To Captain Stewart.
Please supply bearer, Pte. Pilk, with 2 bottles Scotch.
                                        S. Craig, Lt.

There was one more commission for the waiting Pilk.

To O.C. 'A' Company.
No. 12 billet.
Sir,
 This billet, occupied by my platoon, is very close and the yard manure heap contaminates the air.
 If it were possible for the sanitary section to open up a clogged culvert, the basin would be drained of much of the filth.
 I have had the billet floors, walls, and ceiling sprayed with creosote, but until the yard is improved this billet will be unhealthy. Several men have complained about the air.
                                        S. Craig, Lt.

Pilk took the messages, saluted, and disappeared. Stephen threw himself on his bed.

The luxury of it!

3

The night was dark. It hung before Stephen like a material curtain through which he must press his way. The horizon flickered and the darkness pulsed, a winking and flashing of blue lights, and a throbbing terrible because of the knowledge of its significance. A fine, soaking rain fell, and Stephen lowered his head to it. His trench coat rustled in the darkness.

When he opened the door of the estaminet he took with him part of the night, and the sour odours of the great pyramid of dung through which he had floundered, cursing. It was ammoniacal, astringent, sour.

The room they had reserved was at the back. A withered woman led him to it. Piers was already there, and Grant and O'Reilly. And two subalterns from 'B' Company. They sat at a table covered by a coarse linen cloth. The floor was of sweating stone flags, the walls unadorned, save for a framed Royalist medallion upon a crimson velvet ground.

A dark girl brought them glasses.

O'Reilly said unctuously, "I've ordered fizz."

Stephen got out of his dripping trench coat and sat down. They were all sitting relaxed, slack, but expectant. Champagne! The thought of it!

It came, laughing out of the gold-necked bottle, dancing in the glasses. Captured sunshine, living sunlight.

They drank swiftly, inexpertly, as a thirsty man drinks cold spring water. They called for more. Great comfort came to them and sense of well-being. O'Reilly praised the war. He said it was a bloody good war, and he didn't care how long it lasted. And to pass the bottle and not to hog it.

Grant broke into a succession of lewd limericks, each one more lecherous than the last. He then said that all he needed to complete his happiness was a woman.

They drank steadily, bottle after bottle.

Stephen felt life pouring into his veins. The bare room took on a graciousness. He liked it. And he liked the sombre girl who carried in the bottles, opening them expertly, filling their glasses, disappearing silently, with expressionless face. He felt a gush of affection for Piers, for O'Reilly, for Grant even. The two fellows from 'B' Company were the best in the world.

The room swayed gently. What was in these bottles? It was not champagne. Not at all. It was a miracle. Magic. An elixir. Faith, Hope and Charity. Bottled.

If you could remain in this beatific state for the duration you might almost say with O'Reilly that it was a damned good war. No more worrying. No more heartache. No more melancholy.

It sang in your blood, sang in your head, in your ears. Dancing bubbles, rushing upwards. Excited and exciting bubbles.

Stephen pressed the thin glass-stem between thumb and finger. Gracious stem, ballooning out to that great yellow tulip. He gazed abstractedly at the gold of it, loving it, losing himself there in dreams. The bubbles rose swiftly, broke through the surface, danced upon it, up and down. Mad bubbles. Up and down. Ecstatically. Queer how it danced along your blood, sang in your ears.

O'Reilly said: "Boys, what about a song?" And without awaiting an answer, began in his deep baritone:

'We were rolling along,
Down Moonlight Bay.
You could hear the darkies singing,
They seemed to say . . .'

And they joined in, unsteadily, but lustily. They sang song after song; and between each they drank from their glasses. And the songs they sang were the old ones: sentimental, loaded with sentiment, rich in memories. They sang *Drink to Me Only With Thine Eyes, Poor Black Joe, Gone Are the Days,* and many others.

They rose presently and stood in a ring, arms round each others' shoulders, swaying, grinning, beatific, drunk.

Two faces watched them from the door: the dark face of the girl, the dark face of the withered woman.

"Les Anglais!" The eyes and hard mouths seemed to say: "But they pay, les Anglais, they pay."

Voices were all about Stephen, a confusion of sounds, waves of sound. And faces in the blue of the smoke, blobs floating; moons. The room was a glass of fizz, and O'Reilly's face was a bubble in it. Piers' face was a bubble. All faces were bubbles.

Stephen started to laugh weakly, holding his sides. He subsided into a chair, laughing. He was drunk. But he knew he was drunk, because behind the drunkenness of one Stephen there was another Stephen, stone sober. A Stephen who contemplated the scene critically, disdainfully; a Stephen who whispered things one did not wish to hear. A Stephen altogether too sober, so that he was spoiling the fun. Therefore a Stephen who must be silenced.

He rose, took up his chair by its back, raised it above his head and brought it down on one leg. The leg snapped off with a sharp report. He looked round, laughing inanely. Three times he raised the chair again until all four legs were gone. And now they all laughed, bellowing. Then he flung the legless chair from him and burst into peals of laughter.

He collapsed into a chair. Better now. Smash everything. Push the estaminet over. Push everything over.

Blobs floating around everywhere. Blimps. Old Mother Grundy, she got drunk. Who was that singing? Grant, of course. Old Mother Grundy. Ha, ha! He banged with his clenched fist on the table.

O'Reilly burst into song again:

'Keep the home fires burning,
Though our hearts be yearning . . .'

And Grant, in opposition:

'Old Mother Grundy,
She got drunk, fell in the fire
And burnt her bonnet . . .'

But smashing chairs did not silence that other Stephen. He merely withdrew a little, and from his separateness spoke more coldly. He did not seem to think much of Stephen drunk. The drunker the one became, the more sober seemed the other. There was disharmony between them, until Stephen drunk debated with himself the pulling down of the gas chandelier as reprisal on Stephen sober.

The mute girl helped them into their trench coats; the grizzled woman handled dexterously the crumpled notes they pulled from their pockets.

"La chaise cassée?"[7] she asks, spreading lean hands.

They pay, having small idea what they pay, and lurch from the over-heated room into the cold darkness of the night.

Stephen stood a moment, swaying unsteadily. The reek of ammonia smote his nostrils. He turned aside and vomited. A cold sweat broke out on his forehead. He shivered. Piers took his arm and they moved unsteadily forward.

On the horizon lights still flickered, and down the air came the throb of the eternal guns.

From the lighted doorway the dark girl watched them go. Then she shut the door, and it was as though she had said: "Les Anglais!" and said it in contempt.

4

Moving through the darkness towards the rue St. Petersburgh, Stephen sober talked with Stephen drunk, chiding him. He watched him walk unsteadily and pointed out the indignity of it in an officer, in France, on active service.

Stephen drunk retorted that it was obviously too dark to endanger the dignity of a Field Marshal, too dark for even a sanitary fatigue to be demoralised by the spectacle he presented.

But Stephen sober answered, pointing out that both indignity and demoralisation were ignoble conditions in themselves, not dependent in any way upon an observer. Moreover, he contended, there was a spectator, since he, Stephen sober, was contemplating Stephen drunk with painful emotions.

And Stephen drunk defended himself hotly. He asked: How many officers forewent their rum[8] in the line as he did, on the principle that one should face danger and stand up to responsibility cold sober? He was, he reckoned, entitled to the odd wild night, out of the line.

But Stephen sober was not to be silenced. He capped the argument with the incontestable proposition that Stephen drunk had been spending money needed over there in Kent; needed for food, for clothes, for straight necessities.

To this Stephen drunk returned no answer.

Piers, his arm in Stephen's, guided their steps along the puddled road. The rain still fell, a fine, drenching watering from the dark dome above them. The railway embankment on their right was a black parapet; the little miners' houses on their left, troops attacking it. The wet road through which they splashed their way uncertainly was No Man's Land. And the steady throbbing on the night air lent force to this illusion in the disordered mind of Stephen drunk.

The money was certainly wanted over there in Kent. He was a beast. Underneath, he always would be a beast. And Stephen sober said that this was mere lachrymose alcoholic contrition, and contemptible. The thing to do was to cut out wild drinking.

And Stephen drunk started to sing feebly:

"Old Mother Grundy, she got drunk, fell in the fire and burnt her bonnet . . ."

He broke off, suddenly. Stephen sober was listening; his contempt was not easy to be borne.

They were at their billet. Piers stopped and turned his face to the north.

"Listen to the guns!" he whispered, awed.

They listened, heads up, as animals, scenting danger from afar, and senses quickened by it.

Down the avenues of the dark sky floated that steady drum beat, a pulse in the night, and with it the distant flashes of the untiring guns. At once both felt sobered. Stephen shivered, uncontrollably.

"God, but I'm cold," he complained. "As cold as death."

They went quickly to the shelter of the house. Light flowed out to meet them and the warm human smell of the little living room. From the far corner, the lank gendarme looked at them out of expressionless eyes, a long cigar pendant from his loose lips. What were they to him? Nothing.

Notes

1. Seaford: port on the south coast of England, just east of Newhaven.
2. C.E.F.: Canadian Expeditionary Force.
3. drafts: drafted soldiers, i.e. replacements.
4. "sold out to the Japs." See *The Eternal Forest* (pp. 88 - 95 esp.) and *Japan's New Empire* (1942) for further comments on the Japanese. (Extracts of both can be seen at the Godwin site: www.godwin-books.com)
5. Bob England: the Newcomer's (i.e. Godwin's) realtor in *The Eternal Forest*. The "Old Dunn" referred to is Ferguson's Landing's outspoken Socialist intellectual. He and "The Newcomer" become close friends and discuss a wide range of topics: politics, government, economics, war, etc.
6. Iscariot: i.e. Judas Iscariot, the disciple who betrayed Christ.
7. "la chaise cassée": the broken/smashed up chair..
8. forewent their rum: approx. two ounces was issued to each soldier each day. Some senior officers refused on 'moral' grounds to issue rum to their men; some men hoarded it and sold it for profit.

CHAPTER XII

1

WATERY winter wore on. The battalion returned to the line, rested, refreshed, re-equipped; yet without the buoyancy of fresh troops, without enthusiasm. They marched as men habituated to their lot and resigned to it, knowing escape impossible, knowing the inevitability of it all: hardship, hunger of heart, hunger of body, and the darkness wherein the future lay concealed from them, a menace and a hope.

They marched in column of route, swinging along at an easy pace, a brown serpentine organism moving slowly across the dun face of a dispirited land. They progressed along straight roads, and roads that curved comfortingly about the flanks of naked little hills. Their moving length bisected loamy fields and passed between small clusters of graceless farmhouses and tiny hamlets, unbeautiful, malodorous, but evocative of creature comforts now far behind them – of dry beds in dim wattle barns, beer, steaming coffee, succulent chipped potatoes, fried eggs. But most they were reminded by these meagre habitations of the boon of dry beds, of nights of unbroken slumber, relaxed, at rest.

Avenues of stark and lonely trees advanced towards them, breaking the monotony of the flat landscape, flanking the road along which they passed, indifferent spectators of their passage.

And as they marched at ease, equipment huffed to comfort, rifles anyhow, they talked, shouting one to another, quips, grousing, joshing; or, man to man, in undertones, soberly.

They talked of the bones they had rolled on the beaten dung floors of dark and smelly billets, of feasts in steamy estaminets, sweet with the smell of food and of the women who served that food, there in the warmth, in the comfort and the security. Homely memories of homely things, now very precious as the miles dividing them increased with each rhythmic, swinging movement of loins, of sturdy legs.

A loud voice shouts: "Shorty got his last night when he tried to kiss Fat Rosy, didn't you, Shorty, you little runt, you?"

The men near Shorty jeer. And Shorty, chagrined at the memory, putting the best face he can upon the remembered discomfort of the open-handed slap, jeers back at them: "Gee, but ain't you fellers jealous? Rosy weren't the only bit of skirt in that dump, believe me."

And there is in his voice the knavish hint of secret adventures, adventures that exist only in his lying mouth.

At home they talked as though every girl in every village behind the line was a whore. Whereas, in these little villages the women were most virtuous, repulsing the advances of the foreign troops, guilty of nothing but the coarseness of the peasant.

True, there were prostitutes to be found. But they were few up near the line. The shortage of supply was shown by the evidence of demand: at Lillers one might see men in a line, in a waiting queue, outside the house of the single prostitute who served them. Horrible? Revolting? Yes; but there it was, a fact and not to be denied, explained away. Men had their bestial moments. Yet they were not beasts. Oh, no, they were not the beasts they seemed, standing there, waiting, waiting to take their turn.

So they josh Shorty without mercy, jeering at him for the braggart they know him to be.

"Plenty o' skirt, eh?" shouts one. "Then you'd better see about a short arm, Shorty boy."

And there are men who talk in undertones, one to another, talk of their intimacies 'way back home, of what they will do after the war. Of what they were doing before it plucked them from their lives in the towns, in the little settlements, among the orchards, in the bush, from the wide and flashing rivers of far-off British Columbia.

Slow movement of moving feet and rhythmic swing of sweating bodies, moving in unison, as one. Not men marching together, but a unit, an entity. A battalion, and a seasoned battalion at that; a battalion with a record, and proud of that record. A battalion that was an organism in continuous process of change and renewal. A battalion that lay, for the most part, in the region of the Somme, and yet somehow lived on, lived on in the renewal of its parts as a body in the renewal of its tissues, in the men who came to it as strangers to be absorbed, touched by the living spirit of the battalion, made one with it.

Slow rhythm of moving bodies, tramp of feet. Left, right. Left, right. Left, right.

And now and then a song rising from the ranks.

Piers, by his platoon, hears the singing from ahead. He says: "Hallo, Craig starting his canaries[1] again."

And the song, weak at first, grows in strength as the voices of the men take it up. Soon the whole battalion is singing. Craig's canaries have started it, for Stephen is forever at it, making his men sing, until his platoon is like a choir.

"Whiter than the whitewash on the wall,
Whiter than the whitewash on the wall,
Wash me in the water where you wash your dirty daughter,
And I shall be whiter than the whitewash on the wall."

Song follows song and the miles unwind. A voice travels along the column. It halts. It comes again, and the column dissolves into its components. A spell for rest, by the roadside, easing up, relaxing . . .

A youngster, newly come, casts down his rifle with a grunt of relief, and himself after it on to the tufted roadside bank.

"Kid," says a rough voice, "your rifle's sure yer best friend in France. Don't let it lie like that, all in the wet."

The boy grabs the wet butt. He has done wrong, is shame-faced.

But the rough voice was a kindly one, for all its roughness. And it is kindly as it adds:

"An' don't go a-sitting on wet grass, or you'll sure get a bunch o' piles, and piles is painful. Keep yer rifle and yer pants dry, kiddo."

Yes, it is Hicks who offers counsel, Hicks the scallywag of the battalion.

On the crown of the road there was comfort for marching feet but on the edge of the road's camber ankles protested after awhile.

So when the column rises to resume the march, each man shrugging himself into his loosened equipment, taking his rifle again, the outside man of each four changes with the left, so that, in turn, each man walks squarely upon the crown of the road in comfort. An army marches upon its belly; yes, but it marches also upon its feet.

There is a limping man. What ails him? It is his Army boots. They are new. When he removes that great barge of a boot and turns down the thick grey sock there will be a patch of congealed blood upon it, blood from the broken blister that has been chafed into a raw wound.

He carries no rifle, does the limping man. And presently his pack is on another's back.

Rifle and pack: too much to be borne with a foot like that. But others there to take the burden.

Comradeship: that was it. Not merely one man to another, but something more.

And that something?

The spirit of the battalion.

As they marched towards the north the sound of the guns grew louder, more insistent, but the men of the marching column heard that sound only as a city dweller hears the roar of the streets through which he passes every day of his life. The ear received the sound, the tympanum quivered, and the nerve signalled, but the conscious brain was unawares. The sound was perpetual, the signal vain repetition. The subconscious brain declined to carry it to the conscious mind. They were unaware of the sound of the guns, so aware had they become of them.

But the sound grew, and presently, out of the moving column, rose a harsh voice:

"Jesus! Hear them guns?"

And now, as though a switch had been thrown over, the battalion is suddenly aware. The air is vibrating, throbbing. A thin rain falls. The singing dies away. They march in silence. To-morrow they will be settling down in their new sector of the line.

The shadow of Vimy Ridge fell upon the battalion. They were going back to the line with an objective. There would be the same old round. But presently the day would come, bringing zero hour. And they would retake Vimy Ridge, or they would not take it. They would come through the battle, or they would not come through.

2

What is the battalion? It is one thing today; another tomorrow. An organism in constant flux, dying, renewing itself, passing away yet prevailing.

What is the battalion but the men of it? They are the battalion today. But it is not they. For they will pass, one by one, and in battle, in their numbers. They will die, and their deaths will be as wounds to the battalion. But it will live. They will die in their numbers, suffering wounds, mutilations, passing. So that tomorrow, as it were, the marching battalion of today will have perished.

But the battalion is greater than the men of it for the men of it come and they depart but the battalion remains. There are new men, but it is the old battalion, greater than the men of it, than any of them. It is the same, unchanged, unchanging, renewing itself.

What, then, is the battalion?

It is a soul. The corporate soul of all the men who have died in its ranks, died leading its ranks; of those who will die in its ranks, or leading those ranks; of all who will survive until its final disbanding.

And even then the battalion will not be dead, for it will live on in the hearts of those who were there at the last. And when the last of them is gone, yet will the battalion live, incorporeal and mystic; a flame burning in the darkness, made immortal by sacrifice and suffering.

What is the battalion? The battalion is a soul.

3

Evening is upon the road. The shadows fall. The battalion is weary now and the marching of it ragged. Come, now, where are the canaries?

A voice rises above the rhythmic beat of lagging feet, others take up the refrain. The battalion is singing, and in the act, quickening its marching pace. Out into the gathering gloom, out over the mist-wreathed fields, go the music and the words of the music:

"John Brown's body lies a-mouldering in the grave,
John Brown's body lies a-mouldering in the grave,
John Brown's body lies a-mouldering in the grave,
But his soul goes marching on."

Why were these men here? For what were they fighting? If they were victorious, what would victory profit them?

Victorious, they would return to their little homes, to their humble vocations, to their loves. And all would be as before. They would gain nothing, and less than nothing, for they would have lost, having given that which could not be returned to them, these years of their lives. Victory would grant them the residue of their days. Nothing more than that.

And defeat?

It would be the same. They would return; those who survived would cross the seas again, come back to their waiting farms, their little clearings, their young orchards. And all would be as before, save that they would pay a little more here, a little more there, for tea, for tobacco, for daily bread.

Victory, then, or defeat: it would be the same for them. They offered themselves, and they suffered all manner of evil, that all should be as it was with them.

Yet all changed. The wounded would carry their scars, the limbless go their ways upon stilts with metal members, grotesque and horrible, mocking their lovely limbs; the blind would grope their way about the world in darkness, asking of others news of the world they knew, hungering for the light. And the mad and the bereft, they would enter a merciful elysium,[2] the disordered realm of the insane.

But the unwounded, the unscathed? They too would bear their scars, the scars of memory, the wounds upon the soul, unhealing, unhealable.

Why, then, were they here, upon this bleak road in northern France, marching in the soft, cold rain towards the line, towards the guns, towards another tour in the trenches?

It was because they had stampeded. That was all. They were here for no other reason, having no quarrels whatsoever with their fellows. But the herd ruled, and the herd had stampeded. And they had gone with the herd. For what steer stands fast when the herd thunders away? The herd is greater than the steer, any steer in it. The herd is the law: the law of unreason, the law of fear.

No. They did not know, not one of them, why they were in France and not upon the fecund Pacific slope, in the garden of the world. And making that garden beautiful. They had hearkened to the voice of the herd, and had obeyed it. Not willingly, nor yet unwillingly, but blindly. They had answered a voice louder than any voice: the voice of the past that drew them back, the voice that had come to them down the centuries, down the aeons of time, the unending corridors of the ages.

Yet for some, the stampede was snorting joy of life, the glad fulfilment of secret lusts; for some the stampede was unreasoning terror; and for others the crucifixion of the soul.

But all stampeded because the herd moved forward, gathering a mad momentum in its blind rush to destruction. They were the Gaderene swine, moving towards the steep place, as they marched down the dim road towards the battle line. They were the Gadarene[3] swine because they were unjustly condemned, because they suffered for the evil spirit that had not been in their hearts, but had been planted there, put there without sanction. They were victims, suffering for offences of which they were guiltless. And in this, what were these marching men as, if not as Christ, archetype of all suffering, sacrifice?

A battalion of swine going to destruction. A battalion of Christs bearing the sins of the world along a northern road of France as day drew towards night and the march neared its end.

Confused and jumbled thoughts!

The marching song of the North, half-hearted, sporadic, full of the ache of pathos, sadness, floating over the crawling column, a tatter of melody:

"John Brown's body lies a-mouldering in the grave,
But his soul goes marching on."

Notes

1. "Craig's canaries": Godwin was very musical. See *Journal,* p. 304 at the end of *The Eternal Forest.*
2. elysium: abode of the blessed after death, according to the pre-Christian Romans.
3: Gadarene swine: from the Bible, Matthew 8:28, where Christ causes the demons possessing two men to occupy the bodies of a large herd of swine, who charge crazily down a steep slope and drown themselves.

CHAPTER XIII

1

LATE autumn had merged into winter, and winter now in turn was upon its course towards spring. Not that there were as yet signs of the great stirring, for the lovely season tarried overlong, the skies continued grey, rain fell, day after day. So that it was seldom that the men knew the comfort of dry clothing, dry feet, or saw the face of the sun, warm and friendly, shining from a tattered sky.

Stephen had now been six months in France.

Six months. A short time-period as men reckon it in the normal way of normal lives, with death away in some distant future so remote as not to merit a moment's uneasy thought. For then life appears as a freehold, a perpetuity. But here, where life was accepted gratefully in little nervous leases, from day to day, from week to week, aye, and now and then, from moment to moment, six months was not so much a span of days as a series of escapes from the outstretched hands of greedy death. Yes, six months in the line drew itself out, drew itself out interminably.

Stephen now reckoned himself a fairly seasoned officer. He was aware, and took pleasure in that awareness, of a change in the attitude of such subalterns as Grant. They had dropped a justifiable condescension as soon as it ceased to be justifiable. They had admitted him to their fraternity, a close fellowship, on terms of equality. And this was sweet.

2

They had been back in the trenches three weeks when Major MacDonald got his leave warrant. It came by runner on a rain-swept afternoon of heavy shelling.

He sat by candlelight at the dugout bench, the paper in his hand, his face expressionless. It was the first leave warrant Stephen had seen. Yet what day passed without talk of leave warrants? They talked and thought and dreamed of leave, as a prisoner talks and thinks and dreams of the day of release, that far-off day beyond a wilderness of days through which he creeps and must creep to that remote sustaining bourne.

To think that possession of that little sheet of official paper conferred upon one the godlike power of escape, of escape with honour! Escape, true enough, for a matter of ten days and no more. But ten days, when one reckoned life in daily, hourly leases. It was a title to life in fee simple! Ten days.

He stood there, behind the major, gazing down at the paper, foolishly, as though expecting it suddenly to reveal some outward evidence of hidden magic, and, not finding it, remained stupidly incredulous. But the major had received his warrant with phlegm, as with phlegm he ignored the thunder of the guns. Laconically, he announced his intention of spending his leave in London.

"Have you any friends in London, sir?" Stephen asked him.

"Why, no." The Major shook his head. "No friends, exactly. But I'll be running into fellows in the R.A.C.[1] And I may put in a few days in the country. Last leave I spent a week in Leicestershire. Say, what bully hospitality you English give us folks! It was a big park with a great mansion, and they treated me like a prince. Yes, they sure did. And me a stranger. I'll say that's wonderful."

Stephen looked at the grave, unsmiling face. He thought: "Well, and why shouldn't they treat you like a prince, who are a prince among men? What could they do for you that would be too good for you?" Aloud he said: "I'll be awfully tickled, sir, if you could fix up to meet my missis. She knows all about you from my letters; and, of course, she knows your brother at Ferguson's Landing."

And the Major, looking up with a slow smile, said: "Fine!" twice. And that he would sure fix it up. They would have lunch together. She should come up to London for the occasion.

And Stephen, knowing him to be a man of his word, knew that he would do as he promised. The Major meeting Alice would be a link bringing them nearer one another. The Major, leaving him there in that dugout, would take some part of him along. And he would give it to Alice, who would receive it. And, returning, ten days hence, he would bear with him, mystically, some part of Alice, and he would receive that part of Alice and so she would be near to him in this mystical way. The Major would pass between them, taking and bringing, bringing and taking.

He would leave the line at dusk, he said, for by then Jerry would have had enough of it, and he would be able to get back to the transport lines without chancing it under this heavy fire. Anyway, when night fell they would likely let up. He would wait.

And so it was. The bombardment ceased suddenly, its monstrous voice broken again. The wavering candle flame straightened itself up hopefully in the quietening air. The snores of O'Reilly, asprawl on his chicken-wire bunk, an amorphous heap at the dugout's further end, became audible – a trial to weary, lacerated nerves. And so it was.

They shook hands. And Stephen admonished, as he well knew, superfluously.

"And you won't forget, sir, to look my little missis up?"

The Major promised once again, and a moment later was gone.

Stephen now occupied the dugout with the stentorious O'Reilly. Piers and Grant were about the trenches. He drew out from his tunic pocket a bundle of soiled letters and bent his head over them, reading by the steady light of the candle, no longer agitated, but burning serenely in the damp, still atmosphere of the dugout.

Alice's letters: he read them all again, one by one. And now, reading them rapidly, the one after the other, he suddenly realised that since they had parted on that black October morning the year before, Alice had had no fewer than eleven different temporary camps, that number of different lodgings. Why?

Her letters made that clear. It was the children. Landladies did not like children. They objected to the noise, so it seemed, to the noise of small children.

Stephen, reading so much between the lines of these reticent records of constant change, considered this. Objected to the noise of children, did they? To the noise of children? He considered it again. Was it possible?

The thunder of the guns had died away, and the line lay bathed in a healing silence.

Objected to the noise of *children?* He gave it up.

And there had been others, it seemed, who had driven Alice and her lean purse away by systematic extortion. And always pleading the war, the high cost of everything. A shilling a scuttle for coal, and that coal purloined overnight, and the theft indignantly denied by morning. And those who catered, stealing her meagre little store of rationed food.

Not that Alice, in these letters of hers, complained. She had never done that. No, never. Not even in the hardest days of their life out there at Ferguson's Landing when, evening by evening, she would sink into exhausted sleep in the old Mission rocker, exhausted by work, exhausted by her lusty suckling baby. No, she made no plaint, but knowing her, these letters, with their ever-changing headings, told him more than bitterest uttered grievances could have done.

He folded the letters up and returned them to his pocket. Then he sat and listened for the guns. But the guns were silent now. The candle burnt, a little lick of flame, a little flattened spearhead of flame, unwavering, steadfast, there upon the bench in the dugout. The air was no longer agitated from without, and now the candle shared tranquillity with it. It was a little pointing flame.

He heard a voice from above, shot his cuff, and looked at the phosphorescent dial. Eight o'clock already, and Piers coming in. He could hear his slow voice on the steps; he caught the word whale-oil and the murmurous response of the unseen N.C.O. to whom Piers spoke. Piers stood in the doorway, breathing heavily, breathing steam into the moist air.

He said, laconically: "What's been the matter with Jerry this evening, anyway?" Then, tartly: "And they have the nerve to tell us he's short of shells. Bunk, my lad, the blighter's lousy with 'em."

3

The departure of Major MacDonald had left Stephen restless and temporarily deprived of the mood of resignation, qualified by resentment, which had become his way of meeting the conditions of life in the field, of this strange life in the labyrinthine ways of the sandbag city.

Escape! If one could only do that. Perhaps it was shameful to yearn thus in secret. Yet, he considered, many men no better and no worse than himself must have secret longings like his own, unconfessed, unconfessable. Only when this great wave of impotent desire was clothed in humour, or masked by ribaldry, was it confessable.

"When this bloody war is over,
Oh, how happy I shall be . . . "

The men sang that and many another marching song, behind whose common words and banal sentiments lay a world of yearning, of yearning for escape. But there was no escape.

Behind the trenches a vast machine revolved relentlessly, ponderously, engineered by a whole civilisation. Munitions, rations, stores, flowed in a mighty stream along the arterial roads of northern France, flowed always in one direction. Theirs. Towards the trenches, clothing them, feeding them, putting weapons in their hands, supporting them. But still imprisoning them.

The dynamic tide flows towards the trenches unceasingly, untiringly, like the tides of the sea, washing upon this shore of death, wave upon wave. And it imprisoned them, making impossible escape.

And minds far, far to the rear, moved the machine, manipulating it, causing it to function, governing its actions, as the nerve ganglion of the brain governs the body, directing it.

There was no escape. No way out. And of this truth one was, from time to time, reminded by impulses sent out from that inexorable unseen will, there in the mystery of the back areas. Then one had to be remembrancer for those inscrutable dictators of one's life, of those minds that controlled one's life. Yes, one had to read, now and then, in Orders, the laconic messages that thinly veiled, without concealing, but rather emphasising, the threat behind them.

'Private Tom Jones, No. 123456, having been duly tried by Field General Court Martial for desertion in the face of the enemy, was duly convicted and sentenced to death. The sentence was carried out on the 8th of February.'

That was what one read aloud. Those wooden faces looked back at one, from the ranks, standing stiffly, looked back woodenly. Did they hearken to the warning? Did they care for the threat behind the words?

Who could tell?

4

When they had been out at rest a captured fugitive had been lodged for the night in the temporary guardroom, the escort drawing rations from the battalion Q.M. store.[2]

Stephen had seen the fugitive in his temporary prison. No proper guardroom had been available, but in the farmhouse yard, overlooking the dung heap, an empty sty served the purpose. And there, sitting like a cornered animal, in terror, Stephen saw the face of the deserter.

He sat (since in that place he could not stand), and before the low door stood the man who guarded him. Tomorrow he would take the road again with his escort. And presently he would stand before the seat of judgment. And he would be tried, this little man with the close-set small eyes, the low, receding brow. He would be convicted and sentenced. And the Provost Marshal would take him in charge until, ignominiously, at dawn, he would stand, blindfolded, before the firing squad. Against a drab prison wall he would stand, and by that wall he would die.

And over there, in British Columbia, in the forest, on the swift rivers, or in the great mountains, such little men as this were living, free and happy.

What was the offence of this so pitiable human being, degraded from the dignity of manhood to this condition, this plight? It was that he had proffered more than he had to give. His coat had been asked of him, and his cloak also. And he had yielded them up. But they had wanted something that he had it not to give. That was his offence: he had been unable to give that which he had not. He had tossed away the liberty of the wilds, of the beautiful free world he loved, because within his poor simple mind were notions of chivalry and sacrifice.

And so he was reduced to this. He had sought honour, seeking to serve, and had reaped dishonour and ignominious death. It was the last infamy: desertion in the face of the enemy. And it was laid to his charge: truly laid.

Stephen had turned from those tragic eyes, ashamed. He had turned away sick at heart from their pleading, from the terror that looked out from behind them. Somehow, he shared the guilt with those who would presently rise from their mess,[3] file into the place of trial and carry out this duty. Yes, he shared the guilt with those who would presently nip out that pitiable life, take from this so great giver that which they had asked of him, but which he, not possessing it, had failed to give.

An infamous end. But whose the infamy? Was this cringing man there in the sty one whose offence could be wiped out only by death? Did he merit death? Or was he merely a human creature tortured beyond endurance? A subject for compassion, pity? Or for the skill of the understanding neurologist?[4]

Sometimes officers were evacuated and there was talk of nervous breakdown, collapse, neurasthenia. That was all. What were such diagnoses, but merely names less terrible for the thing that stared out of the fearful eyes of the prisoner of the sty?

5

No: there was no escape. One had to see it through.

For one man, as for that man now remembered with pity, physical fear dominated, driving on to the culminating point of collapse and surrender to the deep instinctive urge. And with another it might be sheer revulsion from the bestial life of the trenches unsupported by faith in a cause now seen to be without spiritual significance or moral sanctification. But no escape. There was but one way, and that resignation.

6

Stephen came up from the dugout on the sucking heels of Sergeant Glenny, for it was two o'clock and the hour of his duty round. The night was dark. The rain had ceased. The stars shone from a moonless sky. They moved in silence along the trench and, the enemy being quiet and the trench thereabouts in bad condition, they clambered up the steep side of the parapet and walked upon the sandbag top of it, visiting the posts, giving attention to details, mechanically: bombs needed there, and here a periscope.

And Sergeant Glenny, who usually spoke so freely, in a steady voice, so beautifully assured in his manhood, was silent. Tonight he uttered no unnecessary word, but went, head down, about his business.

And as they returned, in silence as they had come, dawn was at hand, and with it the general stir of 'Stand-to': men upon the fire-steps, at the machine guns, on guard against the dawn and the surprise attack that it might bring.

The night sky slowly blanched, and soon in the east there was a faint blush, a coming to life; it was the birth of day, warm and comforting. Out of the shadows the symmetry of the sandbags, tier on tier, was articulated, still redeemed by this soft, gentle light from the stark details soon to be revealed by daylight.

Stephen turned to the man at his side. He said: "How are things at home, Glenny?"

"The baby died." The voice is toneless.

Stephen said nothing. What can one say at such a time?

Piers would be asleep. And he too would sleep in the warm luxury of his sleeping bag. No Kapok, just a green thing out of Ordnance stores, but heaven. But Piers was wide awake, sitting there by the bench. He greeted Stephen.

"We're detailed for a bombing course," he announced. "Get your gear together and let's beat it."

Escape!

Temporary escape, it was true. Yet escape. Escape with honour.

Notes

1. R.A.C.: Royal Armoured Corps.
2. Q.M. store: Quartermaster's stores. This is where soldiers were issued whatever they required: uniforms, boots, weapons, etc. Sometimes the Q.M. store consisted of only a tent.
3. mess: officers' dining room-cum-bar.
4. neurasthenia: a term introduced by Beard (1869) to describe a syndrome of chronic mental and physical weakness and fatigue which was supposed to be caused by exhaustion of the nervous system (*Dorland's Illustrated Medical Dictionary*). Several of Godwin's writings show a keen interest in psychiatry (*Cain, or the Future of Crime*, 1928; *Peter Kurten, a Study in Sadism*, 1938; *The Great Mystics*, 1945).

CHAPTER XIV

1

EXPERIENCED Piers overlooked nothing.

He said, "We want[1] to get out of the line clean." And he set about binding sacking round his legs, securing it with string; boots, puttees and leathers of breeches were sacking encased until, when he stood up, satisfied, his legs appeared as monstrous members, elephantine.

Stephen started upon a toilette which began with a cigarette tin that served in turn as wash basin, shaving mug and tooth glass, and ended with the encasing of mud-cleansed boots.

The sun was up when they set out for the rear, wading laboriously along through mud knee-deep in places, glutinous, greedy. But the sun that made their spirits rise, presently brought trouble. With clear daylight the shelling began again.

Their way lay parallel with the Arras road and beside it. The road, cratered by endless shelling, was above them; they moved under its lee. Here and there a blackened tree stump bore witness that once this road was tree-lined, shady, pleasant to pass along. How desolate it was now to look upon! The two batmen followed them.

"We're getting on towards Suicide Corner," said Piers, lifting his head to take in their position.

A shell whined its way towards them, stung the air with a bitter snap above their heads, and passed emitting a descending scream. Its trajectory ended on the road above them, a splitting and a rending. Hot metal hissed about them and fell in the trench, spluttered in the mud, disappeared. Little rotating, jagged fragments travelling at high velocity; little crumbs and splinters of hot steel. Nothing more. But death, even so, death and mutilation; blindness, severed nerves, lacerated bowels. But they fell harmlessly enough, and the four men, in file, moved laboriously on towards Suicide Corner.

A notice board, projecting from the broken parapet, told them they were there; beside it leaned crazily another sign with an arresting " 'Ware Snipers!"

in large black characters. And here was no parapet at all.

Through the tear in the sandbag defence an open expanse was revealed, deep-pitted, churned, scarred by shell-fire, by great craters, the zig-zag scar of old trenches half obliterated, littered with debris, tangled wire and corkscrew stakes, rusted and awry.

"Sort of bright spot where a fellow going out for a week would get his," Piers chafed. He drew his monstrous legs up laboriously, struggling against the suction of the sucking mud. "Just the sort of hole," he added bitterly.

Sporadically, as though fired by gunners in an idle mood, shells whined overhead: a sound, bitter and hateful, that swelled and sank and ceased in a splintering detonation beyond the Arras road. The whiplash of the passing shells made Stephen wince like a nervous horse.

But Suicide Corner was now behind them. A friendly parapet rose once more, promising security. But it was close upon two hours before they had cleared the line and emerged, their coverings cast away, upon a good, hard road.

The country lay before them, its flatness broken here and there by black pyramids of slag. And presently they came up with a field. It was very beautiful. The green of it came at Stephen violently. And he melted towards this green and quivered to behold again a field of grass. After the yellow of the line, after the weary monotony of desolation.

They stopped, cast packs aside, and rested. And Stephen kept his eyes upon the kindly field. He could never have enough of its loveliness; could never possess as he would possess it. His eyes drank in its loveliness, hungrily.

Was that enough? No. It was contact by one sense, and one alone. There remained the others, having no contact with the field.

In ancient times men and women had gone out into such fields to perform there symbolic rites, stimulating the earth to fruition by union upon her wide, sweet bosom.

Stephen desired union with the green field of grass, and fusion with it. He would touch it, smell it, taste it.

It was wet with dew. He lay, face down, upon it so that he saw in minutest detail, lovingly, each pendant globe of glistening moisture, each curved suspending grass blade. And beneath his hand he felt the wetness of the earth, and the wet of the grass was upon his face. Cool and fragrant it was. And the soft smell of it rose to him: friendly, kind, evocative.

Presently he saw a little orchard, grass-sowed, and little trees like seven-branched candlesticks, and among them one tree, gnarled and ancient, but bearing abundantly. And it was an apple tree.

So he lay and gathered refreshment, renewal of body, of soul, lying there prone upon his face in the green field of grass, and his face and hands wet and cool with the dew of it.

He returned presently to the roadside, walking freely, tasting the freedom. The two batmen, a little apart, sat smoking, bare-headed, happy. And Piers, alone, chin on hands, a cigarette pendant from his lips, sat in a deep reverie. He did not move when Stephen came up, but continued to stare straight before him. Stephen saw his eyes and saw that they were listless, remote and filled with a sadness.

The bombing school in other days had been the large farmhouse of a small village. It had some pretensions to grace: a little inadequate turret, Lombardy poplars flanking its approach, and, at the rear, garden and orchard with high warm southern wall upon which grew, transfixed, sturdy scented cherry trees.

The quiet comeliness of the place had been defaced by military occupation. Nissen huts obtruded unloveliness among the trees of the orchard; the green grass of the approach had been destroyed utterly by the feet of tramping men.

But the Nissen huts were not unlovely in the eyes of these men for whom they were the sure promise of warmth, comfort and coveted creature enjoyments. They had cots in rows upon either side, and ample windows let in the light of day to them. The Nissen huts[2] were very pleasant; very friendly they were.

And soon Pilk was busy about his business, setting out cleaning equipment, preparing for a grand cleanup; moving about swiftly doing simple tasks and doing them adroitly, efficiently.

A lank captain, sporting three blue chevrons, said:

"To the dickens with bombing! Here I've been a bombing wallah[3] since Festubert and the silly fools send me down for this jerk-water course." And he sprawled upon his cot luxuriating, announcing, without ado, his intention to cut the bally[4] lectures, the dummy practice.

And later he disappeared and was missing for twenty-four hours. He returned, puffy about the eyes. He had lorry-hopped it to Barlin, he said, had had a binge and found a fairy.[5] They envied him.

Nobody seemed to take this course seriously, Stephen noticed. He was told, "It's a way of giving us a rest from the line." Yet the commandant seemed keen and quite oblivious of the mild contempt in which his bombing course was held.

When they had arrived Stephen had been without sleep for more than forty hours. The excitement of the adventure had sustained him throughout the long tramp back. But now he suffered the reaction. Nature presented her account; he slumped upon his cot, inert, exhausted. He was overdone. His voice became husky, and presently the vocal chords failed entirely; he formed words, but no sound came from his mouth. Moreover, he became wracked with cramp. And Pilk, solicitous, tended him, filling a wine bottle with hot water, placing it, thrust into a thick grey sock, upon his belly. And so he lay.

Having nothing to do, there in the Nissen hut, Stephen a little later began to occupy his time with the only literature at hand: manuals on bombing, treatises on high explosives. He read them contentedly, in his cot.

The M.O. looked in on him, and having examined him, said:

"How long have you been running this temperature?"

Stephen did not know. The M.O. wagged his head.

"Probably for weeks," he opined. "Heaps of fellows carry on with a more or less consistent hundred or more and never know it unless they crack up."

For six days Stephen lay there and studied bombs and the actions of high explosives to while away the hours. Presently he became interested. On the seventh day, the last, the commandant set a written paper to his indifferent class. Stephen, still weak, but lacking other occupation, passed a morning with pen and paper. Drawing the anatomy of bombs, British, French and German, was rather amusing.

The commandant had never seen such a paper, and said so. He shook hands with Stephen heartily.

So it came about that Stephen was reported upon eulogistically. He had been back with the battalion only a fortnight when he received orders to report to headquarters. He went, mystified, and was told crisply by the adjutant to report back to the adjutant of the newly formed Divisional Training School.

A week later he was in the tiny village of Lières, as an Instructor of the drafts that were to come in next day for final intensive training before being drafted as reinforcements to battalions in the line.

Then Piers arrived, riding in a lorry. He, too, had been detailed for this new job. Stephen rejoiced.

3

Would there be men from the West, with homely faces, homely phrases? Would there be links with the valley, with the Settlement?

And now they came. And they came eagerly. For in the camps in Canada there had been a single unifying objective: to get overseas, to see the fighting, to make the world safe. Safe for democracy, for their children. Their morale was marvellous.

What made these simple men so earnest about this business of killing and being killed? Why had they protested bitterly against each delay in their transportation overseas, like children cheated of a treat? And in England, why had they chafed at the routine of the camps?

England seemed a promise near fulfilment, and then had ensued months of monotony: drill, route marches, days on the ranges, fatigues,[6] petty restrictions of liberty, irksome discipline concerning trivialities having no ultimate bearing upon the purpose on hand, the winning of this war.

These men who now came had been looking forward thus eagerly, grudging the days and weeks that kept them from the stupendous enterprise for which they had abandoned businesses, thriving homesteads, rough clearings. They had joined up to fight, and the fighting they sought was denied to them. It was their grievance, very real with them.

How could they help win the war by the performance of useless evolutions upon a parade ground in southern England? They were practical men, men used to seeing labour yield things desired and desirable.

So orders for France had come as the fulfilment of the great wish, long deferred. There would be now an end to the tedium of camp life. The adventure was at hand. And they came gladly to meet it, happy to march from Kentish camps behind the booming bands. A draft, outward bound, bound for France. Boom. Boom.

In that moment they were almost reconciled to the loss of their identity, to the disappearance of their proud battalions, each one of the finest out of Canada and now but a memory and a name. Yes, it was true, those battalions had become but memories and symbols of a great purpose. And they were gone, destroyed by the wanton hand of authority, by the inexorability of necessity.

Yet they still lived, and would live, under other names, in other units. The rich blood of them would pass to sustain the drained veins of the tried battalions.

4

The commandant sat at a trestle table in a bare room overlooking the village street, sat sizing up the thing that had been created by a thought and the penstroke of a directing mind: this new-born unit, of which he and these subalterns before him were the brain, the heart, the bowels and muscle; this dead thing that awaited the vitalising soul of the coming men.

It was, he explained, a new idea, the idea of the new corps commander. And that idea? Nothing less than the introduction into the Canadian Corps of the Guards' system of training,[7] the Guards' standard.

He was a Scot, lean and gaunt, with the grey look of a man long in the line. The signature of many battles was upon his face. War had inflicted suffering upon him and he was prepared in turn to inflict it. His eyes were grey and cold, the long nose predatory, the mouth cruel.

"Our job is to knock discipline into these drafts," he concluded. "If you have the slightest trouble, peg the offenders and I'll deal with them." He glowered ominously. "Discipline!" he ejaculated, dismissing them. "Discipline, gentlemen."

5

Poor, simple-hearted men: poor eager hearts.

Stephen found himself with the powers of a senior officer; for the training school ranked as a detached post, so that the subalterns upon its cadre possessed a field officer's[8] authority. So Stephen now had his own company from these newly-come men. It was to be known as the 'Untrained Draft Company.'

And the designation of it was out there, on the further side of the door of the room that served him as living room, bedroom and orderly room.

"Untrained Draft Company! Hell!"

"That's sure the limit."

"Say, I'd sure like to see the old Colonel's face if he saw us guys of the old battalion figgering as untrained troops. I sure would."

"A goldarn insult, that's what I call it. Untrained! Say, fellers, wot we been doin' these last six months? Holy, goly!"

Stephen heard. The voices came through his window with the air now soft with the first breath of spring. And he considered the ways of the army and marvelled at them. So much talk of morale, of *élan*,[9] and the priceless value of the will to win. And he wondered at this crass folly that destroyed so wantonly these sacred things, that trampled upon the pride of such men as these.

Oh, the dear, familiar faces of them, the simple homely ways of them. The frank eyes that looked into yours, man to man. The simple friendliness, good faith, trust. And, as they had been buoyed up, believing the worst behind them, they found the worst was yet to come. They were to suffer more tedium. And after that, the reality: the line, and more monotony.

And then battle.

For what had this training school been organised? It was for the coming battle. For the attack upon the Ridge, towards which their lives moved with the firm purpose of a great machine.

And the worst was yet to come.

The commandant had adjured: "Peg them for the slightest breach of discipline. Put 'em through it." And Stephen was no longer an individual, a man, moving among these simple ones, but a cog in the machine, responding to the command as the machinery answers the orders of the master switch.

Stephen saw the priceless treasure being poured away and he was doomed to help on the wanton folly. Orders were orders. And they had meant (if the commandant's face and words meant ought at all), that he, Stephen, was expected to put these new-come men 'through it,' to make their lives a misery. Yes, he was a part, if an insignificant one, of this machine that ground up human souls, snuffing the flame of enthusiasm, setting up in its place a mechanical obedience based on fear; the obedience of mechanical men.

And he had thought this escape!

He considered his problem, seeking some course that would reconcile duty with humanity.

6

It was dusk when the first of the drafts had marched into the village. They had been nearly a week in France already, moving up from the base, without sleep for two days. They had marched throughout the day, but their weariness was forgotten in the long-last fulfilment of their wish. They were "at the front," at the front at last. Free and easy they were, calling: "Say, lieutenant. Hi! Sir."

They did not understand, but they would understand very soon.

Stephen went among them, sick at heart. And it seemed to him that they had brought their valleys and their rivers and their mountains with them.

And now, aware that there was fresh delay, new torments of routine before them, they looked at him as he moved about their billets, the moving symbol of their servitude; they sensed the gulf that lay between him and themselves.

How did they sense that gulf? By little things: the quiet air of experience, of the man doing familiar things, self-assured, competent. By the blue battalion badges, weather-faded, upon the leather-bound sleeves of tunic. By that seasoned air which is composed of a hundred minute details, and recognised at a glance.

This was their officer, this thin guy, with the dark-rimmed eyes. What sort of guy would he be? Not like their own officers. There were no officers like the officers of the old battalion: the best ever. But what sort of guy, anyway?

Stephen moved among them, giving orders.

The latrines must be used and any failure to take that walk to relieve nature would mean trouble. There would be no smoking in billets, since they were, all said and done, only wattle barns that would burn like tinder and ignite, likely as not, the farmhouse, too. Damage to these wattle barns, however, would involve the authorities in claims from the French. And as a careless foot went freely through the hardened mud of those walls, they would be careful. Whole provinces of France lay waste; cities, towns and villages lay razed, but the wattle barns of this village were sacred.

Nor must they pay for water, if asked to do so. They must report the demand. And they must drink only the water duly doped, rendered safe from contamination. How was it the French took no harm? They had acquired a tolerance.

Upon the dung-encrusted floor of their new habitation they would lie symmetrically, a row of men on either side, and the straw of their bedding would be plaited about its edges, and in line. That drawing on the door would show them how their kit should be laid at their cots' feet for inspection. It must be laid like that: precisely. Not as they had done it in the old battalion? Well, perhaps best to forget how things were done in the old battalion and to do them in this new way. And without too many questions. And they were now in France. They must remember that. What was a triviality in England might be serious here. The penalties were harsh. They might as well know it.

And again, with regard to letters, listen attentively, please. All letters would be censored. They must give no particulars that might be of use to the enemy, no address. And the penalty for smuggling news by cypher would be Field

General Court Martial and the prison at Lillers.

Had they any idea what Lillers prison was like? They might as well know. It was a little hell upon earth. There men did Field Punishment No. 1. What was it? He hoped none of them would ever know. But this would give them some idea. In Lillers prison yard there were two four-foot pits. And men carrying a weight to and fro, placing it in one pit, lifting it, carrying it the length of the yard, dropping it in the other pit: returning. For hours. That was Lillers. But they need not think too much of it: it was not for men who did their job, and did it on the hop.

7

Well, what would they be thinking of him? He did not know. But he was determined: he would work with them and for them. He would, somehow or other, cheat the machine.

And so as the days passed into weeks the Untrained Draft Company got to understand the unwritten code that governed them. And it was this: keep clear of the commandant.

In time they learned to perform the balance step of the Guards, going through this folly with something like good grace, forgiving the indignity put upon them; doing their drill like manikins, perfectly.

And why? Because there was between them and this long, lean officer an unspoken pact. He stood for authority and rigid discipline but somehow he was on their side. They sensed his hatred of it all; they came to understand he was as impotent as themselves in the ordering of their tedious lives.

They talked in the estaminets of evenings, talked over their coffee, their chipped potatoes, comparing notes with the men of the other companies . .
.

"Our officer is a reg'lar feller, yes, sir."

"Say, why don't our officer let us have a bit of boxing, like your guy?"

And the man of the Untrained Draft would josh, saying:

"You oughter got a proper guy like we got. Boxing? You bet, up there in the orchard, when we done our drill. But that aint all. Yesterday he got out a blackboard and spouted a lecture about the strategy of the western front, told us about this Ridge we're due to take."

And another chipped in, aglow:

"Yes, siree, we got a bunch of games too, we play, and we're going to have a football from the Y.M.C.A."

8

One day, as the men of the Untrained Draft were watching a furious mill, the commandant stalked into the little orchard with the adjutant. He was not seen at first, and he came up as a wild whoop greeted a swift left to the jaw that dropped one of the contestants. And he stood there unnoticed, watching the scrap, his thin face grim. But when his presence had become known, and the ring was broken up, he said tartly to Stephen:

"Ten minutes is enough of that. Get them back to the manual of arms."

And Stephen saluted. "Very good, sir." And his men watched, knowing that their officer was in bad odour for their sakes.

But they still boxed. With discretion. There would be someone on the road, mysteriously. And word was always passed when authority approached. The ball came from the Y.M.C.A. They piled arms, doffed tunics and played football, furiously.

And presently came a circular from Headquarters. Men in the Training Schools were to be given a varied day. Boxing, football and the games set forth herewith were recommended. So now they played openly, and without fear of disapproval.

After all, a way had been found. And these men were sound; as they had arrived they were sound. And sound they would go up the line, new blood in the thin veins of the exhausted battalions.

9

At the further end of the orchard a beautifully turned-out[10] staff captain was eyeing the men as Stephen marched them onto the now-familiar improvised parade ground. There was to be a lecture.

He looked them over as a professional spell-binder, shrewd and cynical, estimates the feel of an expectant audience. He was about to offer them strong meat. How would they react to it? He decided, pulling delicately at his ironed moustache, that they were not a very likely lot, these simple-looking Canucks, these men from farms, little businesses, camps. They were rubes, hayseeds . . .

Many a time, in the big arena at Havre and in little villages behind the line, this man had worked his will upon audiences of simple men, men who would have drowned a cat with a pang of pity, and had watched them changing from kindly human beings into potential savages.

Stephen told himself that it was ridiculous to feel this loathing of the blood-lust wallah. He considered, "Well, after all, this is war and this is his job. Snipers may be necessary evils and so, too, perhaps, was this professional gospeller of murder as something to be done with zest and for the enjoyment of it.

"At heart every sniper must be an assassin, since he becomes a sniper of his own free will. Probably never knew or suspected in civil life that he was suppressing a deep hunger to destroy, to take life, to inflict pain . . . Queer, how they all looked the same, creeping through the trenches silently, absorbed man-panthers, with their telescopic sights and notched rifle butts. Doing it for the love of it. Rivalries among themselves, cursing the days when they failed to pick off a man; a day without sport, luck . . .

"This fellow, too. Probably decent enough man in civvy life. But surely a sadist[11] now, fulfilling himself for the first time, and happy at release from the dimly apprehended inhibitions of civilisation. . ."

The lecture had commenced. And Stephen was glad that it was no part of his duty to look interested or appreciative. He could look wooden, like the reporter at the revivalist meeting who was there to report, but not there to be saved.[12]

Now he was well away. Well, good luck to him. If the Hun was like that, well, he did not deserve much mercy. Tale after tale of atrocity, told with art; anecdote after anecdote of the joys of cold steel against human flesh.

And the technique of it. Folly of ramming a man in the breast. Why? Because you'd have to shove your foot against his stomach to get your bayonet out. Madness of thrusting between the ribs. Why? Same reason. No, the way to go to work was to jab to the kidneys, one inch, two inches. It was enough. And the steel came away easily. That did the trick!

A dash of humour to keep 'em going. That old one about the Cockney lad, bayoneting his first Hun: "Gor blimey, ain't it grand!"

Didn't seem to go down with these stolid fellows. Damn glad too. Perhaps a story to be told one remove from reality. All right about an ancient war, told in a snug bar. Get the laugh then, probably. But here, now. No. It wasn't what these men had looked for.

They had considered war, forgetting the nature of it, in the simplicity of their hearts. And now it was revealed to them as bloody murder, calculated assassination.

Stephen looked over the faces of the squatting men. Good lads! Not a smile, not a crack. But not indifference, either. Disgusted, feeling just a little sick at the stomach. That was all.

"Well," he considered, "there was such a thing as psychology. If you would appeal to simple souls you must understand their simplicity. If you would appeal to decent men, calling upon their chivalry, you must call upon a silver trumpet, must surely address yourself to all that was fine in them.

"These men had left their families and their farms, their wives, their sweethearts, and their jobs, because little Belgium had been raped; because the world had to be made safe for Democracy; because Nurse Cavell had been shot like a dog in Brussels; because the *Lusitania*[13] had been sent to the bottom. Not men to become apt pupils at assassination. Poor converts to the Gospel of Murder for the fun of the thing.

"Queer and horrible," Stephen considered, "this herd instinct that swept away individual decency and left only a pack of wolves where men had been. Just followed the herd, and whatever the herd approved was right. The herd, that interpreted absolute moral values, the herd that was a God and a bloody God at that . . ."

The lecture was over. The lecturer was hot. He wiped his forehead. Evidently took it out of him. Still, he enjoyed it. A decent lunch, and then push on to another unit and repeat the performance. Doing good work, jazzing up the fighting spirit. Necessary, too, by God! in the third year of the war. And with a big scrap in sight.

Stephen heard one man say:

"That guy was castrated by the Huns, that's why he gets all wound up like that."

Stephen said: "I wouldn't believe that, if I were you."

But the man remained firm in his conviction. He said:

"Believe it's a fact, sir. And why wouldn't it be likely? I see they're boiling down their own dead to get chemicals out of the boilings. They'd do anything, them Huns, it's my opinion."

A pink-faced boy chirped up.

"They crucified one of our fellows against a barn door, sir." His voice quivered with rage.

Of course that story of the boiling of the dead was a palpable lie. Only so few people knew a word of German. The newspaper that circulated the lie knew that. Propaganda. Banked on nobody knowing that the German word 'Kadaver' connoted the carcasses of beasts, and not the dead bodies of men. Too difficult to explain to these fellows, though.

And the crucifixion? The sort of thing one would require evidence of. No, that was just another propaganda lie. Germans were not like that. Militarism had brutalised them but it brutalised those on the top, not the poor devils who were its victims.

He fumed and fretted. Why couldn't one fight clean, if fighting had to be done? Chivalry. They had chivalry in the old days. But did they? Odd tales of the Crusades came into his memory. No prisoners. Butchery of women and children. No, war has always made men the same; probably would always make them the same. Savages. Trouble was, savages armed with scientific weapons.

Well, anyway this staff wallah had failed – well, practically failed. Some of those fellows would start nourishing a desire to kill for the sake of killing, maybe, flogging themselves into a misplaced righteous anger. But the line would cure all that. Old hands would laugh at their enthusiasm; or sneer at them.

Those stories of the prisoners. Pretty foul, that. Started with fourteen, arrived with three. "All the others tried to escape, sir."

Ha! ha! Very good.

And here he was, this hot gospeller of murder, cooler now; infernally handsome, this sadist, this unmentionable swine. A bunch of ribands,[14] too.

"Not exactly first-class fighting troops," he grinned. Stephen shrugged his shoulders. "The corps commander had another opinion," he snapped savagely. The parade moved off.

Notes

1. "want": this word has the British meaning of "to need, to require."
2. "Nissen huts: tunnel-shaped huts of corrugated iron with a cement or wooden floor" *(Oxford Dictionary).*
3. "Wallah": high-ranking officer or official. Used ironically. Another Hindustani borrowing via the army.
4. bally: "bloody," confounded.
5. "found a fairy": i.e. found "a drunken, debauched, hideous old woman" (*Macmillan Dictionary of Historical Slang,* New York, 1974).
6. fatigues: e.g. digging support trenches, building small-gauge railway lines, transporting food, barbed wire, stakes, ammunition, etc., towards the front. Work party.
7. "Guards' system of training": The Guards' system was the most rigorous and exacting training regimen in the British Army, especially regarding physical fitness (Prof. Jonathan Vance).
8. field officer: army officer above captain and below general i.e. majors, colonels, etc.
9: 'élan: boldness, 'dash,' energetic fearlessness.
10: "turned out": i.e. in uniform, with the implication of spotlessness.
11. Sadist. Cf. Godwin's *Peter Kurten, a Study in Sadism* (1938).
12. Godwin treats revivalism (e.g. Wesley, Booth) in some depth in *The Great Revivalists* (Watts, London, 1951, 220 pp).
13. *Lusitania*: a 32,000-ton British liner, torpedoed by a German U-boat off the Irish coast on May 7, 1915. At the time the Allies claimed that it carried no war materiel; the Germans claimed otherwise. History has proved the Germans right in this assumption. 128 Americans were among the total of 1,195 people who went down with the *Lusitania* and this event did much to push America into the War.
14. Ribands: ribbons, i.e. rectangular cloth, color-coded to stand for medals.

CHAPTER XV

1

PARADE in the soft Spring air, in the little orchard of the village. Stephen stands facing the commandant: behind him his draft company, rows of ramrods. The air thrums. The hedgerow is a shrill green; he fixes his eyes upon a bud.

What was this bud?

It was childhood. Dusty lanes and lanes sparkling in early morning dew. Country lanes of home, hedges a-bloom with wild roses. Little leafy villages of old thatched cottages and gardens of all the homely flowers; hollyhocks, irises, pansies, mignonette, yellow marigolds. Women in low doorways, and ancient men beneath great trees . . .

It was green fields, clover-scented, daisies, dandelions. The smell of rosemary, the sharp remembered prick of thorns. Pale blue mottled eggs in tiny nests. Mother birds. Daisy chains with green and slimy stalks, golden hearts . . .

It was church bells from grey Norman towers, heard from beyond old chestnut trees. It was laburnum spilling over lichened walls; lilac-scenting evening air. And, yes, the apple trees over there were studded with fat pods, breaking out already, cupped tenderly in transparent baby leaves.

Over there, the Gravenstein would be much more advanced. In blossom soon, maybe in blossom now. Five-petalled blossoms in little friendly clusters. Formed in leaves, wide open to the sun. Up close, you would see the fat and sticky pods, each one filled with crumpled pinkness. Yes, and the young leaves would be dew-wash fresh, because the old road, that was really but a trail, would not yet be powdered by heat of summer sun . . .

The old Gravenstein, there by the riband of road, there in the corner of its field, like an old man upon a seat in the soft sun, mellow, a little wistful, but beautiful in age.

Just to plump down there in the long cool grass and look up through the twisted branches, through the green leaves, to the blue beyond: that would be something.

The Garden of Eden myth. How beautiful it was! One could understand how that began. The legend, likely enough, of some gardener of ancient days. A story told and told again, at harvest time, in fields of yellow corn on summer evenings beside old tavern doors. The most perfect thing imaginable: man in a garden of trees, man in an orchard.

And all that folklore stuff that Frazer[1] told about. Trees, always trees, trees as the home of gods, magic trees. Yes, and apple trees, magic, too: poor women rolling in their shade to conjure children from barren wombs.

A tiny bursting bud in the hedgerow of a French village, a podded apple tree. Things seen for a moment in the pause between orders, standing there at attention, on parade, with the Untrained Draft Company. Seen for a little moment, but a moment half as long as life . . .

The buds, quivering, returned his stare; carefree, they seemed, and truculent.

Well, you, standing there, stiff and still, look your fill. You may not see another spring. Take your eyeful of us, of our beauty . . .

Nostalgia, that was the name they gave this pain that came all unawares at the sight of a budding hedgerow, at the sight of the podded trees . . .

Dear nascent hedge! Sweet buds that pressed into the aching heart sharp thorns of happy memories!

"Battalion . . . !"

A rasping voice. A movement in the ranks, slight, nervous, of alertness, like a breeze through saplings. The parade rustles. The word of command comes: an ejaculation, short and metallic. The parade is at attention.

2

Through the village street cattle were passing, gaunt and dung-soiled, melancholy. A blue-smocked boy drove them before him with a stick, striking their lean haunches, scolding them. Already the flies, hatched in the warm spring air, were at those mournful eyes, in clusters, voracious.

Piers, standing by Stephen, watched them pass.

"And the flies, feasting at their bloodshot eyes," he quoted.

They came forward in little nervous spurts, swinging tortured heads from side to side; the boy called, scolding them in his shrill voice, belabouring the laggards. Half-starved they look, as they moved, apprehensively, with foreknowledge of doom, towards the abattoir.[2]

An orderly came up, saluted. Piers took the chit from the waiting man, opened it. He crumpled it in his hand.

"I'm recalled," he told Stephen laconically. He turned to the orderly. "You know my batman?" he asked. "Well, tell him to put my kit together and his own as well."

The man saluted and went.

Stephen looked at Piers, distressed immeasurably. "Why only you?" he asked stupidly, bemused.

Piers shrugged his shoulders. "I've no idea," he answered, "but there it is."

The cattle had passed them now and were down along the road, the sound of their hoofs came back, evocative of country lanes of home, of peace and the sweet quietness of old English places.

The two men walked in silence through the village street, and their way was past unlovely little houses that proclaimed the poverty they hid, poverty of goods and chattels, poverty of spirit. Flat-faced they were and scabrous. Great barns reared gauntly above the little roofs; the tang of ammonia came to them, and the strong stench of wet manure, tainting the soft spring air.

The cattle sensed their doom with foreknowledge old as time; and they knew it with surety. What then had looked out of Piers' sombre eyes just now if not a like foreknowledge?

"I never knew a ranker officer who didn't get this," he said bitterly. "Yet I somehow thought, when I was detailed for this job, that I'd be the exception."

He paused, and they walked a space in silence. Then he added: "Well, this chit means that I was wrong."

"Grant told me," said Stephen, argumentatively, "that he'd a hunch like that. But he was wrong. Those hunches aren't worth a damn. Forget it, Piers, old man." He took Piers' arm. "One day, when the war is over, I'll remind you of this day, this hour, and we'll laugh about it together. Silly old ass! You and your mouldy hunches!"

But Piers did not respond to this badinage, his mood was sombre. He walked in silence. And Stephen looked at him, slantingly, at a loss for words.

Was it possible to know a man only eight months or so and to love him thus? And could it be that as those cattle sensed the abattoir, Piers felt fall upon his soul the dark shadow of approaching death? No, no; a man so sweet, so lovable as Piers could not, should not be killed.

They were now outside Piers' billet.

"I must get my stuff together," he said, laconically. "See you later."

And he was gone.

3

Stephen walked quickly down the street to headquarters. The commandant was at his littered table.

Stephen saluted.

"I would like to go back to my battalion, sir," he said.

The commandant looked up, quizzing him: "What's the matter?" he asked.

Stephen protested. "Nothing, sir; only I'd like to go."

"Oh, you would, would you?"

"That is so, sir."

"Well, you won't."

"I thought, sir, I was entitled to put in to go back," Stephen persisted.

The face of the commandant reddened in anger against him.

"So you understood you were entitled?" he mocked. And now it was Stephen whose face flushed dark.

"I mean, sir," he stuck to his guns, "that a written application would be considered by Division."

The commandant sucked at his cigarette. "Make one out," he snapped.

4

Why do such a thing? Why not take things as they came, the good with the bad? Walking swiftly and uplifted by action, he came with his news to Piers.

No, the last thing he wanted was to be again in the trenches. O God, how he hated the filth of them. No, a thousand times, no. To go back would be hell. But hell with friends, and so, no hell after all.

Why, then? Because Piers was going. What was friendship if not eagerness to share all things both good and evil?

But Piers reacted strangely.

"You bloody fool!" he shouted. "You infernal fool!"

Stephen stood still, wounded. Piers was casting his gear about, without method, ineffectually.

"But, Piers," Stephen stammered after a pause, "I thought you'd be glad. We should be together, in the old company."

Piers now faced him.

"Look here, Stephen," he began in a slow, low voice, "can't you see the difference between our cases? I'm unmarried, a freelance. I'm necessary to no one. If I get mine, nobody stands to lose. But you go under, what's to become of your wife and children?"

Stephen stood silent, stricken. Loyalty to Piers and that other loyalty at issue! – clashing, unreconciled, irreconcilable.

He said quietly, as one who confesses: "Well, I'm putting in my written application, fool or no fool, father or no father."

And looking up he saw Piers with twisted face looking back at him. They stood, eye to eye, for a long moment. Then Piers said: "You know you're a crock as it is, don't you?"

"A crock?"

"Yes, of course, you blockhead! A blind man could see it a mile off. Good God, man, why d'you suppose you are speechless half the time if there's nothing wrong with your throat? Stick where you are, stick where you are."

Stick where he was? Eat his own words? Go back and crawl to the commandant, explaining that he had changed his mind, thought things over, would carry on? No. Impossible.

Piers went off. They said little. But they held to each other's hands, and looked into each other's eyes.

It was three days before word came from Division. The application was refused.

Stephen never knew until long after that along with his written application to Division had gone a chit from the commandant to the effect that this officer could not be spared.

Stephen carried on.

5

The Untrained Draft Company, now trained, was under orders to move up. Drab London buses clanked into the village and stood grotesquely there, unpainted, all their glory of red and white gone. How filthy to train men for battle and then stand by and watch them go! . . .That's egoism. Don't think as an individual: you aren't one any more . . . The men were climbing up the steep stairs, holding their rifles, trailing their kit . . . It's their turn today, yours tomorrow. Spare your pity for yourself . . .

He knew every one of these men, oh, so intimately. And he knew their backgrounds, for, reading their letters, how could it be otherwise? Their hopes, their troubles, their loves, these were an open book to him.

O simple hearts, O dear, familiar faces from the West, O kindly ones become dear through weeks and weeks of closest contact! Farewell!

A cheer rose from the leading bus as its driver threw in his clutch. Stephen waved a hand. He heard their voices, the throb of the machines and their voices above the machines. Then he turned aside.

Oh, what a fool to feel things so! His eyes swam and in anger he brushed the springing tears away. But they were his men, his children. And he loved them. And now they were gone. And Piers was gone.

He walked quickly away, and as he walked the sound of the guns obtruded upon his inward ear. It came to him down the clear blue sky: a thrumming, ominous and hateful, a baleful pulse upon the air.

6

Surely one was entitled to one's batman?

Stephen came, in anger, to the Orderly Room.[3] Why, when Pilk had been detailed as his batman, was he now ordered back to the battalion?

He was ordered back to the battalion, it appeared, because he had been given a lancejack's stripe. And N.C.O.s were wanted. Did Craig expect an N.C.O. for batman? If so, he had another guess coming.

He returned, defeated, to his billet. Pilk was sitting there outside the door, upon its step, and he scrubbed vigorously, like one working against time, at a boot, working the soap into the leather with bared piston arm.

Surely Pilk must be thinking sombre thoughts, going back to the line, back for the impending battle. He would be thinking of those two boys of his, over there, with the mother who drank and was unsatisfactory in other ways as well. His heart would surely be heavy within him.

Why, then, did he squat there in the soft sunlight scrubbing those old boots, carrying on to the last minute? Not because there was need of it, for as he went another would come to take his place.

He said, "Aw, how many guys do boots properly?"

What did that question mean, coming from Pilk, head low over his task? It meant that he was doing the last service in his power, a menial one, true enough, but in its simple way symbolic.

And presently Pilk was standing there in full marching order, his thin face showing nothing of what troubled his aching heart. He grinned, and his teeth played their old trick upon him, making him comic when he would most be dignified.

They shook hands: a long, firm clasp. Not officer and servant, just man to man, and each with much for which to thank the other.

Stephen watched him go with springy step down the village street, his rifle bobbing as he went.

He went slowly to his room and sat down. He looked about idly. There was the cleaning kit set out, neat and orderly; and over there those boots, set by the window to dry. A clean towel beside the bed, and on the little table, the whisky and a glass.

Stephen got up and poured himself a stiff drink. Then he sat down. The liquor warmed him. And so he sat. And presently the glass before him began to quiver and behind him the open window set going a tiny castanet.

Dear God! How could they keep it up, that terrifying gunfire?

7

A new draft came in and it was the same story again: they were hard-done-by men from the best battalion that ever left Canada. And their battalion had been broken up. They had lost their identity, suffered in their regimental pride, become mere draftees for alien units.

And soon they were knuckling down, learning that absurd goose step of the Guards, suffering humiliation and loss of dignity with some outward show of patience. Even so, it was not easy to teach old lumbermen, ranchers and the like, to mince in line like young ladies at an academy for deportment. But it was the Army's way: the Guards' way.

And who were the Guards that they, Canadians, should imitate their methods? Weren't their Canadian ways good enough? And, anyhow, how could this monkeying about win the war?

One might tell them of the Guards, but it was by no means so easy to explain how the balance step was helping matters on. Stephen himself hadn't the faintest idea. It was the idea of their new commander, Sir Julian Byng. That was all he knew. In England they called the Canadians the Byng Boys now. But the Canadians did not refer to themselves in that way. They preferred to be known as the Canadians; if necessary, as the Bloody Canadians.

But for Stephen it was not the same as before. Now the draftees were coming, men called up to the colours and without appetite for war; men chafing to get home to work left half undone. And who could blame them? They were not like the lot just gone.

Stephen had emptied himself upon those men who had gone. He felt that he had nothing to give these newcomers. He merely carried on, mechanically, conscientiously, but without enthusiasm.

8

One day, while physical drill was in progress in the now-familiar orchard, he watched a clash between the instructor and a man in the ranks. Was feeling getting so bad that it had come to insubordination?

"Put them arms up!" bawled the instructor.

"Put 'em right up!"

The man raised his arms shoulder high, but no higher. His broad face had upon it a look of obstinacy, a dogged look.

The instructor fumed. "Say, what's the idea? Can't you get an order?"

Stephen watched. Something unpleasant brewing? Perhaps. The order was repeated and now the squad was an audience watching a duel, keyed up, suppressed. You could feel the tensity. Authority was challenged. The men stood, neutral, watching.

Once again the offender raised his arms, shoulder high, but no higher. The time had come for action.

"Fall that man out!" bawled Stephen. A ripple of excitement passed over the ranks. The climax was at hand.

The man stood at attention before Stephen and Stephen looked directly into his eyes. Sombrely they returned his steady gaze. The man was flushed, his chest heaved; his emotional stress hurt like the unhappiness of a small child.

"Now, what's the matter?" Stephen asked.

"That's the matter, sir," bitterly.

He had opened his grey shirt and bared a shoulder that was livid from the surgeon's knife and laced with the surgeon's stitches.

"I can't get that arm up, sir," he protested, his face dark. Yet even now, with a grievance heavy upon him, his eyes were those of one who laughs easily and often.

"Why have you been sent back?" Stephen asked, shocked.

"Well, sir, there was a call for men and I was put on the draft at the reserve, marked G.S."[4]

So that was how it was, they were now shovelling the wounded back into the line; it was enough, it seemed, if the man could march. Stephen thought. That does not go out here. He said: "Do what you can. I'll report the matter."

He made a report and it lacked somewhat the coldness of official language; yes, it breathed his indignation. And presently he received orders to have his casualty ready to parade for medical inspection. A R.A.M.C.M.O.[5] was going to oblige his Canadian comrades, since he was the nearest M.O. available.

He came on a horse and drew up in the lane outside the orchard. Stephen had his case ready. He was paraded, complete with N.C.O. But there was no examination. Only a few indifferent questions. An a moment later Stephen stepped back to avoid the restive horse as the rider swung its head. The M.O. had made his diagnosis, it seemed, without dismounting. The man was a lead-swinger. He reported him G.S.

The commandant merely shrugged. It was the Army.

And Stephen went off, fuming. To send a man back into the line who could not handle a rifle; it was monstrous! He was G.S., was he? Well, they should see.

So it came about that when the draft departed, their exit was watched by a ruddy-complexioned man from the field kitchens. The casualty was now on the strength of the Training School for rations and discipline. Stephen chuckled. But he said nothing. And that was the Army too. It was known as a 'wangle.'

Notes

1. Frazer: Sir James George Frazer (1854 - 1941), author of *The Golden Bough* (1890), influential study in comparative folklore, magic, and religion.
2. abattoir: slaughter-house.
3. Orderly Room: a room in a barracks (or a tent) which was used as a company office.
4. G.S.: General Service, i.e. fit for any military duty.
5. R.A.M.C.M.O.: Medical Officer, Royal Army Medical Corps.

CHAPTER XVI

1

ON the other side of the wall a young girl was playing upon a tinkling piano some jingle as paltry and infectious as *Sur le Pont d'Avignon.* The tinsel sound penetrated the flimsy wall. The girl played her piece over and over again until Stephen found himself waiting for the passages where she would surely hesitate, stumble and pause, incompetently, then begin all over again.

Playing jingles on an ancient instrument in a meagre little room to the counterpoint of the guns! In the pauses while (as he imagined it) she sat, stiff fingers splayed over yellow keys, head craned to baffl ing score, he heard the recitative of the guns, low and terrible. Such a bombardment! Rising to a mad and maddening climax after a week's long crescendo, a climax that meant one thing: that the hour of the assault upon the Ridge was at hand.

How strange, to be here and alone, in this little room, with a girl playing jingles beyond a dividing wall, with the homely clack of hens from the yard below, and all the soft, murmurous sounds of village life on the soft air – somnolent, sweet – with the hour of battle at hand.

Such gunfire could not last indefinitely; this storm of death that drenched the trenches (and the men in those trenches, cowering, unnerved, fearful, knowing the import of it) must pass, must surely pass.

This means the climax. Battle.

So he sat, thinking. And the music tinkled on, an absurd little jingle picked out by faltering fingers. And behind it the dark music of the guns that filled him with a strange excitement.

2

The adjutant said: "We've taken the Ridge and they're consolidating the position." And he spoke as though he himself had had a hand in it. When he rose from his littered table in the bare Orderly Room, and thrust hands into pockets, there was satisfaction in his manner, and when he added: "If there's a bar, we'll be entitled to it, too," he artlessly revealed the quality of his mind.

A bar for a battle one had heard from afar! The false note jarred on Stephen. A bar!

"Any details yet of casualties?" he asked.

But there were no details. They would filter through later.

The adjutant said; "We'll probably hear something from Major MacDonald, he's coming to us as second-in-command. He should report in to-day."

Stephen had heard from the Major in one short chit of his meeting with Alice in London; and Alice had told of that meeting, too. But neither had said very much about it. So he was coming. Good, good. A familiar face, a friendly face.

"The Major's had a touch of fever," the adjutant remarked, "that's why he's been detailed for this job. He's lucky. Just missed this show."

Piers? O'Reilly? Grant? Pilk? The men of his old platoon? The men of the draft? How had things gone with them?

Yet there was nothing for it but to wait, to wait with a patience that was endurance, suspense.

3

On the evening of the 10th of April Stephen saw a familiar well-knit figure in the street, the swift stride, the erect carriage of Major MacDonald. They shook hands, holding each other, eye to eye.

"Any details of casualties, sir?" Stephen asked, his heart heavy within him.

"Nothing very definite," the Major told him evenly. "O'Reilly came through all right, a blighty on the knee, but nothing very much, I hear. Grant distinguished himself. Piers did well and is all right. But the casualties were heavy. We'll have to wait for details," he added. And his words sounded casual, indifferent.

Yes, they would have to wait. But now, knowing his friends safe, Stephen swung up from despondency to an easy optimism. Pilk would be all right too. Of course he would be all right. And the draft. And the men of his old platoon. Miraculously, this battle was to be unlike all other battles: there were to be no casualties at all.

They walked together down the village street, exchanging their news. To have the Major there was something; it made a man resigned to this hated job.

4

Reports filtered through. And presently there was word of Piers and Pilk. Both had fallen.

Stephen heard in silence. Then he said, stupidly: "Not Piers! Not Pilk!"

But in his heart he knew that he had had foreknowledge of it, knew that his faith had been mere self-deception. He had lied to himself, knowing, with instincts old as time, that his friends would not come back; brother officer, servant and friend.

Later, he sat down and wrote to Alice, finding in the task of writing relief:

"I am feeling very sad," he wrote inadequately, "at the death in action of Piers. We had perfect sympathy from the first and his death has affected me as much, perhaps more even, than if he had been my brother. He went over in the attack on the 9th, and came through unwounded, and next day went with his platoon to 'exploit our success.' Lucklessly it was against a position not properly shelled by our guns. And so he was killed. He was a man of most lovable character, quietly humorous, but chiefly I remember he was one of those understanding ones. He loved poetry, and I remember him reciting the 'Hound of Heaven'[1] in the dugout one day. What I feel aside from the ache that never again shall I see his loved face is a mutinous feeling of revolt that so sweet a man should be cut off before his promise was fulfilled. I am thinking of the day we joined the battalion and stood, side by side, as Vimy Ridge was pointed out to us through the grey mist."

It was not until four days after the battle that Stephen learnt the fate of Pilk. It was a warm day, and all the tender young greens had been brightly painted by an early morning shower, so that now they sparkled in the sun. It seemed only yesterday that Pilk had been about the yard, talking his pidgin French to Madame, whistling, grinning his toothy grin. And now he was dead.

What would happen to those two boys, left with their drunken mother? That would have been Pilk's last thought, likely enough. Well, they would have to do without their father. Like hundreds of thousands of other little boys in bibs and tuckers,[2] in little knickerbockers.[3]

Later came fuller details, so that Stephen learnt the manner of Piers' death. He had had orders to attack a position with his platoon, and he had got battalion H.Q. on the 'phone. The job was impossible and would mean the sacrifice of his platoon without any possible gain. He had wished to know from the Colonel whether he was to carry on in face of this fact.

And the Colonel's voice had come back over the wire: "Piers, I'm sorry. But the order's from higher up."

So Piers had taken his men, had been shot down leading them, knowing his own death inevitable, and inevitable the annihilation of his platoon. And knowing, O bitterness! the futility of the sacrifice.

News of Pilk's end drifted through. Pilk had been shot in the groin. He had been seen staunching the flow of blood, but too weak to fix a tourniquet. Pilk had bled to death. Many men had bled to death. They could not get them back to the advanced dressing stations fast enough. They lay and bled until there was no more blood in them for labouring hearts to pump from gaping wounds.

No miraculous battle, after all, but like all other battles: paid for in blood, in sacrifice, in suffering, agony of body, agony of mind. And, even so, not then paid for.

For the price of victory was like a funded debt, bearing interest in suffering from year to year, long after the last man wounded had passed, after the last widow had stood, dry-eyed, beside the wooden cross of an ordered cemetery where the battalions of the dead lay, line upon line, beneath the new-sprung grass. Vanished battalions of the dead. Yet battalions that somehow lived.

Who shall say what such a battle cost? And who among men shall declare the victory worth the price?

5

And now Stephen felt a revulsion of feeling against the Major. To have had someone to whom one could have talked: it would have helped. But the Major, beyond a toneless: "Poor Piers, I'm sorry," or: "Piers, he was a good officer," was untouched. A moment later he would have put the death of Piers away from him, would be concerned, even more concerned, it seemed, with some return to be made or a report that should go without delay to the Commandant.

So Stephen felt the distance grow between them, because of this grief which they did not share. Was the Major callous, insensitive, unfeeling, more mechanism than man? It must be so. He had become a human instrument of war. For, after all, had they not shared a daily life together with Piers in the close companionship of the trenches?

The Major, then, hadn't a heart. He simply did not care. And if he, Stephen, got pipped,[4] he would merely remark: "Pity. A married man with children," and pass on to other thoughts, dismissing the dead man from his mind entirely.

Even so, Stephen, yearning for consolation, went more than once to the Major's billet. He wanted to talk about Piers, how fine he was, with one who shared with him knowledge of that fineness . . .

The Major sat at a table upon which he had set out the homely contents of a parcel just received. He had set his treasures out methodically, geometrically, and now sat looking at them, at the pink oblongs of chewing gum, at the yellow box of cigarettes, the square tin of maple syrup.

"Isn't it foul, sir, that poor old Piers' life should have been simply chucked away? Simply wasted. It wasn't as if he accomplished anything by dying. I call it murder. And some damned fool at headquarters is his murderer."

The Major regarded his treasures absently, and said, absently: "I remember several things like that on the Somme," he began, seeing no longer the table or the objects upon it, but some remembered episode of the great battle.

The Somme! The Somme! Always the Somme.

Stephen looked down on the grey face. Poor chap, he was spent. He hadn't anything to give; he was dry, dry and empty. He had poured himself out. The Somme had stunned his brain, and it was still stunned: it had numbed his heart, and it was still numbed.

Could you blame him for that? He would grieve, likely enough, only he had forgotten how to grieve. His emotions were entombed in a dark sarcophagus before which a great stone had been rolled. He could not feel.

6

But it was important to pity. To pity fallen friends, the Major, the enemy, the people at home, the people who suffered everywhere. Because if one ceased to pity, then war triumphed and one was smashed by it. Love one another. One couldn't love without pity; nor could one pity without love.

Muddled thoughts, one always came back to them, fumblingly, like a child in the dark.

Stephen left the Major with his parcel and its consolation, with his memories, his slow, dull thoughts, and returned to his Orderly Room.

It was the 11th of April already and the sky was cloudless, the air warm and soft, caressing, as Stephen passed up the village. But coming Spring had lost all savour for him. He was thinking how once he had scrambled with Piers out of the trenches under cover of a wet, white mist. They had stumbled upon the remains of Souchez village, its broken walls coming at them out of the mist eddies. Why did he think of that now, why re-live that experience upon such a day as this?

It was because that experience had brought him into close contact with Piers and remembering it would bring him close to Piers again. It was because Piers was dead and he desired to be with him again, in memory. What was the past? It was the present, when one cared to make it so . . .

They had alighted in a demolished house, simultaneously. And simultaneously had called to each other across a broken wall. Stephen had come upon a dead *poilu,* a mere skeleton flung back across the broken wall. The long vertebrae of the neck obtruded from the empty tunic collar. The half skull lay on the ground where it had fallen. Ribs, yellow and bare, showed through the rent tunic. The man had disappeared, but the uniform remained; he could read the number upon the red epaulettes. The uniform had outlived the wearer. The man had gone; the clothes remained.

And Piers, his head showing over the wall, had held up a small black object in his hand. "A Jerry notebook," he announced, adding: "Complete with roll of Iron Cross riband."

Stephen beckoned, pointing, awed: "Look!"

Piers scrambled over and they sat among the débris side by side. And the white mist, cold and clammy, drifted about them. Between them they had found a dead man and a dead man's belongings, the one French, the other German.

"I've seen so many stiffs, said Piers, "that the sight of 'em doesn't trouble me any more."

He turned from the uniformed skeleton that reposed uneasily across the broken wall so near to them, and said: "Let's see what this Heinie wrote in his notebook." He thrust a small black object into Stephen's hand: "Here, you translate," he said. "You know the lingo."

It was a shabby little book inscribed in gold lettering, now faded, *Notizbuch*. Probably cost no more than five pfennigs, Stephen considered. He turned the damp pages. In the flyleaf, in long, sloping Gothic characters, was written: *'Fritz Muller, Unteroffizier.'* Stephen turned the leaves, translating slowly the characters blurred by the friction of the dead man's warm moving body, and later, by exposure to the weather.

Into this little book the dead non-commissioned officer Muller had put his most intimate thoughts, his poetic fancies; they jostled side by side with entries relating to his regimental duties, his pathetically small exchequer, reckoned in pfennigs.

There was a list of names, those of his *maschinengewehr*[5] crew; there was a rota of duties, an inventory of trench stores.

"Hullo, picture postcards!"

Three of them. How German! Always picture postcards in peace, and picture postcards even in times of war. They looked at them and in particular at one inscribed: *Gluckliche Stunden*. Happy hours. It depicted a German soldier in field grey. The man was smiling up at the little boy who rode joyously on his shoulder. His wife was smiling up as she walked, her arm in his. Happy days! The colouring was crude, the appeal – what was the appeal? Sentiment? Perhaps. And yet one could walk anywhere in peace time and see little family groups of common folk like that: happy, content, self-contained, complete.

"A bit of a poet, our friend," he had remarked.

And Piers had suggested: "Try a free translation." And he had done so.

The thing was headed: *Stolzenfels-am-Rhein*. Four lines of it, as though, in the arduous process of composition, some trench duty had intervened and no later chance or inclination to complete the verses had come.

"It's something like this," he said:

"On the field of honour
A German hero lies,
'For Fatherland and Kaiser,'
He murmurs, ere he dies."

"As bad as that?" Piers had grimaced. "Cripes!" He had turned the postcard of the hero over. "What's this say?"

Stephen looked. "It's from his wife. She writes: 'With many, many greetings, dearest Fritz, from Anna.'"

There was no sign of the owner of the book, which might have been dropped in stampede of flight or in confusion of attack. But there it had lain, keeping company with the dead Frenchman in the wrecked home of a shattered village.

There were so many memories of Piers, and each one of them was very dear.

But there was work to be done. Stephen addressed himself to it, to the routine work of running this company. It was the best way. It helped one to escape. He took his Field Message book and wrote:

Box Respirators. Nine (9) men of this Company have not passed gas test.
                                              S. Craig, Lt.

Notes

1. "Hound of Heaven": poem by Francis Thompson.
2. tucker: frill of lace worn around the neck.
3. knickerbockers: trousers gathered in at the knee.
4. "pipped": hit by a bullet.
5. Maschinengewehr: machine-gun.

CHAPTER XVII

1

STEPHEN tried to make conversation with the guard as the slow train clattered along the uneven track. But it was not easy, for Stephen's French was schoolboy French, while the little guard had no English at all. So Stephen sat upon a little elevated seat from which he could see the length of the swaying train peaked with its plume of smoke.

Below him, standing, the little guard held a paperbacked book close to his myopic eyes. He read Zola: *La Terre.* And he swayed with the movement of the train, absorbed.

It was leave at last, after nine months of it, and an extra clear twelve hours ahead of time. A wangled parade and expert lorry-hopping had done that. An extra day, or an extra night: either very precious. His spirits rose, and against the rhythmic music of the train he chanted to himself; and the wheels of the train beat time for him. A sense of well-being flowed in his veins. So he sang, but not with his voice, for words came nowadays with a thick harshness that no amount of self-doctoring relieved. It was in his heart that he sang, thinking of England, of Alice, of the children.

On the boat were Australians. In the bar they greeted him with: "Hullo, Canada!" and, "What's yours, Canada?" And he returned their salutations with a "Hallo, Aussies!" and, "Mine's a Scotch and a darn good long one, too."

The boat docked. How familiar the scene! Yet how unexpectedly strange. Newhaven, with rising green upon the left, the flat sweep beyond the low wharf towards Seaford. Steadfast faces looking up at one, and an English air all about, warming, intoxicating. Something solid about it all.

Then London and, circuitously, back to Brighton. Alice was now at Port Slade, her latest lodging.

2

It was past midnight when the train ran into Brighton. Exhilaration had subsided now. He had slept heavily all the way down, lank and shabby, in his corner. An elderly man awakened him as the train came to a halt. He smiled upon him with sympathy, a fatherly friendliness.

But this time Alice had hidden herself well. It was an hour before Stephen found her. A long, low row of cottages facing the harbour of the place, it was, and he came, after much searching by match-light, to the door.

And presently there was Alice at the door, peering out nervously into the blackness, amorphous in her white night-dress, furtive, fearful.

She led him into the bedroom. "This is all I have," she explained, apologetically, standing there in her night-dress, sleepy-eyed, remote, a stranger.

He saw two cots and a narrow single bed. He looked about him and said: "That'll do. I've seen worse."

He threw his Sam Browne from him. It fell, and from the further cot there was a movement, a humping of bedclothes. A tousled head emerged. He moved towards it.

She said: "No, don't wake the child. Wait till morning."

So he looked only. But the look was long. He saw, by candlelight, that the boy had grown. The baby he forgot.

"It'll do," he said, slumping into the narrow bed, "We'll have to sleep familiar."

They turned towards each other. They were weary. Soon they slept.

3

Alice asked: "What's wrong with your voice?"

Stephen shook his head: "No idea, it's been queer for some time."

They were at breakfast in the shabby little front room, with its melancholy lace curtains and patterned wall-paper, its plush chairs. Alice was feeding her man, and seeing to it that, manlike, he took that margarine ration of hers for granted, eating her own bread dry, with care, cunning.

"Surely it ought to be attended to?" she suggested, anxiously. "You're most fearfully husky. It must hurt."

Stephen nodded. "Well, yes," he admitted, "it is the very devil, especially as on my present job I have to use it so much. And sometimes it peters out altogether and I'm stuck, hopelessly."

She watched him eat, watched him as he babbled at the boy, grinning fondly and striving to evoke a demonstration where there was only excited curiosity, and the first glimmer of a new interest. Nine months had wiped out all memory of this man from the baby mind. They were strangers, but strangers bent on rediscovering each other again.

And Alice, self-contained, tranquil, watched him with seeing eyes. He looked much older, and his face was grey, his eyes pouched. And thin! How thin he was! A wreck, she thought he looked.

"You ought to be medically examined," she announced firmly.

He raised his eyebrows: "On leave?"

"Why not?"

He shrugged: "Oh well, you know, if I did report sick they'd simply think I was swinging the lead.[1] That's all."

"You can only just talk," she told him. But she said no more, for she had her method, and it was one not unknown to war; it was the method of attrition, the wearing down of opposition by persistence. Eventually, she would make him report sick. Eventually she did.

The voice went, and with the rasping huskiness came again the old hacking cough. Not even this early summer air seemed able to stay those paroxysms. In France such things had been among the minor troubles of existence but here and now they assumed a new importance and prominence from the attention paid to them, from the solicitous preparation of homely remedies: hot lemon drinks and glycerine (ruinously expensive). Chest rubbing, Friar's Balsam. He took these attentions quietly, but gratefully.

But Alice prevailed. Stephen reported sick.

4

He was standing stripped to the waist, chilled by the cold disc of the stethoscope.

"What's the trouble?" he rasped at the tall, impersonal M.O.

"The cause?" The M.O. held the clinical thermometer up to the light. "The cause? Well, we'll know better after a bacteriological examination. You'll have to go to hospital."

He patted Stephen's sharp shoulder blades. "Step on the scales," he ordered. He manipulated the bar and then: "Gee! A hundred and eighteen pounds," he announced. "Say, how tall are you?"

" Six foot," Stephen told him. And the M.O. grimaced.

"Yep, you're sure for hospital," he announced.

"But I'm on leave," Stephen rasped at him. "On leave from France."

The M.O. had now seated himself and was writing, cigarette in mouth: "Forget it," he said.

Stephen got into his clothes. He was vaguely alarmed. A hundred and eighteen pounds. What was that? It was eight stone six. And he had weighed over twelve! The M.O. looked up. Calm, matter of fact, he seemed.

"Ever take your temperature?" he asked. "No? Well, I guess you've been running one for months. You're a hundred and two right now."

5

But Stephen did not go into hospital. The bacteriological test was negative. He was boarded and passed as fit for home service only. So it was that on a warm June day he walked from Seaford station to the south camp that lay in a fold of the downs ramparted from the sea by the green flank of the cliffs.

6

Alice had found a cottage, a little workman's cottage that had passed through the hands of an artist. The Croft had been homely, then beauty had been bestowed upon it, and now, neglected, it was making a wild beauty of its own. It had a little garden, unkempt, but friendly. An old pear tree dominated it.

The rooms of the little place were small, dark and damp, for it lay cupped in a hollow, surrounded by rolling pasture. Beech trees, old and mellow, looked down upon it.

A hand pump supplied spring water, and it was cold and sweet. Very sweet it tasted after the chlorinated water of France. Humble it was, primitive, unadorned. Yet for Alice it possessed one supreme quality: independence of landladies. Here she could be her own mistress. Moreover, Stephen, thirty-seven miles away, would be able to come sometimes, on weekend leaves, by cycle, by push-bike.

7

When they had found The Croft, empty and neglected, forgotten in its little hollow, and had secured it at six shillings a week, it seemed that half their troubles were over.

But furniture? How were they to buy furniture? Stephen carried in his pocket several curt intimations from his bank; they drew his attention to his overdraft. And still the cheques came through from France, from the field-cashier. One after another. Was it possible he had spent so much out there? It was cash spent and forgotten, but it was cash gone, cash to be repaid from future pay.

Alice was shabby; she needed clothes, underwear; the children were shabby; they needed clothes, underwear. But the cottage needed furniture more than Alice or the children needed clothes, more than Stephen needed kit. How to find it? Relatives? No.

"Nothing would induce me to ask," Alice declared.

Stephen was glad. "I'm with you there," he agreed. He still had his memory of the reaction of a kinsman to a request for money. Never again!

8

But the money for the cottage came, and the manner of its coming was along the route of the improbable.

Stephen had taken train for the Sussex village with three days' leave to run before he was due at the Reserve Battalion. He had drawn a cheque, and it was the last he could draw until payday.

He felt desperate. There were men, he considered, earning £20 a week in munitions; there were households, he had heard, where the combined wartime incomes had soared to over £40 a week, households wherein a pre-war income of £5 a week had been considered opulence. And these people were living riotously, were buying unwonted luxuries: grand pianos, whippets, gramophones.

That was the trouble: he was not free to earn money. He was in the Army. Tied. Impotent.

And the cottage had to be furnished; Alice had to be moved in. No money. Yes, here he was, riding first-class, wearing the King's uniform, the uniform of a commissioned officer, and he was harder pressed than the man who greased the wheels revolving under his feet.

He turned over the problem in his mind but found no solution to it. He walked the three miles from the little station, and entered the empty cottage. He passed from little room to little room, calculating.

What was the minimum? Beds were an essential: two at least. A table and chairs, and some sort of chest of drawers. For the floors? Have to let 'em go.

He passed into the tiny brick-floored kitchen. The range had been wrenched from its place: there was no cooking apparatus whatsoever.

What a lot was needed! Another table here, a couple of chairs, cooking utensils, a stove, china, knives and forks. He suddenly remembered that they had linen. That was something. Yes, and they had brought their silver back with them. Not so bad.

How much could it be done on? He stood there trying to estimate the cost. But it was beyond him. He knew nothing of prices.

He left the cottage and cut across the fields. The day was hot. As he went he debated with himself. He was very lonely.

Every problem had its solution. Then this problem could be solved. Couldn't see it? Perhaps not, but it was there. Somewhere. What bunk! He hadn't any money, had no chance of getting money, could never, never ask for money.

Stephen the Optimist and Stephen the Realist, arguing.

Meanwhile there was Alice waiting in her lodgings, where the shillings melted, waiting for word from him, for her fare, for her tiny home.

He halted in a lush meadow full of languorous summer odours. He slipped the belt clasp, loosened his tunic, flung himself upon the grass. Great idle clouds drifted, white and opulent, across the blue sky. He lay, head clasped on hands, watching them. Floating continents and isles, monstrous and grotesque faces, moving across the high sky, beautiful, untroubled, serene.

But the solution?

There was none. Stephen the Realist asserted it with malice. But Stephen the Optimist held fast. It would come. No good reading the conditions of the present into the future, you know. The kaleidoscope twisted, and there you were: new computations, fresh avenues. Hope.

He scrambled up and walked slowly on. He came to the village, to the grey church, to the sleeping station.[2] The last train had just gone.

Cogitating one problem in the meadow, he had created another for himself: he had scarcely sufficient money for a night's lodging. And, even so, it was precious money.

A bed in some cottage, perhaps? Cheaper than the inn. He entered the general store. Behind the counter a trim woman glittered at him from behind gold-rimmed glasses. No, she knew of no such cottage. But the lieutenant's face seemed familiar. Ah, yes, hadn't he stayed at the Tudor house – years ago? Of course, that was it. But they had left the district, those people. Well, this was too bad.

He stood there, fascinated by her brightness and air of efficiency. She cocked her head at him, birdlike.

"Why not give us the pleasure?" she invited.

Stephen coloured. "You mean . . .?" he began.

"Yes," she interjected, "we should be proud to have you. An officer, back from France."

Stephen said: "Thank you very much. Thank you."

One problem solved, at least. He passed through the counter trap and found himself in an rambling old-world house that breathed peace, prosperity. Serene and mellow it was.

Stephen, his hostess insisted, must rest. He looked tired. Ill. Dear, oh, dear, this war. Yes, he must rest until noon the next day and then quietly take the train to London.

She took him to her garden that was ringed by a high brick wall. She set a chair for him among the flowers, beneath a tree; she carried to him a cooling drink. There was no doubt she liked having this guest. As for Stephen, he accepted it all with simple gratitude, saying little.

But next morning, when he was again in the garden, as she had determined he should be, she came to him, shy and embarrassed, stood before him, glittering down at him.

"You know," she started in the tone of kindly condescension used with children, "you aren't only ill: you're worried."

Stephen admitted it. She cocked her neat head.

"Money?" she suggested. "Is it money?"

"Yes, money," Stephen admitted, with like directness.

"Then you must let me lend you some," she began, in a nervous little rush, searching in her kind, honest mind for tactful words. "Yes, you must allow me to lend you some. Be your banker."

"Thank you, you're really kind." Stephen looked up into the radiant face beaming down upon him. A woman he had never seen, so far as he could remember; a woman upon whom he had no claim of blood or tie of sentiment, and she opened her purse to him. And he had accepted, as a child accepts, simply and without protestation.

"It's settled, then," she declared, radiant. "Now, the question is, how much do you require?"

And Stephen said: "Fifteen pounds."

Had he meant to say fifteen pounds? Why fifteen pounds? Oh, yes, that was what he had calculated in the cottage: his minimum.

And when she handed him the money she said nothing of repayment. And Stephen made no promise to repay. Neither condition nor pledge was made.

So his problem, his insoluble problem, was solved. Alice could be moved into the cottage. Alice was to have her heart's desire, a place of her own again. Not much of a place but still, a home, a home of sorts. She would move about there with a light heart, happy because there would be no one to complain about the boy, about the baby. The dark shadow of the last landlady would have passed.

So Stephen the Optimist triumphed and Stephen the Realist took thought. Among the realities, it seemed, must be reckoned golden hearts.

Notes

1. "swing the lead": to feign illness, try to shirk.
2. sleeping station: these were like hostels, set up for men who were on leave and either traveling to the front or leaving it (Prof. J. Vance).

CHAPTER XVIII

1

STEPHEN sat on his cot in his quarters in the lines of the Reserve Battalion. He was reading a letter, a letter from Bob England. And he was thinking of another letter he had read from Bob England. Then he had been in France, and Bob here. Now the positions were reversed.

He wrote:

In the field.

Dear Craig,

Just a few lines. We are out at rest after a fearful grilling. I went down with some trouble with my back, lumbago, I think, but I did not make Blighty with it. I'm a bit too old for this, I'm afraid. I've had my bellyful. It drags and drags. And friends go. I've lost so many. I hope you are now out of it. I shan't have any friends left soon, at this rate. Believe me, Ferguson's Landing would look good to me now. But I must stop, have got to clean up, and I'm tired before I start in.

Yours sincerely,
Bob England.

A changed Bob England, this, a disillusioned Bob England, a Bob England sticking it out, like so many more, because there was nothing else to be done, all enthusiasm gone. Stephen's heart went out to him, somewhere there in France. Not difficult to see it all: the little man of fifty, in the ranks and regretting the folly that had brought him there. A little man drawing on an exhausted vitality, struggling along. No more glamour or brave masquerade of the dyed moustache. That which had been worn with so heroic a gesture was now worn like a clown's motley, a mockery in the presence of tragedy. Poor Bob. Stephen folded the flimsy sheet and made his way to the ante-room.

Life in the Reserve Battalion went sluggishly through each day's routine. These men, who loafed in the deep armchairs, reading the illustrated journals, gossiping, playing bridge, wore an air of boredom. Yet they had once been keen, enthusiastic. And now? Fed up!

The Reserve revealed no enthusiasm in the ranks nor any among the officers of it. There was the routine round; they did it, conscientiously, but without any driving enthusiasm. They lived for London. Wangling had become an art, practised with skill and cunning. Leave warrants were its prizes.

There were the officers on the cadre,[1] well-pleased men who, having done their bit, knew when they were well off. They mostly sported gold stripes.[2] They did not like life in the Reserve; but less they cared about the prospects of France and the trenches.

And there were other officers who drifted in from hospital to carry on until put again on draft. Some stayed many months and were glad to stay; others disappeared after a few weeks. And they went uncomplainingly, but also without enthusiasm.

You might suspect a dry rot in the Reserve Battalion, might see it as a simulacrum of the living organism, a lifeless thing; in this view there might be justification. The Reserve Battalion had no soul.

What, then, was amiss with it? It was composed of war-weary men, war-weary officers, and a sprinkling of scrimshankers, lying low, getting through as easily as might be.

2

In the ante-room a grey-haired captain came, smiling, up to Stephen.

"D'you care to sit in on a game of bridge?" he asked. But Stephen did not care. Neither did he care to take a drink. No. It was best to go T.T.[3] from the start. There was that furniture to be paid for. And, by the same token, there was no money to be hazarded at cards.

A lank subaltern said in an aside to Stephen: "He thought you were an easy mark."

Stephen didn't understand. "Whom d'you mean?" he asked.

"The M.O.," the thin man grinned. "You watch for yourself. There are two of them on the cadre, and they always ask a fellow just back from hospital to sit in, or some fellow just gazetted.[4] I'll say it's a bit too hot."[5]

"How d'you mean?" asked Stephen, still mystified.

"Holy smoke! Can't you understand? They win right along. Oh, I don't say they're crooks. But I'll sure say they skin the babes and make a darn good thing out of it."

Stephen looked across the room. An awkward youngster in brand new uniform, ex-N.C.O. stamped upon him, was diffidently sitting in on a new game.

3

Stephen discovered that light duty in a Reserve was a licence to loaf. No parades, no physical jerks, practical immunity from work.

But presently he found himself officer commanding the Casualty Company. And even so there was little but the veriest routine work. The monotony wearied him. He was preoccupied with the payment of his debts; he lived for weekend leaves, when he could escape, and, trudging his thirty-seven miles by bike, spend a few happy hours in the little cottage with Alice and the children.

In the ante-room the talk was always of London, of wild nights, of girls. The gramophone ground out the melodies of *The Maid of the Mountains.* It ground out *Dear Old Pal O'Mine.* It became a torment. There was some boozing.

Yes, there was a dry rot in the Reserve, and not so far below the surface. And how could it be otherwise? They were men housed and fed and given immunity from the toil of the open market. And they had not enough work to do, or work interesting enough to keep them keen. Their best they had, most of them, already given. Now they were giving their second best. Sometimes, their third best.

4

The summer sun blazed down on the camp, on baked parade grounds, on corrugated iron roofs of the lines, set there in a geometrical pattern on the green flank of the cliff.

And now a band boomed, and away went a draft, out of the camp, down the trim roads of red-brick villas to the railway station. Boom! Boom!

But indifferent men. And indifferent populace. Drafts, what were they? The town, thriving on the military, had seen so many of them. If some went, others came. The town was prosperous. The Canadians had made it prosperous. The town hated the Canadians, but it dissembled its hate. The Canadians were unaware of it, moving about, friendly, smiling.

Men moved about the lines languidly, doing fatigues; on the sweltering parade grounds battalions went through their evolutions, moving automatically at the bark of commands. Sick of drill they were, and those who drilled them were sick of drill, of parades, of all routine.

And bugles sounded in the still air throughout the day. Once or twice the Last Post blared significantly before dusk; from the cemetery it sounded. And it was a wail, plaintive and soul-chilling, a farewell, and a farewell without hope. Hopeless and final.

5

The adjutant was busy, too busy to prosecute. He tossed the papers across the Orderly Room table to Stephen.

"It's a clear case of desertion," he explained. "The man got across to Ireland on a forged pass; he's been drilling Sein Feiners[6] in a Dublin cellar."

Stephen took the papers. Yes, a clear enough case. Where was the prisoner? He was in the guardroom. He must be paraded to the M.O., and certified as physically fit to undergo imprisonment.

The grey-haired M.O., feet on table, shook his head.

"Can't certify him," he objected, pushing the form back. "V.D. Syph."

Very well. The trial must wait. The man must go to hospital. Obviously.

There were four men in the guard room, and the four had each one and the same complaint. They objected to the deserter; they feared contagion. And. there, in that place, they were unable to protect themselves against the infected man.

And the man himself, young, alert, truculent, complained. He had been kept a fortnight there already, awaiting trial. And now another chancre on his leg!

Yes, time to get the poor devil into hospital.

But now more trouble. The man was under arrest and awaiting court martial; therefore the hospital would have none of him. But neither would Justice deal with him. Meanwhile he rotted, there in the guard room.

"My job," snapped the M.O., "is to certify him if he's fit to undergo imprisonment. Well, he isn't. I've reported the case to the hospital. It's up to them."

The M.O. played his cards according to regulations, just as he played his bridge according to Dalton. He played according to the written rules. But perhaps there were other rules, the unwritten ones. Officially, he was correct, and with that he was satisfied. Something must be done, for the prisoner was upon a 'Morton's Fork':[7] on the one prong, no trial for the diseased; on the other, no cure without trial and sentence.

So Stephen drafted a letter and took it to the prisoner and obtained his signature to it. And he took the letter to the Colonel. The Colonel spluttered. Within six hours the Brigadier was in the lines.

Then an ambulance came and the prisoner vanished.

6

The Padre is indignant and in the ante-room speaks his mind like a man. It is encouraging immorality to provide men going on leave with prophylactics; it is putting evil suggestions into their minds. It is countenancing wickedness. Yes, yes, it is shameful, wrong, utterly wrong.

A meagre little man is the Padre, with sallow face and dark, brooding eyes. An insignificant Savonarola,[8] burning himself up with zeal for righteousness. He cannot get away from this thing, this monstrous thing. And sometimes, as he expostulates, walking with nervous steps up and down the ante-room, tears come to his eyes, so upset is he.

But the Army ignores him. In the huts in the lines wisdom has seen fit to deal brutally with brutal reality. There are notices there, in large block characters, and they admonish the troops: Keep your conscience in your pants.

But then, if men will not do that? Which is the better way: to leave them to take their chances of disease or to arm them against it? Exactly; that is it.

The Padre will not temporise. Right is right; sin is sin. These boys will be morally ruined, even if they escape disease. Yes, they will go back from the war, this war of righteousness, morally ruined.

From a deep armchair in the corner comes another voice. It cuts across the Padre's, so that he is suddenly silent, fingers to lips. It is the grey-haired M.O., refreshed and replenished by a profitable rubber.

"There are plenty of you holy men at Cherry Hinton Hospital," he sneers.

The padre looks at the speaker, and it is as though he has been struck across the face. Then the tears come to his eyes. He looks around as though taking upon himself the guilt of these lost sheep of the fold, then walks from the room without a word. The M.O. has not made himself more popular. Oh, no. After all, the little Padre, damn it, meant well. Sincere as hell.

7

There were rumours of a mighty drive to roll up the Hindenburg Line, and not all of them were latrine rumours. The drafts departed, one after the other, so that it seemed every day troops left the camp. And in the officers' mess were many newly-vacant places, and presently they were filled, were filled by shy young men in uniforms painfully new; ex-privates, ex-N.C.O.'s they were – resplendent, but just a trifle ill at ease in a new magnificence.

The smiling M.O. invited these newcomers to sit in for a game; they accepted diffidently, sat in, played and lost money. Then, one by one, they disappeared. Back to France.

What was it they said out there about the ranker officers?[9] That they always got their packets? Yes, one by one they disappeared. And if you would know the inwardness of it, why, there was *The Times*. It made things clear enough. They were about to roll up the Hindenburg Line but meanwhile the Army bled, and bled, and bled. The casualty list was now as fixed a feature in *The Times* as the stock market reports, but it was read in a different way: read with the heart in the eyes.

It was in *The Times* that Stephen saw O'Reilly's name among the killed.

What had O'Reilly said about the war, in that estaminet, the night they had got completely drunk? He had said that it was a bloody good war and he didn't mind how long it lasted. Well, it had lasted O'Reilly a lifetime.

He had his wish.

8

And Stephen did what he was told to do, mechanically. He prosecuted without enthusiasm at district courts-martial.[10] He defended men before them, acting as prisoner's friend, fighting obstinately for acquittals; getting them, with his rasping voice, his face white and drawn, the ghost of the man he had been.

Sometimes now as he crossed the parade ground he felt it swaying gently under foot. At night he coughed, and there was a pain that shot, hot and cruel, in his side. The men in the adjoining cubicles banged upon the thin partitions. He was keeping them awake, damn him.

9

But there was always leave. He lived for it.

He would set off on the old rattling machine with a prayer for a following wind, for a wind that would blow him exulting along the cliff road between Newhaven and Brighton. But the winds hereabouts were prevailing westerly winds, off the Atlantic, keen and strong. Sometimes he was blown off the machine; at other times he had to walk.

Alice was settled in now at The Croft, settled in and making do. She was three miles from the village, isolated and alone with the two children. He smuggled bully-beef to her, brought home his army blankets. They lay beneath them. Nor did their consciences trouble them.

The children were thin, but active. And the boy, how good he was, the tiny fellow, running the errands of a larger child, money clenched in tiny fist, self-reliant, reliable. It was not an easy business, this rationing.

"Do the kids get enough?" he asked.

"It's the fats that I can't get, particularly butter."

Oleo-margarine, what use was that as substitute for body-building butter? No use at all.

But there was plenty of coal. She bought it by the sack, taking in the pram the three miles, dumping the sack therein, wheeling it back again. A little woman wheeling a pram with a sack of coal, and people passing her, motors, carts, lorries. People, it seemed, had little use for a woman in a tiny cottage, a woman with two small shabby children. But they were content. Already the loan was repaid. This furniture was theirs. They were getting their finances on a firm footing.

And once when he came she told him she had found a friend. "The only people in the place who have recognised my existence," she told him.

So now often a large Daimler car stood before The Croft, and from it a dark-eyed woman beckoned Alice with a smiling face: "Come on, out you come, and bring the kiddies."

So life was more pleasant for Alice and she was grateful. Grateful in her own way, showing nothing of it, but feeling it, deep down; and returning it with a staunch friendship.

10

Yes, Stephen lived for these weekend leaves which were escape from the boredom of the Reserve Battalion.

Along the windy road he forced his old machine, counting the landmarks. Wind to Brighton, but presently, beyond Old Shoreham, huddled by its shallow river, the road would turn inland and there would be shelter. He knew it as the back of his own hand. He did not go by train, because he had no warrant and no money to spend on fares. So he pedalled, laboriously, against head winds, the thirty-seven miles.

Often it was night before he glided down the steep hill in whose shelter the old cottage stood. Once it was midnight.

11

Under a brilliant moon he pedalled along the road that winds through meadowlands where Chanctonbury Ring crowns the high hill on the western side. The full moon poured out her beauty upon the countryside; her beauty austere, yet soft and lovely as the response of a woman.

He rode steadily, the magic of the perfect night stealing upon him. The moon seemed near. Her empty face was a luminous disc riding in the clear night. The dead planet yielded the sleeping earth its dead, white light; earth fresh from the fierce contact of the male sun. The landscape, so familiar in the hard light of day, had become a magic realm filled with this soft, intoxicating radiance, unreal and dreamlike in its beauty.

Stephen was riding slowly now, passing through this strange glory of night, the beauty sinking into him. His heart sang; his feverish blood exulted. O the beauty of the earth. O the loveliness of Mother Earth.

He pedalled up the long incline towards Storrington, over the brow of the steep hill. The machine, a moment since protesting, now sprang forward in effortless momentum. The cool air blew upon his face. The low stone wall of a great park now flanked the road, and presently a rise in the ground took him up to common-land, larch-patterned. It dipped down steeply again and a hump-backed little bridge switchbacked him to a right-hand turn. The first cottages of the village were now in sight. Small and mean they were, of red brick and slate, yet in this light, reprieved until dawn of their ugliness and poverty.

Presently, towards midnight, he stood in the narrow lane; the cottage, its window dark, gleamed in the moonlight. The old pear tree in the little garden spread black branches outwards and downwards, fruit-laden. It was asleep.

He wheeled his machine into the garden. It would be necessary to waken her, to call up to her window. He had no key. He set the machine against the creeper-covered wall and stood back, head upturned to the silent window.

Behind him, where a small field rose to an ancient farmhouse, hard silhouetted against the dark sky, great beech trees spread their branches. He turned and faced them, his head up towards their branches. A nightingale had burst into full song. He stood breathless and enthralled. The magic notes ceased suddenly. From a neighbouring tree came now answering notes.

There was a catch in his throat. He stood utterly still. He felt the beat of his heart against the walls of his chest. He felt his heart expand. The music burst out afresh: passionate, urgent, unearthly. Bird to bird. He heard them, there in the dark branches of the beeches, singing in the moonlight, the one to the other, urgently, crying an imperative need; a madness and a frenzy, a love frenzy – sublime, spiritual.

The singing stopped. Those unseen birds were waiting, there upon their high perches, watchful, expectant, palpitant. Then the song came again out of the silence. It ran like a silver stream of sound out of the black rock of the silence. It gushed.

He turned and cast a pebble up at the silent window. It tinkled against the glass and fell back at his feet. And he cast small stones until her head appeared at the casement.

"Listen!" he called up to her in an urgent voice. "O listen to the nightingales!"

She peered down at him from the little window.

"Hush! Hush! Do!" she called in a low voice. "You'll wake the children."

From the dark beeches the song broke forth again, pure and perfect. But the magic had gone. Magic of moon, magic of birds.

He wheeled the machine into the darkness of the little entrance and saw her white figure flit up the narrow stairs before him. She was already in bed when he entered the room. A shaft of moonlight lay like a pool on the bare boards of the floor, and by its light he undressed.

When he got into the bed beside her she was already half asleep, an arm flung back above her weary head. He lay still beside her, for she was surely tired; most weary she would be. And presently he too slept, dreamlessly, the peaceful slumber of exhaustion.

Notes

1. "on the cadre": officially listed as part of a unit but left behind the lines during an attack; in this way the cadre could form the nucleus for bringing the unit up to strength if it suffered severe losses in the attack.
2. "gold stripes": wound stripes.
3. T.T.: tea-totalers.
4. gazetted: mentioned in despatches ('M.D.') i.e. mentioned for being promoted, showing outstanding ability, bravery, etc.
5. "too hot": i.e. too much.
6. Sein Feiner: member of the Irish Nationalist political party, which urged the Irish not to serve in the British Armed Forces.
7. "Morton's fork": a situation in which there are only two choices, of equally unpleasant consequences.
8. Savonarola: Florentine religious leader (1452 - 98). Morally extremely strict. Burnt at the stake in the Piazza della Signoria when the Florentines turned against him.
9. ranker officers: privates and non-commissioned officers were sometimes offered a commission if they were thought to have leadership potential.
10. courts martial: military tribunal. Godwin had trained as a lawyer and wrote a history of the Middle Temple (1954). All the books of Godwin mentioned in these notes are out of print, with the sole exception of *The Eternal Forest* (1994).

CHAPTER XIX

1

IT WAS noon. Stephen stood at the cottage door. The garden rustled, the November sun still gave out warmth. Across the fields, that were in stubble now, came the sound of bells from the village church, over the green meadows. But this was not the customary peal, no. This was a mad peal, wild and free. Something odd about such bell-ringing.

He listened, wondering at it. As he stood, facing the sound, he heard from the lane the rumble of a lorry and the shouts of the men riding in it. He turned. An Army lorry hurtled past. He had momentary glimpse of shouting Tommies. But it was enough. The lorry was down the lane, and the dust cloud in its wake was eddying. Those bells and these shouting men. Yes, it was enough. He dashed into the kitchen.

She stood above the ironing board, pressing down upon the hot iron, and her fair hair was moist upon her beaded forehead.

He told her that an Armistice had been declared, and commanded that she come, forthwith, to hear the carillon from the village church. He was very excited. He could not keep still. He grabbed her and kissed her, caught her round the waist and swung her from the board. But Alice was at her ironing, and she returned to it until the last small garment had been pressed, and thereafter hung upon the line to air.

But presently she was at the door, listening. She gazed out over the fields towards the square, grey tower; but she did not speak, standing there, listening, her work-stained hands folded before her, her blue eyes looking out across the fields, across the yellow fields of corn.

2

The Colonel sent for Stephen. He said: "Report sick, Craig, there's something mighty wrong with you."

And Stephen reported sick, for orders are orders. He stripped for examination, hating it, hating the man who handled him, resenting the physical exposure, the critical eyes upon his thin body.

"You'd better have a board."[1]

The examination was over. Stephen got into his clothes in silence. They were hostile, these two. Wasn't this the M.O. who played bridge rather too well? Wasn't this the smart-Alec who interfered about that V.D. case? There was some revenge in having this lean fellow there – sick.

There was the humiliation of exposed and appraised infirmity in this submission to rough vetting. The medical board decided too that there was something wrong. The thermometer told its tale. Then there was that pain in his side; worst at night, when the coughing was worst.

This time the bacteriological report came back and it was marked: *positive.* Freedom was at last in sight, and then the door closed once more.

Stephen went into hospital. They put him to bed and at night a V.A.D.[2] turned him about. She did it expertly. She spoke of pleurisy. There was a chart above his cot.

He looked about him at the rows of cots that flanked the long hutment; neat they were, and in each a man. From across the ward the face of a boy gazed from the pillow; very pink it was, with starry eyes. But when you looked down you saw that beneath bed-clothes his belly ballooned monstrously, like that of a woman far gone with child.

A New Zealander, he was, from Otago. And between long silences, he talked of what he should do once home. "It's only sun I need," he explained. "That'll put me right, but I'll never get right here."

And the sister listened, impassively. She told him not to tire himself; that he should sleep a little now, while the ward was quiet, no gramophone going. So she passed, and left him with his dreams of Otago.

But one night they placed a screen about the bed of the boy from New Zealand. And in the morning he was gone. But not to New Zealand. Not to Otago.

"What was it?" Stephen asked of the man in next cot.

"Tubercular peritonitis," he was told. "And what's wrong with you?" he added.

"Same as yourself," came the answer from white pillow. "T.B."

"T.B.? What's that?"

"Tuberculosis."

Stephen had not got tuberculosis. Oh, dear, no. He was there because of the pain in his side. Pleurisy. And because of his damnable cough, and his voice, that went back on him.

"Well, I'm glad to hear it, but you're the only man in this ward who hasn't."

And the tone of this answer brought a dark doubt into Stephen's mind. He questioned the little V.A.D., but she said that she could not stop to talk, that she was very busy. He asked a nurse what was wrong with him. And she told him to ask the M.O. when he came on his rounds.

But when the M.O. came Stephen did not ask him. He remained mute in the presence of this famous physician, for all that the Army had made of him nothing but a captain.

So it was the little V.A.D. who told him the truth in the end. She turned upon him, distressed.

"Why did you make me tell you?" she reproached. "I hate to tell the fellows. It's beastly, *beastly.*" And she went quickly away. She was very young.

Stephen accepted the sentence with bitterness.

3

But the pleurisy cleared up and he was allowed to get up. There was to be a dance in the hall of the hospital that evening, the hall that had once been the assembly room of a big girls' school.

Stephen stood by the door. The band played '*K-K-K-Katie, beautiful Katie,*' and the nurses danced with the patients, their white aprons against the hospital-blue of the men. He saw the little V.A.D. from his ward dancing madly with a tall man, smiling up at him from her five-foot-nothing.

Into what did she smile? She smiled into the eyes of the man who looked down to her. And those eyes returned her smile, glittering above the bandages of that smashed face beneath them.

How many facial cases! Noseless men, and men with gaps for mouths, and men with mutilated cheeks, criss-crossed with scars, faces moulded laboriously by the patient hands of the plastic surgeons, built up, as a modeller in clay builds up his model. But modelling, this, in human flesh. And sometimes bones. Ribs for noses. Strange, fantastic makeshifts to undo the work of war. And men, there were, with hardly any features left at all; men whose faces had been blown away. Yes, blown away. By what miracle had those shining eyes so often escaped?

This was the hospital where they dealt with facial injuries. He remembered now. He had heard of it.

4

New faces for the faceless (or for those so mutilated as to need masks, partial or complete), were made in a light room set apart for the purpose.

To this room came the men for whom the surgeons had done all that they could do. Their cunning, their skill and patience, could do much; yet there were limitations, and when these were reached surgery made way for art.

There was the man as he was, looking out from some photograph taken of the young civilian turned soldier and there, beside it, sat the man as war had left him. There was no resemblance between the two, none whatever. Yet there soon would be, for over that obliterated face, the artist would soon place a finished mask of silvered copper, a death mask for the living, and painted with such loving care, such skill, that ten yards off the deception was complete. The painted metal face might pass for flesh and blood.

How will that metal nose and forehead be kept in place upon that half-obliterated face? Like this: by eye-glasses, false moustache, false eyebrows. It may be removed at night for comfort's sake, and put on in the morning.

Dear God! Where would they go, these men with metal faces? How will their children greet them, coming for kisses? And their sweethearts, their girls? Where will they hide away? And how will it be with them ten years hence?

5

The liveliest man in the hospital lay in a surgical ward. When he wished to get out of bed he put out a tremendous arm, swung his wheelchair about, and with one mighty heave of shoulders, leapt into it. He spun the wheels and raced along the yard, his bland face all smiles, a joke for everybody. The heart and soul of the ward, they said he was, and it was true.

How many re-amputations was it? Ten. But now the left stump that had given all the trouble looked a bit better; it was going on well. Even the table, which in the end mastered the bravest spirits, had failed to break the spirit of this Canadian. He had gone, each time, smiling to the knife. What was he going to do when they were done with him?

Go back to the old job; yes, sir!

And that job ?

Driving the old Ford van, the good old 'flivver.'

Couldn't crank her now? What, not on two artificial pins? You could bet your sweet life he could crank her. Yes, sir!

But when ten amputations had become twelve, he whimpered just a little as they wheeled him off. Not much, for there was comfort in that morphia, though less comfort than before.

6

When the agony wagon, silent and efficient, bright with glittering instruments and white porcelain vessels, is wheeled into the surgical ward, all faces turn towards it. It will stop at each bed, and from it the M.O. will take this instrument or that; the nurse will hand him what he wants. Watchful and expert she is. And now and then a groan is heard, a small groan quickly suppressed.

There is a fleshy part of the hand that runs from the fourth finger to the wrist. There a man may bite as hard as he likes and do little harm, though some men bite their thumbs.

When the wagon stops before the double-emphysema case the men in the adjoining beds watch the little tube inserted in the patient's back where there is a little hole. Presently a thick yellow fluid will flow out and there will be a sickly, evil smell. This man bites his thumb, and now and then holds his breath.

When he holds his breath, forcing it to his lungs, the fluid spouts from the little tube. It is quite interesting, that. They watch, fascinated.

Double empyema: not much hope for him. But he does not know there is not much hope; he spends long periods planning for the future. His wife comes to see him, and she is young and pretty. She sits beside his bed holding his hand, shyly, for fear the other men will see and perhaps grin a little. And they see; but they do not grin, they do not grin at all.

7

The big man, who was once a lumberman, has no patience. He says: "Take the damn leg off, I'm sick of it."

But the surgeon merely smiles. Just one more little operation, only one, to make a really handsome job of it. He explains quietly just how it is with that vein that has been short-circuited. It is delicate work, he says, and requires patience: patience in surgeon, patience in wounded man.

But the big fellow is only partly mollified. He complains that at best his leg will be stiff, his occupation gone.

"And what can a gink like me do out of the bush?" he asks. But the surgeon cannot answer him, never having been in Canada.

8

A great lady comes, a great lady who was once a queen. She passes, tall and stately, through the wards, smiling on the men. And she is gone. They are interested in the passage of this lady and watch her pass. They look upon her as a curiosity. She carries no bed-pans, nor does she dress wounds expertly. But in her way she does them good. And when she has passed they are free to disarrange their beds a little; to set the gramophone a-going.

And the Commandant comes, spruce and dandified, with his ironed moustache. And he too goes, attended by the matron. These are figures from beyond the immediate world of the wards, of the men in the cots. These are diversions merely. It is the ward sister who rules that little world, and her they propitiate, fear, yet somehow nearly love. She is a dragon, yet such a dragon as might one day wag a tail.

9

The little Scottie, who has daily massage, desires to get up and walk. It is a feat he has not performed since the bullet grazed his spine. The masseuse says she thinks – though she cannot be sure – that the legs are showing signs, *just* showing signs.

So they take him under the arms and raise him and hold him upright. His legs dangle, limply. He writhes his trunk. They encourage him, shouting from their beds.

"Come on, now, Scottie, lift them feet up, lift 'em up!" imitating the voice of the drill sergeant. "Make it snappy, lad, make it snappy."

But Scottie cannot make it snappy; try as he will, these legs will not respond. They are dead legs. And dead legs they will remain. He may live a year. He may live ten years but he will never walk again.

And presently they lay him, exhausted, back upon the cot. The right leg had a little kick in it, he claims. And they agree. Yes, the right leg certainly moved a bit. No doubt about it.

10

In the T.B. ward there are no such diversions. Each patient is absorbed in his own case, his own symptoms. The nurses find it tedious work. There are men in the cots who cough a lot, and thin men who stalk about the ward, and they cough, too. No, there is no interest for the nurses in this ward, for there are no surgical cases here.

It is tedious being in the T.B. ward, hearing always the gossip of the other patients.

"My right lung's O.K., but the apex of the left is affected."

"I think I'll take my temperature."

". . . And now her people are all against the engagement and have made me promise to wait at least a year . . ."

Alabaster faces and eyes too bright, cheeks with a warm pink flush; hollow chests and sunken cheeks. Yes, the T.B.'s are an uninteresting lot. Nothing very heroic about a disease. But an unpleasant packet for all that. Perhaps even worse than a lost arm, a missing eye. Yes, worse than many wounds, this slow unseen eating of the body's tissues, the sure poisoning of the life-blood.

Besides, the T.B.'s are none too well behaved. Give them leave to go out and they come back drunk. The worst thing possible for them, alcohol. They have no self-control, none at all.

Yes, they are a bother, these T.B.'s. But there is always interest in the surgical wards. Always.

11

Stephen was boarded and marked for transport home but he had no wish to go. What about Alice and the children? Alice and the children would have to stay where they were. His pay would go on; he would be in hospital. He could assign the whole lot of it. Yes, that was true enough. There was nothing for it but to submit. He submitted.

A fortnight later he sailed out of Liverpool on a hospital ship bound for Portland, Maine.

Notes

1. a board: military review board.
2. V.A.D.: Voluntary Aid Detachment. Women volunteers who served in many capacities: nurses, clerks, cooks, etc.

CHAPTER XX

1

NINE days out, so that soon the ship, with its strange human freight, will make a landfall, will find Casco Bay somewhere along that dim arc of the horizon, and come to rest in Portland harbour.

Bringing home the débris of the war, carrying home a little of the reality of it. A ship steaming steadily, because with spine cases a man must do whatever is possible to lessen the agony of men who murmur in their swinging cots below.

Stephen has been a pariah, eating his food alone for fear that he will carry the disease to others. But, still, free to walk the decks, free to mix with all who are up and about. Yes, even free to peep into the cabin opposite where lies a man, and at liberty to make friends with him, standing in the doorway, swaying, passing a friendly word.

"How goes it today?"

He shakes his head slowly, slowly. Not so well, evidently. His eyes close. Time to go away. But sometimes he rallies, this man whose face has fallen all away, so that you can see the skull beneath the skin that is like yellow parchment, tightly drawn.

"Well, you're looking fine and dandy today, old-timer."

And he smiles slowly, pleased at the compliment but scarcely believing it in his heart. Hoping it may be true, that he is better, that he will get better day by day.

"Couple o' days," he says, speaking in his feeble voice, "an' I'll be back home. Yes, sir."

" And where is that?"

"Halifax."

"Ah, that's something – to have a home at the end of the journey. Many kiddies?"

"Three, and all boys; the eldest's ten years old. Nearly old enough to help about the place and a handy boy, sure enough. Yes, sir, he'll sure be a help when I'm up and around again."

And the weary eyes close again and the speaker becomes silent; and Stephen slips away. Has he stayed too long? Has he tired him?

Expectation fills the ship with electric excitement. Tomorrow, around sundown, they should make Caso Bay, and, before nightfall, should be tied up alongside.

2

But tomorrow morning there is to be a burial, at seven o'clock, before the patients are about. No purpose served by casting gloom upon the ship so near the journey's end.

The morning broke upon a sky of tattered cloud grey and cold; wet mist obscured the mast-heads and came coldly upon the face, wetting it. The sea heaved along the ship's side, hungrily. She rolled.

Stephen rose and dressed. He would attend the burial, this burial at sea. So he walked aft and joined the group that stood about the bier upon the after-deck.

The flag came down to half mast and there lashed angrily. A bell sounded from the ship's heart, and the rhythmic beat of her great engines stopped. She rolled in the trough.

Sailors stood beside the bier, and behind them, nurses, their white aprons a-flutter. And all eyes were upon the flag-covered mound that rested there, one end hard by the scuppers.

The old Captain began to read in a voice wind-blown, so that the solemn words rose and fell, as the ship herself rose and fell in the trough of the sea. Presently he is saying:

"We therefore commit his body to the deep, to be turned into corruption, looking for the resurrection of the body (when the sea shall give up her dead) and the life of the world to come, through our Lord Jesus Christ . . ."

Four sailors stoop swiftly and up-end the bier. It slides from beneath the flag and disappears. A bugler steps forward and the Last Post blares out across the grey waters.

A gong sounds from the ship's heart, and she stirs, her great heart beating again. She has been dead, and now, death done with, comes alive. The bunting is run up, it flaps triumphantly from the mast-head.

3

Nielson, the blond giant, is preparing; he has been preparing ever since he came aboard. His mother and his girl will be at Portland to meet the ship. One must make a show. He has blue eyes, and they are very blue indeed, and his chest is the chest of a bull. When he smiles, which is often, there is a flash of white teeth.

Every morning, up and down the swaying deck he has walked, an orderly on either side, a magnificent man, a giant. But Stephen had seen him when in his bunk, the masseuse at work upon him, and he knew that Nielson was but half a man. Two stumps he had; for legs, two moving thighs.

Every day the masseuse had been working on him. A wonderful case, Nielson's. Only three re-amputations. That is all. But he will get fat. That is the trouble with these cases. Already his belly is soft and round and full: the belly of an elderly man. He must fight that off as best he may in the years ahead or in a couple of years he will be too obese to move upon his aluminium limbs, or work the straps of the shoulder harness.

When Nielson loses balance, as he does directly the orderlies at his request release his arms, he swears softly. It will not do at all. And time is short, if that good showing is to be made at Portland.

But when he rests in the long chair he likes to talk of the future, for he is full of plans, and such grand plans they are that they might be those of a man with two whole legs to go upon.

They tell him all is ready to carry him ashore.

Carry? Like hell! Nielson is going to walk. You bet your sweet life. To hell with stretchers: keep 'em for the stretcher cases. What are those legs for, anyway, if not to walk with?

But, they explain to him, to-day the ship will tower above the low wharf of Portland dock. He could not get down that steep gangway on his aluminium pins. Not possible. But when you look into Nielson's blue eyes you know better than that. So many things are possible.

What will it be like in five years' time? Will she love him as much then, this trunk of a man, this relic? And Nielson, how will it go with him when the glamour has departed, facing the struggle legless, maimed?

Like a fantastic robot he jerks his monstrous limbs, using his mighty shoulders. Better every day. And today? Marvellous! He smiles. They'll hardly know that he has lost his legs, those women, when they see him come down the gangway on these pins.

4

Yes, for all these men Portland was the first glimpse of home, as it were. Soon they would be in Canada; meanwhile there was America, and the difference seemed small.[1]

But for Stephen each day widened the distance between himself and Alice and the children. It was exile for him. Alice and the children might have returned to Canada with him and in Ferguson's Landing have awaited his discharge from hospital. But there was no money to bring them there, no money at all.

Towards evening word went round that land was in sight. Stephen went to look. Yes, there it was, twinkling of lights across the gathering darkness of the cold waters.

He went below. The man whose wife waited at Halifax would be pleased. He would take him the news. The cabin door was closed. He opened it. The bunk was empty.

5

There is the town band on the wharf below blaring a welcome. And there are women, faces upturned. Yet it is dark and it is raining. Gifts sail through the air, fall on the deck or are caught by outstretched hands; all sorts of things they throw up in their enthusiasm, in the kindness of their hearts, and many of them fall back into the water of the harbour.

The wharf is indeed far below the mighty height of the great ship's flank. A pygmy wharf, it seems, as they gaze down on it. And presently the gangway is out. And it is steep.

Too steep?

Nielson looks at it and braces himself. No, by cripes! not too steep. He grabs the handrail and moves slowly forward – slowly, like an automaton. And so he goes to his mother, to his sweetheart, walking like a man, like a man who goes upon two legs . . .

At Liverpool there had been no demonstration They had merely embarked, and that was all. True, in each cabin there was a letter in the hand of the King, thanking them, wishing them God-speed; but beyond that courtesy there was nothing.

But how hearty the welcome here!

They filed to the waiting train, or were carried to it, and it was white and very beautiful. Beside each cot were gifts: books, fruit, chocolate, cigarettes, everything a man might care about with a journey to last six days ahead of him.

So presently they steam out and settle down.

"Better turn in," says the sister.

Yes, that snow-white bed-linen, how inviting it was!

The long hospital train gathered speed and thundered through the night but above its thunder there came another sound, the whimper of the youngster in the end cot. Each movement of the speeding train tortured his shattered spine.

6

Stephen arrived in Vancouver six days later. The air had tinged his face with bronze and though he was lean, he looked a healthy man.

It would be a year's job, they told him at the hospital, before he was right. He must go up into the mountains, live in a tent, give the lung tissue time to heal. Then he would be as well as before. Well, nearly as well: an arrested case.

Meanwhile he was free to go about the city, and it was as he strolled slowly along Granville Street one morning that he saw a familiar figure ahead of him. Yes, it was the Major all right. But a Major shorn of his dignity, a Major in store-suit[2] and trilby hat. And suddenly he realised that, after all, the Major was a very ordinary little man. They shook hands.

"Well, sir, I suppose you are tickled to death to be back at your old job again?"

"I'm not back at my own job," the Major told him. "They've handed my job over to another man, a man who stayed at home. I'm teaching again. Well, I guess it's no use complaining, but it's kinder hard to be patient with the kiddies now. Besides, I'm down on my pay. We're moving to a smaller house. You must come along out some time and see the family."

Stephen promised he would come, but he knew that he would not. Men say: "You must come along. What about tomorrow? The day after, then? Well, the day after that?" Or they say: "Come along some time," casually. And there is a world of difference.

Stephen asked after the fellows of the old battalion, but it seemed that the Major, strangely, had lost interest in them. He didn't know, he said, where they were, what had become of them.

"What happened to Grant?" Stephen asked. The Major thought a while.

"Grant, Grant," he cudgelled his sluggish memory. "Wasn't Grant killed on the Somme? Oh, no. I recollect now. He was killed in London, in the Gotha raid.[3] Yes, Grant was killed by a bomb."

But Grant was not killed by any bomb. The Major, it transpired, was thinking of another man. Grant survived. He always said he would. And he had, miraculously.

So Stephen left his old Company Commander, and he was glad to leave him. Poor old MacDonald, that was not him walking so sprucely down Granville, it was merely his simulacrum. Major MacDonald had been killed on the Somme, killed stone dead. And there was his ghost, his spook, walking along in the sunlight.

Yes, there were more ways than one of killing a man. The Major proved that, walking along the crowded street, and doing a job of work. Demobilised.

Major Malcolm MacDonald. Killed on the Somme, and killed every day for a week or more. R.I.P.

Then Stephen got his orders, and a leave warrant, and took train for the mountains, for the mountains that were to cure him. Well, nearly cure him.[4]

Notes

1. This theme of the Americanization of Canada is developed in *Columbia or the Future of Canada* (Keegan: London, 1928, 95 pp).
2. store-suit: a suit bought 'off the rack,' not made-to-measure.
3. "the Gotha raid": German bomber attack on London.
4. Godwin spent part of 1919 in the Sanatorium at Balfour, B.C. (on the Arrow Lakes).

EPILOGUE[1]

STEPHEN climbed down from the Agassiz local at Ferguson's Landing and looked about him. Nothing had changed. The settlement, it seemed, still slept as it had slept five years ago. The face of the world had changed, and all his life with it, but the settlement was untouched. The bullfrogs chanted still in the damp places by the wide river now that it was spring again. And from up the lane he could hear the clang of an anvil in the smithy. That would be Andy Mac.

After all, what had the war to do with Andy? Andy had been wise.

He thought of the Major, Andy's brother, pattern of patriotism, as he had seen him a year ago, in Vancouver; a neurasthenic, pitiable and tragic, returned from the war to be promoted down in his civilian job, broken, yet pensionless, uncompensated.

Yes, Andy had been wise. He had said: "What the hell is the war to me?" And had answered own question with a "Nothing." And there he was now, up there at the forge, a man at useful work.

A strange face regarded the newcomer curiously, there beside the depot door. Little Tom Preedy must have gone his way, since a new man reigned at the depot?

He turned, and nodding to the stranger, took the old road. It was familiar, yet strange. They had built a granary beside the depot; they were learning cooperation at last, as Old Man Dunn had preached it at them all those years ago. Old Man Dunn, whom they had called the Sage, mockingly, behind his burly back.

Old Man Dunn was gone. No talk now, if he should turn in at the familiar picket gate; no milk, warm from the cow, from the hands of little Mrs. Dunn; no milk from a woman smelling of the byre.

Still, no harm to look at the place. Plenty of pleasant memories it had of the old days.

He walked on slowly, mind inward-turned, so that he scarcely noticed the forest he once had loved. He became aware of a man upon the road, and of the tap-tap of a stick upon its surface. He saw a man walking towards him with the uncertain footsteps of the blinded, using his heavy stick; his eyes were covered with black lenses. Something familiar in that figure? Yes!

"Heggerty!" he called.

"Who's that?" Heggerty asked, turning his head in the direction of the voice.

"It's Craig; I'm just out of hospital," he announced. Then he began: "Are you . . . ?"

"Yep, I'm blind. Got mine in the Salient." He swung his head about, questingly. "Here, let's sit down a bit," he suggested. They moved to the grassy bank.

Stephen said: "I'm sorry, Heggerty. By God, I'm sorry." And he added, remembering the tribe of Heggerty: "And the wife and kids, how are they making out?"

"Not so bad. You see, I get a full pension. It's not so bad as it might be. Back in the bush, we are, three miles, and now I know the trail."

A changed Heggerty, this, a Heggerty changed by suffering into a finer man than the old feckless Heggerty who would boast so down there at Blanchard's store.

"I oughter had the V.C. Yes, sir. But they done me outer it."

A changed Heggerty? Well, perhaps not so much changed after all. Stephen asked: "What about Bob England? Is he back on the old place?"

"Him? Why, he was killed at Passchendaele. Didn't you know that?" And there is scorn in the voice. This is not news; it is history. No, Stephen didn't know. Poor Bob. So keen from the first on this war; then, afterwards, weary of it. And now killed by it. Poor Bob.

"Many changes in the place?" Stephen asked after a pause, for he could not share Bob England with this man.

"Not many," Heggerty told him. "But a few. There's a bunch of Japs come in." He pointed up the road with his thick stick of the blind man; "Japs are in Old Man Dunn's place."

"Has anybody had news of him?" Stephen asked, a thousand happy memories flooding in.

Heggerty nodded. "Why, sure," he answered. "Seems like he went off sudden. On the train, on his way home. They buried him 'way back in Ontario somewheres. I don't know nuthin' about Mrs. Dunn."

Old Man Dunn dead. Well, well.

After a pause, Stephen asked: "Is old Stein still around?"

"You don't know nuthin', it seems," said Heggerty, impatiently. "No, old Stein done himself in. They found him on the wires of his own fence; he'd fixed his shotgun up with string and blown his head off. They sed he was a spy. These bastards back here thought everybody was spies, but it got on the old boy's nerves. And then they got the policeman to come up from Carlyle. It was then he done it."

"And Blanchard?" Stephen asked. He might as well know if all the inhabitants were dead, he considered, bitterly.

"He's in his store. And I'm going there now. He tries to do me, now I can't see nuthin'. But I'm a darn sight too smart for a poor son-of-a-bitch like him."

The same old Heggerty. But changed, because now you could pity him with self-respect, whereas before, you felt ashamed of it.

Stephen got up. "Well, I'll get along," he said.

Heggerty rose slowly, holding his thick stick before him. "Put me right," he requested. "See you again," he added. But of Stephen he asked no question. What was another man's trouble to him?

Stephen went along the road; he passed Old Man Dunn's place and where the ancient house had stood he saw a new house, trim and stark and yellow against the green. The Japs had made it so. And where the old orchard had been were rows of strawberry plants. He saw a little yellow woman moving among them.

So they had cut down the old orchard, and it was gone. Yes, everything was gone. Everything, that was to say, except the old Gravenstein, away up there in the little meadow, standing in its corner, like an old man taking the sun. It would be in blossom now.

Dear Gravenstein! He would climb the fence and lie in the long grass, just as he used to do after a long day's work in the bush; and he would see the evening sky again through the green leaves, through the pink blossom. How often in the past had he come with an empty sack and gone home with a full one, eating apples from the pockets of his jeans, munching them contentedly?

The lane curved about the bend, and he came upon the place.

The Gravenstein had gone.

He stood for some moments there, looking at the spot where it had spread its branches, and then walked slowly down the lane.

After five years how would the old place look, the little clearing that was the beginning of his ranch? Neglected, surely, changed.

And so he came upon it, snug upon its little bench high above the river, with the forest standing behind it, looking down upon it. He stopped and looked upon it.

How could he have forgotten? He had made those graftings just before he went and now, after five years, here was this young orchard in full blossom. He moved slowly forward, and the whispering grass parted before his feet, and after them, bruised but living, rose again. And he considered, standing there among the trees.

The old apple tree was dead but it yet lived, for in the sap of this grassy orchard was the sap of the old Gravenstein, renewed. And he saw in the tree, in the apple tree hewn down and dead, a symbol. It was dead yet it lived. Of what was it the symbol? It was the symbol of life, and of death. It was the symbol of birth, growth, and decay; and, thereafter, of rebirth and renewal.

But the men, the dear ones whose remembered faces had for ever vanished from the valley, whose voices were forever silent, those strong voices that had called to their straining teams, or from among the great trees of the forest, how could it be that they should live again?

Yet, surely, it must be so. The tree was life, thrusting up from the dark womb of earth, spreading wide branches heavy with fruit. It was the Tree of Life, of Life Everlasting.

The sun sank below the rim of the forest and a soft light glowed mysteriously out of the shadows. It was evening. He moved among his trees, caressing them. How they had flourished! How they would grow, year by year, giving forth blossom, and after blossom, fruit!

What was he but a branch upon a tree, fruit upon a bough? And that tree, the Tree of Life, of life eternal, of life and renewal, out of sin, and suffering, and death.

They were not dead then, those dear remembered ones? Ah, no. They were not dead. They lived. And here was the promise of their rebirth and renewal. The ancient Gravenstein had gone up with the crackle of fire but the tree endured, here in this young orchard; here and now, where day itself marched steadfastly to the death of night. Yet night would bring a new day, born of the darkness, born of the death of other days.

He turned and faced the west and its fading light shone upon his face, lending it dignity and a sweetness. He smelt the fragrance of the earth, the sweet earth that he honoured in his heart. And he thought: Soon the dew will form above the earth so that the earth will drink, and hidden roots suck in new life.

And then he went.

Once, he turned, as the trail, descending, lifted a green curtain between him and the orchard. And, turning, he saw the branches of the last tree visible, pink with blossom, ghostly in the gathering twilight. It burnt like a pale pure flame, unwavering, very still in the evening air.

He raised his hand to it, in salutation and farewell.

THE END.

Notes

1. Many of the characters in the Epilogue are well-developed in *The Eternal Forest:* Preedy, Old Man Dunn, Heggerty, Bob England, Blanchard, Mrs. Corley. To order *The Eternal Forest* see my site (www.godwinbooks.com) ot the ad at the end of *Why Stay We Here?*

Left: Elizabeth Godwin (1849 - 1911), George Godwin's mother, and (above) his father, James (1845 - 1893).

Donald Godwin (1880 - 1922), with his wife, Jean, and two children, Kennedy (1911) and Frances (1912 - 1992), mother of the editor of Godwin Books (www.godwinbooks.com). Donald fought in the Boer War and appears briefly in Chapter I of Why Stay We Here? *He signed up to fight in World War I with the rank of Major. Once in England he was furious to find that if they deigned to send him to France he would have to relinquish his rank as a major and go as a captain. He refused this arrangement and remained in England. Donald died in 1922 when, as passenger in a neighbour's car, the car tried to race (and cut off) an Interurban tram at Arbutus and 33rd St. Sadly the tram won the race; ironically, the driver emerged unscathed.*

*Dorothy Godwin (1885 - 1979),
George Godwin's wife ('Alice' in* Why
Stay We Here?*). They were married in
Canada in 1911.*

*Lieutenant Commander Geoffrey Allfree,
R.N.V.R., R.B.A., (drowned in action
October 1918). Close friend of George
Godwin. Godwin named his second son,
Geoffrey, after him. Allfree was a distinguished war painter and doubled this
task with command of a gunboat; he was
tragically drowned a week before the
signing of Armistice.*

*Richard ("Dick") Godwin (1887 -
1964). Another of George's brothers who
fought in the Canadian Army in World
War I. Dick saw action in (at least) the
Fricourt sector of the Somme Offensive
and figures prominently in* Why Stay We
Here? *(Chapter II, 5) as a kind of 'Deus
ex Machina' for getting George a commission in the Canadian Army. In Godwin's
private journal (located at the end of the
1994 version of* The Eternal Forest*)
George describes Dick thus: "Wilful,
wild Dick! Instinctively he turned
towards the open spaces of the world;
streets and offices are not for such as he.
Men like him belonged to times of Elizabethan England." Dick ran a plantation
in Samoa during the 1930s, then moved
to New Zealand at the outbreak of World
War Two. He was a redoutable amateur
boxer: "Bulldog Godwin."*

Looking north to Golden Ears Mountain from near 'Ferguson's Landing' (today's Maple Ridge).

Port Haney, 1908, looking downriver. Blanchard's General Store was much like this one, and located nearby. It has since disappeared (see page 21).

LAND & WATER

Vol. LXIX. No. 2965. [XX]　　THURSDAY, APRIL 26, 1917.　　[REGISTERED AS] PUBLISHED WEEKLY

Canada on Vimy Ridge

"An expert wrote marvellously in Land & Water, *expounding the theory of war, explaining the strategy of the western front, masterly expositions that wrought design and significance out of seeming anarchy" (see page 91).*

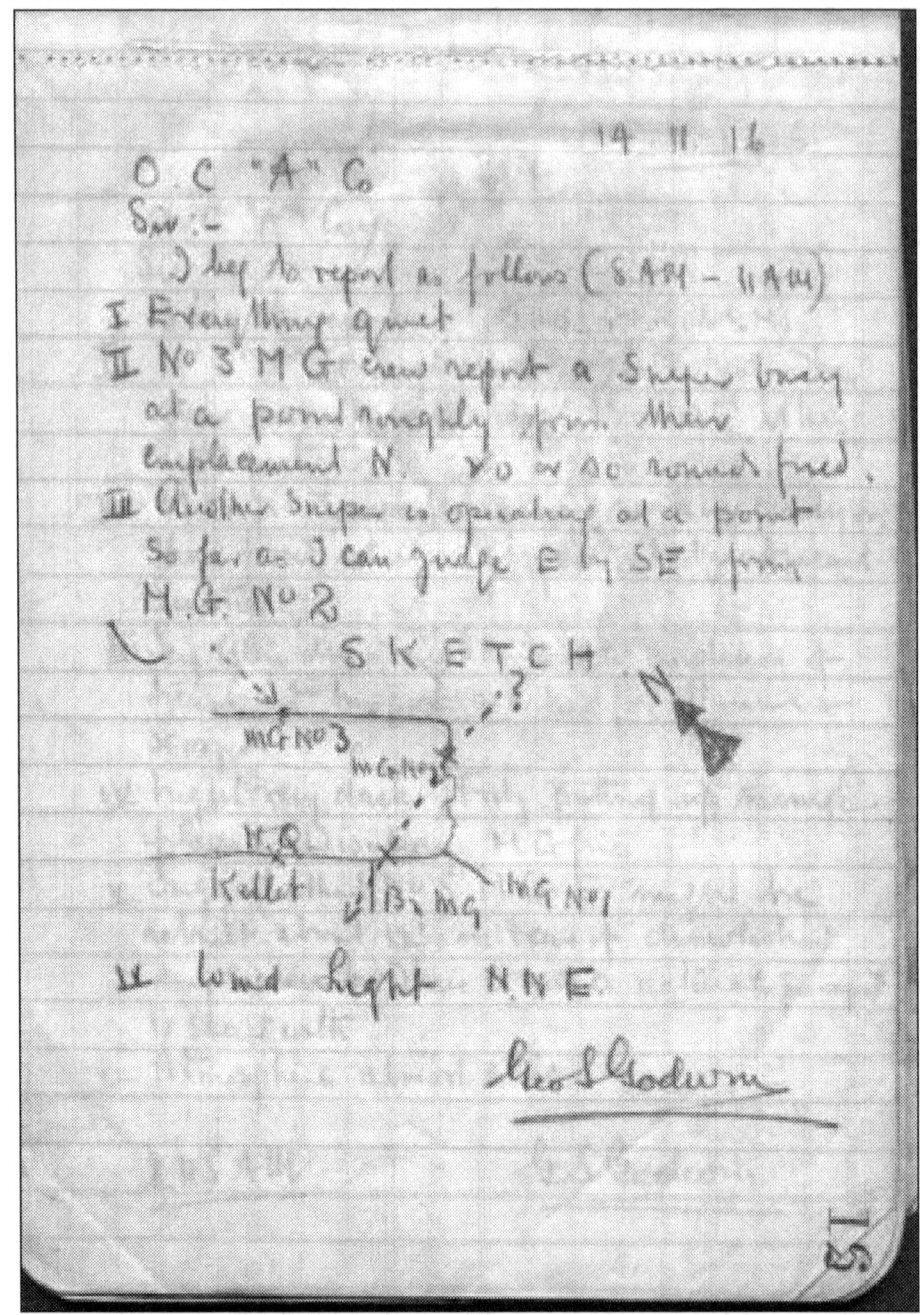

A page from Godwin's Officer's Field Book, attempting to pinpoint enemy sniper activity (see page 54). Courtesy of Mr. William Godwin, one of George's sons.

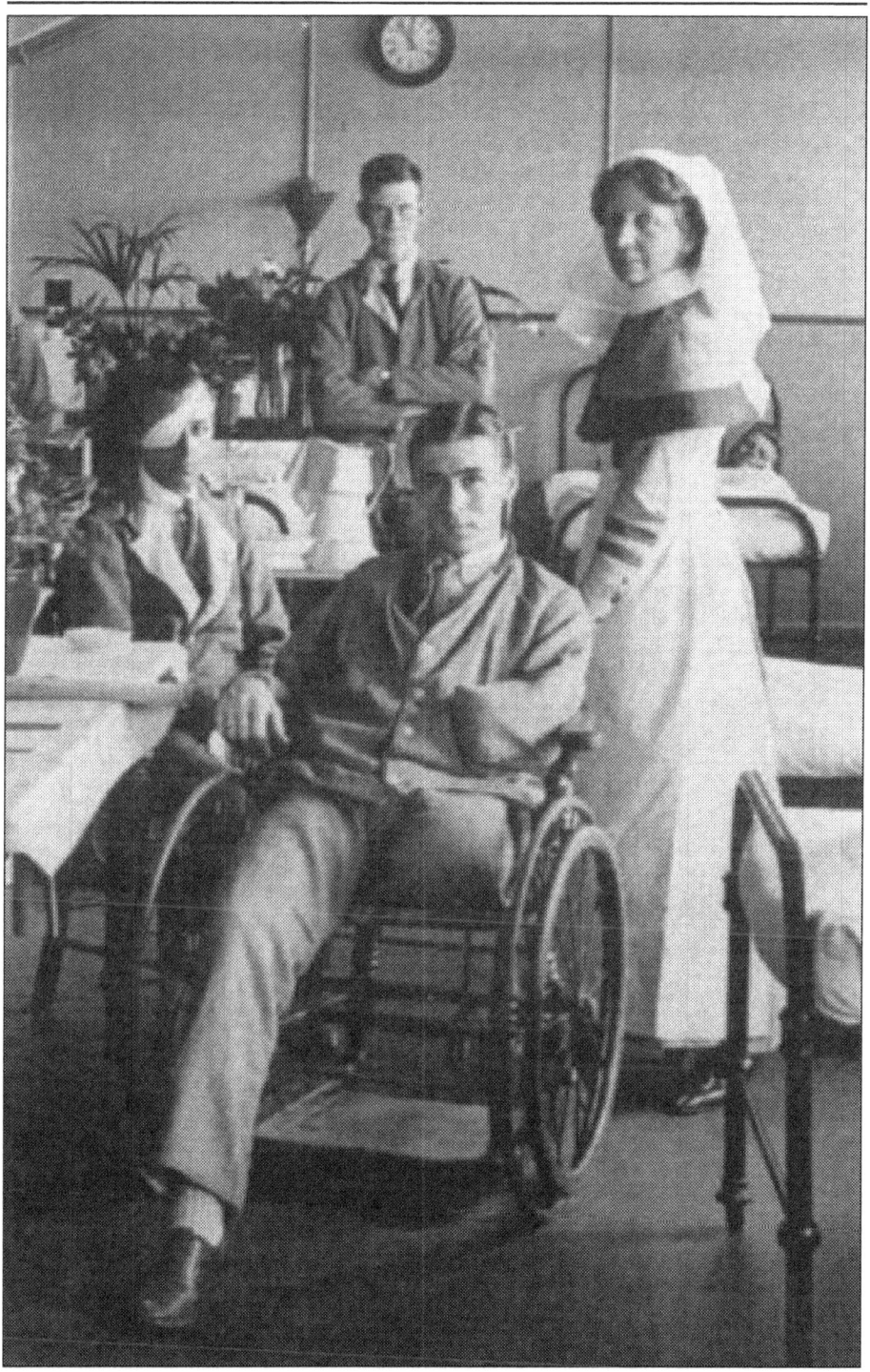

A military hospital in Toronto. Godwin has a great deal to say about the physical and psychological casualties of World War I. (Photo courtesy Canadian National Archives)

OTHER BOOKS BY GEORGE STANLEY GODWIN

1. *Cain or The Future of Crime.* London: Kegan Paul. 1928. 108 pp.
2. *Columbia or The Future of Canada.* London: Kegan Paul. 1928. 95 pp.
3. *Criminal Man.* New York: Braziller, 1957.
4. *Crime and Social Action.* London: Watts. 1956.
5. *The Disciple* (a play in three acts). London: Acorn Press. 1936. 88 pp.
6. *Discovery (The Story of the Finding of the World).* London: Heath Cranton, 1933. 96 p.
7. *Empty Victory.* (A futuristic novel). London: John Long, 1932. 288 p.
8. *The Eternal Forest.* Vancouver: Godwin Books, 1994. 320 p. Preface by George Woodcock, life of Godwin and notes by Robert S. Thomson, archival photos used to illustrate the text. Extracts from Godwin's *Journal.* As stated earlier, this was the first of George Godwin's books to be reprinted.
9. *Geoff, a family memoir.* Godwin's son, Geoff, was lost at sea (1970) while attempting to cross the Atlantic in a small two-person craft. This is Godwin's eulogy to his son; it contains Geoff's log.
10. *The Great Mystics.* London: Watts and Co. 1945. 106 pp.
11. *The Great Revivalists.* London: Watts and Co. 1951. 220 pp.
12. Japan's New Order. London: Watts and Co. 1942. 32 pp.
13. Journal of George Godwin. 20 pp. of selections from this unpublished work are found at the end of the 1994 version of *The Eternal Forest.*
14. *The Land Our Larder* (The Story of the Suffleet Experiment and its Significance in war). London: Acorn Press, 1939. 127 p.
15. *Marconi (1939 - 45), A War Record.* London: Chatto and Windus, 1946. 125 p.
16. *The Middle Temple: the Society and Fellowship.* London: Staples Press. 1954. 174 p. I have enclosed a number of notes about Godwin's association with The Middle Temple in *The Eternal Forest.*
17. *The Mystery of Anna Berger.* London: Watts. 1948. 226 pp.
18. *Our Woods in War.* London: Acorn. 1940.
19. *Peter Kurten.* A study in sadism. London: Acorn Press. 1938. 58 pp.
20. *Priest or Physician?* A study of faith-healing. London: Watts and Co. 1941.
21. *Queen Mary College (East London College): An Adventure in Education.* London: Acorn, 1939. 209 p.
22. *Trial of Peter Griffiths.* London: British Book Centre. 1950.
23. *Vancouver, a Life.* London: Philip Allan. 1930. 320 pp. A study of the famous explorer, charter. Includes charts, extensive notes.

According to Whitaker's *Books in Print* (1994), all of Godwin's books are out of print. We can now strike two novels from this list. The above list of books might not be complete. It will be interesting to see what surfaces in the future. Godwin was once the editor of *Alelphi,* a monthly literary journal, now defunct. Numerous articles have been written on Godwin's books. For details see Combined Retrospective Index to Book Reviews in Scholarly Journals, 1886 - 1974, Vol. Four. Arlington and Inverness: Carrollton Press. 1980. See also *The Book Review Digest* (New York: Wilson. 1931, etc.). and *Contemporary Authors* (Detroit: Gale Research Company).

The Eternal Forest

The Eternal Forest (1929) describes George Godwin's experiences as a homesteader possessed of an acute eye for political and socio-economic realities in British Columbia's early days. *The Eternal Forest* and *Why Stay We Here?* together comprise a saga in which the peace of the Fraser Valley is contrasted with the chaos of the Western Front.

The Eternal Forest

featuring a preface by renowned scholar George Woodcock, is now available from the publisher, Robert S. Thomson, at:

www.godwinbooks.com

What the critics have said . . .

"Godwin's sensibility that nature is not only a resource to be conquered and exploited – but also a source of life has a remarkably modern ring. 'Mother Earth,' he writes, 'the fecund, kindly giver of all life.' (. . .) In hindsight I find it odd that all my literature studies at the U. of British Columbia in the 1960s featured the usual pantheon of literary heroes from the 40s to the 60s with ironic detachment serving as the spiritual template. Now I find myself drawn to this earlier epoch and discover that my present intellectual sensibility was already fully developed in Godwin near the outset of the century" (Tom Shandel, *B.C. Bookworld,* 1995).

"The descriptive passages of the surrounding forest are beautifully written, sensual and evocative. We see it, through the Newcomer's eyes, in all seasons and moods. (. . .) It is here that Godwin's spiritual self finds genuine succor, for the forest 'got hold of you and made you think, it gave you your place in the universe, taught you the significance and the insignificance of man; it whispered of God" (p. 207). Such reflections, which constitute the most moving passages of the novel, are even more striking to the modern reader aware that such places are rapidly vanishing" (Claire Campbell, *National History*).

"A historian once noted that we know more about Ancient Egypt – thanks to the Rosetta Stone – than we know about the early days on the Mississippi. In the same vein it may be said that *The Eternal Forest* tells us more about early pioneer settlements along the Fraser River than we could find in any conventional British Columbia history book" (Jack Gilmore, Surrey, Canada).

"This is not a political novel. It is fiction woven from personal experience containing acute and verifiable observation of an emerging society" (Prof. Brian Elliott, Vancouver).

"A beautiful hardcover package . . ." (Tom Fletcher, *Maple Ridge & Pitt Meadows News*).

Recent critical studies . . .

- *B.C. Bookworld* ("The Great Fraser Valley Novel" by Tom Shandel). Summer 1995, p. 25.
- *B.C. Studies* (journal). *The Eternal Forest,* reviewed by Dr. Brian Elliott. Summer 1995, p. 103.
- *National History,* book review by Ms. Claire Campbell. Summer, 2000.

A typical extract . . .

"The alders were felled easily because they were young and their green and grey mottled bark, beautiful as the skin of snakes, concealed a soft, sappy wood. They reeled under the blows, groaned, swung drunkenly, and spun earthwards. With bent and twisted branches they throbbed for a moment like living things feeling the agonies of death, and came to rest."

Order from: www.godwinbooks.com

www.ingramcontent.com/pod-product-compliance
Lightning Source LLC
Chambersburg PA
CBHW070113260626
47160CB00004B/1443